50¢
HR

THE
ARMAGEDDON
SECRET

A NOVEL INSPIRED BY ACTUAL EVENTS

ROBERT
BURNHAM

Archway Publishing books may be ordered through booksellers or by contacting:

Archway Publishing
1663 Liberty Drive
Bloomington, IN 47403
www.archwaypublishing.com
844-669-3957

Because of the dynamic nature of the Internet, any web addresses or links contained in this book may have changed since publication and may no longer be valid. The views expressed in this work are solely those of the author and do not necessarily reflect the views of the publisher, and the publisher hereby disclaims any responsibility for them.

Cover mushroom cloud image: Getty Images.
New York World's Fair image: Wurts Bros. (New York, N.Y.). Used with permission of the Museum of the City of New York. X2010.7.2.7882, slightly modified for publication with permission of the Museum.
Albert Einstein quotations are used with permission of
The Hebrew University of Jerusalem, Einstein Archives (34-347).
Wood engraving illustration of subway tunnel via Wikimedia Commons.
https://commons.wikimedia.org/w/index.
php?search=pneumatic+subway&title=Special:MediaSearch&go=Go&type=image
Library of Congress. Public domain.

The Armageddon Secret is a work of historical fiction, using well-known historical and public figures. All incidents and dialogue are products of the author's imagination and are not to be construed as real. Where real-life historical or public figures appear, the situations, incidents, and dialogue concerning those persons are entirely fictional and are not intended to change the entirely fictional nature of the work. In other respects, any resemblance to persons living or dead is entirely coincidental.

Scripture quotations marked (NIV) are taken from the Holy Bible, New International Version®, NIV®. Copyright © 1973, 1978, 1984, 2011 by Biblica, Inc.® Used by permission of Zondervan. All rights reserved worldwide. www.zondervan.com The "NIV" and "New International Version" are trademarks registered in the United States Patent and Trademark Office by Biblica, Inc.®

Scripture quotations marked (ESV) are from the ESV® Bible (The Holy Bible, English Standard Version®), copyright © 2001 by Crossway, a publishing ministry of Good News Publishers. Used by permission. All rights reserved.

ISBN: 978-1-6657-1155-5 (sc)
ISBN: 978-1-6657-1156-2 (hc)
ISBN: 978-1-6657-1154-8 (e)

Library of Congress Control Number: 2021917894

Archway Publishing rev. date: 10/11/2021

CONTENTS

PART 1: RISE FROM DARKNESS

PART 2: THE WORLD OF TOMORROW

PART 3: TESTS

ABOUT THE BOOK

1938: In a Berlin lab three years before America's entry into World War II, Hitler's scientists were the first on the planet to split the atom. Suddenly, Germany was the only nation closing in on the secret to possessing the ultimate weapon. If the Nazis' quest couldn't be checked, civilization would vanish. German general Ludwig Beck's heroic Black Orchestra Underground fighters swore to topple Hitler before he extinguished humanity. *That much is history.*

In the heart of the Nazified, terror-slammed German capital, an American expat journalist with an old and very personal hatred of the Nazis is recruited by Black Orchestra for a momentous quest. Their network of spies has uncovered the existence of Hitler's atom bomb project, but no German atomic scientist can be trusted to help them disrupt this menace. They must have a channel to America to piece together the knowledge essential to block the route as they battle the Gestapo, betrayal from within, and their own demons to stop the German atomic bomb. Success or failure of their desperate final struggle to derail Hitler's ultimate weapon lies in the hands of a young German widow. Her courage and intelligence will ultimately decide the fate of not just the war but of all humanity.

The Second World War still commands attention seven decades later. Yet, our collective knowledge of this devastating conflict lacks the comprehension of how narrow our planet's escape was from an unspeakable outcome. The keystone for creating the atomic bomb was *The Armageddon Secret.*

Dedicated to the Memory of
Sandra Campbell Burnham
Miss Canada
Loving Wife of 34 Years

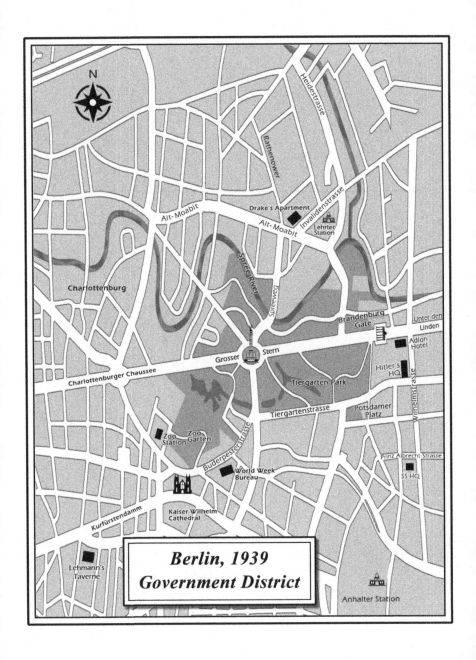

Berlin, 1939
Government District

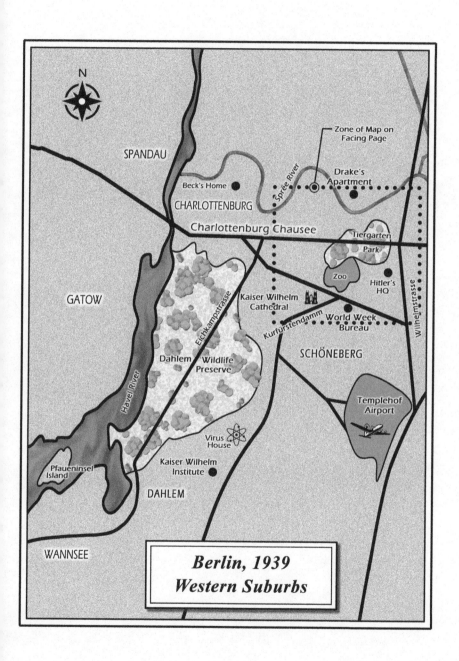

Berlin, 1939
Western Suburbs

HISTORICAL NOTE

Long ago, English writer H. G. Wells imagined a super-powerful atomic explosive he called "carolinum." This concept became a reality with an artificial element, eventually known as plutonium. The first steps in creating this new element from nature's uranium were made secretly inside Nazi Germany more than three years before America began the Manhattan Project.

Many of the people and events described in the following pages were real, while some are fictional. Combined, they portray incidents that could have spared the planet from Nazi destruction.

**We may be destroyed, but if we are,
we shall drag a world with us . . . a world in flames.**
—Adolf Hitler, 1934

ACKNOWLEDGMENTS

This novel is the culmination of my fascination with the early development of the atomic bomb dating back to my student days at the University of Michigan. On an autumn Ann Arbor afternoon that I will never forget, I was walking through the Undergraduate Library when I saw a black hardbound book titled *The German Atomic Bomb* lying on a table. I sat down to read, and was soon astonished to learn of civilization's narrow escape from a Nazi Armageddon. I later read other accounts of the liberation of nuclear energy by the Germans during the period before the Second World War had begun, years before America's successful development of the atomic bomb. Somehow, humanity avoided Nazi atomic weapons despite Germany's colossal head start and well-known engineering prowess. I began a correspondence with Willian L. Shirer, CBS Radio Berlin Correspondent of the 1930s and author of the bestseller *The Rise and Fall of the Third Reich*. He encouraged me to write about this astounding near miss. Still, my many years of intense career focus didn't allow sufficient time until recently for the total immersion needed to complete the project. Although this is a work of fiction, one must believe that something like this must have happened to bring about nothing short of a miracle.

My thanks to my wife, Suzy Russell Burnham, my son, cinematographer Alexander Burnham, and Mary Monte LeMerise, "the best sister a man never had," for unending encouragement and support. Editors Natalie Fowler and Monique Peterson supplied extraordinary recommendations. Best-selling author Hank Phillippi Ryan has been an inspiration with her suggestions. And beta readers Roy Gosse, Dennis Zacharski, Robert Forbes, Dr. Terence Cosgrove, Dr. George Kates, Catherine Ticer, Mitch Ostrowski, and Dr. Shirley Nuss helped shape the final product.

Accuracy in depicting people and events of the pre-war Nazi era could not have been attained without the resources I uncovered and the multiplicity of locations I visited during research for the manuscript. These included investigations at the Kaiser Wilhelm Institute for Chemistry and various other Nazi-era locales in Berlin, in Munich the Deutsches Museum and the location of the Bürgerbräukeller beer hall, the Imperial War Museum in London, the Institut du Radium in Paris, the 1939 New York World's Fair location at Flushing Meadows in Queens, New York, and the American Museum of Science and Energy in Oak Ridge, Tennessee. Among the principal reference works employed in the writing of this novel were: *The Making of the Atomic Bomb* by Richard Rhodes, 1986 (the Pulitzer Prize-winning gold standard for comprehending the history of atomic energy); *Berlin Diary: The Journal of a Foreign Correspondent 1934–41* by William L. Shirer, 1941; *The German Atomic Bomb* by David Irving, 1968; *Before the Fallout* by Diana Preston, 2005; *Manhattan Project: The Untold Story of the Making of the Atomic Bomb* by Stephane Groueff, 1968; *Berlin 1936: Sixteen Days in August* by Oliver Hilmes, 2016; *The Origins of the Second World War* by A. Offner, 1975; and *The Mind of Adolph Hitler* by Walter Langer, 1972.

PART ONE

RISE FROM DARKNESS

CHAPTER 1

UNDERGROUND

"Power. More power than has ever existed in the
whole world, all inside one round ball.
Power—to set all men free . . . or destroy them."

H. G. Wells, *The World Set Free*, 1914

NOVEMBER 9, 1938

THE DAY OF DEATH HAD only a few hours to live. As Alexander Drake hurtled through the tunnel of the Untergrundbahn twenty meters under the streets of Berlin, he couldn't possibly foresee the world-shattering decision awaiting him very literally around the next curve.

The subway train shot through the blackness of the subterranean realm, the clatter of the steel wheels blasting Drake's eardrums. He felt the bodies of fellow passengers move against him. Their starched collars and slicked-back hair marked them as office clerks, minor officials, or merchants. Droplets of sweat tumbled from his forehead as simultaneously an icy shiver moved up his back. A dreaded sensation was coming on—the damned flu or something even more loathsome. He ached to get home, to crawl under the quilted blanket atop his bed, and to block out the tumult of this dismal day.

Someone pushed him in the back—hard—and shoved a card into his hand. A heavy body drove him against the packed U-Bahn car's steel wall. "Do what this says and keep your mouth shut."

Drake glimpsed a hunched shape dart into the mass of riders, leaving behind a reek of perspiration and mothballed winter clothes. An overhead light was close enough that he could shuffle between people to get beneath its beam. He scrutinized the typewritten words:

URGENT

Drake:

Take train tonight at 2010 hours to Dresden from Anhalter Station. Meet our agent in car 2419. You will exit train at Zossen.

Board at forward entrance, count four compartments. He wears black hat, will ask you a single question. Your answer will be: VIOLA.

Help preserve civilization. Avenge the murder.

We are Black Orchestra.

Stapled to the back of the card was a reddish, elongated rectangle of heavy paper, imprinted with the words "DEUTSCHE REICHSBAHN Anhalter Bahnhof nach Zossen." In its center, a handwritten scrawl in blue ink: "Bahnbus 2419 / Stunden 20:10 / 20 RM H und R". He stared at the railway ticket to Zossen—8:10 tonight, coach number 2419, twenty Reichmarks roundtrip.

Preserve civilization? His thoughts lay tangled in a pile inside his head. *Murder?* This bizarre message had landed like a shocking bolt from the blue, but his twenty-five lonely months in Germany combined with disillusionments and torments strung out over fifteen years had galvanized his psyche, serving up the grit and stamina to withstand whatever madness stretched in front of him. He jammed the card and ticket deep into the pocket of his favorite double-breasted Harris Tweed woolen overcoat as he leaned against the vibrating partition.

Viola. The face of his dead fiancée flashed into his thoughts. *Who could know her name here?* A waterfall of sadness dragged down the corners of his mouth.

The press of bodies drove his face against a vertical stainless-steel grab post, its coldness a startling contrast to the hot skin of his jaw. He took a deep breath and gripped the bar, his fingers twitching in a nervous rhythm.

Since morning, news reports had flooded the Berlin bureau of *World Week* magazine. Outside his office, four teletype machines had been clattering all day, spitting out Nazi-censored descriptions of anti-Jewish demonstrations raging across Germany. But as the day wore on, Drake made his way around Berlin, contacting his confidential sources, trying to find the truth about what was going on. The unofficial stories were different—tales of ruthless, brutal murders of innocents that began in the crowded streets yesterday afternoon. Hitler's Ministry of Propaganda was calling the disturbances Kristallnacht—Crystal Night. According to these demented Nazi minds, Germany's great synagogues and thriving Jewish businesses were nothing more than insults to Nazism and required obliteration. But, contrary to the official line, the riots were eating this nation's major cities, and the word was getting out, pouring past the borders, sending shockwaves worldwide as news of the slaughter spread.

Lehrter Bahnhof—the red and white signs flashed like strobe lights past the car's windows. The brakes gave off ear-piercing squeals as the subway train slowed for the stop.

The gap between the subway car's threshold and the concrete platform looked huge tonight, like Drake might tumble headlong into the void. He pushed through the throng of humanity, forcing his way out of the station and onto the sidewalk slick with melting snow reflecting the multicolored lights of the city. The hot, moist air inside the station had intermingled with the nighttime cold, generating a luminous fog that hung like a heavy tapestry above the frenzied mob. He blinked as he tried to comprehend the scene before his eyes. All around him were faces hard with suspicion, apprehensive of their fellow citizens. *Watch your neighbors. Trust nobody.* The shouts, the antisemitic curses, the rage of the populace moving through the streets made it seem like he was inside a steam pressure cooker run amok, having built up too much power, tonight rupturing with devastating results. Fights, screams, windows shattering, blazing fires were everywhere, pounding his eardrums like a thousand jackhammers. The odors of spilled beer mixed with cigarette smoke saturated the air. Drake saw everything but felt nothing except disgust and sickness as the pain burned behind his eyes.

He swung toward three big smoke-belching stake trucks speeding by, horns blaring, as they swerved recklessly through the horde of people, a dozen uniformed soldiers hanging off the running boards. Large black and red Nazi swastika flags flapped from the trucks' roofs. Brass cartridges gleamed in packs of ammunition belts stacked high in the cargo beds. People moved as one single mass of flesh, sweeping one way then another. He caught sight of bright yellow-orange flames licking the dome of the synagogue a block away. A man crashed against his shoulder, screaming, "Shoot the goddamned Jews! Bastards brought it on themselves!" *Nazi lies are fungi,* he thought, *spewing poison spores everywhere.* Drake glanced toward a trash barrel next to a lamppost and, for a moment, considered vomiting into it.

Yellow shafts of light from car headlamps carved through the mist and across his field of vision as he slumped against a cold stone wall. A flickering torchlight lit the word JUDEN scrawled across a store display window. He shoved his way through the crowd, managing to get a hundred meters away from the Bahnhof's portal. It was two blocks to his apartment, but at that moment, it seemed like two kilometers.

The sound of shattering storefront glass reverberated like a bomb blast. He jumped sideways to avoid flying splinters—a metal sign over the display window: ZINGERMAN'S APPLIANCE STORE. The glass was gone, leaving a gaping hole. Electrical sparks spewed from the sockets of broken light bulbs inside the shop. Roughnecks sprinted through the opening like they'd heard a gunshot signaling the start of a race and grabbed everything in sight.

Under the flickering light of burning yellow torches, three stormtroopers waving metal batons pushed the looters aside and clambered into the store.

The onlookers moved toward the opening, then, like an ocean wave, fell back as the soldiers reemerged. Drake glimpsed a bald man being hauled behind them, his legs dragging across thrusting daggers of glass that ripped through his trousers and flesh. The yellow Star of David armband hung in tatters from the sleeve of his shirt.

"Here's what we do to rotten Jew shopkeepers who gouge poor Germans!" shouted one of the brown-shirted soldiers. A baton whacked across the man's head, the blow flopping the victim onto the concrete like a discarded store mannequin. Since the age of eleven, Drake had been the one who stood up to the schoolyard bullies when they shoved some weaker, outnumbered kid too hard, but the reality of this moment told him something like that wasn't going to happen tonight. Powerless, Drake stood under the light of hissing oil torches as a jackboot stomped on the man's neck.

He stared at the black blood accumulating in the gutter alongside windblown papers and shards of glass.

1923 again.

The reporter put his palms against his temples and turned away from the carnage, pushing back remembrances of his own anguish in Munich, Detroit, and London, merging with new sufferings right in front of him. He walked north, away from the River Spree and into darkness broken by a few streetlights. *What has Germany become?* This nation, which had birthed intellects like Beethoven and Bach, Einstein and Goethe, had been grotesquely transmuted. Adolf Hitler had unleashed in the inhabitants of Germany a propensity for infinite violence. As he shook his head, he caught sight of the dim yellow illumination radiating from eighteen tall, grandly arched windows of the train station's grandiose locomotive house, a mammoth cathedral dedicated to the gods of German technology. *So inventive, so bright—so barbaric.*

The ground rumbled under Drake's wet, ruined shoes as a train pulled into the station. He again touched the card in his pocket. "*Preserve civilization?* I'm a greenhorn reporter from Detroit." His words boiled out in English, something that came when he was upset with the world. "How in hell am I gonna *preserve* a damned thing?" He spat into the gutter.

Still, the bewildering message meant one thing for sure: If he were to go to this rendezvous, he'd either learn the secret of this Black Orchestra or plunge himself into a Nazi trap. He had to decide—was the trip to Zossen wise or just a fool's gamble?

CHAPTER 2

RIBBON OF DARKNESS

"Playing it safe is the most dangerous thing in the world."

Sir Hugh Walpole, *ca.* 1915

D RAKE MADE HIS WAY THROUGH the slush along Invalidenstrasse, his wet feet getting colder with every step. The brutal midwestern American winters he'd endured as a kid had made him hate this dreadful season. At times, fantasies would come to him about an assignment in California or South America. Although his work had taken Drake to London, Paris, Spain, more places than most anyone had traveled in a lifetime, he needed a vacation. But dreams must wait for a better day—he faced a huge decision and had no one to talk with. It was in times like these that he wished he'd made more friends in this city. He had a few—very few—and their conversations were continuously filtered through an accretion of caution. Sometimes it seemed the flow of horror stories—disappearances, beatings, and threats—had snuffed out most of their collective brainpower. But next year, he promised himself, he'd labor less for his employer and make a more vigorous effort to get to know people—that is, if he stayed in Berlin. Given the swelling prospect of war, that was far from certain.

A block from his apartment, in front of another row of shops, a new group of SA Brownshirts approached from across the street—*more damned trouble,* he thought.

"Hold it!" a thick-bodied soldier, stick in hand, shouted at Drake. "You look like Jew garbage." Another figure pushed a blazing torch toward his face. "You'd better have a Jew star sewn on yourself under that fancy overcoat." They took menacing positions on either side of him.

"Sorry, boys, but I don't have one, so leave me alone. Look at this. Press pass from Goebbels. Get lost." He winced imperceptibly, feeling a sting of cowardice as he thought of his Jewish grandmother but recognizing that defiance was over for the day.

"Don't tell us what to do, prick. Get off this street before we decide to kick your ass for looking like a Jew."

The one holding the wooden truncheon pushed it into Drake's chest, sending him stumbling back toward the street. A shower of Nazi spit landed on his shoes. His muscles went rigid as rage coursed through his body. *Don't have a chance here,* he thought. Then, turning, he straightened his coat and walked away.

He'd had more than his share of clashes, usually involving government censors, Nazi officials, or rival reporters. In such predicaments, he'd averted calamity by employing a finely-tuned sense for detecting dangerous turns of conversation or ominous expressions and using a gift for talking his way out of jeopardy. It didn't hurt that he was tall with broad and powerful shoulders, which combined with a slather of good luck, had provided emergency pathways away from disaster—so far.

Thick aromas of fried pork and onions infused the vestibule of his apartment building, undoubtedly emanating from the unit occupied by a plump Polish woman who cooked all day and favored bright, oversized, flowered dresses. One of the three bulbs had burned out in the brass light fixture hanging above the hallway, making the place even gloomier than usual. He turned his key in the lock and stepped into the apartment illuminated only by the dim, milky glow from a streetlamp outside the window. Drake switched on the ceiling light and slumped into the small chair by the telephone table. It was another day gone past—the same austere room, the same daily strivings of trying to be an effective journalist in this straight-jacketed realm of Nazi censorship. He glanced at the mystifying card again, then flipped it onto the papers strewn across the table. "Fifteen damned years today," he said to himself, turning away from the light. For the ten-thousandth time, he saw the drunken mob of Nazis and heard the single gunshot. His hand swiped across his eyes, pushing away the mental pictures. He stood, then walked across his room and wrenched off the dripping wet undershirt. Feeling the increasing soreness in his throat, he flung the undergarment against the wall. He slipped a clean white undershirt over his head, put on a woolen cable-knit sweater and dry shoes, and wiped his face with a thin towel.

Drake dropped the cloth on the dresser next to a picture framed in black wood—a photo of a man with clear, dark eyes and a hard, well-defined chin, a person at the height of his powers. Like Alex, he had a slightly arched nose and a broad forehead. The smile was non-committal, a straight line that conveyed neither joy nor sorrow. The photo's expression seemed to say *there is something of great importance you must do.* Drake shifted his view to the mirror on the nightstand and studied his own face. His skin was clear, displaying a permanent beard shadow. His eyes, a rich dark brown and framed by long lashes, conveyed an attentive presence, anxious for happiness but expecting trouble, like a small dog finding itself alone in a strange kennel. Fatigue showed in gray smudges beneath the lower lids, eyes of a man past the age of illusions yet still possessing the optimism of youth. Things had a way of educating him, and even at this stage of life, he was a person to be taken seriously, a clear thinker, and expressive of his ideas. Still, there were moments when an overpowering restlessness struck him. He was a journalist who could seldom satisfy his compelling desire to find the truth, often frustrated by the combination of Nazi control of journalism and the cold realization that tools to be acquired by his apprenticeship as a newsman were not yet his.

The note lay on the small table next to the train ticket. *Avenge the murder.* Could he dare think that after all these years, there might be a way he could somehow strike back? "Nazis can't arrest me for taking a train ride, and if there's one chance in ten million that I could help somebody slit Hitler's throat—" His voice trailed off as his knuckles rubbed along the stubble on his chin. "Day of Death be damned!"

Drake needed an hour to get to the crowds to Anhalter Bahnhof. Whatever research this Black Orchestra had done on him didn't include his address—it was a long way to that train station. He gave a longing look at the feathery floral quilt on his bed as he turned to grab a clear bottle of medicine down from the cupboard. Its black and orange label promised *KOMPLETT HEILEN DIE GRIPPE*, a flu remedy leftover from the frigid winter of '37. He swallowed a mouthful of the foul-tasting concoction and set the bottle on the tabletop as he swung his arm toward the light switch. The container spun and fell to the floor, shattering into scores of gleaming glass fragments—one more wretched incident squaring with this Night of Broken Glass. The pieces would have to remain there until he made it back—*if* he made it back. He donned the belted overcoat, wound a woolen scarf around the opening at the neck, then hurried down the building stairs, out into the darkness, toward the city engulfed in madness. His eyes followed the chain of streetlamps. In the moonlight, Invalidenstrasse looked like an infinite ribbon of black crepe.

CHAPTER 3

BLACK ORCHESTRA

"The curtain of the Universe is shattered . . ."

Percy B. Shelley, *Hellas, A Lyrical Drama*, 1821

DRAKE'S NECK MUSCLES KNOTTED AS he strained to hear the sharp, metallic-sounding words blasting from the ceiling loudspeakers, echoing off the gray granite walls and high steel beams of the vast Anhalter station. The crowding and the jostling here were even more suffocating than out on the streets, with hundreds of voices swirling into a deafening cacophony, the shrieks of people fleeing the horrific rampage, determined to get away from the frenzy of the city.

Drake cut his eyes toward the giant clock above the entrance to the south train platforms. A loudspeaker blasted a vital slice of information: *Dresden Gleis Zehn.* His train was boarding on track ten, just four minutes to get aboard. Half a dozen black locomotives with red-painted noses stood on parallel tracks, spilling clouds of white steam into the air. Their steel wheels and polished running gear shone brightly under the lights of the engine house. Oilers and maintenance workers scurried about to ensure the equipment performed correctly. Working his way through the mass of passengers, he approached the platform, senses on full alert for any sign of entrapment or deception.

He folded the card from the subway encounter and creased it again between his thumb and forefinger before ripping it into small pieces and shoving it into the black mouth of a trash container. He walked alongside the coaches with sky-blue walls and silver roofs. *There—CWL 2419*. A conductor. *That funny mustache—he doesn't look like a conductor—what is he?* Light-headed, unsteady, Drake stepped up into the darkness of the rail carriage.

The sliding door to the fourth compartment was ajar only a few centimeters, allowing an ethereal wisp of smoke to spiral up and into the corridor. Flu symptoms had scrambled every other sense, but his nostrils still registered the smell of burning tobacco leaf.

His eyes scanned up and down the passageway. Nobody else was visible in the wood-paneled corridor. Still, he could hear muffled conversations emanating from other compartments. Dim overhead lights left the floor of the walkway in darkness. Drake moved toward the slit.

"Guten Abend, Mein Herr," said a thin voice coming from the same direction as the smoke. "Something?"

Drake blinked several times. "Viola." He slid the compartment door open wider, allowing him to see the speaker inside. A hollow-cheeked blonde man in a gray sweater, wearing a black snap-brimmed hat, sat motionless on the velvet seat. He held what looked like a photograph, although Drake couldn't see the image from his angle. The man's eyes, set above a face riddled with pockmarks and bordered by fringes of sparse hair, squinted at him, then moved to stare at the drawn shade as if to see through to the Bahnhof crowds outside. He exhaled a deep chest full of smoke, then twisted his head back toward Drake.

"A lovely name for whom I presume was a delightful lady. Pity."

Pity? Drake thought. *Screw you*. A trifling word to use in summing up what she'd meant to him.

The blonde man motioned toward the upholstered seat with a

dramatic sweep of his left arm. "Come in." He smiled with an almost imperceptible shift of his mouth and shoved the photograph into a small blue envelope.

Drake dragged the door shut behind him as he kept a tight grip on its handle. He swallowed hard. "How do you know about her?"

"What kind of silly question is that? In your profession, you deal with spies endlessly. Berlin harbors a swarm of informers. Bribe a secretary, compromise a records clerk." The man stubbed his cigarette out in the stamped metal ashtray embedded in the armrest. "That name shows how much we know about you. Your deceased fiancée."

"Then what's this all about? What am I here for?"

"I think that will be made amply clear in a few minutes. Now sit down."

The piercing, rattling screech of a trainman's whistle rose above the sounds of blasting steam, then a shout of the German version of "all aboard." Two almost simultaneous whacks echoed in his ears as the car's doors slammed. The train lurched forcefully, producing the sharp, echoing crash of the iron couplers. Drake twisted, half-falling onto the seat cushion.

He studied the other man's face for clues of deceit, found none, then spoke in a quiet, controlled voice. "'Black Orchestra'—what is it? What's it got to do with me?"

"I'll come to that. First, we make an agreement."

"You're joking, right? I agree to nothing."

"*Herr Drake*, I'm not joking at all. You're forgetting that we each have ample means of destroying one another."

"Is that why you brought me here? To hang me with a noose tied by the Gestapo?"

"Certainly not. But suppose you're sitting there thinking of turning me over to the police. If that happens, my associates will put a knife in your back." There was a hint of a stammer in his voice.

"I'm sure they would."

"So comes the simple agreement. If you betray me, you get killed, and if I reveal you, you'll tell the police who I work for—the anti-Nazi Underground."

"Underground—like I thought. All right, go on." Drake rubbed his sore eyes.

The German lifted a brown paper bag enclosing a rectangular slab, shifting it to rest on top of the envelope containing the photograph. "I'm going to give you knowledge of how this involves you—you'll have twenty-four hours to decide what you're going to do. You get off this train at Zossen, thirty kilometers from here, so you don't have much time to learn."

"Sounds like a bad deal for you either way. If I turn you in, you get a firing squad, and there goes whatever you are trying to accomplish. Are you risking that? Must be a damned good reason."

"There is, Drake. I know that when you hear what I'm going to say, your chances of turning against us will be . . . infinitesimal. We're dead serious—and we'll soon find out who winds up dead."

Drake wiped sweat from his temple as he stared through the other man's eyeballs and into his brain.

The German stubbed out his cigarette in the ashtray. His hands quaked slightly, belying an appearance of composure. His hand darted into his shirt pocket and fumbled for a second, then withdrew something and moved it his lips. He chewed and swallowed, then resumed talking.

"The fragility of civilization, Drake. Consider ten thousand years of its construction wiped out in a single night. And so, my group has one purpose—to stop something which, unchecked, means that could happen."

"I'm an American newsman you met five minutes ago. You're going to trust me with an earth-shattering secret?"

"We know why you hate the Nazis. You've already come to our side, although you don't yet know it. We require a link to America, and for you, call it *settling accounts*—you need us for that."

"What 'accounts' are you talking about?"

"You know precisely. And we meet today, quite an anniversary for you. Hate? Such an inadequate word. Perhaps there's some other expression for what you have felt for fifteen years. Defiled? Cheated? This fact, at the close of the day, is why we chose you as our *vertraute* . . . our American confidante."

"How do you know about that?" he said after a moment, leaning forward in his seat.

"Same as I said two minutes ago. Informants. Germans record every bit about peoples' lives, and my unit has excellent access. The key point for you to absorb—Adolf Hitler himself ordered your father's assassination. I'm sure you didn't know that."

Drake slumped in the rail coach seat and looked toward the ceiling. "It was a random bullet," he uttered, repressing the notion that deep inside him, somehow, he already knew what this man was about to say.

"Hardly. And it's not in our interest to tell you more unless you join our cell."

Neither one spoke for a full minute.

"You want a link to America? I've been gone since '36. There are thousands of Americans in Germany who might be a lot more effective in accomplishing that for you."

"Here's why you're wrong. Two things make the essential difference. One, you're a journalist, an investigator, and it wouldn't be out of the ordinary for you to be asking questions of people in America, including scientists. Two, your American citizenship enables you to get out of here to meet with scientific leading lights over there—as long as the United States remains neutral. So, combining your hatred of Nazis with your investigative job, plus your passport—no person we've identified has all these things."

Drake raised his eyes. "I don't know anyone in the scientific community across the Atlantic."

"You will—we'll take care of that. You've read H. G. Wells?"

"English novelist. *The Time Machine*—he wrote it around 1900, I think."

"Another of his texts, twenty-five years ago—*The World Set Free*." He grasped the paper bag, pulled a book from it, and ran his hand over its battered dark brown leather cover. The smoke swirling from his cigarette seemed to wrap around the volume and capture it. "He paints a picture . . . a dictator of the *Central Powers* gets his hands on a super-powerful explosive capable of destroying all of humankind. Bombs with colossal energy—Wells called them atomic bombs. Take this, read it. The government has banned this book in Germany. Don't be caught with it unless you want serious trouble."

Drake reached across and grasped the book as a fist banged on the door of the compartment.

The other man's hand became a blur as he snatched the book back and stuffed it under his rump a split second before the door slid open.

"Die Fahrkarte, bitte?" The conductor extended his hand for the red tickets as his eyes scanned the two men. He punched the holes with a little silver press and was gone.

"The next uniform coming through that opening could end our conversation in a rather brutal style. My small Resistance cell might not last out this night."

Drake became aware of a familiar sensation in his fingertips, a signal that a life-changing event was imminent.

The man flipped the book open to a page with the corner folded over twice and handed it back to Drake. "Read what's underlined. Understand why the future rests upon what Black Orchestra must do."

The words were underscored with red pencil.

> Luminous, radioactive clouds were drifting from the atom bomb's center and killing and scorching all they overtook. Such was the last state of Paris and, on a larger scale New York, Chicago, London, Moscow, Tokyo, and two hundred and eighteen other centers of population.

"Armageddon, Drake, from the Hebrew *Har Məgiddos.* The final battle at the end of the world, culminating in forsaken wastelands where once stood civilization's great cities. Frightening concept, you must agree."

Drake looked up, weighing and calculating, then closed the book. "Fiction writer's imagination. I can't help you." The other man's eyes resembled small black pits that flashed with intensity.

"Read the book tomorrow. Then decide."

Drake turned the volume over in his hands. "Germany has these bombs?"

"Thank God, no—not yet. Our informants tell us that experiments are going on inside laboratories in Berlin's western suburbs, attempting to liberate atomic power. Many of the world's best scientists are there, and the Nazis are pressing them to create atomic explosives. But Black Orchestra doesn't know a thing about atoms and atomic explosives—we don't know even where to start if we're going to get in the way of the H. G. Wells bombs."

"You'd better find yourself an anti-Nazi German scientist or two to help."

"We can't depend on anyone in the scientific community here. You know how dangerous communications are in this country—a tinderbox. Children betray their parents to the police for saying the wrong thing."

Drake tapped his fingernails on the black Bakelite armrest and gazed at the floor as if he could conjure some explanation or guidance from the swirling patterns in the dark red carpet. "Atom bombs," he finally said. He tucked the book into the crumpled paper bag and pulled his coat closed. "If your story is true, then all existing ways of warfare— airplanes, tanks, guns, battleships—are useless. One airplane nullifies a hundred thousand soldiers."

The train swayed as it traversed an uneven section of track, throwing the blonde man sideways across the seat. He looked unsteady for a moment.

"We must stop it, Drake." He whacked his hand against the wooden wall. "We fight this bomb because evil will fill the vacuum left if good men do nothing!"

"How many are in this group of yours?"

"Less than ten."

"*Ten?* Against the entire German army and Nazi apparatus? That's suicide."

"That word implies cowardice, failure to face one's challenges, and opting to exit life to avoid them. For us, it's self-sacrifice to stop something which threatens the very existence of nations—that's heroism, not suicide."

A loudspeaker voice boomed through the corridor: "*Zossen als nächstes!*" The Zossen stop.

The German's eyebrows, earlier relaxed, had merged to become an arched bridge below his deeply creased forehead. "Your point of departure is here. Take this—a telephone number and words that look like nonsense." He passed a small card to the American. "You'll receive instructions for decoding the words on the card, which will provide further directions—that is if you choose to move forward." His hands fell into his lap, and he swung his face back toward the shaded window. "Perhaps we'll meet again." He nodded in a gesture that seemed to confirm a satisfaction that he had made his points.

The pain in Drake's throat was interfering with his thinking. In the span of a few minutes, he'd looked into the face of the anti-Nazi Underground, seen visions of H. G. Wells' atomic bombs, grasped the truth about his father's murder, and received a summons to help defeat Nazism—all simultaneously mind-boggling. He slid the door open and shot back a steely glance, then began moving toward the front of the railcar. The ninth of November—the Day of Death. Its name, given by Drake many years ago, had again been validated tonight in the hideous costume of Kristallnacht. But what he had learned in these last few minutes meant that efforts underway inside Berlin's laboratories could soon spell the death of civilization.

CHAPTER 4

INVALIDENSTRASSE

"Civilization: The lamb's skin in which
barbarism masquerades."

Thomas Bailey Aldrich, 1903

T HE STATION PLATFORM WAS A lacework of shadows and lights, icicles
hanging from rain gutters, baggage carts lined up neatly along the
building's side. Alex Drake passed through the swinging doors and
picked out a bench in the dim, concrete-walled Zossen Bahnhof. The
place looked like the inside of a vast bank vault minus the money. Every
one of the dozen or so passengers who sat with him held their heads
downward. The silence of the station was a stark reversal of Berlin's
bedlam.

Drake had never spoken about Munich. Nobody knew anything
beyond a few facts he'd shared with his boss. Throughout the screening
process by immigration *apparatchiks* during his entry to Germany, the
officials interrogating him never asked a word about it, as if it didn't
exist in government records.

Only his editor, Jimmy Keene, knew something of that day. Berlin sustained a labyrinth of connections and discreet understandings, and he had built a long, illustrious career upon his vast quantity of them. *Could Keene have a relationship with Black Orchestra?* The question smoldered in Drake's mind.

Drake stood and walked down the ramp toward the rail cars. He hoisted himself up the steps of the coach and found a seat as far as possible from another human.

"Alle an Bord!"

The train lurched into motion, gaining speed as the cars snaked through the rail yard and across the switches. Drake turned toward the window and saw his ghostly, greenish specter looking back, the image appearing far older than his twenty-six years. He twirled his diamond ring around a few times on his finger. It was his grandmother's gift to him that first Christmas after Munich—his father's wedding ring set with his mother's diamond, the band crafted to fit an eleven-year-old's finger. Before the Day of Death, his existence had centered on the tall engineer who'd provided him with the blueprint of how to behave, act, and feel. And the gift of that blueprint left him with a debt owed to that man, payable by doing the best possible with the underpinnings left to him. *To hell* with a cruel bullet that had shattered his life.

Then there was something called tuberculosis. His mother had survived its destruction—or so it seemed. Not long after her husband's death, her body had weakened visibly. She cried in her room every day, staring out at the Michigan winter as if the man she'd loved so fiercely might come walking back into the house. Within months, the boy stood under a sky that looked like a slab of grey concrete, staring at her carved wooden coffin. He couldn't remember much of the ritual except for the voice of a sad-looking minister praying next to a pile of dirt in the windswept Glen Eden cemetery south of Eight Mile Road. Four men lowered her into a dark rectangular hole, transforming Alexander into a stunned, wide-eyed orphan.

The train was speeding along the tracks, but the rail car was quiet except for the rhythmic clatter of the wheels against rails. As he stared at the sparkling jewel on his hand, his thoughts drifted toward a sobering realization: nothing anchored him to this world. Alex Drake wasn't a fatalist and harbored no death wish. Still, he loathed the notion of squandering his life on a quest which he might—at the last moment—recognize had never been attainable. It was time for him to suppress these ruminations and refocus on the revelation of a superweapon coming into the hands of Hitler.

The train slowed again. The nearly-empty cars rocked as the train crawled toward a station at the center of a little village where freight cars sat motionless on side rails and baggage carts waited for attention on the platforms. Locomotives belched steam and smoke into the cold night air as the train came under the railroad yard lights and edged toward a stop.

Shouts. He jerked upright. *Now what?*

It was nearly impossible to see through the fogged-up windows, but he could hear echoes of anti-Semitic insults and curses. A loud *whack* against a window of the railcar—chunks of glass blasted toward him. Through the opening, he saw a battle raging on the platform. A club whipped through the air, landing on a man who let out a wail. The conductor entered the car with a sneer on his face. "Jews getting a taste of bitter soup tonight." Spittle leaked from his lower lip. "A Jew caused that broken window. He'll pay for it with his life."

"Asshole," Drake said under his breath in English.

"You say something?" the railway employee asked.

Drake looked away, conquering his urge to go to battle but tasting sour bile at the back of his tongue. "Nothing—forget it."

"That window's gone," said the uniformed trainman. "All of you, out of this coach and into the next one. Right now."

The seven or eight tired passengers marched down the corridor and across the inter-car platform. This coach was as empty as the one they'd abandoned—nobody was traveling to Berlin on such a night of broken glass. Drake started to take a seat, but the train's lurch threw him backward, half-falling, half-sitting onto the cushion. Even a riot couldn't delay a German train. Berlin's fires, marchers, and murders weren't far ahead.

A few minutes of somnolence transported Drake out of the disquiets of the hour. After a time, he opened his eyes and saw the big city's lights illuminating the horizon. The train tottered through the thickening suburbs of Berlin and soon glided into the cavernous Anhalter Bahnhof, now nearly empty. A sign:

Südausgang

South exit. Stepping off the train was like pushing his foot from one universe into another. Drake moved down the train station's stairs, scanning the road for a late-night cab to shuttle him back to his apartment.

Soldiers strode along the street, ten abreast, carrying blazing, smoking torches high above their heads. Their hoarse voices bellowed the Nazi Party theme song *Deutschland Über Alles* as they pushed aside those who blocked their way.

He massaged his burning throat and tugged at his scarf, his heart rate accelerating. *Anti-Nazi Underground,* he thought. A taxicab crawled slowly toward him, its roof sign flashing *Frei*—unoccupied. Surprised by his good luck, he waved his arm furiously and jumped into the back seat. Through the side glass, he surveyed the rioting crowds and clenched his teeth.

"To 910 Invalidenstrasse, *bitte,*" he said.

The driver nodded as Drake switched on the overhead light. He slipped the old novel from the paper bag, pulled the card from the inside cover, and looked at the scrawled telephone number. He closed his eyes and confronted the imaginings of hundreds of blazing cities, millions of charred bodies, swastika flags flying over *The World Set Free*—or whatever sort of world might remain after the Nazi Armageddon. The mission ahead was clear. Although it was almost certainly doomed to disaster, he must risk everything to stop Hitler's bomb.

CHAPTER 5

INTRUDERS

"In criminal hands, radium might become very dangerous . . ."
Pierre Curie, speech at the Nobel Prize Awards, Stockholm, Sweden, 1905

"GUTEN MORGAN," ALEX DRAKE SAID to the bright-eyed, recently hired receptionist as he walked past her desk. He was moving slower than usual this morning, the combined effects of flu and the residue of last night's mysterious meeting. The frosted glass door of his *World Week* office rattled too loudly for his aching head. He slung his wool overcoat over the wall rack.

She brought in a cup of coffee and flickered a shy smile as she placed the porcelain saucer atop his desk. She was pretty in a pleasing, baby-faced way, a round face with full lips and rosy cheeks. Her perfume was sweet. *Maybe, when he felt better, he'd ask her to dinner,* he thought. *Or not. It wouldn't lead anywhere.*

"Thanks," he said. "Not feeling real great this morning. I've got to rewrite my piece about Nazi war preparations and then get started on one about these riots. I need a few hours with no visitors. Please—try to keep folks out of here as best you can till midafternoon."

"Of course."

A young man with a bit of international name recognition, good-looking, personable, and professional, should have a florid love life, especially in this city where much of the eligible male population was off to the military and lonely ladies abounded. There were flirtations, not all of them unsuccessful, but too much work and too many rotten memories quelled his interest in female companionship. He coughed, then leaned forward and snapped a handkerchief from his hip pocket. A wavy lock of black hair fell forward against his forehead, which he swept back in a habitual jab.

She closed the door behind her as Drake spun his chair around to face the beat-up green Olivetti typewriter. He gritted his teeth, then started banging the keys.

In a half-hour, he'd reworked the paragraphs to the point where he judged it would pass the censors who monitored all his journalistic work. He took one more readthrough, then walked it across the hall for the proofreaders to flyspeck before filing it with the Ministry of Public Enlightenment and Propaganda officer.

He dropped back onto his desk chair and spun a blank sheet of paper into the typewriter platen, then twirled the roller and slapped the carriage return a few times.

"So," he said quietly, "what lies do I make up to tell the world that the slaughter of Jews last night was not a slaughter of Jews?" Then words began to spill from his brain, through his blood and fingers, and onto the paper:

Night of Broken Glass

By Alexander Drake

Station Berlin, November 10, 1938. In the past twenty-four hours, Germany has progressed further into being a nation dramatically unlike all others and far different from itself as it existed only five years ago. It is being called Kristallnacht, Crystal Night, the Night of Broken Glass.

He plunged forward, painting word images of smashed windows and burned synagogues, struggling to remain inside the shrinking boundaries he knew he must obey. If he failed, he'd draw another Nazi rejection and the wrath of *World Week's* publisher Henry Crown in New York City for being late with the story.

His last sentences appeared on the sheet:

> German Jews will ultimately be forced to give up their possessions and leave this nation forever. It is now clear—crystal clear—that German leaders will accept nothing less.

That was it for now. Drake pulled open his battered leather briefcase and removed the paper bag containing the forbidden book, sliding it out and turning it around in his hands. The first page:

The World Set Free
A Story of Mankind

By H. G. Wells London Copyright 1914

He read the introduction. "Dedicated to Frederick Soddy for his work *Interpretation of Radium,* published 1909." *Who's that?* Drake wondered. The name sounded English. *An English atomic scientist?* This had to be more than a fictional daydream. Wells had based it on some quantity of scientific scholarship. It would take him four or five hours to read this thing, but he was a fast reader. If he zipped through the text and landed only on portions relevant to atomic bombs, he'd get the overall message in an hour or two.

The door burst open, its window glass vibrating loudly, like it might shatter. The receptionist had already failed.

"Alex!" The door shot open. Bureau chief Jimmy Keene held the knob. Drake shut the book in the blink of an eye, then dropped it face-down at the side of his typewriter. "What the hell's wrong with you?" Keene crossed the office and sat down on the chair across from the desk. "You look sicker than an egg-suckin' dog!"

"Touch of the flu and out too late last night."

The editor's face creased with an insincere smile. "Take care of yourself. If you miss the mark with your articles anymore, you'll be recuperatin' on a slow boat to New York. Kleiner, the S-O-B from the Nazi censorship office, called me, complainin' about the article you turned over to the censors yesterday—your thing—*Germany's gettin' ready to fight a war.* You sent it over there without lettin' me read it. You're forgettin' I'm the editor! I'll read *every goddamned word* you write before it goes out of here, understand? It took me a long time to evolve a sense of what can pass through to the United States. Learn it from me or get another job. You're not catchin' on to ways to fight through this censorship." His West Virginia drawl was more noticeable than usual. As he leaned forward, his colorless face was taut. "Writin' for me, you have to be much more than a writer. To be a good journalist, by God, requires more than writin'. Means learnin' to follow a narrow road with steep cliffs and no guardrails—takes a helluva dose of guts, concentration, hard work, sacrifice. Remember that in days to come, whatever happens. Recognizin' Nazis' quirkiness and whims will get you a long way. Still, they've got Thor's hammer until something happens to take it away from 'em. And they'll kick your butt out of Germany, and mine too. Or worse—much worse."

Drake raised an eyebrow. "You don't like me much, do you?"

"It's not that. You're green as hell, even though you've been at this now for a few years. Long way to go, and I'm not a real patient man. By now, you ought to know what's gonna work with these censors. You're so fixated on being a proud journalist that you won't work within their boundaries. Maybe you're too bullheaded for this job. A nice desk to write from back in New York City might be your ticket."

Was this what it felt like to be fired? He'd never been thrown out of a job before, and maybe this was it coming.

"Boss, you'll get the rewrite before the censor sees it, not after—and it'll make our owner in New York happy."

"Get to be a better liar, son. Sensible caution, not surrender. It's a feelin' you need to get. This game changes every day, but our readers and our owner know that you can't tell things quite as they exist here. To stay alive in these parts, everyone's gotta be compromised. Morality here in this country can't be seen in black and white. It's many shades of rich, strange shades in between. So humor the bastards a little, get 'em to trust you."

Drake nodded as he shook a cigarette from the pack on the desk and offered one to Keene.

"No, thanks," he said, pulling his dark brown carved briar pipe from a vest pocket. "What's that you're readin' there?"

Drake shifted in his chair, struggling to hide his sudden unease. He glanced toward the edge of the desk. "Just something I found at the bookstore a few days ago."

Keene shrugged. "Let's not sit here makin' more chin music. Just be sure you get no more rejections for a while."

"No more rejections. Count on it."

The editor gave him another half-smile and stood, then took two steps toward the door.

I told Keene a year ago about the murder, Drake thought. *He's the only person who knows about it here. Now he's curious about what books I'm reading. A man so intertwined within the deceptions of Berlin—can he be trusted?*

"One more thing—before you go," Drake said.

Keene paused and glanced back, a startled look crossing his face.

"I told you about my father's death."

"What about it?"

"Ever mentioned that to anybody else?"

"No. *Hell no.* Why ask me somethin' like that?"

"Never mind. You're the only person who knows about it, and I want to keep it that way."

"It's your business, not mine, not anyone else's." The brass knob rattled in Keene's shaky grasp before he slammed the door shut.

Drake reached for the book, unsure if he could believe Keene. He tapped his fingertips on the back of his chair, then walked across his office and reopened the door to see the scowling receptionist.

"It's okay. You tried," he said, then turned back toward his workspace.

The gloomy blue twilight of early winter had crept across the intersection of Thielallee and Faradayweg streets in the western region of Berlin. A thin, middle-aged woman in a fur-trimmed black cashmere overcoat and fancy shoes stood at the intersection, waiting for traffic to clear. She carried a brown shopping bag and watched the Christmas lights twinkle in the darkness of the patrician Berlin suburb of Dahlem. The woman's name was Helga, and she was the personal secretary of Dr. Otto Hahn.

She looked up at the top corner of the three-story Kaiser Wilhelm Institute, at the decorative turret roof shaped like a gigantic Prussian Pickelhaube spiked helmet. The structure was built with a royal grant before the Great War, and she'd always suspected this fact had motivated the architect's laughable choice for styling the form of the roof—the Kaiser's headgear.

Reichsführer Heinrich Himmler's Schutzstaffel, SS for short, had recently taken sudden new notice of the Institute. Unbeknownst to Hahn and other directors of the KWI, several secretaries and janitorial workers of the laboratory held second jobs—as employees of the SS or the Army Intelligence Office. A bit of extra income from keeping an eye out for specialized paperwork or new test equipment combinations was certainly not wrongful gain. Covert eyes infiltrated many places within German research centers and academia.

Helga had a taste for elegant, stylish possessions, far more exquisite than she could afford on her modest KWI academia salary. She appreciated the SS officer providing her with the means to enjoy some comforts here and there. Helga had no way of knowing that her SS contact wasn't sending the fruits of her work to the Nazi government at all. Like her, the slightly built blonde man also led a second life. His was being a member of a small coterie of dissidents called *Schwarze Orchester*—Black Orchestra.

CHAPTER 6

SHOCKWAVE

"A sudden bold and unexpected question doth many times
surprise a man and lay him open."

Sir Francis Bacon

DRAKE SLID HIS HAND ALONG the railing of the steps leading to
the door of the apartment building. The flu symptoms lingered,
which, coupled with the workday's struggles, left him with zero
energy. It would be dark in a half-hour, and he toyed with the thought
of just going straight to bed with no supper. Twisting his key in the
lock, he pushed the door open, switched on the light, and tossed his
coat across the small, dark sofa. Maybe he'd open a can of soup and
heat it on the single hot plate next to the sink. *So tired.* He sat down
on the sofa and closed his eyes, venting a sigh of relief that this day
was over.

A sharp knock, two taps with a knuckle. *"Telefunken Telegramm!
Öffnen, bitte!"*

Drake straightened his back. "Yeah, gimme a second." He'd lapsed into English.

He stood and shuffled across the floor. As he reached for the doorknob, a split-second twinge of suspicion crossed his mind. He paused, then twisted the knob.

The door instantly sprung into his face, smashing the side of his cheek and firing him backward and against the sofa. Yellow auras flashed into his field of view as a leather-gloved fist hit him across the chin, snapping his teeth together. Strong hands locked his arms behind him as another pair of hands shoved a rag into his mouth.

"Don't make a sound, Drake, or you die right now." The words were whispered but harsh. "Keep your eyes shut."

Drake fought for consciousness, his knees wobbling. One of the hands slapped him hard.

"Listen to me carefully. Stay quiet, or you go with us on a ride that will end most unpleasantly for you, do you understand?"

"Um-uh," he answered through the cloth.

"Now, open your eyes."

Drake looked at his two attackers. Even though his vision was fuzzy, he could see that they wore uniforms adorned with silver "Death's Head" insignia. *SS officers!*

"Take the rag out of his mouth."

Drake leaned onto the sofa to steady himself. "What do you want from me? I'm an American citizen, and I've done nothing wrong."

The SS man on the left showed a threatening grin. "Nothing? Really, now."

A fist again lashed out and caught Drake's left ear, leaving him sprawled face down on the floor.

"Stand up! You're an American—a spy."

As Drake started to rise, a vicious kick landed on his ribs. He fell back down, groaning, and rolled onto his back.

"What were you doing last night on that train? You were plotting with a bastard who used to call himself SS but has now been exterminated. What traitorous acts were you planning with him?"

Drake felt his mind clearing slightly, but the pain in his side was not going away. It *had* been a trap, and now—his next stop would be a torture chamber.

"I wasn't on any train—I was here all night and sick. Ask my landlady. You've got the wrong person."

"Like hell, Drake. You're a liar and will tell us every detail of your little meeting with the turncoat. Your choice is to talk or die. What do you know about Ludwig Beck—another traitor?"

"Never heard of him."

"Another lie. Tell us what you know about his gang of subversives!"

"I told you. Nothing—I was here. I don't know what you're talking about. Threaten me all you want, but I'm not your guy. Get out and leave me alone. You want America to know what you're doing to me? Kill me, and the world will hear about it."

"So, we'll just shoot you here and make it look like you killed yourself." He glanced at his accomplice. "Hold his arms."

The gun was pointed directly at his temple—it was time for him to join his father. It was an honor to die like him, resisting this scum. "Go to hell, asshole."

The SS man smiled from one side of his mouth, then waved the shining black Luger as he carefully steadied it. *"Auf Wiedersehen, Amerikaner!"*

The gun's hammer snapped against the frame, the sharp, hollow *clack* bouncing off the walls of the apartment. Drake's eyes stared straight ahead, surrendering only the flicker of an eyelid.

"Seems we've run out of bullets tonight, *Herr Drake*," the man said as his arm dropped to his side. He pulled at the top button of his shirt and unbuttoned it. Drake blinked to try to clear his vision, still foggy from the beating. He couldn't be sure of what he was seeing.

"Who are you?" He gazed at the clerical collar suddenly visible under the knot of the tie.

"You aren't afraid. You have the guts to risk everything to stand up to Nazis with a gun sticking in your face."

Drake coughed and wiped a trickle of warm liquid from the corner of his mouth.

"We're not SS members. We got these uniforms through our Black Orchestra connections. I am a cleric and a comrade of General Beck. I believe you'll meet my associate and me again soon. Sorry for roughing you up, but we had to know how strong you are, see if you could be trusted."

The second man in German uniform spoke. "The Reverend is a tough war veteran despite the collar. He hit you pretty hard."

"Damn—" said Drake, shaking his head slowly.

They turned toward the door, and the one identified as a minister looked back.

"And put something cold on your ear. It's turning purple."

CHAPTER 7

THE RUBICON

Alea iacta est ("The die has been cast")

—Julius Caesar, January 10, 49 BCE,
as he led his army across the Rubicon river.

B IG SNOWFLAKES SPUN LAZILY IN the sky, dancing around the glass
bulbs of the streetlight, then vanishing as they flicked against the
pavement. The remaining light of day was just enough for Alex Drake to
make out the numerals on the brick pillar leading to the walkway. The
quick phone call four hours earlier had given him what he needed to
untangle the instructions for the meeting. Entering the garden courtyard
a few minutes past the agreed-upon time, he glanced toward the low-
hanging full moon illuminating the walkway flanked by fir trees. A
sense of dread flooded his mind. He switched the small parcel he carried
from one hand to the other and reached to punch the doorbell button.

The door opened, and a man who introduced himself as *Generaloberst*
Ludwig Beck's butler asked his name, then took his overcoat and
escorted him through the foyer and into the main room. Drake took

notice of the dark French furniture that dominated the sumptuous decor. Rose-colored damask draperies provided a backdrop to antiques and comfortable-looking couches.

A figure stepped from the shadows in the corner.

"*Herr Drake,* I am Ludwig Beck."

Drake nodded toward the former Chief of Staff of the German Army—the land component of the Wehrmacht, the overall German Armed Forces.

"My side still hurts after your thugs damned near kicked it in." Then, extending his arm toward the German general, he added, "Here's your book."

Beck took the brown paper sack. "The beating—sorry, but I needed to know if you could stand up to what's coming—that is, of course, if you join us."

"Glad your "Reverend" didn't make a mistake in checking if his gun was loaded."

Beck projected a studied air of confidence, what some might call *command presence.* He was dressed in a gray suede leather jacket and black trousers. His eyes were bright, but his mouth seemed to be set in a permanent scowl, something like an inverted smile. Beck's hands were tightly clenched fists. Drake sensed great anger inside this man, his discipline holding it at least temporarily in check.

"This way." The general led him into the library, furnished with hand-carved wood tables and chairs. The peaceful surroundings did nothing to settle Drake's edginess.

"Sit, please," Beck said.

Well-filled bookcases lined the walls. A writing desk with a tall black-shaded lamp stood in the middle of the room. The hearth framed a half-dozen blazing logs that crackled and sent bright orange-yellow sparks spiraling upward in the rising heat. Drake settled into a leather-covered wingback chair. It seemed odd that this steward didn't leave; instead, he stood to the right of the hearth, staring, like he was waiting for a cue. He was thick-chested, with muscular arms, contrary to the reedy butler-type.

"Something to drink?" asked Beck.

"No. Nothing."

"We know of you as an up-and-coming news writer."

Drake cut his eyes back toward Beck, his senses on full alert. "I'm a writer, true."

"I've seen some of your pieces in the translated version of your American magazine—quite good. So, I'll go straight to the point. Aboard the train, my associate told you about us and spelled out why we've summoned you, why we believe you can help us in our task ahead, and how you might be motivated to help yourself. And you must have many questions."

"Correct." Drake cast his fingers through his hair as he spoke.

"Then, before you ask them, I will reveal to you that it was not unanimous among my confrères to ask you to join us. Some of us are adamant that you should be called on to help. Others are—shall I say—less convinced. They argue that adding another variable, you, to the mixture increases risk."

Drake shifted slightly in his seat before cocking his head to one side. "Then what the hell am I doing here?"

"Because most of us believe that you'd add significantly to our odds of success. I'll explain after we clear up some necessary things. You've read the book?"

"I've read it. Huge bombs—unlimited power to destroy. Fiction so far, but I gather there may be things happening now. If so, how are you going to stop this from getting into Hitler's hands?"

"In point of fact, that's the fundamental question, and the answer involves you."

"That makes no sense."

"It might if you knew more."

"Then start with what your man aboard that train said. Something about Hitler himself ordering my father's murder in 1923. Where'd he get that?"

"Are you ready to learn the truth?"

Drake nodded. "Whatever it is, it was long ago, and my calluses are well in place. Go ahead."

"You'd been in Munich for more than a year—just a boy, accompanying your father on an overseas assignment. A renowned power systems engineer, he'd been hired by the Weimar government of Germany to help rebuild the nation's electrical supply network after the Great War. He wanted to educate you—immerse you—in the ways of another culture. You'd learned the language with no accent, possible only with the very young. Am I correct so far?"

Drake exhaled, drew his shoulders up, and slowly nodded his head. "Keep going."

"Then came the day of Hitler's aborted attempt to seize power in Bavaria. That morning, three thousand Nazis led by a young Adolf Hitler marched toward the city's center to battle government soldiers. But they ran into much stronger resistance than they'd expected. The soldiers crushed the Nazi rabble. Hitler escaped by running away like a scared rat, and his number-two-man Göring got shot in the balls."

"I know some of that. Mind if I smoke?"

"Of course not. And here's where it gets complicated for you. After the battle, a traitor in the local government decided to let Hitler know your father had played a role in its undoing."

"What? How?"

"The word was that Nazified workers at the electrical plant had talked of the plot; elder Drake overheard their conversations. He told the plant manager, who tipped off the police before the Hitlerites started their attack. The Munich police were ready and waiting in front of the *Feldherrnhalle.*"

The words were coming in a rapid-fire cadence that made Drake's mouth feel like he'd been eating sand. He snapped the brass-cased lighter shut, its lid emanating the hollow Zippo *clunk.* "Before the Bavarian police captured Hitler, he'd ordered your father hunted down. There weren't many Americans around Munich then, so it didn't take long."

Beck stood and paced across the room, then back to the fireplace before turning toward Drake. "A man and his young son walked out of a restaurant and started crossing the street to their hotel. A single shot. Done in the flick of a sniper's finger."

Drake closed his eyes as he comprehended the words. The bastard who now ruled Germany had been personally responsible for his years of torment.

The door chime rang in a melodious four-note sequence. "On that somber note, there would be my oldest friend, Holger Speier," Beck said. "A trusted member of Black Orchestra, probably accompanied by his lovely wife, Sondra."

Drake's eyes caught the motion of approaching figures. A servant re-entered the library, followed by two other people. The reporter stood. *Frau Speier* had one of those faces that one might see in a cosmetics ad. Her skin was pale, slightly reddened at the cheekbones by rouge powder or the cold air. A stylish black hat with a lacy veil adorned her head, and her lipstick was a subdued ruby red tone.

Beck took steps toward the new arrivals. "Sondra, Holger, meet Alexander Drake."

Drake shook hands with the somewhat oddly matched couple. Her grasp was firm, her hands strong with long fingers.

"*Guten Abend,* Drake," said Holger Speier in a thin voice as he looked over the gold frames of his glasses. "I've read your magazine. Quite like *Time*, though you'll probably disagree with me there."

"We play the game better."

General Beck fixed his gaze on the crackling fire dancing in the fireplace. "We are not here to discuss your writing, Drake. Sit down, all of you." He paused as they did as he'd requested.

"Sondra is unique. As a result of my friend here, she knows well the activities of Black Orchestra and is a *de facto* member. I like to think she's his muse—like a guiding spirit."

Sondra looked into the flames. Drake contemplated her face. *And so what is she?* One imagines a woman simply out for easy money and a comfortable life. She might have had her pick of any man, but she'd chosen a husband twice her age. *Explanations abound.*

"Do all the wives come to meetings of Black Orchestra?" Drake asked. "Kind of a family get-together? German one-pot suppers?"

Sondra's mouth turned down. "Sarcasm, *Herr Drake?* I come here only because my husband requests it. Holger asks for my advice and thoughts on many things. Others might resent my presence, but like good soldiers, they pretend to accept me. I go to some of the meetings and keep silent. Holger pays the bills for Black Orchestra. Bribes get costly, so nobody complains very loudly."

Beck dropped his frame onto the chair behind his desk and tapped a shining brass spheroid paperweight on the leather writing pad.

"She's essentially right," the general said. "You certainly know that I resigned as Chief of Staff of the Army High Command three months ago in opposition to Hitler's plans to invade Czechoslovakia. The trappings of wealth you see around you—I couldn't afford this on a German general's salary. But Hitler pays out extravagant bonuses—bribes—to leaders to maintain loyalty to him. Since I left, my income dropped so dramatically that *Herr Speier* must provide for Black Orchestra's work. Now I'm suspected of plotting a *coup d'état,* and I see the black-suited, black-hatted Gestapo agents lurking around, keeping me under surveillance."

"Why doesn't Hitler just have you killed off? He doesn't hesitate when it comes to murder—why would he even think twice about eliminating you?"

"Arresting me would anger the leadership of the military, which still harbors many of my supporters. He knows that. So, I'm in perpetual peril of being hit by an imaginary bus or having a fictitious heart attack."

The servant had disappeared. Drake's fingers drummed the tabletop.

"Who's shadowed us here tonight?" he asked.

"Listen, if I didn't think we were safe, I wouldn't take the risk. The shades are drawn tight; this place is frequently checked for listening devices."

"Your impression thus far of Black Orchestra, Drake?" asked Speier in Pomeranian-accented German.

"'Impression?' Well, I'd say your courage is astonishing, but before you can find a way to get rid of this hypothetical Nazi wonder-bomb, the Gestapo will have you in their teeth. The game will end before it's begun." *Say no more,* he thought.

Sondra Speier crossed her legs and adjusted her dark-colored satin skirt. "You're quite right. I don't have a vote, but I've told my husband that I oppose your becoming part of this intrigue—I don't think it's smart or necessary, and, quite candidly, you'd be well advised to leave things alone and stick with your life as a magazine reporter. You are *compos mentis.* Stay away."

A German wife, speaking out and using Latin words. *Unique*—Beck's comment had been correct.

"Eight men, nine with you, fighting the vicious government of this country of eighty million," she continued. "Someone will be caught and forced to expose Black Orchestra—soon. You'll be rounded up and sent to the torture chambers. I despise everything about the Nazis and their terrible actions. Still, Black Orchestra has no chance of interfering with the Nazi government. You're wasting your lives to try to change things that can't be changed."

"These atom bombs—what they'll do to the world if Hitler gets them. You're telling Black Orchestra just to let this happen?"

"With these bombs that you talk about," Sondra said, "Hitler could threaten to kill the whole world with impunity. I hate him as much or more than you or the others do, but I'm a realist. He's not going to be stopped by this little group. You'll need an army,"

"We *have* an army, Sondra," said Beck, "a big one. General Klaus Würter represents factions in the military who've declared they'll fight on our side against the Hitlerites and support our new government."

Drake tapped his fingertips on the arm of the chair and studied her face.

"How do you know that?" she asked. How deeply do you trust him? Will he actually do what you need him to do?"

General Beck sat straight as he replied. "I—we have no choice but to trust him. Without the armed forces on our side, we've got no chance. He's absolutely essential." The flickering firelight had turned his face crimson. "You've read about these weapons in Wells' book—countless millions of people dead. I could sit here in my house with my servants and books, ignore the idea of Nazi atomic bombs, then my grandchildren—if they survive—call me a coward because I stayed back."

"Your man on the train," Drake said, "disclosing startling secrets to me, a stranger. I'm a foreign national. You're either fools or have lost your minds."

Beck's eyes narrowed, an angry expression creating crinkles on his forehead. "Had we not known of your father's murder, we would have never taken such a chance. But it's *that* fact that made us very certain where your loyalties lie. It's a question of how much courage you possess. You're here because we need you, and by our design, you've acquired knowledge that makes you very dangerous. Which do you choose— cooperation or an untimely death?"

"You're threatening me?"

The general's hand sliced a swinging arc in the air. "Call it your new reality."

Drake nodded and stood up.

"Save your threats. I'm one-hundred percent in, with one-hundred percent certainty of getting killed." And the new reality was that he'd just crossed the Rubicon.

"Indeed. So, ask your questions," said Beck.

"Your man on the train—who is he?"

Another heavy log fell from the blazing pile. "A complex story. I believe I hear him at the door just now. I hope you're prepared for some surprises."

CHAPTER 8

IGNITION

"I answer him who asks, "What was God doing
before He made heaven and earth?"
He was preparing hell for those who pry into His mysteries."

Book 11, Chapter 12 of *Confessions of St Augustine*, ca. 420 AD

THE BUTLER USHERED IN A man with thick, wiry hair and heavy, black-rimmed glasses. Drake was surprised. *That's not the guy from the train.* He wore a long black wool coat, plain, buttoned up to his Adam's apple. He reached an arm up and yanked a wig off his head, then removed the dark glasses and fluffed up his thin hair as he shivered from the Berlin night air. Drake began to rise, now recognizing the face.

"No, don't get up. Good evening to each of you," the newcomer said. "All Hallows' Eve has passed, but I've kept this disguise around for just such a night like this. I tried a big mustache too, but it made me sneeze." He unbuttoned the top buttons of his coat and began to pull it open. Drake sat straight up as he instantly recognized the clothing underneath—black uniform, white shirt and black tie, the right lapel adorned with runic letters, like a pair of lightning bolts.

Drake jumped in his seat. "You—you're Hitler's SS?" he said, voice rising.

"And we meet again, Drake, so soon, and I will tell you my name this time. I am SS *Oberleutnant* Gunnar Schoe."

"An SS officer in a meeting of the Underground. This gets more amazing at every turn."

"As the others already know, it's complicated," the newcomer said. The servant was carrying a chair toward him.

Beck waved and said, "Sit down. Drake has questions. Your little tête-à-tête with him was effective. He has committed to join our movement. He has things to ask you and the rest of us."

Drake looked directly at Schoe. "A traitor to the SS. That means you'll betray anyone."

Schoe twisted his mouth and stared back. "You don't know my circumstances—you can't judge."

"Circumstances?"

"It was 1930, Drake. You weren't here, and you didn't experience the despair this nation had fallen into—a time of poverty, hardship, and loss served on top of the devastation of the World War and a global economic depression that commenced the prior year. A loaf of bread in Berlin in 1922 cost 200 Reichsmarks. By the time Hitler tried to seize power in Munich a year later, that bread price had risen—just a bit—to 200 *million* marks for a loaf. The currency was worthless, the economy hung around in the trash for years. Then Hitler came along with his shining promises for restoring the German people who'd lost everything in the financial collapse and hyperinflation. Germans like me went for it like a dog biting into sweet meat. I found inspiration in the idea of this nation becoming a better place, and I joined the Nazi Party, eventually entering the SS. But after a time, I realized the obscene truth. My job positioned me to comprehend what Nazism really was—earlier and more clearly than most. Then something happened. Something which changed the world for me."

"Which was?" Drake asked.

"Call it mass extermination or genocide, but I was assigned to investigate poisons. I was handed orders signed by Adolf Eichmann, SS *Hauptscharführer* of Department 112—Jewish Affairs Department." Beck held up a single finger and leaned forward. "Was it now one year ago?"

"Yes, and that memo said, 'You are to determine the fastest, most efficient way to exterminate *useless eaters.*' That meant human beings—Jews, Serbs, the sick, anyone the Nazis deemed undesirable. I'd heard Himmler talk of slaughtering 30 million people across Europe to make room for 'pure Aryans.' That was my task: kill 30 million people. With my doctorate from the University of Aachen Institute of Chemistry and as an SS officer, I was the perfect investigator of poisons—to efficiently murder humans."

Schoe dropped his gaze and moved his hands up and down his sleeves as he continued in a low voice. "And I found it, a formula of hydrogen cyanide, which became known as Zyklon B. Used to fumigate ships, warehouses, and trains. My intellect—my soul—rejected participation in this colossal crime. I used the word *despair.* But I vowed to fight it, not let it destroy me. That's when I decided to use my job, my career, to help destroy Nazism. I sought out the general, convinced him I was real, and found hope with Black Orchestra, which I joined just a few months ago."

Drake felt the muscles of his brow relax. "And how long has this group existed?"

"Two years," Beck answered. "As recently as September, it looked that we would move against Hitler after his demands that the Sudetenland be turned over to Germany. Events were heading to a declaration of war from Britain. Then the stuffed-shirt English coward Chamberlain prostituted himself, gave in to Hitler's demands, and ruined our plans to leverage that Nazi madness into our army-backed overthrow of this damnable corrupt government. Then a few weeks ago, we learned of this H. G. Wells atomic bomb moving toward existence, and here we are, *Herr Drake.*"

"Beck eventually came to trust me," said Schoe, "unlikely co-conspirator as I might be. That I suppose describes you, too, an American journalist. So, who will betray us? How long before our pathetic throats get cut? These questions loom over us every second."

Drake leaned against the back of his chair and looked up at the ceiling.

"Welcome to Black Orchestra," said Beck. "Here's your membership kit." Beck handed across a white cardboard box about the size of a matchbox. The label bore the inscription Wrigley's P.K. Kaugummi. "Open it, shake out the bits."

"Wrigley's chewing gum?"

"Yes, but manufactured in Frankfort since 1925. Popular here, you've seen it in stores, but it's a hell of a lot different than what's in that packet. This gift comes courtesy of one of our most essential associates, whom you will soon meet."

"Gift? What is it?"

"Concentrated arsenic. Bite into one, and death follows in a matter of seconds. If you get yourself in a position where you're going to have to submit to the SS, that's the time to have a nice, refreshing piece of chewing gum. Otherwise, you'll end up in a show trial and disgrace the United States before you go to the torture chamber and the firing squad. That's the potential outcome for which you've signed up. It's not too late to back out."

"General, I said I'm in, and I meant it."

DECEMBER 2, 1938, THE KAISER WILHELM INSTITUTE, BERLIN-DAHLEM

"Fifty million times the power of TNT!" Professor Otto Hahn shouted at the smoke-darkened walls of his laboratory universe. He staggered backward from the blackboard, dropping the fat stick of chalk on the floor, then turned to slam his worn, ivory-surfaced K&E slide rule against the desktop. The blow shattered a delicate porcelain cup, spattering droplets of coffee across the starched white cuffs pushed out from the sleeves of his woolen jacket. He pressed his hands against his temples. "Because of me!"

A chest-crushing pressure flowed through him as his intellect fought to grasp the reality of the mathematical integrals and differential equations scrawled on the slate wall. He glanced at the backs of his hands. The reddish light of the setting sun spilled across his leathery skin, creased by decades of work with radioactive substances and caustic chemicals. Maybe the massive radiation exposure would do away with him as it had recently killed *Madame Curie,* but it wouldn't be soon enough to deliver him from the coils of guilt encircling his neck.

Touching his gray mustache, he took wheezy breaths as he turned toward the window. Heavy, dark eyebrows hooded his large eyes, focused on the shadowy Berlin cityscape eastward from the Kaiser Wilhelm Institut für Chemi.

Hahn swept away the puddle of coffee and shards of porcelain as he closed his hand around the report lying on his desk. His index finger passed slowly, carefully over the pages, as if he might press their contents back into the paper, keeping the words and numbers from coming into the world.

"Burn the papers! Now—before anyone else sees them! Hahn thought as he looked around the laboratory, the trembling of his lower lip infuriating him. His fingers jabbed against it.

The worktables were messy. Cubes of a whitish, semitransparent material were stacked next to something akin to an oversized Christmas angel food cake—a big white toroidal ring made of paraffin wax. Hahn had placed small cylinders of highly radioactive radium in the center of the ring more than a day earlier. Against the outer skin of this cake of wax, he'd pasted thin foil sheets of the purest uranium obtainable, thinking he might find that the uranium would change in some way when atomic particles spewing from the radium passed through the paraffin wax and hit the strips.

It changed alright. But the change was an unforeseen, startling thing. Most of the uranium had simply disappeared. Whatever substance remained wasn't uranium anymore—instead, something bizarre had happened, something never before experienced in the history of humanity.

He tapped his pencil on the stack of graph papers and notebooks illuminated under the greenish shade of the desk lamp. He reread his co-worker's computations and notes, retraced the results a dozen times before replicating the calculations himself on his blackboard, expunging all residual doubts. Over many hours, some of the uranium metal had transformed directly from a solid substance into energy. Working with Einstein's mathematics, he'd calculated that if the uranium atoms were instantly and entirely converted to power, the explosion would be *fifty million* times greater than ordinary bombs!

"Why?" he asked aloud. "Why wasn't this laboratory blown to a godless hell along with the rest of Berlin?" *Speed* was the answer. The enormous energy had bled out slowly, over twenty-eight hours, instead of a tiny fraction of a second as with an explosive. *If the power were to be released all at once,* he thought, *yes, although the data said that couldn't happen with uranium. But with a new element—like H.G. Wells' carolinum—the instant release would . . .*

He erased the numbers and symbols on the slate while thinking of the face of a dark-haired, plump man with thick glasses. This emissary from the German War Office would come calling again soon to check the progress of the "atom experiments." Naturally, government officials probed everything he did.

That bastard Kurt Diebner. A Nazi nuclear physicist employed by the Reichswehrministerium, the Reich War Ministry, this unpleasant man already knew too much about the atomic energy research and suspected that Hahn's work could lead to instantaneously unleashing the great energy inside each atom. He barked his words like an angry dog—*what happened? Where's your data? Show me everything!* Hahn would have to provide a written report on this latest experiment, which Diebner would undoubtedly send to Himmler, even to Hitler. He dropped himself onto his desk chair. Incinerating the information would accomplish nothing. Others in the laboratory understood the results and procedures. Diebner already knew far too much, and if Hahn made excuses, destroyed calculations, the project leader would order another experiment, and next time he'd stand there in person.

His eyes fell upon the empty birdcage in the corner of the room. Empty since '37, yet there it remained. The wires had enclosed Ralf, Hahn's richly-colored friend of twenty years. He'd died in the spring of that year, a pity since parrots of his kind lived to fifty or more. The growth on his neck, probably due to radiation, took his strength, then his life. So, the innocent bird dies, not the evil scientist. It should have been the other way around.

Hahn gripped the tarnished brass drawer clasp, glided the drawer open, and stared at its contents. Rulers and pencils hid the small glass vial, but soon his shaking fingers dug far enough to find it and pull it out. His lip quivered with increased intensity, intensifying the shame.

Dear God, Otto Hahn thought, *I am the destroyer of humanity. As it was in 1915—when I made the chlorine gas—it comes to me again, but this time . . .* millions *will die.*

He jerked the cork out—white, chunky crystals fell from the vial and into his open palm. The face of Lise Meitner, his collaborator of thirty years, appeared in his mind's eye. She had helped him investigate radioactivity and had given sparkling insights into the world of the atom. But she was now far away. *Lise would know what to do.*

The sodium cyanide granules in his hand were just a few centimeters from his lips. His nostrils picked up the pungent smell of bitter almonds. He was completely aware of what would happen in the next seconds. This chemical would paralyze his central nervous system, his body would convulse violently, terminating his crimes against humanity. That is, if he had the guts to put the crystals in his mouth. His hand was now shaking violently, his jaw set hard. There was only one way to atone for what he'd done. He must surrender to the ghosts, past and future.

A fist slammed on the laboratory door, the noise jarring, reverberating.

"Hahn! Are you in there?"

The door rattled again, then the knob twisted. Hahn looked down at the white flakes in his hand. He snapped his fist shut.

A bespectacled man swung the door open and pushed through. "Stand up! I am talking to you!"

The professor remained in his chair, his only gesture of nonconformity. "Just give me a minute, Diebner. I'm not well."

"Your office is a mess—what are you doing?"

"Leave me alone, please." Hahn glanced at his watch, twisting his wrist just enough so that the crystals sprinkled against his pants as they quietly dropped to the floor.

"Why all that crap on your papers?"

Hahn straightened, rubbing his eyes. "Nothing—a small accident."

Diebner walked to the opposite side of the laboratory, keeping his eyes on the experimental apparatus near the window.

"The uranium tests—where is your report? By now, you and your cohorts must have results." He turned back to Hahn. "Is that the report there on your desk? Give it to me!"

"It's just a letter . . . from a friend." Hahn brushed bits of porcelain and flakes of poison from the papers and slid them into a drawer. "I need time."

"You have until tomorrow, Hahn. And I will see the work repeated in front of me, even if I must sleep here on a chair next to you." Diebner walked toward the door, then turned back, pulled down his glasses, and looked over the rims with a flat gaze. "Seven in the morning—not one goddamned minute later! *Heil Hitler!*"

CHAPTER 9

PURE URANIUM

"There is not the slightest indication that
nuclear energy will ever be obtainable."

Albert Einstein, 1932

BERLIN, DECEMBER 15, 1938, SS
HAUPTAMT (SS HEADQUARTERS)

THE PILLARED GRAY STONE BUILDING ahead loomed over SS *Oberleutnant* Schoe. He looked up at the six-story structure capped by greenish sloped roof panels and took a breath. He didn't feel right— were the chest troubles getting worse? *Damned cigarettes.* He needed to quit, but he needed a lot of things right now. In time, perhaps. Walking through the slush covering the sidewalk of Prinz Albrecht-Strasse toward the grim, arching entrance to No. 8, the most feared building address in Berlin, SS Headquarters, he tried to calm himself. A few bars of "Tango Ballad" from Bertolt Brecht's *The Threepenny Opera* boiled up from his throat.

There was a time,
And now it's all gone by.
When we two lived together,
She and I.

That first verse, he thought, *such a time.* Schoe's favorite stage play, Brecht's masterpiece, was banned in Germany after Hitler's rise. *One more reason to hate the bastard.* 1930 was such a grand year, yet horrible at the same time. He was in love during that spring of blossoms and colorful birds, but the nation around him was drawing near the awful abyss of civil war in its streets. They'd look out from his apartment onto the traffic below, then, more often than not, make love before he went off to his new job at SS Headquarters. And so things changed as the year went by. She'd turned colder as the weather did, and one evening when he came home, all her belongings were gone. Except for once more, he never saw her again. *Enough! Silly old thoughts.*

Schoe's desk telephone nagged a few minutes before ten, forcing him to redeploy his mind from a report from the Wehrmacht armaments research center on recent tests of a rocket-propelled anti-tank missile.

"*Hallo!*"

A pause, then a too-familiar voice blasted from the earpiece. "This is Herrmann."

"Yes, sir. What can I help with this morning?"

"I have something I need you to do. Ignore your schedule and go directly to Dahlem. I have just received news of an important conference setting up there at this moment. Kaiser Wilhelm Institute."

"But I must—"

"This is imperative. No arguments."

"What will be the subject, sir?"

"A new development in weaponry. Wehrmacht people will be there. I can't go—I have a meeting with *Reichsführer* Himmler himself. Use my driver and get details from my secretary. I have already announced that you will be there on my behalf. Now get over there and go to work. Report to me what happens."

The line went dead as Schoe pressed the telephone handset against the side of his jaw and clutched at the pain in his chest. "Wehrmacht people will be there" meant something big concerning "weaponry" was about to happen. Anyway, as one of the SS technical staff's primary intellects, he was the logical choice to attend. Maybe it was about the same anti-tank rocket tests. He stuck his hand into his shirt pocket. He kept his supply of pills in a tiny envelope—glyceryl trinitrate, known commonly as nitroglycerine, the active ingredient in dynamite. *Oh, the irony.* Highly diluted, nitroglycerine worked to keep him alive—to fight against the creation of a vastly more violent explosive than dynamite. He chewed and swallowed the pill dry, with no water.

The official SS car sped across Berlin's western suburbs through a light snowfall, the driver splashing pedestrians with smiling abandon. After a half-hour ride along Eichkampstrasse, which cut through the Dahlem Wildlife Preserve, it stopped in front of the Kaiser Wilhelm Institute building topped by the Pickelhaube. The car's rear door swung open, and Schoe clambered out and took the steps up to the entrance.

The SS *Oberleutnant* was ushered into the large conference room, where he signed a document acknowledging his presence at the meeting. His nervous stomach was acting up, adding to the pains below his breastbone. There were a dozen others already seated at the polished walnut conference table. Schoe knew some of the faces, but no one exchanged greetings. A man with thick glasses, sitting at the head of the table, nodded to a soldier standing stiffly at attention to the right of the door, who moved to close off the room.

The man pushed his spectacles to the top of his forehead and began turning an object over in his hands. A highly polished block of blackish metal, the size of a sugar cube, glistened in the light of the chandeliers. He placed it on the table and tapped it as he looked at the others who sat watching wordlessly.

"My name is Kurt Diebner," he said. "What I'm holding is the purest exemplar of natural uranium ever produced. Pick it up and feel it—it's not radioactive, don't be afraid. Here—pass it along to the others."

"Why do you bring us here on such short notice, Diebner?" The question, aggressive, angry, was asked by a man in uniform. Schoe recognized the face of Ernst Kaltenbrunner, the top security enforcer of the SS.

Diebner tilted his head away. "I am in charge of a War Office project to investigate the explosive potential of uranium. We know very little at this early stage, but things you will hear today may be critical to maintaining Germany's supremacy. Everything discussed here is at the ultimate level of secrecy. Keep that in mind as you listen. Introduce yourselves and be quick about it."

Each man declared his name and responsibilities. Schoe was familiar with most of them, including German scientific luminaries such as Werner Heisenberg, Carl von Weizäcker, and Hans Bothe.

"Dr. Otto Hahn, my top radiation scientist at this institution, is the man responsible for the new discovery. Proceed, Hahn."

The gray-haired professor rose and took hesitant steps toward black draperies, which he slowly drew back to reveal a large white cardboard panel embellished with hand-printed words and arrows. Deep wrinkles above his hawkish eyes bespoke a reluctance to share his information, but he took a step closer to the board.

"I will be brief and do my best to explain this. Hand me that cube."

The shining metal block was passed down the line of men, the last person lifting it onto Hahn's outstretched hand.

"Did you notice how heavy it is? You might know that uranium is the densest of all metals—three times the weight of a piece of steel the same size."

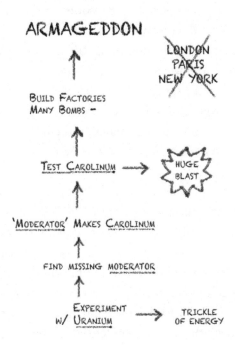

Hahn leaned over and carefully placed the cube near the center of the table, the overhead light bringing out his hands' leathery look. "Natural uranium from the ground is not explosive. But we've now found it will release energy—a great amount of energy—under the right conditions." He pointed to the bottom of the chart. "Down here—my experiment with uranium. Energy came out, but over a span of days—a trickle. Then, I used Albert Einstein's equations to calculate the power let loose. Of course, you realize that an *explosion* means it has to be released suddenly—all at once."

Kaltenbrunner turned his face upward. "Einstein—the traitor scientist, living amongst the Americans now." He spat out the words in contempt.

"You probably have heard speculation about atom bombs," Hahn continued. "It's impossible unless there is some way to unbind the energy in an *instant*, not days."

"Bigger bombs do not guarantee victory in war, Hahn," said Kaltenbrunner. "Doing what you said—exploding instantly—how much more powerful might this imagined bomb of yours be than our bombs of the current type? Three times? Ten times?"

Hahn hesitated and looked at Diebner for authorization to speak. Diebner nodded slowly.

"Fifty million times more powerful on a gram-for-gram basis, by early crude calculations."

A collective gasp went up.

Raising his voice and slapping the tabletop, Kaltenbrunner said, "You can't mean that one of your fanciful atomic bombs replaces fifty million conventional bombs!"

"That assumes every atom of the metal would burst, which is unlikely. Remember, ordinary uranium does not explode at all. If it did, this planet would have vaporized long ago. A new, unknown version of uranium must be created—an artificial element that yet has no name. It doesn't exist. There is no little cube of it to pass around. And if and when it does come, it might not be something to pass around because of a small problem. If it turns out to be radioactive, it will kill you. Creating it will require technology of which we have no concept at present, something quite unlike anything previously done."

"Absurd, Hahn," said Kaltenbrunner, pushing back his chair. "There's nothing new here. You're just talking about burning uranium, like wood burns. Many metals burn, including the magnesium inside our incendiary bombs. Same thing."

"No. Totally wrong. Know this, all of you!" Hahn's back stiffened. "Nothing 'burns' in this. And element uranium will not burst *all at once*. We now know of the vast energy lurking inside atoms, but to get it out will require something all-new. How to make it? That's what men of science have wondered about for more than twenty-five years. This thing right here." Hahn tapped his finger against the line on the page marked "moderator."

"This is needed to transform uranium into a new element. Like adding yeast to the dough to make it into bread. So, whoever finds the yeast here can make the bread to annihilate the world."

Hahn ambled back to his chair, sat down heavily, and slumped forward, his right hand shaking as he ran it across his eyes. Schoe looked closely at the aging scientist and saw a tear running down the side of his face.

Diebner was polishing his glasses with a white handkerchief. They sparkled under the lights as he put them on the table. "So far, we don't know much more than what he's said. A huge amount of scientific research lies ahead to understand how to make this thing. We know with some certainty that we are first to split atoms, based on what my people have gleaned from reading international journals and technical papers. Schoe! Are you paying attention?"

The blonde SS man's heart jumped crazily inside his chest as he heard his name called out.

"Of course!"

"You," Diebner shouted, "of all people in this room! Your job in the SS technical staff. Why in the hell don't you know what our future enemies worldwide—England, the United States, France, even Japan—are doing concerning splitting atoms?"

As he cleared his throat, Schoe sensed his vision going black. He pressed his chest to try to make the pain stop. "I—all of us—learned of this atomic bomb possibility just minutes ago." He heard the pitch of his own voice rising. "My research people and I already have atomic energy on our list of subjects to watch for in worldwide scientific literature. Due to this disclosure, the search for information about nuclear bombs will be prioritized on the list of—"

"Dr. Hahn," Heisenberg interrupted, "forget your ideas of the instant release of atomic energy for a weapon." They all knew of his 1932 Nobel Prize award for formulating quantum physics theory and his eminence as one of the world's most renowned scientists. "Forget about this bomb idea like most of the international scientific community already has. Your slow release of energy from uranium atoms is perhaps the world's first, but it couldn't explode. Without your 'yeast' to make the new element, nothing. Even with it, probably still nothing. In the past, Einstein has said the same thing. So if you people report back to your respective bosses that atomic energy bombs are about to start coming out of Germany's war production factories, you're fools."

Hahn lifted his eyes, suddenly widened with hope.

"Then why waste our time if it's going to lead to nothing?" asked Kaltenbrunner, again slamming his big hand on the table.

Diebner grabbed the cube from Hahn. "Because despite what the esteemed Dr. Heisenberg states, there is a chance that this line of research might indeed result in a tremendous weapon for Germany— or England, or America. Which one of you would like to tell the *Führer* that the British have this weapon and we do not? Consider this information to be like a 1903 announcement to Germany's military that Americans have made a crude preliminary flight of an airplane, the weapon that would play a major role in the Great War of 1914 and an infinitely greater one in the next. Which of you wants to take that chance with the uranium block sitting there?"

They were speechless. Diebner's eyes searched back and forth at the men. "There is no purpose in further questions," he declared. "The point of this conference has been achieved. You have been informed of this confidential step, and each one of you must be watchful that our potential advantage gained with this research is not wasted. Total secrecy and vigilance are required to safeguard the fatherland. Be careful how and to whom you report the information, and don't forget that this is only a tentative first stride along a path that could lead to a complete dead end. We meet again in seven days to coordinate the atom bomb project's formation—people, resources, and responsibilities. Be prepared. You are dismissed."

Schoe sat for a full minute, contemplating the words he had heard as the others left their chairs and filed out. *It's coming,* he thought. *I must get this to Beck.*

The snow had intensified under a gray sky, building up in white stripes along the streets' curbsides and against buildings. Schoe looked around for the brown Opel Kadett with the number 52 painted on the rear fender. *There.* He heard the motor's sputtering sound and saw thick white exhaust smoke bubbling out of its tailpipe. The driver rolled the window down.

"I need lunch. They served us nothing in there. Take me to the Zehnder restaurant on Regenerstrasse. I shall find my own way back to my office."

The car made its way across Berlin as Schoe contemplated what to tell Herrmann and how to convey this atomic weapons development information to the members of Black Orchestra. He bounded up the stairs and into Zehnder's, a place specializing in fried chicken American-style. He passed between the tables to the telephone booth at the back of the restaurant. The light inside the compartment was burned out. *Just as well,* he thought, *I don't want anyone seeing me.* Dropping a coin into the slot, he stabbed his finger at the holes in the dial, twirling it around with quickness.

"General Beck's residence," said a voice. Schoe paused to listen for telltale clicks or static on the line indicating wiretaps. There were none. When the general answered, Schoe issued his coded instructions for a meeting.

The SS officer ordered a cup of tea from a stocky waitress with multiple chins. He was the only customer in the place. A cat was curled up in a corner next to the staircase, and an old-fashioned radio with a round glass dial sat on a shelf and played orchestral music. The tea was hot and robust. He added cream English-style from a porcelain cup and waited. The jet-black animal crossed the eating area and turned to stare at him with unblinking green eyes. *Was this cat a spy?* He checked his watch and looked toward the radio.

A deep voice sounded from behind him. "What's this about?

Schoe turned to see General Beck. "Why in God's name risk a code red? Since there are no other customers, I will sit with you here. Be brief and save the details for another time."

Schoe cleared his throat before speaking in a hushed voice. "I just came from a War Office briefing session for German scientists and senior military people—the subject being the atomic bomb. It's going to move fast from this point. Germany probably already enjoys a huge lead over other nations."

The general looked confused for a few seconds, then his eyes narrowed, his brain linking the words he'd just heard. "We meet tonight to learn what you know, then lay out a plan of action. Let's get out of here. I'll start the fan-out process to alert our comrades. Twenty-one hundred hours at the warehouse. Tell your story then, and be early."

The dreary December winter produced a cover of near-darkness by half-past five. A thin coating of ice made descending the steps in front of the *World Week* Berlin bureau office sufficiently perilous that Drake stopped halfway down to lean against the railing. He cupped his hands around the lighter to shield the flame from the wind as he lit a cigarette, then looked over his hands to see a male figure standing to the side of the last tread. The lighter snapped closed as he turned quickly and continued down the steps onto the snowy sidewalk. A Mercedes-Benz sedan was idling smoothly at the curb a few meters away. Drake gave it a momentary glance.

A female voice came from inside the car. *"Das ist er!"*

The figure, silhouetted by headlights of oncoming vehicles, came toward him. "Do not move, *Herr Drake*."

He shuffled back a step or two. "Who's that?"

"Come over here." A familiar voice.

The car's right rear window was rolled down a quarter of the way, but it was impossible to make out the facial features of the person inside. Nevertheless, Drake could feel eyes upon him. The interior light suddenly switched on as the door swung open.

"Get in. Don't attract attention."

Sondra Speier slid over to give him room to sit. He knew the scent of Chanel perfume, which was by unlikely coincidence his late fiancee's favorite.

The driver slammed the door shut and moved around the long hood to take his place behind the wheel. The car moved smoothly away from the curb and into the early evening traffic.

"Tell him your address. We will drive you home."

"All right. 719 Invalidenstrasse."

Sondra reached forward and turned a hand crank to close the glass partition between the rear seat and the driver's compartment.

"To what do I owe the honor of this invitation—or should I call it a kidnapping?

"Sarcasm?"

"Maybe. You and I didn't get along especially well at our introduction."

"I've come to tell you of an urgent meeting at the warehouse basement—nine tonight. Beck says all must attend, all to be informed. I tried to call, but I didn't have your direct number, your switchboard was closed. My husband is not feeling well, and he's asked me to go in his place and come here and tell you to be at the meeting. And there's another thing."

"What would that be?"

"You're a newborn to Black Orchestra, yet I'm turning to you about something dreadful. And I have a reason for doing so."

Drake gave out a little laugh. "Here we are in your car, and unless I'm completely wrong, what you're about to tell me is even more ominous than Black Orchestra's struggles which I'm already aware of."

"Correct, but you must know this before you become so involved that you can't possibly back out."

"I'm probably way past that already but go ahead—say it." Drake stared toward her nearly invisible form. The car had stopped for a traffic signal in front of a theater. The illumination of the colorful windows backlit her delicate profile—high forehead, sharply pointed small nose, full lips, strong chin.

She swung back toward him and said, "I think . . . there is a traitor within the cell."

Drake sat bolt upright. "A traitor. How do you know this? What's Beck say?"

"I haven't told the general yet. This involves someone my husband cannot know about." She turned away.

"Why not?"

"The person is pursuing me relentlessly. Someone inside Black Orchestra"

"*Pursuing*? To kill you or make you his lover?"

"Perhaps 'lover' in his mind, not in mine."

"Okay, maybe he's a scoundrel, trying to make a cuckold of your husband, but does that make him a traitor to this bunch?"

"Cuckold." She tapped a finger on her chin. "Meaning the unfortunate husband of an unfaithful wife. That won't be happening, *Herr Drake*. But, I have my reasons to believe this."

"What are they?"

"I've come to understand his personality enough to know that he has motives that don't square with those of Beck and the rest.

"Why haven't you told the general of your suspicions?"

"Because I might be completely wrong. A woman's intuition can be a fickle guide. I can't say anything until I know for sure. When the time is right, I'll tell him, but I can't allow my husband to suffer over this."

"How could this hurt your husband? You mean he'd be jealous?"

"Beyond jealous—he'd be devastated. I've thought about this endlessly. Beck will not believe that I am faithful to Holger. In his opinion, I'm only with my husband because of money." As the limousine passed the streetlamps, yellow light flashed rhythmically across her face.

"I'm telling you too much, too soon, but I sense that you can be trusted, and you have the slimmest ties of anyone to Beck and my husband. To know of my relationship—although platonic—with another man would destroy Holger. His heart is weak, and . . . you're the only one I can communicate this to. In the event something happens to me, someone must know."

Drake sighed. "Who is this *Kerl* you suspect of being a rat? Goerdeler? Schoe?"

"I said I won't tell you. I don't yet have proof."

"How's that going to work? A group of us fighting for humanity and can't trust each other?"

"I need time. For now, you will say nothing to Beck. Not yet."

Drake struggled to control his anger. Every additional scrap of information about Black Orchestra yielded some bizarre new way to get killed without ever accomplishing anything. If this illusory Judas decided to open up to the Gestapo, it's over before Black Orchestra can take its first swing at the piñata.

Raising his voice, he said, "This is insane!" He grabbed the sleeve of her coat. "You *must* tell Beck of your suspicions and make known who it is!"

"Don't touch me," she said loudly, pulling away.

The chauffeur's head bobbed up. He reached back for the crank handle, lowering the partition glass a few centimeters. *"Something, Frau Speier?"* he said.

"The gentleman will get out of the car right here. Pull over, Joachim."

The sedan began to head for the curb.

"Out of my car—now!"

"I apologize. I was out of line."

She waited until the car was stopped. "I'll tell you when I think the time is right to say something to the general. Not before."

Drake leaned back against the velvet-upholstered seat and, in the darkness, imagined the tormented expression that must be on her face. Something had changed her; she was second-guessing her mindset against Black Orchestra. A sweep of wariness enveloped him. *Battling the Nazi atom bomb while trying to grasp the state of mind of a colleague's wife,* he thought. *That's self-destruction.*

"Never mind, Joachim, keep driving to his address."

"Of course, *Madame.*" He rolled the glass closed.

"At Beck's place," Drake said, "your words were that Black Orchestra was foolish to take the oath to stop the atom project and kill off Hitler and his pond scum. You told me to stay away from Black Orchestra, to go to America. Now you're dragging me in even further. Why, *Frau Speier?*"

She took a deep breath, and in the dim light, he could see she'd turned her face in his direction. "The simple answer is *you.* I've believed right along that Black Orchestra is a journey that will destroy Holger and everyone else. But now, with you on board, you might be its key to success. The other men in Beck's group are smart—a lawyer, a businessman, military leaders, a politician. But they aren't physical. One's a preacher, another a bony intellectual chemist. They're incapable of any real action." She moved her hand toward his and touched his wrist for a second before she pulled away. "You are independent, with much courage—Holger told me of the bravery you showed when Beck's men put you to the test. You could be the catalyst to transform Black Orchestra from a debating club into a real force capable of doing something."

Drake sat back in silence.

"God knows," he said, "I want Hitler and the Nazis exterminated as much as any of us—more so. But your proposition of a traitor, if it's right, makes our failure certain. We must tell the general."

"That might be true."

Drake caught a better view of her face in the glow of a passing truck's headlamps and tried to find signs of deception. The eyes looking back at him displayed only sincerity and resolve. Even so, his training as a journalist and his midwestern American horse sense were kicking in. Something about this encounter wasn't adding up. Not at all.

CHAPTER 10

A SUPERNATURAL ELEMENT

"Carolinum . . . the crowning triumph of military science,
the ultimate explosive . . ."

H. G. Wells, *The World Set Free*, 1914

REDDISH-ORANGE NEON TUBES FLICKERED ABOVE a door opening at the end of a pathway, nearly invisible in the weak light thrown off by the sign.

Warenhaus Speier

Alex Drake looked around for signs of movement, then walked to the side of the building and found the handle of the dimly lit door. He hadn't known of the Speier Department Store warehouse building before, but he'd arrived at the meeting of the Black Orchestra membership by following directions. It seemed to be an obvious place for the Gestapo to storm in and arrest them all. He pulled on the heavy door. Rusty bolts crunched as it inched open, revealing a descending staircase. Going down those stairs meant getting that much closer to hell.

"Drake, you're last. Lock the door behind you," said General Beck.

The journalist's eyes were fixed on the large round table surrounded by seven men and a woman sitting wordlessly. Although there was only one remaining unoccupied chair, he was several minutes early. *Germans are preoccupied with time.*

Drake tugged at the collar of his dark green woolen sweater as he approached the table.

"This will be a swift meeting, consisting of only one topic aside from introducing you. Unfortunately, Speier is ill tonight and sent his wife, Sondra, in his place."

So, this was the coterie known as Black Orchestra.

"You're in distinguished company, *Herr Drake,*" said the general. He was introduced to each person one by one, shaking hands as he walked around the circle. Beck motioned for Drake to be seated at his side. Doing so, he again looked around the table at each face, memorizing names, as worthwhile reporters do, and searching for any display of unusual traits. The former mayor of Leipzig, Carl Goerdeler, presented a broad forehead, bright eyes, a politician's high collar with black necktie. Hans von Dohnanyi, a lawyer of some eminence in Berlin, scowled and fidgeted with his tiny glasses. Reverend Dietrich Born's lips held a cigarette dangling precariously from the left corner of his mouth, a stern look absorbing his face. This Lutheran minister and war hero had blasted French gunners out of numerous pillboxes, supposedly killed dozens before he took a bullet in the neck and went home to enter a seminary. He looked more like a well-built longshoreman than a preacher. Next to him sat General Klaus Würter, High Commander of the German Army. Two facial scars were evident on his right cheek, presumably *Mensur* dueling scars, esteemed among the German military as badges of individual courage. He held a cigarette near his mouth, his hand covering his lower face, head held in a position that made him look supremely confident, his eyes narrowed to slits. And then there was the jovial-appearing *Generalmajor* Hans Oster, second-in-command of the Abwehr Division of the German Army. Oster's *confrères* had the know-how to provide false papers, supply intelligence, and kill people.

SS member Schoe was next to Beck, and at the far end of the table sat *Frau Speier.*

"Drake is our link to the United States," declared Beck with a sweeping motion of his arm. "Establishing the necessary connection to American atomic scientists will rest squarely on his shoulders. We will ask you to do many dangerous things, Drake. Do you remember your oath to Black Orchestra?"

"Of course," he declared as he looked at the faces around the table.

"Then it's done," said Beck, slapping the tabletop and turning to his right. "*Oberleutnant* Schoe, please enlighten us with your new information about building this bomb that we must stop Hitler from possessing."

"Just a minute," Würter said. "We sit here in this basement, waiting for the SS to come down here and arrest us, just to get a science lesson?"

"General," Beck shot back, "you've pledged your life to prevent this unimaginable weapon from falling into Hitler's grasp. Don't you wish to know *what in the name of God* we are talking about?"

Würter crossed his arms, his smoldering anger radiating out from him as he stared at the tabletop. *Nailed him*, Drake thought.

"If you want to leave, *then do so*," Beck shouted. "That goes for all of you!" He slammed the palm of his hand on the table. "I'm in charge. You come to my meetings, and you will take the actions I tell you to take. You are either with me or get out!"

Schoe cleared his throat, waited a few seconds, then stepped closer to the easel supported by a tripod perched at the edge of the table. "Since nobody has shown an interest in leaving, I proceed. Until now, we have had no knowledge of atomic bombs beyond H. G. Wells' decades-old fiction. But today, I attended a War Office meeting where I was briefed on German atomic research."

The others looked around at each other. Schoe picked up a large silver marking pen and removed its cap in a quick motion, instantaneously releasing the powerful odor of benzine solvent. He built a diagram on the paper in thirty seconds, similar to the one Hahn had sketched.

"It all boils down to this," he said, holding up the figure. "Doctor Hahn's experiment at the Kaiser Wilhelm Institute means that the way to mass destruction through atomic chain reactions is real but requires a new element, which way back in 1914 Wells named carolinum. To make it from uranium requires a mystery additive called a neutron moderator. Without this, there's no carolinum, no explosive. That's what Hahn told the group today—the moderator is the key to an atomic bomb."

"But Hahn used nature's uranium, right?" Drake asked.

"Uranium is no good. Results in only a slow energy release—over days. For this to become a colossal explosion, a fast—*very fast*—reaction is necessary. For that, it takes a new, much more unstable element."

Schoe tapped his hand on the paper and swung his foot as if kicking an imaginary ball. "So Doctor Hahn has now politely informed the German military of this super bomb possibility. I did my own calculations. If this Nazi atomic weapon can change every atom of this new carolinum element into energy, then one of these bombs with a few kilograms of it would be equivalent to exploding ten thousand ordinary bombs *every single day for fourteen years!* That could be quite literally earth-shattering."

"*Scheiße!*" Born shouted, his face crinkling.

"Now imagine," Schoe continued, "Hitler, with hundreds of these bastards in his criminal hands!" A collective murmur went around the table, heads shaking side to side, eyebrows raised.

"It's all coming into being. They've decided to call the atom research building in the Kaiser Wilhelm Institute complex *Virus House* to frighten off anyone thinking of snooping around."

"And so, when does your wonder bomb come to humankind?" Beck asked.

"Very soon, unless we stop sitting on our hind ends and do something." Schoe dropped his gaze and crushed his cigarette into a large glass ashtray already partially filled.

"What 'something' do you have in mind?"

The SS man looked down, unable to meet Beck's eyes. "Sir, I have nothing more to offer you tonight."

For at least a minute, the subterranean hideaway was quiet. Then Drake gripped the edge of the table and rose. "As your newest collaborator, I can offer fresh eyes—an outsider's viewpoint."

All faces turned toward him.

"Since nobody else seems to have any ideas, let's hear yours," said Beck.

"Maybe it's all right there in front of us," Drake said in a clear voice. "That 'moderator' written up there—whatever it is—it must not be discovered by them. We must block them from converting Mother Nature's uranium to super-explosive. I mean, find a pathway to dupe the German atom scientists, throw them off, keep them from discovering how to create carolinum. Exterminate Hitler before he has access to any of these bombs. Replace him and his slimy friends with a new government, and the madness stops. Finally—the Nazis can't be allowed to go forward with making these bombs alone, without other nations knowing about it and creating equivalent weapons. So we push the United States to develop atomic bombs of its own to counter the Germans. In America, we'd call that a "stalemate." And General: *do all these things simultaneously*—make it a scattershot—and one of them will work." Drake sat down and looked around at the others.

Sondra Spier was staring at Drake, her eyes wide.

Goerdeler crossed his arms. "Good ideas, Drake, but as you've stated, you lack knowledge. In normal times, I'd declare that you should gain much more understanding before you speak out. But these times are far from normal, meaning I must agree with you," he said. "Success with just one of these ventures would prevent world destruction by Hitler. General Beck, you've got to make someone responsible for each one of these routes Drake proposes."

"And soon!" General Oster said. "To say time is of the essence is a gross understatement. I know I speak for us all when I say we're pissing fear about this thing, with apologies to the lady in our presence."

Beck looked around the room, studying each person's eyes as he collected his thoughts. "We immediately alert the Western Allies," he said, "especially America, with its scientific and industrial might. Oster, you're in the best position to identify essential persons in America to alert to this threat, and Drake will use his acquaintances to contact them. Schoe, you're the scientist—I'm putting you in charge of stopping carolinum production. And Goerdeler, you will come up with a workable plan to assassinate this monstrosity who calls himself the *Führer*. You have your assignments. All infinitely risky, but look at Schoe's diagram—we can't let this put the whole world in a grave. Our little group finds itself at the most crucial turning point in human history. Now go. We meet again in exactly seven days. Schoe, Goerdeler, stay here."

The three remaining members sat silently until the door slammed shut. A gray cloud of stale smoke hung from the ceiling.

"And now we have a most unusual new member," declared the general. "Your impressions?"

Mayor Goerdeler crossed his arms before speaking. "A smart young man, unhindered by the German mentality of total obedience, our unquestioning deference to hierarchy. There's a strange quality about him. Something about his eyes—I can't yet put it into words."

"Drake was right," said Beck, "when he said that he has the clarity of coming to us from the cold outside, and he isn't afraid to speak up."

"Very startling to have an American as part of a German Underground alliance," said Schoe. "And without his life experiences, this would make no sense. But now we have our link to the neutral and mighty United States."

"Crisis makes for strange bedfellows," General Beck declared. "Go home and try to sleep tonight. I hope the common sense of the morning agrees with our decision."

CHAPTER 11

DOCTOR SZILARD

"Evil's shrewdest trick is to persuade us that it does not exist."

Baudelaire, *Le Spleen de Paris*, 1862

NEW YORK CITY, DECEMBER 23, 1938

H EAVY SLEET AND FREEZING RAIN had pelted the metropolis all day. Lousy weather commingled with constant rumors of imminent war in Europe were depressing everyone. The stock market had sunk to depths not seen since the devastating crash of 1929, making millions of New Yorkers miserable during the holidays.

Manhattan traffic was thickening in the waning afternoon light as businesses were locking up, people riding the elevators to the streets. It would be a night of long taxi rides to get inhabitants of the island to apartments, restaurants, or late get-togethers.

Hungarian émigré Doctor Leo Szilard loved the holiday season in New York, the invigorating hubbub of Christmas. This energy was a welcomed contrast to the somber atmosphere of Berlin from which he had escaped five years before. Walking along the rainy street, he passed the glittering window displays of Macy's—chock-full of shimmering tinsel, toy trains looping around Christmas trees hung with ornaments, and fake frost dusted on the glass. A group of carolers sang near the north entrance, dressed for a Dickens Christmas in long mufflers, top hats, and bonnets. Tonight, despite war worries, it was still the New York of his dreams. Szilard took a moment to look around and enjoy the spectacle, then hurried across the avenue as the traffic light turned red. His thick, wavy hair framed a round face with full lips and sparkling dark brown eyes. He had been among the brightest of the nuclear physicists of Germany. Still, his departure was generally seen as a good thing in German scientific and Nazi Party circles.

One less egghead Jew.

He paced in circles at the corner of Fifth Avenue and 33rd Street, fidgeting, turning his head from side to side as if to say, *what did I do to be standing in such cold?* Ahead of him, the grand display windows of the Empire State building splashed multi-colored lights off the shimmering wet concrete.

Days earlier, *Generalmajor* Hans Oster had nosed around the Abwehr *Gruppe I-K* technical research unit, asking questions and eventually learning the name of a scientist who occupied a singular position in American academia. His researchers had provided brief but revealing background data on Leo Szilard. Born in Hungary, Szilard had studied at the University of Berlin, where his mentor was the pillar of atomic physics, Albert Einstein. Shortly after Hitler's rise to power, pressures bearing down on him because of his Jewish ethnicity caused him to hunt for a way out of Germany. Just in time before his persecution could begin, he got himself to England.

Moving to New York City in the early months of 1938, he quickly rose to prominence among the elite nuclear physicists of America. All of this made the Hungarian genius the perfect person for Black Orchestra to enlist to stop the German atom bomb. Oster relayed the contact information to Drake, who began a communication process that would, if successful, span the Atlantic Ocean.

Leo Szilard again glanced up and down the busy street. The phone call a day earlier had been quick but very troubling. A man identifying himself as "Herb" said he had vital information from Germany. Leo had thought momentarily of hanging up, but then the voice said the message was coming 'from the Pickelhaube.' That bit of erudition was enough to compel him to listen to the instructions for a meeting.

A passing taxi splashed slush toward him, causing him to hop backward. *Reckless clown!*

The voice on the phone had told him to watch for a man wearing a black coat with a purple scarf. Leo leaned against the cold stone wall. How was he going to see purple in this dim light? Images of Berlin flooded his memory—listeners, spies, uniformed guards, everyone watching everyone else—constant fear. He felt freedom here, but this man named Herb could be a spy for someone, maybe the Nazis. Or even an assassin. He looked across the street toward the corner of the Empire State skyscraper.

There! Under the streetlight—purple scarf. Szilard crossed the street.

"You are Dr. Szilard?"

He nodded at the words.

"Thank you for coming. Unfortunately, my train was delayed—I hope you aren't upset due to my being late." The man with the purple scarf turned against the freezing wind funneling between the towering stone walls.

Szilard spoke in broken English with a strong Hungarian accent. "Is not for you to worry. Shall we go for coffee, out of this wet? There is a place nearby."

Herb List nodded his head. They walked in silence to a tiny, white-tiled coffee shop.

Szilard held the door and carefully observed the other man as they entered. He was small, stout, with a tiny goatee beard, like those he'd seen on the chins of Frenchmen. This man had warm, believable eyes. The two new acquaintances walked to a corner booth. List slid in first, Szilard continuing to look around, watching for signs of danger. The fast-footed waitress slammed white ceramic mugs filled with steaming coffee onto the table between them, then retreated.

"I am sent by a friend of mine in Berlin," said List, his voice so low that Szilard had to strain to hear. "We worked together closely in Europe. He trusts me, I trust him. I located you because his coded cable said there is a crisis you need to know about."

"Crisis? Who exactly sent the message to you? You mentioned the Pickelhaube. That's why I came here to take this huge risk."

"I can only say that he is a person in Berlin—and knows what's going on. I can't tell you anything more."

Szilard tapped a finger against the tabletop and twisted his head in anticipation.

"The message I am to pass on to you says this involves 'the Hun.'"

"Yes. The Hun—Adolf Hitler." Szilard looked around to convince himself no one could hear them, then swallowed a mouthful of coffee. Fear of spies and informants from his former life in Berlin rested on his shoulders. He could barely contain his anxieties as he waited to hear the remainder of the communication.

"A short message," List said, his eyes narrowing. "I say this to you exactly as I memorized it and was ordered to repeat it. It sounds to me like silly talk, gibberish."

"Yes, yes," said Szilard, taking another sip of coffee. "Get on with it."

"Here it is. 'The world is set free. Holsten has appeared to Hahn under Kaiser's spiked helmet. Core is split. We need help to stop Holsten. Contact us via Herb.'"

Szilard felt the blood drain from his face as he fought to keep from spewing coffee onto the table. "Spiked helmet! *Gross Gott!* Say it all again."

List repeated the words.

An involuntary jerk of Szilard's arm sent his mug flying, shattering into a hundred pieces as it hit the floor. He jumped to his feet and put both hands in front of his face.

"Oh, dear God! Wells was right—he was *right!*" Szilard tottered for a moment and turned toward the door.

"Before you go, take my card, Doctor. My name is Herb. We must communicate back to the sender in Berlin. Call me at my number—written there. Vermont 70995."

Szilard snatched up the card and ran out the door, flagged a passing cab, and shouted to the driver to take him to the King's Crown Hotel in Morningside Heights, near the Columbia University labs. As he grabbed the door handle and climbed into the vehicle, the small white card fluttered down into the slush at the curb.

The King's Crown was the home of both Szilard and Eugene Wigner, another expatriate European nuclear physicist. As the cab splashed through the wet streets, Szilard's mind reeled back to their endless discussions, conducted in Hungarian Yiddish, late into a hundred nights. He and Wigner had dreams of a glorious future, a planet without wars, ruled by a world government consisting of logical yet compassionate intellectuals.

"Open!" The pounding on the door was thunderous. "Jenó!"

The door pivoted, but Szilard's fist kept swinging in the air. "It's happened!"

Szilard pushed the other man into the room and slammed the door behind them. "A message from Berlin—came to me just now! Jenó—the energy of the atom has been released!"

"What are you saying? Who has spoken to you?" Wigner spoke in a low-pitched Hungarian dialect that his fellow countryman Szilard often found to be too slow for his comfort. "I don't think so. That cannot be true."

"Someone from the Kaiser Wilhelm Institute sent a man—a messenger—to meet with me. He relayed to me a coded message, startling information. I have a card with the name and telephone number of this man whom I met." Szilard fished in his pockets. "But . . . I had it! It's gone!"

Wigner leaned forward, eyes unblinking. "Leo. Calm down and sit. Exactly what did he tell you?"

"The message—it said Otto Hahn has done it, he's become Holsten now."

"Done what, Leo? What are you talking of? *Holsten?* That's a German beer. But you mean a person? I've not met this Holsten. Someone who works with Hahn?"

"No, Jenó, *think, dammit.* Holsten was the make-believe character in *The World Set Free.* The scientist who builds the atomic bombs!"

"Ah, yes," Wigner said with a heavy sigh. "Wells' amazing book."

"You sit there fiddling with your watch, looking unconcerned. But this message—if true, it means Germany has found the terrible secret."

"Not necessarily. They might not know as much as we do. But, unless Berlin no longer exists, this must have been the slow release of energy, not the cataclysmic explosion."

"You're correct as usual. The fast reaction would require the production of the new element, which Wells called carolinum. When Germany makes carolinum, bombs can happen right away."

Szilard pressed his palms to his eyes and hunched his shoulders. "I must alert the Americans through my partner in patents, Dr. Einstein. We will go see him. He alone possesses the reputation required to get Roosevelt believing there could be German atomic bombs—the great danger this poses to humanity. He must start to *believe.* He must compel the American War Department to get their atomic project started."

"We were there, Jenó, under the Pickelhaube. You and I first read Wells' The World Set Free and foresaw the horror that will come with Wells' new element. God forbid the Nazis have already found the secret to the creation of carolinum."

Wigner turned his head away, the gray shadow of sadness crawling across his face.

CHAPTER 12

HEART

"After great pain, a formal feeling comes
The nerves sit ceremonious, like tombs—"

Emily Dickinson, *The Complete Poems*, no. 341, 1862

ALEX DRAKE STRUGGLED TO BELIEVE his eyes. On his desk lay the most recent issue of his arch-competitor *Time* magazine, dated January 2, 1939. It had been brought into the building minutes earlier by a courier from the Ministry of Propaganda. Its red-bordered cover bore a creepy drawing of a uniformed man playing a bizarre calliope. Hovering over its pipes were what seemed to be the figures of tortured victims of indistinct events. And under the illustration, cryptic lines:

The Man of The Year 1938

From the Unholy Organist, a Hymn of Hate

Drake stared at the cover illustration, and then his fingers flipped to the article, lines he had quickly skimmed moments before. It told of

Hitler's early life and his rise to power, his successful efforts to rearm Germany, and his political triumphs during 1938 over Czechoslovakia, England, and France. The article concluded with these ominous words:

> To those who watched the closing events of the year, it seemed more than probable that the Man of 1938 might make 1939 a year to be remembered.

Hitler—the man of the year? Madness, he thought. Drake took the magazine in his hands, rolled it up, and threw it onto a shelf in the bookcase. *With atom bombs in his pocket, he'll be the man of burnt-to-a-crisp eternity!* His loathing of Hitler had found new fuel. The next meeting of Black Orchestra would take place in a few hours.

Sondra Speier's bedroom was simple and elegant, like the gold hand mirror resting on the dressing table. She gazed at her reflection as she stroked the bristles through her shoulder-length hair parted to one side and swept across a high forehead. Gray circles were visible under her eyes, so maybe some makeup would improve her look and her mood. She had slept badly again last night, so she smoothed foundation cream on her cheeks and dabbed a bit of pinkish lipstick to brighten her face. In the small frame in front of her, between bottles of costly fragrances and jars of delicate skin cream, she saw the picture of an older man with possibly only a few years of life remaining. She remembered how his hands quaked as he'd fumbled with the buttons on his shirt a few hours earlier. Tonight, Holger had gone off to a dangerous meeting with his comrades across the city at his company's warehouse.

The appearance of his lined face and age-spotted hands as they looked in the dim light of the late afternoon made her think about life-changing transitions. Her life of thirty-one years had brought pitiful depths and exhilarating heights. Yet, the comforts she had enjoyed were in great jeopardy of vanishing due either to Holger's decline or the devastation of war. Or maybe both.

"I must go out," she said to herself in a low voice. "I need a drive in the city." She picked up the telephone handset to call her chauffeur.

The Mercedes 380K W22 limousine swung smoothly right and cruised down the dark, silent street in the direction of Sondra's Charlottenburg home. The hour spent in the broad rear seat of the limousine, the partition between herself and the driver closed for privacy, had soothed her thoughts and calmed her stomach. She knew it was past ten, and Holger would probably be home from his meeting and sleeping by now. A single light shone from the kitchen window. She'd dismissed the servants before leaving and remembered that the lights were shut off when she left. Holger might still be up, getting a bedtime snack.

As they turned into the drive, she noticed the headlamps bounce light off the red reflectors of a car parked in front of the house. Perhaps the neighbors had a visitor.

The chauffeur pulled up to and under the archway next to the side entrance in his usual manner. He stopped the car and sprung out to open the rear door.

She walked past the driver as he reclosed the car door, then moved toward the front of the vehicle.

"*Frau Speier,* do you have anything else for me this evening?"

"No, go and catch the next streetcar. Have a good evening with your wife."

The driver bowed and spoke a polite *Guten Nacht.*

She hadn't been out long, but the house seemed different, cold. She could hear the distant, hollow footsteps of the chauffeur, starting his walk to the streetcar stop. She twisted the light switch inside the entry, pulled the door closed, and walked down the tiled corridor connecting the side entryway with the kitchen. She turned the corner at the end of the hall.

A figure was sitting at the small table in the center of the room, head down, his back to her.

"Dear Holger. How was your meeting?"

The man jumped up and whirled toward her.

"Good evening, *Frau Speier.*"

She gasped, recoiled backward, and screamed. "Who are you—what are you doing in here?"

"Gestapo business. Sit down—now!"

Sondra walked quickly to the opposite side of the table, her heart beating so loud she could hear it in her ears. "*Gestapo?* You have no right . . . where's my husband?"

"I will tell you again to sit. Or would you prefer police custody right now?"

"I'm not sitting anywhere. *Where is he?*" Her voice was strained, brittle.

"He had to make a little trip to talk with some people at Gestapo headquarters. As you know well, he is a close friend of Ludwig Beck, which is not a good position to be in during these times. I'm so sad to tell you that he became rather agitated when we arrived to take him away for interrogation. I do believe he was having heart trouble. Severe heart trouble." The stranger offered a mocking smile, his eyebrows rising. "Don't scream again, or I'll shove something truly nasty into your mouth."

Her hands shook as she moved to cover her eyes.

"My associates left me here to . . . console you when you arrived home to find him gone. And to give you a solemn warning." His prominent Adam's apple moved up and down above his collar as he spoke. "Come over here. You are very lovely. I like what I see, and I'd like to feel what's under that dress. You can save yourself and your husband right now by obliging me. Tell me about your husband's relationship with this traitor Beck."

"I've got nothing to say to you, bastard! Where have they taken him?"

"Gestapo headquarters. Did you know that my somewhat barbaric cohorts have recently been starting autopsies before the criminals are yet dead? Why, the butchery—so disgusting."

She looked at the doorway and considered making a break for it.

"If he—or you—won't talk, the interrogation will result in his death. Punishment for his treason with Beck. And I will see to it that you'll go out in a way worse than his unless you cooperate."

She clutched at her throat. "I want to see my husband, damn you!"

"Play the game with me. It will go much better for you."

"Get out of my house. I have rights—"

"I determine your rights, *Frau Speier.*" The man moved toward Sondra, grabbing her arm. "You're tough, and it will give me great pleasure to extract the truth from you, starting right now!" He jerked at her dress, revealing her rounded breasts only partially covered by a white brassiere. The man twisted her body toward the light. "We are going to have a wonderful evening getting to know one another and talking about your husband's friends, are we not?"

"You dirty *swine*—!"

She pulled back from his grasp, stumbled, and caught herself on the edge of the table before she fell. Her eyes caught a glimpse of something bright, golden, on the floor. Shattered spectacles—Holger's glasses, the broken lenses splashed with blood.

Her captor laughed. "We know everything. You are common trash, a whore from the *Kabaretts.* I'll have to teach you about friendliness and manners."

The Gestapo agent locked her arms behind her back. A long tress of deep brown hair slumped across her face. Her torn dress had fallen open again. "We need to be more comfortable for the next portion of my inquiry. I'm already feeling excited. A slut knows how to please."

"*No!*" she wailed, shrinking as much as she could from his grip. Then, a brutal punch burst against her right eye, exploding her vision into a cascade of tiny bright stars. As she dropped, the Gestapo agent tightened his hold on her and hit her again, then slapped her hard across the mouth.

"*Leave her alone!*" She swung her eyes toward the voice coming from the servant's entrance to the kitchen.

"*Joachim!*"

He began running toward Sondra.

"Stay back! I'm Gestapo!" He whipped a gun from inside his jacket and lifted it.

The chauffeur reached for Sondra's hand and pulled her away and toward himself. She gathered her torn dress and pinched it closed. Her teeth clenched as tears ran down her cheeks, reactions from the pain of the punch and the realization of Holger's fate.

"I witnessed what you were trying to do to her. You will have to shoot us both."

Sondra propped herself up against the tabletop and pushed her hair back off her face. "Be careful whom you shoot," she said. "I have a name for you to think about: Sophie Müller. If you don't know, she's the wife of your boss Heinrich Müller, Gestapo Chief of Operations. I had lunch with her last week. Shoot me, and she will be distraught, to put it mildly. When she learns I'm dead and my husband has died in your custody, that's going to cause you trouble, *Herr Gestapo*, or whatever the hell your name is."

The intruder waved his pistol toward the shattered glasses. "This is a warning, an example to your Ludwig Beck. Any further attempts to interfere with the government will be dealt with brutally—unmercifully. Prepare for your husband's burial or what you will have done with his corpse. You must have the body removed from Gestapo Headquarters within twenty-four hours, or it goes in the garbage."

Sondra fell against the tall, stone-faced chauffeur and sobbed.

CHAPTER 13

TESTIMONY

"To live in the hearts we leave behind is not to die."

Thomas John Campbell *ca.* 1810

THE MIDDAY SUN WARMED ALEX Drake's sleeve, a welcomed
sensation amid the chilly office air and his drafty window.
He could feel the hostility of February in North Germany— more
intimidating this year for many reasons, not just the weather. The
paper in his typewriter carried today's effort to paint a word picture that
would pass the regime's censorship authorities yet convey something
of informational value to his readers. His subject was inoffensive in
these times, namely the launching yesterday of the *Seydlitz*, a heavy
cruiser of Nazi Germany's Kriegsmarine, the fourth of the *Admiral
Hipper* class of vessels. While he could fill the allotted 500 words
with technical specifications and compliments about the technical
competence of German shipbuilding, what he really wanted to do
was to scream at the world of the menace of yet another colossal
war machine being added to Hitler's collection. By ratcheting up the

awareness of *World Week's* readers' to the existential threat of Nazism, he could advance Black Orchestra's purpose of toppling Hitler before he achieved world conquest—or world destruction. But he was fully mindful that he couldn't do it all at once. This was a whale to be eaten one bite at a time.

The buzz of the telephone startled him. He slammed the typewriter carriage across to start the next line as he raised the handset to his ear—three quick clicks, then a voice. "Zephyr brown. One-half hour." It was the distinctive voice of lawyer Hans von Dohnanyi. Months of code-talk messages between Black Orchestra's colleagues gave Drake knowledge of what was being said.

"Ja." He put down the handset and grabbed his wool overcoat from the wall rack, then opened the door of his office. *Why would Dohnanyi request a meeting?*

Steam wafted from the street vendor's cart a half block from the *World Week* bureau entrance. *"Pommes frittes, mit mayo,"* Drake said, pulling a few coins from his pocket. The little paper tray of fried potato strips covered with mayonnaise was a favorite street food in Berlin. He used his fingers to pop the tasty bits into his mouth as he walked across the Budapesterstrasse toward the Berlin Zoological Gardens. He passed through the Zoologischer Bahnhof's grand entranceway. He headed to the ticket windows in the stately stone buildings topped with massive carved lions facing each other like mortal enemies poised for combat. He paid the admission price and headed east through the riveted steel gate.

It would be a ten-minute walk to the aviary where Dohnanyi would be waiting. He watched for curious eyes, but there were none to be seen in the cold expanse of the zoo except the eyes of the indomitable penguins and musk oxen.

"Back here!" It was the voice of Dohnanyi, coming from behind the hay barn. The air was deathly still, the animals quiet. Drake walked in the direction of the voice.

"Here—inside the barn."

"What is it, Hans?"

"It's life or death; otherwise, I wouldn't risk us coming here. There's something you've got to know."

The air was still. A distant bird call sounded like a whistle or a flute. Drake lit up a *Jonnie* and blew tobacco smoke away as he steeled himself for whatever was coming next. "Okay, go."

"Holger is dead."

Drake whipped the cigarette from his lips. "Dead! How?"

"Here's what I know. Gestapo agents came to his house, and he was taken somewhere. His wife was away, but one Gestapo man waited for her. Beat her up and said they were going to get Beck next. Holger might have had a heart attack right away. I don't know. Her driver returned, found that scene and stepped in, got a gun pointed at him. Gestapo decided to let her live to tell us Beck is in trouble regardless of his military standing and reputation."

"Damned bloodsuckers."

"Sondra sustained injuries. Her chauffeur took her to a hospital. They let her have a phone, and she called me as her attorney. The phone line was, of course, monitored, every word heard by the police, but she managed to tell me what I'm telling you. They might have tortured Holger into revealing Black Orchestra. We don't yet know if they extracted anything about us from him before he died, but I suppose we'll find out soon enough."

"How bad's she hurt?"

"Said she has bruises and a blackened eye. Had her man not heard her scream . . ."

Drake kept his eyes downcast as Dohnanyi continued in an unsteady voice.

"We're damned close to being exposed. Since we don't yet know what they could have extracted from him, we've got to assume the Gestapo will learn everything about Black Orchestra. That means we're all going to be picked up and arrested."

"Surprised they haven't already pulled something like this."

"Hitler can't risk an uprising in the military if General Beck is arrested. But if they prove he's leading a revolutionary group, that shield is lost." Dohnanyi looked around, scanning for unwelcomed observers. "So they target his suspected collaborators."

"Have you talked to Beck?"

"For a few minutes. He's trying to figure out what to do next. Maybe every one of us has to try to flee Germany. For you, Drake, my earnest advice is to use that American passport of yours *right now.* Pack a few essentials and head for England or the United States tonight. If you need money, I can get you money."

Drake threw the cigarette butt to the semifrozen ground and stepped on it. "I'm not going anywhere."

"Things might change fast and soon, so keep your options open, pack a shaving kit and underwear. I'd tell you to put a gun in too, but I know you don't have one."

"What about Sondra?"

"She's not in the hospital anymore and wants to talk this afternoon. Her driver will bring her to the Pfaueninsel—the Peacock Island—on the Havel. She wants you to come also. Five this afternoon. We meet at the white wooden castle."

"Why me?"

"Not sure. Your job with us, Drake—one of several jobs—is to eventually tell the world the story of Black Orchestra, assuming you survive. It might be because of that."

"We're all in this dance together. So if she wants me there, I'll be there."

"I'm anxious about General Beck," Dohnanyi said. "Something efficient—a truck swerving to run him down, or an intruder injecting an undetectable poison into him as he sleeps."

"And what becomes of Black Orchestra?"

The lawyer looked straight ahead into the midday light flooding through the denuded tree branches. "It will cease to exist, having done nothing but talk, and the atomic bombs will come to Hitler."

"Let's get this job done before that happens. I'll see you at the island."

Drake watched as his colleague turned and walked past the bird sanctuary. He knew nothing about this woman and trusted her not at all—a hundred "what-ifs" shot through his mind, all unvaryingly bad.

"This place is a long way from the wrong eyes and ears," Drake said, looking past Dohnanyi and Sondra and toward the prominent white wooden façade, a remnant of the party thrown on this island park that celebrated the closing of the Berlin 1936 Summer Olympic Games.

Sondra had tried to conceal a deep-blue bruise with makeup powder, still visible under her right eye. Her upper lip was puffed out like that of a prizefighter. "The Gestapo wanted information out of him," she said. "They killed him, and we don't know if they forced him to reveal anything. He had a weakened heart. I hope it gave out quickly before they could torture him. General Beck sometimes said he thought I was Holger's protector. The biblical meaning of my name Sondra is 'brave defender.' For my husband, I didn't do a good job of defending."

"What about you?" Drake asked.

"I will survive, as I always have. They are *Scheißedreck*." Her face had gone rigid. "Holger was . . . genuine." She paused for a minute, maybe more. "He showed me unselfish love. He found me in a bad situation, protected and helped me. Never in my life did I feel what I felt with him."

Drake found himself sinking into a glut of clashing emotions. Sondra's plight reconnected him with his state of mind when diphtheria—a kid's disease—took the life out of his wife-to-be. He knew the ache—centered someplace in the viscera—that accompanied such a loss. He was confident that she would deal with it in time, but in his own situation, he'd fallen flat in the efforts to conquer his grief. He wanted to tell her to get tough, move ahead, but how could he give that counsel when he hadn't done it himself? "I'm sorry," was his pathetically inadequate, almost-laughable utterance.

She cried softly, the coldness evaporating from her face. "I'll get past this. Cuts and bruises will heal." Her eyes darted between Drake and Dohnanyi. "Holger's money will continue to support Black Orchestra, and I'll throw all the strength and resources I have into stopping that devil from getting the atom bomb. Nothing else matters anymore."

Drake and Dohnanyi stayed silent.

"Somebody's walking over there," Drake said. "Two of them."

"They're coming this way," said Sondra, grasping Drake's arm with her deerskin-gloved hand. "We must go, but again I tell you both, from this point forward, I fight in place of my husband. Tell that to General Beck."

Alone, Drake crossed the iron bridge back from the island. A walk of a block brought him to a small tavern, one he'd never seen before. He was hungry and in need of a drink. Inside, he walked through the small vestibule and entered the main room. It was dimly lit, the walls decorated with the standard German tavern treatment of painted scenes depicting pristine valleys in the Bavarian Alps. He took a seat at the empty bar and pulled his gloves off.

The thin, fortyish bartender got off his stool, threw a towel over his shoulder, and sauntered toward Drake.

"What'll it be, stranger? Not seen you in my place before."

"Beer. And a whiskey."

"Whiskey? All I got is schnapps."

"I'll take it. Double."

He swung the towel down to wipe the bar in front of Drake, then switched it across to the other shoulder as he walked off.

Drake clenched his jaw as he thought through the things he'd heard in the park. *Sondra had walked into her kitchen to find a Gestapo thug. Her husband killed—how could they know his timing and hers? What benefits would accrue to her from his death?*

The bartender whacked a beer stein onto the wooden bar, then placed the glass of schnapps, filled to the edge, beside it. "Anything else? Get it now because if nobody else comes in, I'm closing up and going home."

Drake didn't look up. "Chicken soup."

Visions of Viola's face crept back, then reeled out of control, his thoughts shifting to that miserable day in London—the rattle of the black Austin taxi's idling motor, a whitish cloud of exhaust drifting from the tailpipe, the car's rear door held open by the driver under a gloomy, drizzling sky. He'd stood in front of a small grave marker at the edge of the Royal Leamington Cemetery in Warwickshire, next to a vast landscape of towering gravestones in the English style. Carved marble florets topped the etched words: *Viola Lobdell 1914–1936.* She was a flower at the edge of a rain-drenched forest of cold stone monuments. Above all, she was gentle and loving, accepting of his silliness and frequent foolhardiness, and capable of what seemed to be infinite kindness. He thought of the mornings when her hair spilled across his pillow like a silky swirling storm. Then came the day her soft eyes closed for the last time. And so came his aversion to forming bonds with others. His life became that of a solitary man.

Then a telegram a few weeks later. Would he consider a new assignment at the *World Week* Berlin bureau? His excellent German language skills, a need to start anew, and the excitement of the upcoming 1936 Olympic Games in Berlin all said *yes*. Goodbyes were said, trunks packed, official papers signed—all prerequisites for his journey to Germany's capital. Now nearly three years on, his constant sparring with Nazi censors had dulled his reporter's skillfulness and sometimes physically sickened him. Although he longed for another love as he'd had in London, his emotional bank account was empty.

The schnapps had helped. Maybe he should take up heavier drinking. *Another dumb idea.* It was time to move on.

CHAPTER 14

THE WATCHER

"Recent developments in nuclear physics might lead to
the production of an explosive far more powerful than
any yet known, and any country possessing it
would have an unsurpassable advantage."

Letter from Paul Harteck to Erich Schumann,
German Army Research Director, April 24, 1939

ALEX DRAKE ADJUSTED THE WIDE lapels of his double-breasted
overcoat and reached for the restaurant's shining brass door handle.
A nicely dressed twosome pushed the door open toward him just as he'd
started to pull. The orange neon light from the sign above Lehmann's
Taverne washed down on them, illuminating their unsmiling faces.
The man's arm was firmly around the waist of his much-younger lady,
who wore heavy makeup and strong perfume. Maybe she was less of
a girlfriend and more of a hireling at this point. Drake moved out of
the cold night and into the warmth of the Italian restaurant—three
linked rooms, always noisy, usually filled with Berlin's celebrities and

important Nazi Party members. He strode across the spotless tile floor and saw in the far-right corner couples dancing to the energetic music of a brassy four-piece band. His nostrils registered the smells of white sausage and sauerkraut intermingled with tobacco smoke and the aroma of freshly cut onion.

The foreign correspondents usually began arriving around nine p.m. after they'd cabled their articles to America or elsewhere and often didn't leave until two or three in the morning. Even though he'd endured a long and frustrating day at the bureau, he wasn't tired enough to head straight to bed and elected to instead go out for food and conversation, both of which were always in ample supply at this place. The usual delegation of journalists, minus a few on this particular evening, sat around the reserved table marked *Ausländische Korrespondenten* near the restaurant's front, smoking, drinking, and talking with arms moving in agitated communication. The Nazi Ministry of Propaganda believed in providing first-cabin treatment for foreign correspondents, expecting that they would achieve a *quid pro quo*—favorable treatment of reporters in exchange for positive stories about Germany. It often worked.

As Drake approached, overflowing mugs of beer and silver trays of food carried by determined-looking waitresses flew by. Edward R. Murrow of CBS—the Columbia Broadcasting System—stubbed a cigarette into the ashtray and speared a sausage with his fork. Next to him sat Bill Shirer, the voice of the nightly CBS World News Roundup broadcast that was heard worldwide. Pulling out a chair and plopping himself down at the long table, Drake glanced toward the handsome, confident Murrow, a heavy drinker who alternately bragged and complained that he smoked three packs of cigarettes a day.

"Who got deported today?" Drake asked Shirer. "Looks like the CBS News team survived more or less intact."

Shirer laughed as he pulled the meerschaum pipe from the corner of his mouth. "Well, there's always the thrill of tomorrow to look forward to, and along with it, the likelihood that a truck'll hit me after I broadcast something the Nazis decide is wrong. Anything even slightly resembling journalism has been abandoned someplace along the way. If I live to get out of here, I'm going to write a book about this nightmare."

"Yeah, bye-bye to journalism and investigative reporting," said

Drake. "To probe for facts around here is equivalent to self-annihilation. We have our informants, but even if we get something worth knowing, the Nazi censors—you know the deal—I'm just blowing off some steam."

Shirer nodded, rubbing a hand across his bald pate. "Murrow and I were talking about the state of affairs Hitler finds himself in if there's a new world war. If he attacks France and England, he could likely beat them, 'cause they're still burned out from the last war and haven't kept up big armies. But if the United States comes in, as they did in the first one, you and I both know the American factories' muscle. We've seen it first-hand—General Motors, Westinghouse, US Steel—they have factories galore and can make anything, and the U.S. commands all the oil and iron ore they'd ever need to overwhelm Germany. If that happens, Hitler's only hope is some kind of breakthrough weapon, some secret project to counter the American power. Like this thing that I learned of today from my informant, a whore who hears a lot from her sex partners in the military and the government. My newsman's spark of investigative reporting remains, although it will get me killed one day. What the hell do you suppose is something called Virus House?"

Drake lifted his chin, momentarily stunned. "Virus—a sort of germ," he said, maintaining a tone of ignorance.

"Not this time, I don't think. The word is that it's some sort of new program at the German War Office. Moved a lot of people into an old building on the Kaiser Wilhelm Institute property out in Dahlem," said Shirer. "They might be working on germs, but a lot of electrical equipment has been shipped in—doesn't sound like medical stuff."

"I'll see if I can learn anything about it, Bill." Drake looked away as he mulled over the message that had been sent to Szilard in New York— still no reply. For a few seconds, he thought of using Shirer or another reporter to send another message to America about atomic research in Germany. Still, he realized that getting more people involved was a terrible idea and would further jeopardize Black Orchestra's already wobbly secrecy. No, it was time to get Herb List to make another try at contacting Szilard, or maybe a different American scientist.

Jimmy Keene and Ed Murrow were talking quietly. The *World Week* editor was small and pale, in sharp contrast to the rugged good looks of Murrow. Unless he was angry, Keene spoke in a soft voice, working his delicate hands as though he were holding a valuable object in them. His was an unlikely combination of God-given talent and backwoods indifference to formalities. Nevertheless, almost everyone who met him instantly liked him, and when they listened to him or read his reportage, they soon gained respect for his intellect.

Intent on fetching a beer, Drake looked around the room for a waitress. His eyes spotted the figure of a woman standing alone inside the doorway of the restaurant. The upper half of her face was obscured by a dark veil hung from a small black hat, partly concealing thick tresses, but he knew her instantly. She turned toward the correspondents.

"Bill, that's my landlady. I owe her rent money. I'd better go talk to her because she's seen me."

"Oh?" said Shirer. "Quite some landlady from what I can see."

Drake rose and walked toward the shrouded figure, subconsciously brushing back the hair that had fallen across his forehead.

"Hello, Alex Drake," said Sondra Speier, hands in the pockets of her wool coat. Her slight smile accentuated the delicate proportions of her jawline.

"This is a surprise. Not a good place to be seen. The Gestapo keeps a watch on these reporters, including me."

"Can we go over there?" She gestured toward an empty table positioned on the opposite side of the room. "All those men are news correspondents?"

"Yes, so better keep that veil over your face."

Drake noticed several of the reporters staring at Sondra.

"Would you care for wine?" He drew his chair up to the table.

"See if they have a bottle of Médoc Château Beychevelle 1928. If not, perhaps a 1929 Bordeaux, an excellent year for the vineyards. Something from Château Margaux."

Drake lifted an eyebrow as he contemplated her knowledge of French wines. "I'll give it a try, but this is an Italian restaurant."

"Holger once mentioned that foreign correspondents come to this place, so I thought perhaps you might be here tonight. I decided to take this risk despite my fears of Gestapo killers coming at me again. The police have left me alone since that night, but I'm sure they keep watching."

Nodding, Drake motioned to a waitress in a dirndl dress, barely concealing her overflowing breasts. *"Kellnerin! Komm!"* he said. She nodded as he conveyed his wine request, then she moved off in the direction of the bar.

Even behind the black veil, the candlelight accentuated Sondra's bright eyes as she looked toward the end of the room, only briefly glancing toward him. Her shoulders were small but straight, with a hint of strength. The tailored black jacket fit her perfectly.

The waitress wasn't gone more than three minutes, but she approached with a satisfied look on her rosy face.

"I have exactly your Médoc, *Mein Herr.*"

"Miraculous." Drake poured the wine, then raised his glass and said, "Well, 'cheers,' as we say in America."

She nodded as she, too, raised her glass slightly. "And sad birds still sing."

"What's that mean?"

"An old toast, that's all."

They both drank their wine without further conversation. Still, there was a reason for her presence, something more than just the need for company and a few breaths of Berlin's crisp night air. Drake remained patient.

"I imagine you came here tonight because you want to talk to me about something."

"I do. Before Holger died, I told you of my sense of a traitor. And now—I feel it even more strongly."

"Are you finally going to say the name of this person?"

"It's not the time yet. I still don't have any actual proof."

Drake took a deep breath and made a *hmmm* noise in his throat. "Well, then you've got to get proof. *Soon.*"

She nodded as he split the remainder of the bottle's contents between them. Another loud argument erupted at the correspondents' table.

In a shadowy corner of the Taverne, a man sat down in a booth, his hat pulled low over his brows. A fast-moving waitress brought a stein of beer and a loaf of black pumpernickel. He sipped the beer and chewed on a heel of the bread, his eyes focused on one couple seated across the room. Rather than sit inside his car and watch her house as he often did, tonight, he'd followed Sondra to the restaurant and entered through the back doorway.

His double shot of vodka arrived from the bar. He wasted no time downing it in a single swallow. It felt good almost instantly. *Der Mann mit Zwei Geheimnissen*—the man with two secrets—that's what made him very different from the pack of running dogs aspiring to reach great heights in the Nazi regime. Klaus Würter was, without a doubt, very different in other ways, too. Like the blade of a sword make from Krupp steel, he had been hardened by the thousands of hammer blows he'd taken and the scorching coals which had hurt him in the early years of his life. The harder the blows came at him, the stronger he grew. The alcohol was now beginning to infuse into his brain, calming him while summoning deep emotions from some subconscious region.

A disciplinarian Prussian Army officer, his father held tremendous expectations for his son and made impossible demands. The oxhide belt with its heavy brass buckle was the brutal enforcer. *Less than a perfect score on that composition?* That usually meant a roundhouse punch to the ear and thirty welts across his buttocks. More than once, bound to a post in the dark, wet basement for two days without nourishment or water. And his mother? She'd sustained her own nightmarish abuse, and her protests cost her an eye. One particularly memorable incident triggered by his "failings" resulted in him being thrown across the dining room and crashing through the door glass of a china cabinet, lancing his face along his cheek. He later in life passed it off as a dueling scar, one of two he claimed. The other scar, below his left eye, was deliberate. Klaus told his military school classmates that it had occurred during a fencing championship match in his hometown, but the reality was that it was self-inflicted. To prove his strength, he had resolved to slit his face deeply with a straight razor and not pass out in the process. He succeeded, confirming to himself that he was at least as strong as the dead old man had demanded. *So,* he thought, *why did he want Sondra Speier at his side?* Above all, it was the thrill of pursuit. He had the cards to play that would catapult him into the place where he should be and must be, right beside Adolf Hitler. She would revel in the power, money, and prestige which she would possess as his wife. Yet there she sat, looking into the eyes of a damnable weasel. Maybe Drake ought to be the next Black Orchestra instrumentalist to play his own funeral dirge.

He was lonely and bored, but these were only temporary problems. In a few weeks, maybe months, he would become a leader of the Third Reich, and she would be completely his. It was only a matter of time.

CHAPTER 15

THE HERMIT

"Whosoever is delighted in solitude
is either a wild beast or a god."

Aristotle

S ONDRA SPEIER, HER HEAD RESTING against the rolled porcelain edge
of her freestanding clawfoot tub, stared out of the windows of her
bathroom and drank in the beauty of the apple trees flowering in
white and pink outside her house. The late May sunshine was warm
and allowed her thoughts to drift away from the myriad problems that
seemed to shadow her endlessly. Above the scented water, the golden
faucets and crystal handles shone brightly in the sunlight. She focused
her eyes on the two large vases of white and violet flowers from her
garden sitting on the flat marble surface of the sink. The warm water
relaxed her shoulder muscles, and she could feel the tension flowing
from her back and into the water like wine pouring from a bottle. She
loved hot baths, and the water made the porcelain warm against her
buttocks and back. A crystal chandelier above the bathtub sparkled with

a rainbow of colors as the sun, having now fallen far enough for its rays to catch the lowest diamond-like bobbles, played games with the light.

She took the tan sea sponge with one hand and ran it along her opposite shoulder and upper arm, across her still-youthful breasts, and she pondered for a moment the smoothness of her skin, its freedom from flaws. Such a figure doesn't last a lifetime, and she was aware that the years were passing quickly. Her body had changed from what it was a decade ago; still, it was a source of self-esteem. She wished that the sponge was instead the palm of a man's hand, moving along her hips and caressing her. What had it been now? Eight years, ten years since a lover with strength and desire had touched her? Now her lover was a sponge in the bathtub. She possessed qualities that few women could match but comprehended the mockery that there was no man in her life and none on the horizon.

The knotty complexities of Black Orchestra, culminating in the death of her husband, made the prospects for another relationship nonexistent. It hadn't been much more than four months since she'd become a widow, and her muse of positivity whispered that in time, all of this would heal. She had a visitor coming in the hours ahead, so the luxurious bath must come to an end. She reached for the shining brass telephone handset to call the housekeeper to help her from the porcelain tub.

Alex Drake slammed the door of the taxi. Only a sliver of moon hung over him as he turned away from the street, walking in the direction of a baronial three-story stone and brick home. He stumbled slightly in the near-total darkness as he ascended the steps. No porchlight and the lack of streetlights in response to air-raid blackouts made it hard to find the doorbell. *There,* to the right of the portal. He moved the lever, and the hollow tinkle of bell chimes followed instantly—there were no signs of movement from inside the house, no answer.

Yesterday, two weeks after their bottle of Château Beychevelle at the Taverne, Drake had sent a coded message to Sondra Speier requesting they meet. In her reply, she'd agreed and asked him to come to this house where the Gestapo had murderously confronted her and her husband a short time ago. It was an unexpected suggestion—would Nazi Party agents be watching again?

The night air carried a sharp chill, causing his shoulders to hunch slightly. He turned his back against a sudden wind rushing across the dark expanse of lawn spreading toward the street. The moving air swirled cascades of doubt over him. He took two steps back. Then, from the sidelights of the door, he saw movement. Fingers pulled back a tiny portion of the thick lace curtain, sending a small beam of light across his face. The bolt clanked as the substantial door slowly swung open. Drake felt his heart skip several beats as Sondra reached for his arm and swiftly pulled him inside.

"Guten Nacht, Alex," she said in a soft voice. "Come in."

He moved into the large foyer. Sondra had wrapped herself in a full-length deep red robe, its collar high, the waist tightly cinched. Thick, deep brown hair fell across her velvet-clad shoulders.

"I hate being alone in this house." Her almost imperceptible accent suggested a northern European birthplace, maybe Danish. He thought it odd that he'd not noticed this before. A note of anxiety? A fire glowed from the arched stone hearth behind her.

"It was quiet enough with Holger here, but now . . . *"C'est une belle tombe, n'est-ce pas?"*

"I don't know much French, but do you mean 'a beautiful tomb?'"

"Accurate. Holger was a lover of precious things. I feel his presence here among the possessions he adored. I miss his gentle spirit. I have my society friends, ladies who come here for tea or visit restaurants with me, but how often can one discuss other peoples' grandchildren and the dreadful state of art prices before becoming completely bored and dissipated? And evenings are dreadful. I requested my housekeepers to leave me alone tonight to tend to their families. That's why, despite the dangerous possibilities, I suggested meeting here with you. I am going mad by myself in this place."

Drake shifted his weight from one leg to the other, raising his eyes to meet hers. "Come," she said as she led him into an impressive-looking library, stocked with volumes of fine leather-bound books. The lamplight was inviting and cast a comforting glow throughout the room. "Sit and relax." Her arm extended toward the plush sofa.

Looking down as he walked, he felt himself engulfed in a sea of vibrant red and gold patterns displayed in the largest intricately woven silk rug he had ever seen. He gingerly sat down on the sofa as he continued to scan the room—high, gilded ceilings seemed to hover above sizeable antique oil paintings hung on the white-paneled walls. A life-sized bronze statue of a ballerina bowed toward him from across the room.

As she lowered herself next to him, he caught the subtle scent of her fragrance.

"I see it in your eyes," she said. "You're uncomfortable here."

Drake turned toward her. "Aren't you worried too? Your husband is gone just a couple of months, you are under Gestapo watch, yet here we sit."

Sondra shrugged her shoulders and nodded. "It's a chance I'm willing to take. We've both learned to live dangerously at times—most of the time. Why did you come here?"

He rubbed his chin, the day-old beard scraping against his fingers. "I had to talk to you about this thing you've confided in me."

"All right—go ahead."

"Stopping the atom bomb—how's that going to happen if you're right about a traitor?"

"I know." She looked away. "It's a mess, but we can't do anything about it. At least for now."

"Can't do anything about it? Of course we can! Tell me his name, for Christ's sake!"

"You know it would cause horrible things for Black Orchestra if I'm wrong."

Drake drew a breath and released it before speaking. "We're going to go to Beck with your suspicions."

"The next meeting is Sunday night. So I'll do it then. But please, no more of this tonight, Alex."

Somewhere in his subconscious, he wanted to explore this new place of emotions he found himself in, complicated and ill-advised as it was.

Turning away from him, she opened a drawer, took out a stack of thick paper cards, and placed it on the table next to the sofa.

"Do you know of the Tarot cards? Some say they can accurately predict the future, could tell us things about ourselves that we don't know—or don't want others to know."

Sondra moved the deck of cards across the desk and in front of them. "Holger bought these cards two years ago to be a fun birthday gift. He hired a gypsy woman to teach me about the cards." Then, smoothly, she flipped them over and fanned out the deck.

"Not that I've become a Tarot expert. It's something to play with, to make me think more deeply about life."

Drake remained silent.

"Seventy-eight cards, and each card has a figure and an inscription. I've studied them and know their interpretations. I'll draw one for you, and you pull one for me. Then we place our hands together and draw one, and the deck will tell us what our future will bring."

His eyes scanned the room. A bit of relief came as he saw the full-length drapes pulled across the windows. Two side panes flanking the fireplace were uncovered but high off the floor.

"The gypsy taught you the meanings of these inscriptions?"

"Yes, I learned they were used for divining the future. Like the Ouija board, I suppose."

"And about as accurate."

Sondra smiled at his skepticism. "Then, you don't care what the cards might say?"

"I'll play. You draw first," he said.

Drake watched while Sondra skillfully shuffled the cards. She slid a card from the middle of the deck and turned it over.

"*The Hermit.* Is that you? It means a person who is not just isolated but also searching inward, trying to know himself. Withdrawing from people and relationships with others."

"That's not me at all. I'm no hermit—far from it, Sondra."

"Now for mine. You draw."

Drake reached for a card and turned it upward. Sondra gave out a slight gasp. "The death card. But it's upside down. Not terribly bad, because in that position, it means change or destruction followed by renewal. New life follows death."

"I feel like I should be taking notes," he said.

"Let's draw a card together." She placed the deck under the lamp.

Drake began to feel a tiny give-and-take between them as they moved their hands toward the cards. Her soft caress was delicious.

"Is this the one?" she asked.

Drake nodded. "Pull it. What's it say?"

"It's *The Lovers*. Show me the cards before and after that one."

He pulled the cards and turned them over to be seen.

"Those put it in the *future* position," Sondra said. "A good omen—it means we're backed by others who will face the future with us instead of us having to go it alone."

"That sounds believable. We're trusting Black Orchestra to be strong, for all of us to support each other in this little bitty recreation of saving the existence of civilization. Draw another card."

"*Queen of Swords*. Mmmm—a regal-looking woman, sitting with a sword beside her. I don't recall much about that one. I must get my book."

Sondra faltered, unsteady, as she stood to pick a small volume from the nearby bookshelf and held it under the lamp, flipping pages. "Yes, now I remember. Here it says, '*The Queen of Swords*, representing a woman's strength and powers of intuition. Her sword stands for her ability to use intuition and improvisation to defeat her enemies. Her intellect is sharp, and she can be intimidating to those that do not know her well.'"

Drake was a trifle amused. "Is that you?"

"You'll have to answer that for yourself. Could mean something about things to come."

"It's horoscope gibberish—nothing."

"Remember it," she said. "Perhaps someday the words will have meaning."

Drake looked away from the card and into Sondra's eyes. There was an aura about her in this light, her lips curved into a Mona Lisa-like smile.

"Do you have a woman—here in Berlin? Or perhaps elsewhere?"

He glanced away. "There was someone in England."

"I learned from Holger that you had a fiancée."

"Yes."

"What happened?"

"A disease killed her. I thought of going back to America, but then this Berlin assignment came along. Now she's in a place a million kilometers beyond the moon."

"I'm sorry, Alex. Have you, uh . . . are you better now?"

"It passes slowly. People tell me it takes a couple of years, but it's been that and more, and still, it doesn't seem much different."

"Your words—it's what I also deal with. My love of my husband was something unlike what you and she would have had. You had a future—with fat little babies, new adventures around the world, decades to build your love. And you would have been an amazing father—you will be that someday. Holger was a wonderful man, but I knew that his time was minimal. I find a bit of comfort in recognizing that truth."

To his surprise, he placed his arm around her shoulders.

Without hesitation, Sondra continued. "Alex, I think we're starting to have feelings for each other."

Drake nodded. "That's confusing—and dangerous."

She took his hand in hers and moved it down along her long skirt. He didn't resist. Then she moved his hand up under the hem until he touched the calf of her leg and up toward her knee.

Drake sat upright. An image slammed into his brain.

He was touching a prosthetic leg.

Turning to look into his eyes, she spoke in a soft, sad voice. "Alex, you must know that I am not the whole woman you might expect. This I live with every day of my life."

Drake sat back and reached to grab her arm. "You didn't have to."

"Yes, I did. Now you know," she whispered. "I'm part real, part fake, and you must decide. You need to know this about me because it might interfere with my ability to achieve Black Orchestra's essential ends. All I can do physically is to sit on the sidelines."

"But you move so well—I've never noticed."

"I can't walk very well sometimes, I can't jump, and when I make love, well . . ." She leaned underneath the table and fussed with the limb for a minute. "Holger saw to it that the finest maker of these things in Europe fitted one to me after I had recovered from the amputation. Have you heard of sepsis?"

"Yes, an infection. Bad."

"My leg got infected."

Drake listened as he pressed her hand.

"The leg had to come off below the knee to stop the raging growth of infection. It worked. They gave me a new leg below the right knee. Straps hold it on, and with training, I regained my ability to walk. I'll tell you something very dreadful to remember, Alex." Sondra seemed to tense up as she continued, a tear building at the corner of one eye.

"Don't, Sondra."

"No—it's good to let this out."

She clenched her jaw as she looked away. "Summertime—1931. I had a job at one of Berlin's *Kabaretts*—nightclubs where nearly nude models stood around or reclined on sofas for the patrons, men and women, to look at and get their excitement. We were called *Schönheit Mädchen*—Beauty Girls. One night . . . a drunken Nazi rat shouted something at me. He pulled a knife as I passed his table. My costume was practically nothing—that was life as a worker in those places. He grabbed my leg and made a degrading comment. I slapped him hard—a wild, insane look came to his bulging eyes. His filthy knife sliced and twisted through my leg below the knee—I almost bled to death. The last thing I remember before I passed out was the pain. It was more than I could bear. My savior that night eventually became my husband. Holger has—I mean had—been at my side every moment since, until he couldn't anymore. Holger, a man with such high integrity, to also suffer at the hands of a rotten Nazi!" Her eyes blazed.

"Sondra . . ." Drake's words caught in his throat.

Her eyes had become like pools of calm waters. He wanted to pull her into his arms and feel the warmth of her body.

"This madness has already cost me my husband." She looked down at the cards. "Will the Nazis take you also?"

Regaining his mental compass, Drake said, "Understand this: you're more whole than any other woman I know. The most important thing in this universe right now is stopping Hitler's bomb. You're under surveillance by the Gestapo. We could be caught together, forced to talk, exposed as conspirators along with the rest of Black Orchestra. Then would come a Nazi show trial—the United States would become involved. This would explode in our faces—like an atomic bomb. Our efforts would die along with us."

Sondra sat for a few seconds as his words sank in. Drake studied her, watching her face for signs of a reaction. Her jaw set as she turned back to him.

"So, you're thoughtful, well-spoken, even philosophical," he said. "Seems contradictory that you would begin working as—what—a poser, a dancer?"

"I suppose it does. But I had no money and a lot of responsibilities. I needed to work, and I found work."

"I get that."

"When my mother was about forty, she began losing her vision. My father had died on the Western Front, so we were alone, and she couldn't keep on with her job. We lived off my father's military pension, but after the financial collapse of 1923, that was gone. I managed to finish what is called high school in your country, but in 1927, the job opportunities for an inexperienced woman were none. I worked for a year in a clothing store, but that ended when the owner died. We had absolutely nothing, and she needed a new drug called insulin which had become available in small amounts and at high prices, but we had no money for it. So, I investigated work at the "Femina Palace," got hired, and that allowed for the purchase of the drug and paid for a little apartment. I don't know what we would have done after my leg was gone had it not been for Holger's presence." Drake discovered he had taken her hand in his.

"She's still alive?"

Sondra put her other hand over his. "She is and lives in the Schöneberg district, in a small apartment I pay for with money from my husband. I see her once a week. She has friends and is now in her mid-fifties. As bleak as things looked a decade ago, we have arrived at this place out of harm's way for now."

"Admirable. You've satisfied at least some of my curiosity. Remember, I'm a journalist, and snooping is part of my job. A German *Kabarett* girl who speaks French, cares for her mother, and uses Latin phrases."

"I read a lot, and I've got an excellent memory. Actually, I'm quite ordinary."

Describing herself in these terms, he understood why he was feeling these things for her. She was multifaceted, intelligent, strong, and beautiful, a dangerously attractive combination that might hopelessly entangle a man.

"We're much alike, Alex. Tough times for each of us as children, the suffering at the hands of Nazis, a shared hatred of Hitler brought on by death and pain. And now, the fate of the entire world balances on us accomplishing our task." Her words came deliberately, in a firm voice.

She lurched in her chair as logs fell in the fireplace and a sudden flash of orange light flickered across the room. Her eyes darted to a window above and next to the fireplace.

"*Alex!*" she screamed. "*Up there!* A face!"

Drake swung around to follow her gaze but saw only blackness in the square windowpane. He sprang up and ran to the door, flung it open, and burst out into the night. He couldn't see and struggled to keep his footing on the wet, slippery grass. Approaching the window, he followed the light falling to the ground. His fingers wrapped around the Zippo in his pocket, and in a few seconds, he had a flame that flickered in the wind but gave off some light. Wood was stacked under the window next to the fireplace. Shoe prints, barely visible, could be seen in the moist grass near the woodpile. Somebody had been standing there, in front of the window. He knelt and scanned the patterns. He couldn't be sure without more light, but the impressions of the soles seemed to be saw-toothed like those of boots, not ordinary shoes. The marks led to total darkness behind the house. In front of the logs were three cigarette butts. Drake scooped them up, then looked in the window. Sondra was in the middle of the room, her hands covering her mouth and lower face.

A watcher had stood here in this spot moments ago. Maybe a Gestapo agent, keeping surveillance on the widow of a suspected dead anti-Nazi conspirator. Or maybe her would-be lover.

Drake retraced his steps and came back into the library where Sondra stood, petrified with fear.

"I saw it," she said, "a face. But it was too dark—I couldn't recognize it."

"Looked like boot marks out there. Big boots. Could be Gestapo or maybe the character you suspect."

"Yes—"

"Look at these. They were in the grass under the window."

"Burned out cigarettes. What's that writing on the ends? Something's printed on there. Hold one under the lamp."

Drake twisted the white stub under the light as they tried to read the lettering.

"Melachrino," Sondra said.

"Yes. Not a common brand, but I've seen them."

"So, a smoker was outside there, standing on the log pile, watching us. Long enough to smoke three cigarettes."

"I'd better go, but I don't like leaving you here alone."

"No, it will be all right. I've made sure the locks are strong, and I'll call my chauffeur to come. He'll be here immediately."

Her eyes had closed to perfect slits. Her face was framed by her dark hair, backlit by the glow of the ornate cut-glass shade of the lamp. He nodded slowly and contemplated for a long moment the invisible barrier that stood between them.

"Kiss me before you go," she said, stepping toward him. Their lips touched, and he leaned into her kiss. He felt her tongue moving against his and pulled away.

"We must stop now, or we'll keep on going," he whispered.

She looked toward his chest. "Yes, go."

He fished a *Jonnie* cigarette from his pocket and lit it up with the shining silver lighter on the desk. He turned toward the door as he again glimpsed the Tarot card on the table, the thing that had started to unravel his defenses. *The Hermit.*

Sondra closed the door behind Drake. It had been a strange evening, but one question was answered: would her body again respond to the touch of a man after all this time? It did—ardently. She reached down and adjusted the straps of the prosthesis and thought of the comforting words he had spoken earlier. An ache spread up her legs and back, something like the sensations she'd experienced when she had the infection. Insecurity, a fear of "crying wolf"—these intense emotions were holding her back from revealing the identity of the man she suspected of betraying Black Orchestra. She now had only one way to proceed—keep careful watch over this possible traitor within their ranks. She had to become his personal Mata Hari.

CHAPTER 16

POLAND

"I now call my people at home and my peoples across the seas,
who will make our cause their own.
I ask them to stand calm, firm, and united in this time of trial."

King George VI, speaking in a live broadcast, September 3, 1939.

THE REICH CHANCELLERY, BERLIN

AFFAIRS WERE COLLAPSING VERY QUICKLY for Adolf Hitler.
Only a week earlier, the world had been shocked by the signing of the historic non-aggression pact between former antagonists Germany and the Soviet Union which seemed to give the Nazi kingpin a powerful ace to play in his game of high stakes European power poker. His next wager was to launch the invasion of Poland, confident that his pack with Stalin would guarantee that Britain and France would remain cowered and incapable of doing anything but giving more blustery speeches.

Germany's Foreign Minister Joachim von Ribbentrop walked down the marble-floored hallway, his head lowered. Outside Hitler's office, several high-ranking Nazi Party officials had collected, awaiting the Foreign Minister's arrival with the rumored letter from the British Ambassador. As he walked toward them, Ribbentrop looked gray, his face heavily wrinkled. He silently passed by the others and entered the room where Hitler sat.

"*Führer*, I have a communication just delivered to me by courier from the British Embassy." Ribbentrop walked sluggishly to the window and turned the paper toward the light as he slid it from its envelope. Hitler sat behind his desk. *Generalfeldmarschall* Göring rested his fat body on the heavily patterned sofa. "I will translate, but I'm afraid I will not have every little—"

"*Get on with it!*" Hitler roared. Ribbentrop flinched at the words and shook the piece of paper.

"It reads as follows: 'German attacks on Poland have continued since September 1. The Government of Germany is informed that, unless not later than 11:00 a.m., British daylight time, today September 3, satisfactory assurances to the effect that hostilities have been stopped have been given to His Majesty's Government in London, a state of war will exist between the two countries as from that hour.' End of communication."

The dictator had long held confidence that he could continue his bluffing and feigning, making demands and bloodlessly getting territory he wanted until he'd achieved a Nazified Europe.

But that dream had evaporated along with the moisture in the ink bearing Prime Minister Neville Chamberlain's signature. The bloodless conquests were over, and British bombers could be heading for Berlin right this minute. The men within the office were completely silent; the only sounds were of the traffic on the Wilhelmstrasse, three stories below.

Hitler glared at the ashen-faced Ribbentrop. "What now?" he shouted. "You *guaranteed* this would not happen."

It had been four months since Chamberlain made his first real stand against Hitler's aggression. This stunning turnabout followed years of British indecision and attempts to appease the Nazi appetite for conquest. In his speech before the House of Commons, he'd seemed energized, like a new man. He vowed that Britain would come to the aid of Poland in the event of an attack. But few in Hitler's government believed him. Chamberlain had become the icon of weakness and indecision within the Allied governments.

The restaurant in the Berlin suburb of Potsdam was almost devoid of patrons. The walls of the place were of polished mahogany panels hung with a large portrait of Adolf Hitler and a smaller picture of a face with an ashen complexion, probably the owner of the establishment. Sondra Speier sat across from a man in a gray wool jacket. Three waiters stood in the entrance to the kitchen, looking anxious, most likely due to the lack of business.

"Your favorite 1929 Bordeaux—do you like it?"

She nodded and smiled for an instant as she sipped from a stemmed crystal goblet. Decent French wine would be getting scarce with the declaration of war by France and England hours earlier.

"It's odd to see you without your uniform."

"They say a man always looks good in uniform."

"You even wear it to meetings of Black Orchestra."

"Why not? Most military men wear the uniform almost all the time."

"You're quite proud of your position in the Nazified German army."

"Not the Nazified army, but yes, the German army. Unlike the old version, this army wins. I prefer winners."

"Well, you're about to get tested. War is here, Poland is first, and it won't amount to much against the Wehrmacht. But with Germany now fighting both the English and the French, I guess we'll soon see who's a champion."

"Sondra, my dearest, do you doubt for even a moment that Germany can crush all of them?"

She lifted her wine glass and took a sip as he concluded his sentence. "Oh, I forgot for a moment," she said, swinging the wine glass in a broad sweep of sarcasm. "We're talking about the great Fatherland which can conquer the whole world blindfolded and standing on one leg. If that happens, then what?" Her face began to redden.

"Keep your voice down. You're going to get us into difficulties."

With a shrug of her shoulders, she went on. "When the last war ended, all the nations murdering each other had recovered to a large extent in a few years. This war is going to be very different. Things won't go back to normal afterward. We know what's at stake this time."

"And I win, whatever happens. I simply need to predict the winning side correctly."

"Meaning you have no loyalty to Beck or your uniform? Well, that tells me a lot about you."

"I didn't mean that. I'm simply saying that if Black Orchestra can destroy Hitler or Germany can't win the war for some reason, atom bombs or otherwise, I will eventually be on the side of whoever is victorious. All for the good of humanity, of course. I'm loyal to Germany *and* to General Beck."

A waiter in a tuxedo passed nearby, adroitly swinging his platter of food away from them in something resembling a ballet dance.

General Klaus Würter smiled self-assuredly, took another sip of coffee, and stared across the table at Sondra.

"You're going to marry me. When that happens, I'll take good care of you."

Sondra was disgusted by his proclamation, but she flipped her hair off her forehead and offered a bit of a smile. "If you knew more about me, you wouldn't be so eager to say things like that."

"I am going to become a figure in this country that will amaze you. The day is not far off when people like Himmler will work for me, not the other way around. When that time comes, you will beg me to be part of it."

"How does any of that work with our sworn duty to exterminate Hitler?"

"We'll get rid of him, and no matter what or who replaces them, I'll have power. It doesn't matter if that's Goerdeler, Himmler, or Beck. And I'll stop any use of atom bombs in the unlikely event that they somehow become real."

She touched a starched napkin to her lips and moved her head up and down slightly.

"I am my own man, and I do exactly what is necessary to make me stronger. Others might think that I bow to their commands, but soon they will bow to me!"

A master schemer, she thought. *Playing both ends against the middle.*

She looked around to confirm that there were no restaurant patrons within earshot before she spoke in an almost inaudible voice, lifting one eyebrow. "And Black Orchestra, Klaus?"

"You tell me. Has Beck's group served its purpose? Has it stopped Hitler or this atom bomb fantasy? The answer is *no*, of course. Nothing but talk. I'm a man of action, and I'm tired of talk." Würter exhaled smoke and stretched his arm toward the green glass ashtray, stubbing the cigarette and twisting the butt. She looked at the paper covering the remaining centimeter of tobacco—black letters wrapped around the circumference of the little cylinder. Mel—she couldn't quite see the rest of the word. Würter's watch brushed the side of the ashtray, moving the cigarette butt slightly. *Melachrino.*

Sondra shuddered as she comprehended the evidence she'd become aware of within the last two minutes. Finally, Würter was confirming what she'd suspected all along. He needed to control everything around him and cared about nothing except furthering his own interests. And, he was a voyeur. She had enough now to reveal her suspicions to Black Orchestra's leader. The time had come. Sondra swallowed hard as she thought about what she must do.

Twilight slid across the big city on this first day of the European conflict, which had erupted into bloody combat only hours after war was declared. Radio reports came of the British ship *Athenia*, allegedly a troop carrier, torpedoed just west of Ireland by the German submarine *U-30*.

Members of Black Orchestra had received varying forms of summons from Ludwig Beck. One by one, they arrived at the meeting place in a cadence spread out over an hour and requiring various diversionary means to get there—streetcar, U-Bahn, taxi, walking, or automobile.

Alex Drake slid into the rear seat of Beck's *Grosser Mercedes* at the corner of Invalidenstrasse and Rathenower. For a half-hour, the expert driver crisscrossed the city to shake off any tails. He got out of the car a block from the meeting place and walked through an overgrown alleyway lined with dormant lilac bushes and willows. Ahead was the portal of the brooding old warehouse. The neon *Warenhaus* sign no longer glowed.

Drake stepped back into the brush, tangling himself in sticks and branches, then stood still, waiting out of sight. Soon he heard footsteps moving toward him. He narrowed his eyes to slits and watched Goerdeler pass him first, *Generalmajor* Oster a minute or two later. Another figure approached. He stepped forward.

"Sondra," he said quietly.

She stopped mid-stride and stumbled slightly. "Oh, Alex—you surprised me."

His key twisted in the lock cylinder. "You go down first—I'll wait a minute or two, then follow." She flashed a smile, turned, and went through the portal.

The stairs creaked as Drake made his way down into the underground meeting room. As he sat on a chair and slid close to the table, he felt a surge of apprehension, a sense of change. The declaration of war on this third of September had made the world feel like a very different place than it had been only a day earlier. The subterranean chamber was already thick with tobacco smoke. His colleagues were talking and waving their arms, absorbed in separate conversations.

A hand loudly slapped the tabletop. General Beck lifted his arm and said, "quiet!" The leader looked around the table. The voices went silent. "The war we hoped could be averted is upon us," he said." Men are again dying in battle." Beck's sad countenance was reflected on most of the other faces. "The German people . . . responsible for two wars in this century, not even half over! Are we madmen?"

The Reverend Born fidgeted uncomfortably.

Beck continued, "Now that war has come, the pressure from Hitler on his scientists to produce the Wells bombs will be even more intense. I have given you assignments. Oster, you and Drake have contacted this Dr. Szilard to alert America of this threat, but nothing was heard in return. Schoe, you have come up with nothing to halt carolinum production. You, Goerdeler, using your clandestine channels to 10 Downing Street, you've been pressing the British to help us overthrow the Nazi government, but they give no signs of support. Nothing."

Born's face was red with rage. "Nothing, nothing, nothing!" he shouted." "That's all I hear! We're getting nowhere. God has placed us here, *now!* What are we going to do?"

"The fastest way to accomplish what must be done," answered Beck, "is to kill the snake, chop off its head."

Carl Goerdeler drew a deep breath. "General Würter, we thought your boss General Halder would act to arrest the bastard before this war started, but he lost his nerve at the last moment. So, we dispose of Hitler ourselves. But somehow, we must get access. Then, we require the *means* to kill. And lastly, even if successful, we will not change anything unless we eliminate Göring, Himmler, and others who would continue his terrors!"

Drake cut his eyes toward Goerdeler. "Unless they're all exterminated, a new snake will slither out of the old skin and bare its fangs to inject venom into the world. *Radioactive* venom, according to Schoe here."

Beck looked around the table at the Black Orchestra members. "Said like a true writer, Drake. So, is anyone not with us?" asked the general. "Anyone not one hundred percent behind liquidating this monster?" He pulled his glasses down and looked at Drake over gold rims.

Drake could feel the eyes of the others upon him, making him uneasy. They'd never unanimously approved of his presence. Were they looking at him because they were concerned about his loyalty?

No one volunteered to leave, nor was there any talking. Finally, Beck spoke. "Then, this is a solemn pledge we make at this moment. We shall kill Adolf Hitler. Carl Goerdeler will become the new Chancellor of Germany, backed by Würter, Halder, and the entire armed forces. We put an end to this nation's nightmare."

Beck looked around the table as each man nodded assent.

"General," said Oster of the Abwehr intelligence agency. "The Munich *Putsch* Festival."

Drake knew all too well that this Nazi commemoration was the annual celebration of Hitler's 1923coup attempt to seize the Bavarian government—the events that led up to his father's murder. It was the gathering of the *Alte Kämpfer*—the Old Fighters.

Beck looked up. "Ninth of November. Hitler goes every year and never misses."

The mention of that date—the Day of Death—made Drake's eyes squeeze shut for a few seconds.

"Yes," Oster said, "in the meeting room of the Bürgerbräukeller beer hall. Drake, your German is nearly flawless, but just in case, that's Citizens' Brew Celler in English. The main hall can seat a few thousand. Hitler gathers top Nazis all around, makes speeches, and slaps everyone on the back. They're all going to be there. Very predictable. I see a big bomb going off right near the bastard."

Schoe ran a hand through his wispy blond hair. "Under Hitler's chair, ready to send him on a tumble back to hell before he makes another asinine speech."

"My thoughts exactly," said Oster. "Activate a bomb by radio at the exact moment it would be most effective. All the top Nazis will be in the front row. Hitler and anybody else with the power to unleash atom bombs killed in one moment. Rodent extermination."

No one moved. "I have been there, to that site," Beck said. "Perfect place to set off a bomb with maximum effect. At least three hundred people are going to be in the hall when Hitler takes the podium. A bomb will kill nearly everyone in the room."

Sondra spoke for the first time. "General, you say this, but how can our little group go inside that place, the Burger—whatever you called it, and plant a bomb? There will be guards all around."

"Drake, go to Munich, get into the Bürgerbräukeller. As a reporter, you have credentials giving you good reasons for being inside there—to cover preparations for the event. Devise a detailed plan of the place and how a bomb could be concealed and detonated."

The general straightened his back and continued in a deep voice. "My orders are to be precisely carried out, no excuses. Oster, your experts will locate bomb materials. And you must find a trusted technician to make and place a bomb that will eradicate Hitler, including a foolproof means to install the device and trigger it. Goerdeler, through your contacts, we need to ensure the governments of England and France are going to stand behind us. Dohnanyi, from you, we shall receive a legal blueprint of how we'll restore a legitimate government when the attack accomplishes its objective. How will we control the government once Hitler and most of his first rank are eliminated? Würter! Generals

Halder and Fromm must be completely aware and supportive, ready with troops to move against any remaining Nazi strong points. You and I will meet with them, get their commitment to arrest or kill off Nazi leaders throughout the country in the first moments after the explosion."

Around the table, all heads were nodding, but each person's eyes revealed apprehension.

"One more thing," said Beck. "Sondra, you have many friends among Berlin's business community and wealthy society people. Learn all you can about their loyalties to Hitler, now that war has been declared. In the past, they have been emphatically pro-Hitler. Will they back our new Goerdeler government?"

"I'll try to measure sentiments," she said. "Attitudes are quickly changing, this I know."

Drake glanced toward Sondra, and she returned his look. Her fingertips were shaking almost imperceptibly.

Beck stood up and leaned forward, placing his hands on the table. "I repeat—trust no one! That means spouses, fellow officers, relatives—" He paused, then declared, "We meet again in five days to report progress. So do your jobs—but be vigilant every second!"

Nearly simultaneously, each person pushed back their chair and stood except Sondra, who said quietly, "General Beck and *Herr Drake*, can I have a moment with you privately, please."

General Würter paused his steps and looked back, his eyebrows arching. Beck glanced at him, his eyes declaring *this is none of your business. Keep going.*

No one spoke until they heard the last steps on the stairs and the closing of the door. Drake checked the stairway to ensure no one had remained inside. What was she going to say? She was articulate and intelligent, but her choice of words might make the difference in the actions Beck would take once he'd gained this knowledge. He returned to the table, tapped the oilcloth table covering, and dropped himself into a chair across from her.

"What is it?"

Sondra cleared her throat before speaking. "General, this you won't like."

Beck cocked his head and sat back, arms folded. "On with it."

"I've already mentioned some of this to *Herr Drake,* and he's urged me to come to you. I have my reasons to believe there may be a traitor, a double-crosser—right here among us," she said.

"That's crazy." Beck's eyes narrowed. "Who are you talking about?"

"I suspect Klaus Würter will betray Black Orchestra."

Drake sat up and touched his lower lip. A solemn expression crawled across Beck's face. "*Würter?* Where in the hell do you get this idea?"

"Things are adding up, General. He's pursued me romantically, especially after Holger's death. I've come to know him well enough to understand that he has only one loyalty—to himself. He doesn't care if Hitler, Goerdeler, or Charlie Chaplin is the leader of Germany, as long as he gets himself near the top rung."

Beck sat back in his chair. "That's not evidence of treason. I've known Würter for a long time. He worked closely with me every day. His superior, General Halder, precisely positioned him as a member of our group, ensuring that the German General Staff aligns with Black Orchestra's goals. Würter's undeniably bigheaded and self-centered, but he's no traitor. He's done everything I've asked him to do, and Halder trusts him completely. To make this kind of dangerous allegation, you must have more than just a vague feeling. Get me proof!" Bulging veins in Beck's neck went purple, his eyes widening.

Sondra nodded before speaking. "I'll continue whatever relationship I have with Würter. I'll keep being friendly with him, stay in a place where I can get the evidence you need for the protection of us all."

Drake tightened his fists. "I've listened to your suspicions. *No proof.* Both of you—go," Beck said. "Leave me alone."

The general watched the pair walk up the stairs. He leaned forward under the lamp as he curled his shoulders and allowed his chest to sink. *Würter!* He was a tough, sausage-necked German general but had never evidenced any sort of treachery. If Black Orchestra lost him, it would be devastating to their cause. And if they succeeded in eliminating Hitler, the Wehrmacht's divisions loyal to Beck and Halder would have to roll in to occupy centers of Nazi entrenchment, places like Munich where Hitlerism was strongest. He desperately needed Würter to ensure that the German Army would be on their side in the ensuing struggle once they had slain Hitler. There would be no charging off to Halder, making rash accusations, unless he had something concrete to go on. This was all conjecture—no evidence of any disloyalty on the part of Würter or anyone else. If there was a traitor in their midst, *anything* they did was at risk of exposure and failure, a stunning thought since he knew the fate of the entire world rested on their shoulders. He sat back, slipping his hands into his pockets, his mind searching for a basin of cool water, strength to meet the mounting dangers threatening him and his colleagues.

CHAPTER 17

BÜRGERBRÄUKELLER

"It is better to fight for the good than to rail at the evil . . ."

Alfred, Lord Tennyson
Maud, pt. 3, sect. 6, 1855

TUESDAY, OCTOBER 17, 1939

ALEX DRAKE LISTENED TO THE locomotive vent a powerful head of steam, followed by the screech accompanying the first belch of pressure from the pistons, inching the long train forward. It was barely daylight. He'd boarded the train early, eager to get to Munich. As the cars gained speed, he stared out at the bare branches on the trees whipping by—signs of early autumn, portending a severe winter.

He thought of tales he'd read of other conspirators who'd fought against corrupt governments, their fears that an insider would betray them. Paul Revere and his men ended their meetings at the Green Tavern by swearing their secrecy pledge with a hand on the Bible. But what would promises of loyalty mean to a determined traitor?

The dark, clear eyes of Sondra Speier knotted his thoughts. Why wasn't she also murdered the night her husband died? She brought nothing to Black Orchestra except her dead spouse's money and the matrons of Berlin's high society. The tingling feeling in his fingers was returning. He had to refocus his mind and energies on destroying the German atom program.

The train trip to Munich would take just over six hours. He had again concocted a hokum story to serve up to his boss, Jimmy Keene, telling him that he thought it was an excellent idea to go to Munich for a few days, get a better sense of what Germans outside of Berlin were feeling about the new war. He would craft an article out of the visit, but the reality was that he was going on a scouting trip to finalize the plan for killing Adolf Hitler.

Spandau, the westernmost of the *Bezirke*—municipalities—of Berlin, had grown up at the confluence of the Havel and Spree rivers, and life there had evolved to move more slowly than at the frenetic pace of the center city. Alex Drake sat in a subway car that sped along the tube of the U7 U-Bahn line. His point of debarkation was the Spandau Rathaus station not far from the western bank of the Havel.

Beck's orders were for him to wear workmen's clothes and meet at a wooden bench located 700 meters north of the Charlottenburg Chaussee bridge. He walked half a kilometer east from the station, the blue water of the river coming into view. There was the bench between two giant oak trees losing their leaves with the onset of colder temperatures.

Drake sat in solitude, admiring the bridge's graceful steel arches and rethinking what he'd seen and heard in Munich. The autumn sky was cloudless and resolutely blue. The sun on his face felt genuinely pleasurable against the slight embrace of cold in the air. He caught sight of a figure wearing dark glasses and a gray plaid wool hat striding toward him.

"*Guten Tag*," the general said in his usual austere manner. His face was craggy, the wrinkles much more pronounced than the last time he'd seen him.

"And to you, sir. I won't waste time—I have a plan to go over with you."

Beck looked around the immediate area, surveyed the people in the distance, and then glanced back at Drake before sitting beside him. "Tell me what you've got."

Drake squinted one eye against the bright sun. "The operation will be physically possible, but my plan is far from complete. I'll need help from you and others to finish it. I went inside the Bürgerbräukeller three times this week, managed to slip into the meeting room each time."

"Good. Continue."

"Excellent situation for planting an explosive. There are white-painted hollow posts behind the speaker's platform, spaced about twelve feet apart, several right behind the stage. A bomb could be stuffed inside one of them and be set to trigger just when the place would be full of top Nazis."

Beck's eyes registered a look of skepticism."And explosives?" asked Beck. "How will we gain access to them?"

"Oster hasn't come up with nitroglycerine, TNT, cordite, or anything else. It's a big problem with no solution, not yet."

Beck exhaled heavily through drawn lips and rubbed the back of his neck.

"When I used my press credentials to gain access to the room, declaring that I needed to gather background information for a story about the celebration, I came across a contractor, hired to set up an elaborate system of lights and microphones for Hitler and his crowd. We need to bring one of the contractor's people over to our side."

"You're not making sense. Do you presume to trust a nameless worker with something so important?" asked Beck. "No, that's an unacceptable answer."

Drake massaged the beard stubble on his chin. He'd started with a feeling of confidence that he had a workable way to kill the dictator, but the general wasn't buying it.

Beck waved his hand. "No infiltrating of contractors—that's a reckless absurdity."

"Then we choose our own person and put him inside the meeting hall to work."

"That's more like a possibility. We find a trustworthy technician to build the bomb. He goes in there to work while nobody else is around. You'll watch him."

"We'll need Oster's Abwehr to find someone. I'll go to see the *Generalmajor.*"

"Do it," said Beck. "We only have a few days to execute our plan, which right now is no plan at all. Now, let's get the hell out of here."

"You first. I'm going to sit here until you're out of sight."

"Keep me informed." Beck crossed the lawn gone more brown than green, and vanished behind a stand of tall yews.

Drake fought off a wave of melancholy as he thought of the enormity of the task ahead. He had to split the effort into discreet compartments because looking at the whole plan would only overwhelm him. If he ate the elephant one bite at a time, he might have a chance to consume the entire thing, but the chunks of meat were going to be huge and leathery.

Oster's large, highly polished mahogany desk was utterly devoid of papers, pictures, or mementos. Late afternoon sunlight fell across both men in streaks created by the white blinds behind the windows' heavy draperies. Drake stopped talking as the assistant delivered black coffee in ornate porcelain cups with saucers and a small pitcher of cream, then quietly departed, shutting the door.

"First thing, let's make sure you are on record as being here on official Nazi Party business. In my daily logbook—you've got a different name, and you've come to interview me about renegade Polish radio broadcasts intended to prolong the fighting and how the Abwehr is finding the stations and destroying them."

"If that's a fact, maybe I can make that into a genuine article for publication. But right now, I'm here to talk with you about a meeting I just had with Beck. The dirty little problem of getting a bomb built to blow them all up in that meeting hall."

Drake described the needs of Black Orchestra for bomb materials and a technician to put it to use. Oster maintained a look of detached impatience, his mouth downturned, eyebrows knitted. "Yes," he said,

"I must talk to my superior, Admiral Canaris. I cannot move until I have his support. I'll get agreement from him—he's on our side. I don't think it's a problem."

"How much time do you need, Hans?" asked Drake.

"I'll find him immediately and discuss it. He's gone for the day, but I'll get it going tomorrow."

"Find a way," Drake said. "You know what happens if we fall flat."

Oster nodded slowly. "There is nothing more important on this earth, which will become a cinder if we can't kill this serpent."

Enigmatic was the description used frequently in describing Abwehr leader Admiral Wilhelm Canaris. Brilliant, educated, personable, he hated the Nazis but concealed his loathing flawlessly. He was very much a skilled bureaucrat, making a steady rise through the Party's ranks by virtue of his prodigious intellect and iron determination. He was responsible for knowing everything there was to know about matters inside and outside the Reich that could impact the German military machine. In his mid-fifties, Canaris had been an investigator for the Navy during the 1920s, becoming a member of the Nazi Party by 1930. By mid-decade, he'd powered his way into the leadership of the secretive, nearly invisible Abwehr operation.

Since then, he'd stayed on constant alert for ways he could derail the Hitler government—an astounding situation given the magnitude of his job, akin to America's FBI Director J. Edgar Hoover being a closet Nazi, working to unseat the Roosevelt government.

Canaris' desktop calendar showed a full day of appointments. Hans Oster had reserved an hour first thing but had not indicated the subject.

"Willi." Oster swung around the corner of the office door. "I apologize for this mysterious meeting, but things are about to get more puzzling. Take your coat, and let's go for a walk."

"*Ja*," said Canaris. "And be quick." He pushed away from the desk and followed behind his subordinate. They made their way through the office door and out of the building.

Through an avalanche of golden leaves blown off the linden

trees a block north, they strolled along the Friedrichbergstrasse until they reached an outdoor café, one they had used for such delicate conversations before. It was a pleasant mid-October morning, about 17 degrees Celsius, low 60s Fahrenheit—still decent for sitting outdoors. They pulled their chairs up to a table at the farthest corner. Oster drummed his fingers on the tablecloth. "This is about Black Orchestra. It's big."

"Of course. The Beck group," said Canaris, squinting against the sunlight. His bushy brows, sparkling eyes, and thick, silver hair gave him the look of the grandfather every person wanted to have, yet belied his resolve and intensity. "You knew of my trip to the Polish front two weeks ago," he continued. "The devastation rendered by the German military, seeing Warsaw in flames, brought me to tears. I witnessed the burning of a synagogue in Będzin with 200 Polish Jews inside. Our children's children will have to bear the blame for this, Hans. The orders for these atrocities came directly from Hitler. His thirst for killing is without limits."

"Indeed, Admiral. The potential for a super bomb which you and I discussed a few weeks ago—imagine this weapon in his grasp—just one of them might be as powerful as thousands, maybe millions of current bombs."

"*Verdammt!* How realistic is this? What do you know?"

"I don't know how far the scientists are in making this happen. Work is going on at the Kaiser Wilhelm Institute in Dahlem. Top scientists. We *must* stop this."

"No question, Hans."

"I've been making every effort to keep Black Orchestra out of the eyesight of the SS and Gestapo. But, one of the group's members was killed by them. They told his wife they know that Beck is up to something." Oster leaned over, his voice dropping to a near whisper. "So, I'm talking about a plan to kill Hitler and many of his closest cronies—at the *Hitlerputsch* anniversary celebration in Munich soon. Beck has approved it."

Canaris raised his eyes to stare at Hans Oster. "Of course, they want my help."

"Correct. A lot of help."

Canaris gave a nod of understanding. "Assassination would be difficult, very difficult, but it's the most direct way, assuming we exterminate the whole Nazi leadership, and nobody of Hitler's ilk replaces him. But it's not the only way. For example, have you considered eliminating the scientists who would create this weapon?"

Oster smoothed his hair back before speaking again. "Germany's best atom scientist is Heisenberg, but there are at least half a dozen others spread out in various labs and university campuses around the country. It is easier to kill Heisenberg than Hitler, but the Nazis will lock the remaining brains up in prison and force them to produce these weapons even quicker. The assassination of Hitler and his collaborators—yes, it's the most effective solution to stop these weapons from coming."

The spymaster waved out the match he'd used to light a cigarette. "Many people have tried to eradicate Hitler. He is well protected, smart, incredibly lucky. God knows I'd like to see his rotting corpse, but how? Who dares to take that chance?"

"It might be possible with Black Orchestra's plan," said Oster as he lifted his cup and looked down at the coffee, then back toward his boss. In this light, Canaris looked ten years older than he did minutes earlier. "But we can't do it without your support." He outlined Black Orchestra's scheme.

The Abwehr leader leaned toward Oster to hear the explanation. Then, finally, he sat back in his chair and folded his arms. "This just *could* have a chance of success. I'll give you everything I've got for this one. Tell me exactly what you need from me, Hans."

"Explosives. And then there is the tiny little matter of getting a person to design, construct, and plant an explosive device."

Canaris lowered his eyes as his finger traced the lip of the cup. "Perhaps I have someone—there is one man," said the admiral. "I used him three years ago." He looked up. "Do you know what an *idiot savant* is?"

Oster smiled and set his cup on the table. "I do. A brilliant idiot. Go on."

"This person—named Elser—is something like that. A genius in electrical matters and tinkering with bombs, yet otherwise slow and susceptible to suggestions. He made a bomb, wired it, and concealed everything. I simply told him it was a direct order from Kaiser Wilhelm, and he did it without question—perfect job. His bomb killed eleven communists. He may be the answer if he's still alive and not already conscripted by the Party."

Oster nodded.

"I will try to locate him," said Canaris. "In the meantime, I will see what can be done to get explosives."

"What more can I tell you, sir?"

"One simple question. Who will be Germany's new leader after you dispose of the current devil?"

"This Bürgerbräukeller action will make sure the replacement won't be a member of the present infestation. They'll all go back to hell where they came from, and Mayor Goerdeler becomes the new leader of Germany."

CHAPTER 18

SAVANT

"Sorrow makes us all children again, destroys
all differences of intellect."

Ralph Waldo Emerson, *Journals*, vol. 8, entry for Jan. 30, 1842

S ONDRA KNOCKED ON DRAKE'S APARTMENT door at nine in the morning. He invited her in to share some eggs scrambled with cheese, a flat tin of sardines, and a couple of raisin baguets. While he cooked, she ran the coffee percolator and brewed enough to sustain the conversation they both knew would be difficult.

"Dangerous," he said, "meeting here in my apartment, but I had to see you before I go to Munich."

The eggs were good, and in times of war, sardines had to do. Between bites, she talked. "The Bürgerbräukeller—a damned complicated scheme, Alex." Sondra stared down at her hands. "There must be some better, simpler way to kill Hitler. You're going to get caught and killed. Don't go."

Drake looked away, his forehead tightening. "This is a rare

opportunity to get at him. Now that war has been declared, he seldom goes out. I'm in the right career when it comes to having some freedom to move about. My boss gives me leeway, and my press credentials explain my presence in places where I might get questions. I've got to do this, Sondra. Everything is set to cut Nazism out of the body of Germany, and I'm the chief surgeon right now."

She swept her hair back, then touched the corner of his mouth. "If you're going to kill Hitler, do it and get back here safely and soon."

He dabbed a paper napkin against his chin. "I'll come back—count on that." He grabbed her hand, pulled her close, and kissed her gently.

Georg Elser lived quietly and invisibly with his parents in Grunewald, on a peaceful street where children played and dogs sometimes barked. In his room, he read comic books and tinkered with radio sets. He was thirty-seven.

It was early afternoon, and he was walking toward his much-loved candy store, past a pair of zig-zagging yellow terriers. Behind the wheel of a sleek, midnight blue 1938 Mercedes-Benz 320A sedan, Alex Drake pulled up alongside the curb. He held a small photograph in his hand, which he stuffed into his coat pocket as he cranked the window down.

"Georg, is it not?" he asked.

"Who are you?"

Drake tapped on the upper door frame. "My name is Fritz. This baby will go a hundred," he said. "Like to try a run in it?

"Oh? Go right now?"

"Right now. Jump in."

In a moment, Georg was inside the car. The engine built a deep, powerful exhaust note as Drake punched the accelerator.

"Its engine—a four-liter straight eight," said "Fritz." They entered the northbound lane of the Reichsautobahnen east of the center city, heading toward Stettin—no speed limit, few cars.

"Can you feel the power of the engine, Georg? It is running well today." Drake took one hand off the wheel to fiddle with the cigarette lighter on the instrument panel and got a smoke going.

"My friend told me that you love cars and electrical parts."

"I know everything about them."

"And things that explode?"

Elser jerked his head forward and turned toward Drake. "Hold it right there, *Scheißkopf.* Are you the police?"

"No, absolutely not. I hate the police."

Elser seemed to settle down when he heard those words. "I hate the police, too. They have hurt me, Fritz."

"I'll protect you from them. So then—things that explode. You build them, you were saying?"

"I build them great. Great, Fritz!"

"I thought so. What if I told you Kaiser Wilhelm needed you to build some things to blow up a building with a timed explosion?"

"I could do that, sure. I know that our Kaiser still lives but is far away. But how do I know you are not just trying to hurt me? You could go to the police, tell them things. I would be put back in that jail."

"No, Georg. I wouldn't let them hurt you, ever. What if I gave you five thousand Reichsmarks to do this and to keep it our secret? For the Kaiser and Germany."

"Five thousand?" Georg's eyes suddenly went wide. "How do I trust you?"

"Do you trust the Kaiser?"

"I do! I sure do."

"Since he sent me, you must trust me."

"Will this bomb kill police?"

"It certainly will, Georg. Many of them."

"Oh, that's want I want to do. Kill police. Kill Gestapos."

"It will kill many of them. I hate them as much as you do. What if it killed a lot of Nazis? Would you have a problem with that?"

"I hate Nazis and the SS too. They're worse than those Gestapos."

"The Kaiser hates Hitler and this bomb would kill Hitler. If he's dead, the Kaiser will come back from exile in Holland, be our leader again as he was in the Great War."

"*Ja!* I would love that, Fritz! But you would have to get me away before the bomb goes off."

"We will both get away. Count on me for that, Georg."

"When do I get the money?"

"I will give you half now, the other half after we finish our work. Do we have a deal?"

"I will help the Kaiser." Elser fiddled with the knobs of the car's radio and coaxed music from the speaker. "I like this car. When you pay me, I will buy one just like it."

Drake smiled but sensed that this liaison had so far been way too easy.

"That's very good, Georg. You just need to tell me what you need to do your work. I can get things for you."

"I have already got a perfect timer and detonator, just right for this. But no explosive, Fritz. Get me lots of explosives."

Drake glanced toward this human being who, perhaps as a child, had shown great promise to be a positive instrument to the world and was now somehow irreparably damaged. One could imagine the thousands of disappointments that had come to his parents. How many disrupted school classes, enraged teachers, crazy arguments, visits by officials ending in police custody, jail time, buckets of tears? Like children all across the world who experienced varying degrees of mental and emotional dysfunction, Georg never asked to have this kind of existence, nor did his parents anticipate that the joy of bringing life into the world would result in sorrow, regret, even moments of sheer terror. But so it was, someplace far beyond explanation by mortals.

Drake reached into his lapel pocket and pulled out a wad of bills. He eased up on the accelerator pedal a bit as he glanced at the speedometer. "That's 100 kilometers per hour, Georg. Just remember, I'm your friend. So, let's go on a while longer, then we will drive back to Berlin. This is the first half of your money right here. Take it—just a start. We'll meet again at 10 a.m. tomorrow in front of the candy store."

Many months earlier, as the last snows of 1939 had melted, Admiral Canaris had used up a big marker to get his hands on a quantity of an explosive known as donarit. It was powerful but soft like clay, moldable into any shape, detonated by a small electrical blasting cap. For that reason, donarit was used in mining operations. The Gestapo had rigidly clamped down on possession of all explosive materials before the Olympic Games of 1936. However, mining businesses were still able to get supplies of donarit and dynamite.

The owner of a mining concern in the Bavarian Alps had benefited from Canaris' help during the 1938 road-building efforts near Hitler's Eagle's Nest retreat close to the fairytale village of Berchtesgaden. The Nazi Party had planned to run a wide road straight from the village limits to Hitler's property line, the right-of-way slashing through the mine owner's property, wiping out his administration building. Nazi officials regularly and ruthlessly seized private property and paid owners minimal compensation.

Canaris had heard of the miner's problem through a mutual acquaintance and realized he could benefit from helping an enterprise engaged in tunneling in the immediate area of Hitler's abode. Canaris' representative had a meeting with the owner. Not long after, the Berchtesgaden District *Gauleiter*—regional Party leader—found it to be in his interest to modify the route, preserving the mining company's assets. In return, Canaris now had a friend positioned to conceal things in mines near Hitler's compound, items like trucks and soldiers. And one never knew, but perhaps someday a substantial quantity of blasting caps and donarit might be useful.

CHAPTER 19

QUESTIONS

"All things are ready if our mind be so."

William Shakespeare, *Henry V*

BAUER'S SÜSSIGKEITEN WAS A TRADITIONAL German confectionary
store, its display window filled with colorful, mouthwatering sugary
delicacies. Alex Drake supposed that such a presentation of extravagance
would only be possible if the owner were a National Socialist German
Workers' Party member. The building was only five meters wide, its
brick walls crowded on both sides by thick woods. Drake sat in the
idling Mercedes but knew he couldn't linger much longer without
risking some sort of official attention.

"*Ja*, Fritz!" came a shrill voice. Drake jumped as he came out of his
thoughts.

"Hello, Georg. Hop in. We'll go for another drive."

"Sure!" said Georg as he bounced into the car, humming some
unrecognizable tune. "Drive fast! Let's try for a hundred-twenty today!"

Relieved that Elser had shown up, Drake let out the clutch on the rented car and accelerated briskly away from the curb. His Black Orchestra colleagues shared his worries about Georg's trustworthiness, but there existed no alternative now. The choice was to wait and try the assassination some other way or go with this risky plan. Every day they delayed, Diebner got closer to the atomic bomb. More postponement was not an option.

"It's not here in the car, but I have it. Are you still good with our deal? You build and install a bomb, and I pay you the rest of the five thousand?"

Georg let out a bark of laughter. "I never change my mind, Fritz. Once I say something, it is for sure. Never say that I changed our agreement. *Never*, understand?"

Drake nodded as they passed into the Wannsee region. For the first time, he was aware of a threatening side to this man. The lake, rippling and blue, became visible at the edge of the road ahead. Neatly trimmed shrubs lined the water's edge.

"Where is this p-p-p-place where I am to put the bomb? And how much time do I have? And I'll need other parts besides the explosive. And what kind of explosive do you have?"

"Come on, Georg, one question at a time."

Drake used the stoplight to fire up a cigarette. Elser was excited to get to "play" with an explosive substance he wouldn't otherwise be able to get his hands on. He didn't seem as intent on getting the money as he was to show his unlikely genius, not to mention giving vent to a passion for causing explosions.

"Can you go to Munich for a few days, Georg? I'll take care of all your expenses and make sure you have a safe place to stay."

Georg's eyes narrowed in simplistic delight. "When, Fritz?"

"We only have a few days. I have the explosive with me today."

"What kind? I don't use nitroglycerine—it would explode and kill me. Dynamite is fine, though."

"It's donarit. I have it in the trunk of this car. You're familiar with it?"

"I know all about it—the best! It's almost all ammonium nitrate, but about 12 percent trinitrotoluene—that's TNT—mixed with just a little nitroglycerine. I'll control it with double ZZ-42 detonators. Those I have in my bedroom, under my chest of drawers. This is so great, Fritz, doing this for the Kaiser. I will build for him a perfect donarit bomb."

Drake was momentarily knocked back by the comprehensive knowledge expressed by this otherwise simple man. "Okay. And Georg, I will give you another three thousand at the end. A bonus for doing a good job. All right?"

"Yes—for the Kaiser!"

Drake took a last drag and stubbed the cigarette out in the ashtray.

"And if you lie to me, Fritz, I will use your donarit to blow you to hell."

CHAPTER 20

DECEPTION

"General Arnold is gone to the enemy."

George Washington, 1780

DRAKE LOOKED AROUND THE CELLAR of the Speier warehouse. Grim faces revealed a collective awareness of their impending doom balanced by a resolute determination to prevent Hitler from seizing the atomic bomb.

"Go ahead." Beck looked toward Drake. "Tell us exactly where the Munich operation stands."

Drake cleared his throat and leaned over the table. "Canaris' man, Georg Elser, is almost done with the bomb device. He and I get on the train in the morning. We will plant the bomb in the celebration hall beginning tomorrow night. We're moving forward at full speed."

The Reverend Born raised a hand. "If you're caught, Elser will spill his guts. Kill him as soon as he has done his duty."

"He's right, Drake," Beck declared. "He dies the moment the bomb

132

detonates. There will be mass chaos—put a knife across his throat and throw him in with the other corpses."

"I'll dispose of him one way or another," Drake replied.

Sondra touched his leg under the oilcloth table covering. He knew what that meant. She didn't want him going there but also knew his determined mindset.

"So," said Beck, "things are about to get very interesting. We will be working here on preparations, waiting for your telephone call to verify that the explosion has occurred. When we have heard your confirmation, the rest of the plan will instantly push into action, including Halder's and Würter's military insurrection. Goerdeler, give us details of the *coup d'état* that rolls into action as soon as we blast Hitler to atoms."

"*Der Mann mit drei Geheimnissen.* That's who I am, Heinrich. The man with three secrets. I once had only two, but now there's a third, something very critical and imminent. It could turn this nation and the whole world upside-down." Light from the table lamp fell across the speaker's face, highlighting the scars on his upper cheek. "The first secret, which you've known of for some time, is my observation of Ludwig Beck's activities."

Heinrich Himmler, Supreme Leader of the German SS, blinked his eyes in rapid-fire progression. "Then get on with it. Talk."

"Yes, well, before I remind you of the other preexisting secret, I will tell you that this new one comes with a rather steep price. Do you still want to hear it?"

"It'd better be *damned* important."

"You just might agree that it is. Beck is planning to kill the *Führer*—tomorrow night! A bomb will be planted in the Bürgerbräukeller, set to detonate at 9:15, right in the middle of Hitler's big speech."

Himmler's head jerked back. "*What?* Why didn't you make this known to me before now?" The words shot from his tiny mouth topped by a little Hitler-style mustache.

"You should be thankful to me that I found this out, and I'm telling you of it now." Klaus Würter thought of how he'd trained himself to keep his face austere and emotionless when telling lies such as this one. He sat erect, hands clasped in his lap. Only in the past hours had he convinced himself that he'd benefit the most by taking this colossal step to crush the Bürgerbräukeller plan. As he watched the SS leader's face, he thought of another time not long ago when he'd sat in Himmler's Berlin SS office. He'd told him that General Beck's lifetime friend, Holger Speier, financially supported Beck's anti-Hitler organization. That conversation had signed the old man's death warrant and made his exquisite wife accessible.

Himmler seemed to have regained his composure. He steepled his fingers as he swung around to gaze through his window, down to the people and traffic on Munich's Marienplatz. "This pig Beck. He's more dangerous than I thought. I should have him picked up and shot. But his popularity with the Army remains a problem. If I arrest him, I risk substantial dissension. There could be a revolt—Beck has a fair number of loyalists still in power across all the services. So far, the *Führer* has not given me orders to eliminate him."

"Heinrich, you need to use this thing smartly. Make it known to the public that Beck is planning an assassination attempt."

The SS boss walked to his desk, sat down, and began fiddling with a chromed letter opener, passing it slowly, almost sensuously, across the palm of his left hand.

"Ridiculous. Our *Führer* will never permit the people of Germany to think there is any dissent even remotely associated with the military. I oversee every aspect of Hitler's security. How could anyone, especially a cunning individual like Beck, think they could get close enough to him to try something like this?" The Nazi leader's fingers played at the edge of his mustache. He swung back to Würter.

"Heinrich, you're a smart man. Use your brain on this. If you can't risk blaming Beck and his clique, accuse the English. Find a British patsy and set him up. Build animosity against this enemy. The German people will revile such a heinous act and strengthen the hand of this government."

"I'll decide that. Tell me exactly how, where, and when this is supposed to happen!"

"Ah, yes, which brings me to my third secret because you won't learn the full content of the second one unless you give me what I want."

"You want me to have my people extract your 'secret' from you?"

"Now you're the one being ridiculous. Think about the bloody massacre of 1934, *the night of the long knives*—Hitler's murder of Röhm, your rival, the leader of the now-extinct SA. Branded a sex degenerate, he wound up with a lead-bullet headache. Very terminal. That could be you unless you give me the reward that I should already have received from you for not spilling my knowledge to the *Führer* of your very perverse activities. Kill me if you'd like, Heinrich, but remember, there is somebody who has the photographs and the wire recordings of your nights with the little girls. That person has instructions to go directly to Martin Bormann, your most stubborn opponent, if he doesn't hear from me every twenty-four hours. Bormann would so love to have this gift from me, permitting him to plunge a knife into your—"

"Stop!" Himmler whipped his glasses off, his beady eyes cold, flinty. "You're every bit as incriminated in those affairs as I am. We both belonged to that same interest group."

"The word is *pedophile*, Heinrich. Little girls? Some photos show you with girls no more than ten—quite sharp photos, actually. I wonder why you allowed yourself to be photographed and recorded in acts so depraved? Oh, I know," he said, sarcasm dripping from his words. "So, you could relive those activities as you pleasure yourself in your special viewing room."

"You had your nights with them, too, you bastard!"

"Irrelevant. Hitler cares nothing about me, doesn't even know me. *You*, on the other hand—the obvious pinnacle of pure Aryan strength and virtue—with ten-year-old girls? On the recordings, your impassioned blabbering about their beautiful little bodies?"

Himmler's face took on a pinched expression—perplexed, worried. Then his demeanor quickly swung to fiery rage. His fist slammed down on the desk.

"You goddamned pig! Blackmailing me!"

"Calm down. Look at this as an opportunity to wrap this into a personal triumph. You can become a big hero in Hitler's eyes by representing yourself as having found and stopped this assassination attempt. You should be incredibly happy that I came by today."

"Tell me everything!"

"Not so fast. I'll continue to keep my secrets very private and only tell you more about the assassination plot on one solemn condition: You swear to make me your second-in-command. Nothing less. You've done it before—taken men from the Wehrmacht and placed them in high SS positions. Hitler gives you free rein."

"Second-in-command?" Himmler chuckled almost inaudibly. "You've never learned how to bargain, have you? Rest assured that your life will be far better for you in every way if we halt this action. If we cannot stop it, that will be a different story. You'll be held responsible—completely—for it. I will interrogate you in a few minutes, and you will give me every little detail of this criminality. Wait outside."

General Klaus Würter stood and walked toward the door. "Second-in-command, Heinrich. Don't trifle with me. Show me the order for my promotion, signed by you, and only then I'll tell you everything."

"Right, Klaus. Second-in-command it is, then." Himmler hid his face, which crinkled in total contempt for this man and his absurd demand. "The papers will be drawn up."

"You're out of your mind, you fool! Who in hell is lying to you with this trash?"

Adolf Hitler sat in a velvet-covered wingback chair in his quarters at the Party's Munich headquarters called the Brown House. Waking the *Führer* before nine in the morning was strictly forbidden, so Himmler had waited to announce the news until Hitler had started his usual morning meal of sweet pastries and hot milk. The dictator's drawn face showed that he had not slept well again. Since the September third declaration of war, Hitler's nerves had been in an exaggerated state of agitation.

"Leader, you're well aware that I've deposited a spy deep inside one of the anti-Nazi subversive groups in Berlin. He came to me late yesterday with this information. I got all of it out of him, I believe it's valid, and we need to take steps."

"What criminals are behind this?"

"It's Beck's group, and my efforts to monitor them have paid off, sir. You've decided not to apprehend him because of the implications we are well aware of, but this could prove to be an excellent opportunity to secure this nation's unbending loyalty to our plans."

The Nazi leader turned to look directly at Himmler. "War terrifies even the strongest German—death, bombs, economic disruption. Our people need to be absolutely unified behind us as this struggle unfolds. An assassination attempt on me as Supreme Leader of this nation! That could hold for us even more political power than our 1933 parliament building fire—a way to shock the German people into total fusion behind us in the circumstances of this new war." His left hand was shaking as it held a piece of sugared cherry strudel. "The Reichstag fire we sparked worked back then. Who knows what might have happened to our fledgling government had we not decided to burn down the legislative building and blame it on the communists? However, this move is spectacularly dangerous. Me, you, we could all be annihilated."

Himmler nodded. "But if we accuse anti-government conspirators inside Germany with an attempt to kill you, we can—"

"No! I never want the German people to think that any conspiracy exists that could threaten to unseat National Socialism. There will be no mention whatsoever of any 'anti-Nazi Underground' in our midst. Just a few Jews and communists backed by the British." Hitler rose and paced back and forth several times before speaking again.

"I need another Reichstag fire. This thing might be worth the risk, which you must reduce to zero. You said you had an expert to inspect this bomb's apparatus to make sure it is reliable and won't go off early."

"Correct, *Mein Führer.*"

"Then fly him here this minute. Get the airplane motors running!"

"I've correctly anticipated your order, sir," he lied. "He's already in the air."

"Have him go through the device thoroughly, then dispose of him. This action is so critical to our future that the life of one ordinance expert has no significance. Others might learn that we were alerted to this bomb's presence in advance of the explosion. That would become an unmitigated disaster!"

"I will make it my solemn duty to see that nobody remains who can divulge this information. As always, *Führer*, I will make sure things are taken care of."

Hitler dropped into his chair again, pressing down the lapels of his gray field uniform. "Yes. The reward outweighs the risk. And your sole responsibility is to *guarantee* that this thing doesn't blow me to pieces. Be sure this is known as a British-sponsored assassination attempt, no matter what in hell it is. Take special care of the seating arrangements. Put people near the podium whom we would not mind meeting an early demise. And get me out of there soon enough that I don't join them, but close enough to the minute of the explosion that it will be regarded as a very near miss, ordained by providence."

Himmler suppressed a nervous smile and folded his hands behind his back to conceal his shaking arms. "It will be done," he said, but he knew that the perpetrator was a complete unknown, the SS explosives expert might not be found in time to get here in six hours, and a botched outcome could mean both his and Hitler's deaths.

Drake and Elser slept at two separate Munich *Pensions*—boarding houses—on the city's south side. Drake stayed in a large house named *Pension Eidelweiss*. A few minutes before eight in the evening, they strolled individually through the crowded beer hall of the Bürgerbräukeller, a gray cardboard press pass pinned to Drake's lapel, his accomplice dressed in blue workman's garb and carrying a canvas haversack. They drew no attention whatsoever from the hundreds of rowdy patrons and dozens of uniformed Nazis sitting at tables or crowded around the two long bars.

Drake walked ahead. Elser took a quick step and put his hand on Drake's shoulder, twisting him partway around.

"These are all Nazi rats, Fritz."

"They are, but keep quiet and stay back from me. We don't talk until we get through the doors." Drake knew there was a fatal problem if someone had locked the meeting hall. During his reconnaissance trips, the entrance was always left open. They made their way through the anteroom. Drake grabbed the brass door handles—again, the hall was unlocked.

"Let's get to work, Georg," Drake said, pulling the doors closed. In the room illuminated only by his Crone Fisheye flashlight, Drake led the way to a ceiling support post to the left and behind the stage. The column was constructed of four vertical pieces of decorative white-painted wood. Elser held the light as Drake wedged his small saw into a gap high on one of the sections of a post near the stage, then began to work it back and forth. The work was slow and tedious, produced noise, and the specter of a watchman coming upon them was Drake's constant dread.

They worked slowly to minimize sounds—the sawing took forty-five minutes, maybe more. Although he'd made measurements during his scouting trip, Drake remeasured the opening to ensure there was enough space for Elser's mechanism. It would be a close thing, but the hole's dimensions were consistent with the bomb's outlines. The painted wood pillar cover piece was shoved back in place and secured with four small nails. They quietly packed up and separately slipped out onto Rosenheimerstrasse in front of the Bürgerbräukeller. The final step tomorrow night: push the bomb into place and set the timer.

The next day dragged along as if it would never end. Each minute seemed like an hour. He went out of the *Pension* twice to eat, although he hadn't much hunger beyond a fierce desire to kill Adolf Hitler. Then came the hour for the last foray into the meeting hall for final preparations. Making his way along the Munich streets, Drake wondered aloud if Elser would show up for the last step. So far, he'd done everything asked of him and materialized each time. And behold! There he was, standing on the northwest corner of the block, across from the Bürgerbräukeller, just as agreed. They entered the main floor tavern, which was dimly lit and jammed with Nazi Party members and their loud sounds of singing and talking. The meeting hall doors were again unlocked. First Drake, then Elser entered the dark assembly room.

Two SS motorcars pulled away from the Munich SS Headquarters and headed east on the Adolf Hitler-Strasse in the blackness. Inside each car were three SS officers; their destination was the Bürgerbräukeller. The night's orders came from the head of the SS, Heinrich Himmler. The highest-ranking officer of these six had, hours earlier, spoken with Himmler himself to ensure directions were followed precisely and with absolute secrecy. The task was quite out of the ordinary, but their training guaranteed that no one would ask questions. Two of the uniformed men were unusually burly and had different orders from those of the others. Their job was to closely monitor words and actions and eradicate fellow officers who knew about the purpose of their visit to the meeting hall. They were to arrive at the target by 8:45 p.m.

Elser turned off his flashlight, leaving the hall illuminated only by the tiny strands of light sneaking through the gaps at the four entrance doors.

Drake pushed up his sleeve, revealing the greenish-glowing numerals on his radium dial watch. "I'll keep track of the time, Georg. Now we wait thirty minutes. That will bring us past the twenty-four-hour mark before the moment of tomorrow's explosion, and you can start the clock. Then, connect the detonator battery and close up the hole."

Drake wasn't looking in the direction of the doors, but his eyes caught something which drove a sudden flash of new fear through him. The thin shaft of light coming from the center gap in one of the doors had been obstructed by something.

"Someone's at the door," Drake whispered.

Then as quickly as it had vanished, the ray of light returned, accompanied by the sound of shuffling boots beyond the door.

"Gone," Drake said, almost inaudibly. "I'm going out there to cut off anyone who might disturb your final work. Make everything perfect, Georg. If something unexpected happens, go back to your room. Put this rail ticket in your pocket."

"You're leaving me, Fritz?"

"I'll just be outside. I'll come in when we get past nine-fifteen and you've set the timer."

"I don't feel good about you leaving me alone."

"We can't afford another visitor. As soon as you're done, come outside and go across the street from where we came in. I'll meet you there if I don't make it back down here before you leave." Drake turned and walked toward the door, adjusting his press pass.

Outside the meeting room, the noises were of the dining room festivities, the sounds of a band playing. Fingers tingling once more, he eyed the exits. The floor was concrete, illuminated by the yellowish light of the unfrosted ceiling bulbs. Then a firm voice from behind.

"Hey! You're standing around here—why?"

Drake turned quickly. There had been no sound of footsteps.

"No problem, *Mein Herr, Danke schön*. Getting away from all the music and smoke for a few minutes."

"Well, you'd better get outta here. I'm the assistant manager. Nobody's supposed to be near this hall before the big Party meeting tomorrow night. Who are you?"

Drake shifted his weight from one leg to the other and stood straight. "I'm a reporter for a major international news agency—just looking around at all the fine preparations for your leader's address tomorrow night. Would you consent to give me a few words? I surely won't quote you unless you want me to."

"Maybe, but no quotes. Which 'big news agency'? What's your badge there say?"

"Why, *Time* magazine in America. Jim Bryce is my name. Glad to meet you." The press pass was working, the Abwehr's skills once again delivering results. "Let's go have a beer while I ask you a few questions, let my readers know what a superb job you're doing here."

They turned away from the door as the manager began describing the story of the Nazi leaders' big annual get-together. *Elser*, Drake thought. *Is he okay in the hall? Gotta keep this real short.*

Elser's nerves were in tatters, his fright level increasing with each second. It was almost time to set the device, and he needed Fritz to be there with him. Maybe he'd stopped somebody and was taking care of that. Regardless, he wanted to get out of this place. Finally, after what seemed to be an eternity, his wristwatch, illuminated by a flick of the flashlight, told him the moment had come. He dialed the timer's hands to 21:15—carefully and with slow precision. He then closed the timer's glass face and put the butt end of the flashlight into his mouth. Canting his head to shine the light toward the top of the pillar, he stretched himself as high as possible and pushed the box into the opening. Then the wood cover went on, and the nails were tapped into place. His hands were shaking, but he'd done his job for his beloved Kaiser Wilhelm.

Georg switched off the flashlight and sat down in the dark as he listened to the band music coming through the cracks in the doors. The Kaiser was going to be very happy, but where was Fritz? The final assembly of the mechanism had gone together just right. Its heart was a Braun industrial clock timer with twin output contacts, noiseless by design, no ticking to alert anyone.

Voices! Then sounds of footsteps in the hallway. Georg stood up and held his breath, unable to move. The door latch rattled, then another metallic sound. He squeezed the handle of his tool case tightly. The door swung open, and chandeliers blazed into glaring life.

"Drop that case!" shouted one of the men who stood in the doorway. Dressed in SS uniforms, they aimed their guns squarely at Georg. "Put your hands above your head and walk over here."

Elser followed the order. A Luger was pointed against the side of his head. "I had work to do," he said.

"Work?"

"Something for the Kaiser. Something he wanted me to do to help Germany!"

"Kaiser, eh?" The SS officer laughed and glanced toward his companion. "Show us, you jackass."

"My clock. Put it in the post, just as *Herr Fritz* said the Kaiser wanted it done."

The taller SS officer looked around the room. He grabbed the tool case off the floor and dropped it on a chair, then placed his gun down and rummaged through the valise while the other man kept his weapon pressed against Elser's back.

"Right now! Show me where you put your mechanism!" declared the shorter SS man.

Georg remained silent. They had taken his light from his hand and beamed it along the columns. He walked to the post where he'd stood a minute earlier and pulled the loosely affixed cover away. The dial of the timer and the red wires were obvious.

"You've been busy, haven't you? Walk ahead of me," said the SS officer.

As they approached the doorway, a figure loomed ahead of them. This man, also dressed in black uniform, shot out his right arm in salute. *"Heil Hitler!"* he declared.

"Heil Hitler! He was installing a bomb, sir."

The third man grabbed Georg's neck and squeezed until his eyeballs felt like they were going to pop. He heard guttural sounds coming out of his own throat.

"Scheiße! You've pissed your stinking pants." He glanced at the other officers as he shouted, "Wait here with him while I call the *Reichsführer.*"

Ten minutes later, a thin man strode into the Bürgerbräukeller's grand hall. He pushed his *pince-nez* spectacles higher up his nose. Two SS men stood near one of the white columns with a square opening near its top.

"Where is this bomb? Is it in place?"

"My leader, we have not touched it. This man says his name is Georg Elser. He has confessed to everything, of course."

"For whom is he working? The British?"

"I do not know, sir. I'm not sure he even understands. He has an accomplice whom we have not found—yet. Elser says the contact's name is Fritz, but that's all he seems to know. He will give up all his secrets very soon."

"The orders to build the bomb came from our Kaiser Wilhelm," Elser cried.

"Georg, my name is Heinrich Himmler. I am head of the SS." Tapping his index finger against his lower lip, Himmler scanned the man's wild eyes, tiny mouth, and unkempt hair. "Would you like to leave Germany? Take things easy? I will help you."

"Yes!"

"What time is your device set to go off?"

"I s-s-said before. Fifteen minutes past nine tomorrow night."

Himmler rested his finger alongside his nose, his other arm folded across his chest. "Georg, I want you to recheck your bomb carefully. Be *absolutely certain* it will go off at exactly fifteen minutes past nine."

Elser nodded vigorously, his eyes wide. "Yes, sir! Everything is enamel-coated and double-wired. It will work perfectly! *Perfectly!*"

The SS leader wiped his nose with a satin handkerchief and carefully refolded it before stuffing it back into his lapel pocket. "You will be sitting with my associates in this building." He raised his head to emphasize his words. "If the bomb goes off earlier than fifteen minutes past nine, a bullet will rip through the top of your head at the moment of the explosion. However, if it goes off on time, you will have a nice long life ahead of you, and you will be amply rewarded for your work. I told you to look at it again."

"Well, yes, sir!"

Himmler continued studying the face of the strange man. He regarded himself as an excellent judge of character, and while Elser was unusual, he seemed genuinely confident in knowing his craft.

"Do it now. Officers, not a word to anyone about what we've seen and discussed here. When he's done, you men will hold him in a place where no one will see him." Himmler pivoted on one foot and started for the exit, followed by his driver and two bodyguards.

Drake closed his notebook and pushed the pencil onto the top of his ear. "It was good talking with you. Your event with the *Führer* tomorrow will be historically important. Congratulations in advance." His watch read 9:40. He'd taken far too long.

"As I said, don't mention my name. I'll look forward to seeing your story in the German edition of *Time* if I can find one."

The manager was still watching him, smiling and nodding his head. Drake walked quickly across the dining room and into the hallway outside the assembly gallery. *Guards!* In front of each door, there stood a uniformed man with a sidearm. There was no way to check on Elser, no choice but to go through the doorway, onto the front street, and see if he could somehow find his man. Elser had to be done by now, out of the building and waiting for him across the street, or he'd been captured, and their mission was dead.

The crowd on the street was growing, but no sign of Elser! Dozens of revelers were trying to get taxi rides; some were flagging the cabs before he could get close. Elser's boarding house was at least two kilometers away. Drake started walking. The streets were bustling with pre-celebration revelers, but their drunken enthusiasm didn't warm the cold wind blowing on his face.

Elser's rooming house was entirely dark. There was no way to contact him if he were inside. He couldn't try sneaking in because he didn't know which room his man had chosen. He couldn't just go in the front door and awaken the landlord. That would lead to many questions. Drake walked around the nearby streets and waited in front of the *Pension* until 1:30 a.m. Finally, he gave up and set off for his own rented room, went up the stairs, switched on the pink-shaded lamp beside the small bed, and laid down. He thought about the things that were supposed to happen later this day. Drake shut off the light and tried to push the visions out of his mind of his father's murder which took place only four blocks from where he lay. He got maybe a half-hour of actual sleep, the remaining time spent staring at the ceiling. The Day of Death had arrived again—what terror might it bring this time?

In the diffuse light of early morning, Drake packed his briefcase and left the rooming house. The streets were still deserted, and the air temperature was cold enough to slice quickly through his overcoat. A beer truck lumbered past him, then a police car. The rail station was empty except for a few railway workers tending to their chores. He took a seat in the corner furthest from the ticket counters but with a good view of the train platforms. High above the benches, the hands of the station clock showed 7:35. Elser's ticket was valid for the 8:05 train to Berlin. A railway agent came to unlock and open the gate to the train bound for Berlin. Passengers began to enter the railcars. It was getting late. Drake tapped his fingers on the wooden armrest until his nails began to ache.

"Alle an Bord!" shouted a conductor standing on the steps of the first coach.

In minutes, the train began pulling out of the station, generating vast amounts of steam and sound, but no sign of Elser. *Jump out from behind the clouds of steam, Georg!* But no. The fool had missed his train.

If he were already apprehended, the authorities would be looking for an accomplice—if they'd found Elser's ticket, they might be watching the train to see if anyone was waiting for a comrade. Drake stood and made a helpless gesture. He realized there was no choice except to believe that Elser had installed the bomb and had gotten lost or captured. It was time to get out of the station and eat something, although his stomach wasn't demanding food. He had to waste the hours of daylight, and he needed to keep his mind and body alert and hardened against anxiety, flashbacks, and strength-wasting ruminations.

CHAPTER 21

FURY

"The best-laid plans o' mice and men oft go astray."

Robert Burns, 1790

THE AIR INSIDE THE BÜRGERBRÄUKELLER was a blanket of cigarette and cigar smoke. The walls echoed the clamor of voices from middle-aged Nazi Party members, most of them outfitted in military uniforms. Drake stood behind the last row of chairs, peering intently at the stage in front of the assembly of Nazis and selected outsiders. All the lights were dimmed except for the single brilliant spotlight on the figure standing alone on the platform. His giant shadow played against the deep red curtains and white wooden posts near him. Goebbels, Himmler, Göring, and Hess were all absent from the front row! *Where the hell are they?* Drake asked himself.

Hitler bowed the tiniest bit as he took a breath, wiped his mouth with the back of his hand, then continued his speech. "And so, England, the nation of shopkeepers, has declared war on Germany again." His gravelly voice strained as it rose in anger.

Drake checked his watch—9:01. Fourteen minutes until the detonation. He looked again at the door behind him, flanked by two SS guards, automatic rifles strapped to their shoulders. It was time to move through the portal and wait for the blast.

"This fool Chamberlain," the dictator continued, "says Britain fights for civilization. Let me ask you something, my brave comrades." Hitler looked around the room as the mass of men again sat down. "Do they fight for the civilization consisting of the misery in the mining district of Newcastle? Or the decay of central London where the children lay dying, choking on the filthy air? That is *civilization* as defined by Chamberlain and his running dogs! Germany shall bring civilization to the world, and they shall regret their arrogance!"

The audience of yes-men who rose and shouted approval almost every time Hitler paused for breath jumped up again as their idol glanced again at his watch.

"Victory! Great strength as in 1923, and victory now! Good night, my Old Fighters!" He dashed from the podium to the side door twenty steps to his right.

Drake's back stiffened. *Hundreds were about to die for nothing!* All he could do now was hope Elser *hadn't* succeeded in planting his bomb. He turned and looked around. *"Jeder hören!"* Drake roared. "Listen, everyone!" An SS guard shoved him and said, "Shut up, *Arschloch!*" A wooden baton caught him on the side of the head and sent him spinning onto the concrete floor as he lost consciousness.

The caravan of four Mercedes limousines with long, curved fenders, each flying Nazi flags from their front fender tips, passed through the intersection with only the slightest slowdown to detect cross-traffic, then made a sharp right turn. As Hitler's car passed the fence bounding the rail station, the concussion hit them, a hollow, echoing sound like a giant firecracker exploding inside a tin garbage can someplace in the distance.

"It was big . . . a big bomb. Right on time," said *der Führer.*

"Yes, Leader. A complete, unqualified success. My explosives technician from Berlin said it would be so after he checked the bomb setup this morning." His face rose from looking at his watch. "Thirteen minutes after you stepped off that stage."

Hitler let his head fall back against the velvet-covered headrest, his face reflecting a smug satisfaction in what had just taken place. Yet, he knew that many of his Nazi compatriots had just been sacrificed in a scheme to exalt himself as a godlike near-martyr in the wake of starting a new European war. But his best and most reliable associates were nowhere near the building.

"This will deliver a huge return for us, Heinrich—I call you *the faithful Heinrich* as you have been dependable for many years. But if you fail at concealing this action, you will have a different name: *the dead Heinrich*."

The blast had brought Drake out of his stupor, and he sat up, dazed, momentarily confused. An enormous circular chandelier lay next to him, having missed him by barely a meter but crushing two men whose blood gathered in a black puddle. Getting to his feet, he turned and stumbled toward the front entrance. He could barely focus his eyes. Smoke, flames, and screams churned through the fallen roof beams, and crazed people smashed into him. The sound of the explosion reverberated inside his skull, an eardrum-breaking roar that would not subside.

Drake's hand wiped across his nose. Blood gushed in a hot stream down his face and onto his shirt. He reached to the wall to steady himself. Gore-drenched men shoved past him, driving him back with stiff arms and swinging fists, their wails only now penetrating his deafness left by the explosion. A shoulder hit him squarely in the back, smashing his head against the plaster wall. He fell again—hard. A stampede of wounded and frantic Nazis running for their lives trampled over him. For a second time in seconds, he confronted the prospect of death.

Then, a momentary pause in the surge of fleeing humanity. Drake got to his feet and lurched out onto the street. Turning back, he saw smoke billowing from the structure, dazed people struggling through the doorways, and heard sirens from approaching police and ambulances.

His emotions swirled with disappointment and blind anger. Who had betrayed them? Hitler *knew* about that bomb and let it blow up anyway, timed it perfectly! And if the Gestapo had grabbed Elser and linked the attempted assassination to Black Orchestra, they'd soon be as dead as the Nazis lying in the demolished meeting hall. Drake realized that he needed to get to a telephone and call Beck to announce this failure. He made his way to the small tavern scouted out yesterday for this purpose. Entering, he saw that one phone booth was unoccupied, went inside and dropped a coin in the slot, then dialed the operator. After a long delay, a female voice.

"*Anweisungen, bitte?*"

"Call to Berlin exchange, Crest 85822." More delay, then a buzz in the earpiece.

"*Hallo.*" Beck's voice.

"Vulture. Red, do nothing." Four terrible words. Drake hung up and went back onto the street. Was the anti-Hitler Wehrmacht contingent already on the move, falling into a deadly trap due to Hitler's escape?

He hobbled six blocks to the train station through dozens of quickly accumulating emergency vehicles and screaming, shouting, panic-stricken people. How would he explain this horrendous, abysmal failure to Beck and the others? He got to his train and found a seat inside the coach. Drake sliced his fingers through his hair, keeping his eyes downcast and furtively wiping blood from his forehead onto a handkerchief. Their best chance to safeguard the world from Hitler's atom bomb had just blown up in his face.

"Alex—you're hurt. And Hitler is as healthy as ever. So why does this happen?" Sondra stood next to the bed in Drake's apartment, where the reporter sat sipping tea, a three-day growth of beard framing his features. She lowered herself onto the quilted bedcover lit by a stream of sunshine through the single window in the place. "The good never seem to win."

Drake shoved the empty cup onto a shelf of his well-stocked bookcase next to the bed. "That question is way beyond my capabilities as a would-be philosopher. But at least I'm still alive. Can't say that for a hundred who were in that meeting hall."

"It's not possible to kill him. He's Satan incarnate. The forces of evil protect him, whatever happens. Many say it's true."

Drake leaned back against the wall, turning his face toward her, anger showing in his eyes. "I'm sure he was tipped off by some son-of-a-bitch—English term for a *Schurke*. Your suspicions of Würter—do you think he could go so low as to reveal this to the SS?"

"Yes, I've thought about that, but again we have no information."

"Yeah, I don't know what he would have to gain. It could be."

"Or some kind of supernatural intervention. But what kind of god would permit him to escape, to destroy the world and all its creations? *What kind of god, Alex?*" She heard her own voice rising.

"Quiet, these walls are thin. No benevolent deity would keep him alive. Instead, he lives thanks to some power that craves the tragedies he will bring. Evil personified."

"I'm thankful that you made it back—you could easily have died in the explosion or been arrested and shot."

"Which could still happen."

"This whole thing is hopeless!"

"You know the stakes. Is there any alternative to fighting on to put a halt to this wonder-bomb?"

She placed her arm around his shoulders as he turned his face away. She knew the answer.

CHAPTER 22

STRENGTH

"If by herself she will not love,
Nothing can make her.
The devil take her!"

Sir John Suckling, *Aglaura*, 1638, *Song*, st. 3

DECEMBER 15, 1939

THE RESIDENTS OF BERLIN LACKED the spirit of Christmas in this milieu of war. Sondra Speier ordinarily made the holidays a big celebration within her small circle—decorations, gifts, food, and cards, but not this year for many reasons. She was not outwardly religious but believed in God and life after death. Some individuals who think this way call themselves spiritual; she seldom thought about the supernatural, but perhaps in time, or maybe with a child, it might be different.

In these last days of 1939, large numbers of Germans were reconnecting with their beliefs, praying for protection from a rain of bombs falling on their houses, begging the Almighty for the safety of their children marching off to battlefronts. Politicians preferred to employ euphemisms such as "noble sacrifice" when forced to mention the war's human cost, but the reality was that bullets and the blasts of artillery shells meant blind men, legless men, and coffins. These images did not mesh well with lighthearted exchanges of presents and the baking of sugar pies.

Sondra heard the doorbell ring on a cold and gray afternoon and watched her butler cross the room to answer it. She listened to the sounds of a brief, inaudible conversation. The door closed, and the servant walked into the library where she sat.

"*Frau*, a parcel has arrived for you. Shall I leave it with you now, or would you want it later?"

She placed the newspaper on a side table and looked up.

"Who sent it?"

"I'm afraid there is no card with it, just a simple tag with your name."

"Leave it, then. *Danke.*"

The package was small, carefully wrapped in dark purple paper with a pink ribbon. She waited until the servant had left, then slid the bow off and pulled the paper apart. The glue holding the wrapping gave way easily, and she looked at a wooden box with a gold clasp and hinge. Swinging the lid open, she saw the diamond-encrusted brooch with a yellow gold mounting—unmistakably expensive. She fingered the sparkling piece of jewelry and thought who the sender might be.

"No note or inscription," she said to herself. She stared at the diamonds for many minutes. The chime of the old clock in the foyer softly rang as if it were as distant as her thoughts. Then another sound.

The butler reentered the library. "Pardon my interruption, *Madame*. You have a call on the telephone."

She placed the package under the fringe of the divan as the handset was brought to her. The young female servant maneuvered the long cord as Sondra picked the handset off the cradle.

"Yes?"

"Hello, Sondra." The voice was firm, deep, and familiar. "I hope you enjoy your Christmas celebration and your gifts—especially mine if you have it yet."

"It arrived. I was about to find a way to return it."

"Return it? But it will look beautiful on you. You must keep it. You have a friend who cares about you and has given you a token of his admiration. It is time you accept me. We need to talk. Meet me."

Sondra paused before answering. "Only for a short time. My driver will take me to the Hungarian restaurant next to the Gloria Palast. One half-hour." She hung up without saying another word. Then, putting her fingers around the brooch, she took it from the case and held it up. Sondra had a feeling more potent than ever that Würter was a traitor. It was her mission to find proof. Maybe this gift would help her get it.

Two men stood on the sidewalk in front of the Tapioca Café on the Budepesterstrasse, one of them holding the shaft of an umbrella in his left hand and the end of a dog's leash in the other. The canine was a large grey poodle, shorn in the classic style to emphasize its long ears and large, round head. The other man talked excitedly, his leather overcoat pushed back by his arm buried in his pants pocket. The restaurant sold good food and religious articles.

Sondra walked around them and entered the restaurant to the sounds of jingling bells nailed to the top of the door. The air smelled of spicy tomato sauce, and shelves displayed things that the Nazis usually would not tolerate, including crucifixes and Bibles. Yet, a slight amount of religious freedom was still seen as necessary to appease the faithful. The proprietor, a woman in her sixties, came out from the kitchen. The years had bent her and made her hair very white, but her face was still beautiful, with startling bright blue eyes and clear skin. "You must be the officer's guest that he is expecting. He is right over there. Can I bring tea?" she asked, taking Sondra's coat away. "And I have good wine."

"A moment, please."

Sondra nodded as General Würter jumped up to pull her chair back from the table. "You look lovely as always. Please, be seated."

Having disposed of the coat, the owner returned with a small notepad and pencil in hand. "Something for you?"

"Yes. The tea would be fine. With cream."

"And sir, anything else beyond your pilsner there?"

"Nothing except some quiet time."

"Of course." And she was gone.

Sondra took her thin leather gloves off carefully and placed them next to her knife before speaking.

"We could have met at my place."

She smiled and shrugged. "But here we are. Take your gift." She slid it across the table and flipped her dark hair off her face as she looked beyond him.

Klaus Würter tilted his head and said, "You will love me eventually. Much sooner than you think."

"You believe that?"

He laughed. "I am a powerful man, much more so than you realize. The authority and wealth that I shall soon have will amaze you."

Sondra checked her watch and crossed her arms as the teapot, a cup and saucer, and a pitcher of water were placed on the table. A little flowered vessel of cream arrived seconds later.

"Power and wealth don't impress me."

"Then why are you here? You have not been altogether dismissive of my attentions."

"You are part of Black Orchestra. You are my colleague. We trust each other, or we will surely fail."

Würter settled back in his chair and reached into his uniform jacket, removing a long cigar.

"Do you mind?"

"Suit yourself."

He lit the tobacco and exhaled smoke away from the table.

"Exactly what are you, Klaus? Are you part of Black Orchestra, or are you something else? I can't tell whose side you're on."

"What a thing to say, my dear Sondra. I believe I am the most ardent anti-Nazi in the group. But, of course, above all things, I do whatever benefits me."

She looked across at him.

"Meaning tomorrow you could become pro-Nazi, Klaus? Destroy us all at any moment?"

"Nonsense. It reduces to simply this: I am a soldier, loyal to my leaders. And General Halder and General Beck are perfectly aligned, so I have no choices to make."

She studied his eyes; they blinked several times in rapid succession, and the message they conveyed did not match the weak smile that had formed across his face.

"And you will be right there with me—you will be at my side when Halder, Beck, and I replace Hitler. *Der Führer* will come to an inglorious end very soon, either because of us or in some other way. If it's us, we destroy all Nazi leaders, our man Goerdeler takes power, and Germany becomes a democratic, modern nation among nations."

She leaned back and crossed her arms. "And in the end, Klaus Würter is at the top, regardless of whether Nazism or Black Orchestra is victorious."

"It all comes out the same, my dear. The only difference is this atomic bomb, which I don't believe amounts to anything—it's a lot of pseudo-scientific blather. It might come to reality in ten years, but probably never. So let others worry about that fantasy while I get rid of Hitler."

The restaurant owner reappeared through the kitchen door, wiping her hands on her apron, looking around the room, which was empty save for her two guests.

"Klaus, every person in Black Orchestra is there because of different individual motivations, but we unite to stop Nazism. I don't care for your ambivalence regarding who survives. Hitler and Nazism must go. What if Beck knew of your ambiguity?"

"I'm not ambiguous—I'm a survivor and an ambitious man. What's wrong with that?"

"All depends on where your ambition takes you—if you decide to place your bet on Hitler, you're a traitor."

"I'm committed to Black Orchestra, and that is my loyalty, Sondra. If they give up or get caught, that's when I preserve myself—and you. Beck knows I am his lifeline to the German army, and he needs me."

"I admire your intelligence. You're terribly important to Black Orchestra, no doubt about that. You'll get power, that also I'm sure of.

I'm worried about my own well-being. Maybe there *is* a way we might be together." She looked down.

"Where will you find anything better than what I can provide? With the American? Is that it?"

"That's not your concern, Klaus. I remind you that we are in the middle of a fight to the death, our necks are on the line, and romantic entanglements will interfere with what we are trying to accomplish."

Würter took another draw from his cigar. "You're foolish to associate with him in any way other than Black Orchestra's concerns, Sondra. You'll be *damned* sorry if you get yourself wrapped up in something with him. It would be good for you and good for me if we are together. I don't give up, my love. You will realize soon enough the truth of what I say."

"We're comrades in the battle, Klaus. Now I must go. Thank you for the Christmas gift. I have decided to keep it."

"Think clearly about what I've said. This war won't last long, so carefully consider what your life will be when it is over."

Sondra looked directly into his eyes. "Unless you, me, and the others cooperate to achieve our pledge to eliminate Hitler and his atom bombs, we won't need to worry about life after this war."

Würter nodded, then motioned to the waitress for the check.

Sondra thought about her words as they waited in silence. For a moment, she mistrusted her own motives. General Beck believed that she'd married Holger for his money and the stability he brought, and there was an element of truth in that notion. Would she be strong enough to resist the sheltered place that Würter offered? Her fingers wrapped around the diamond-encrusted brooch, then she closed her hand over it. *"Die Kabaretts,"* she whispered inaudibly. She was *Adamas*—in the Greek, hard as diamond.

An uneven smile crossed the face of the German general.

CHAPTER 23

HEAVY WATER

"In one drop of water are found all the
secrets of all the oceans . . ."

Kahlil Gibran, *The Prophet,* 1923

ELGA SHUDDERED AS THE BUZZ of the intercom sounded, snapping her out of a few minutes of unfocused thoughts. It was now more than two decades since her son had perished in the hideous trenches of Western France, yet he was in her consciousness every hour. War was utter waste, and if she could help avoid the next one, that gave her reason to risk her existence.

"You must take a letter," came the voice from the speaker. "Come in, please."

She gathered a sharpened pencil and a spiral-bound notebook, organizing her thoughts before entering her boss's office. She admired Professor Hahn but knew from his correspondence that he struggled mightily with the dire implications of his discovery of atomic energy.

Helga knew Hahn was under dreadful pressure, yet she'd never been able to ascertain if he was genuinely anti-Nazi.

Now in her early sixties, she wanted to retire and travel to places far from Germany. So when she'd encountered a blonde man shadowing her from the streetcar stop to her apartment, eventually asking her to do some work for him, she listened. When he said the work was essential for stopping future wars, her willingness to participate in information-gathering increased significantly.

Secreted in the bottom of her purse was the little camera provided by her contact. She furtively photographed just about every document that came and went from Hahn's office. The VEF Riga camera, measuring only three by seven centimeters, had macro focusing ability and was equipped with a parallax correcting viewfinder coupled to a Cooke triplet-type Minostigmat 15 mm f/3.5 lens. Official papers of possible interest regarding atomic energy were slipped into a manila envelope and taken with her into the restroom once a day. Inside her stall, she pulled the documents out and captured the images. This setup enabled her to take photos in the cramped confines and the meager illumination of the lavatory stall. Each afternoon, she dropped off the velvet sack containing the tiny camera to the owner of a small grocery a block from her apartment. This grocer was well-paid to make the bag disappear until the blonde man arrived to pick it up every night at 6 o'clock. He dropped it off again at about the eighth hour of the following morning. For this, the shopkeeper benefitted by seventy-five Reichsmarks per day, about two hundred dollars, not an insubstantial amount. Helga trusted him because once or twice a week, the shopkeeper visited her room for conversation. He was a good man in more ways than one.

As she entered Hahn's office, she looked down at the letter on the corner of his desk. Its title: *Heavy Water for Converting Uranium.* Werner Heisenberg was the sender. Her enigmatic contact would be very interested in this.

Quickly shifting her eyes to his face, she was appalled by what she saw—his complexion was ashen and displayed the lines of deep, desperate sadness. He closed his eyes and said, "I need to send a very confidential letter to *Fraulein Meitner.* I will dictate it to you now." He gestured for her to take her usual seat for dictation. "Don't question my words—code talk—they won't make sense to you."

"Of course, Doctor Hahn. I miss her so much. Is there any chance she will come back to your laboratory?"

"Never, unless the Nazis disappear. But for her, it is a *blessing* that she is no longer here. She's safe with her nephew Frisch in Stockholm, who shares her love of atomic physics. But they will rue the day that they banished her from Germany because of her Jewish heritage. She knows more about atom physics than any of us, and they kicked her out, never to return. I take solace in the fact that they didn't kill her before she was able to abandon this wretched place. Money is short, she couldn't take cash out of Germany, so I gave her my mother's diamond ring before she left."

Adjusting her reading glasses, she said, "and *my* mother gave me excellent advice: *never say never.* Do you wish to begin?"

The elegant establishment at 27 Kurfürstendamm was the destination of the slim figure hurriedly crossing the street, not quite running but making his way such that three speeding cars went whizzing past his back. Gunnar Schoe trotted up the steps of the Hotel Kempski, then seated himself at a table in the hotel bar. This was Berlin sophistication, a masterpiece in glossy black and white surfaces highlighted by tiny spotlights, palm trees, a pianist in tuxedo playing romantic songs on a shining grand piano, a few well-dressed patrons, and a melodic hum of conversation. He ordered whiskey, leaned back in a leather chair, and focused on a nearby table where an attractive, thirtyish woman touched the rim of her drink adorned with a miniature camel, fused from sugar, hung on the side of the glass.

Ten minutes later, his guest arrived. Ludwig Beck removed his fedora hat, his face betraying ample amounts of anxiety. Schoe gave him an almost imperceptible wave, and the general crossed the room, pulled out a chair, and sat down.

"Now, what is this going to be?" Beck asked as he removed his hat and pushed back his hair. He wore large sunglasses and a fake moustache.

"Hello, General," Schoe said, "you know the routine. It's the usual 'would not have called for you if it wasn't important,' and it is. I have a new assignment. My orders: in my position as chief scientific investigator for the SS, I'm directed to use all the Reich's resources to locate a production source for making a mysterious molecule called heavy water. It's related to a War Office research project, so I've been told. You know what that means. The Heisenberg report."

"We knew this would happen. Can you actually find a source for this material?" Beck lit a cigarette and waved the match out.

"I've already found it, sir. Two phone calls to friends in chemical companies, and I had it. More work will be needed to ensure the answer is correct, but there's only one source in the world—for now."

"Why do they need you if it's so simple?"

"I'm the only chemist in the whole organization. Who else in the SS would know whom to call? And, I'd already made inquiries earlier on after we learned of its existence through Helga's copy of the Heisenberg report." Schoe tapped his cigarette on the rim of the chrome metal ashtray.

"You're on the horns of one very wicked dilemma. The question is: can you escape between the horns? Do your job, and you advance the German atomic bomb project, or lie and plead ignorance, then they will find out the truth later, meaning you will be blamed for delay, incompetence, and probably shot."

"If I were a lesser man than I like to think I am, I'd figure out a way to get over the border to Switzerland and hide until this is all over. But I'm tougher than I look, General. I'll find a way between those horns somehow."

"You'd better. Give me your frank appraisal on this heavy water, whatever the hell it is."

"I won't burden you with scientific babble, sir, but here it is. Heavy water is a very rare variation of ordinary water but has quite different properties. Molecules of heavy water are found intermingled with good Mother Nature's ordinary water in tiny amounts—but extremely difficult to separate. That takes vast quantities of electricity to accomplish. Electric power dams are the best way, but such dams are gigantic projects requiring years to build and a particular geography of mountains and rivers. Germany has neither. But in 1906, to make ammoniated fertilizer, Norway began building the world's largest hydroelectric power plant outside Rjukan, Norway, in one of the deep mountain valleys, and called it the Vermok plant. It took them decades to finish and to switch on the electrolysis. It would take many years for Germany to build similar works. So along with the fertilizer, a tiny bit of heavy water trickled out as a useless byproduct. Nobody knew what it was good for or what to do with it. They sold some to scientific researchers in various countries but mostly just threw it away."

"Unfortunately, that makes the Vermok plant a known quantity, *Oberleutnant,* so you don't have a choice. Unless you report this, you'll be found out."

"To report, or not to report. There's no benefit to playing games with this."

Schoe's story was beginning to tie together with details of a new international development the general had learned of only hours ago. "Consider this," Beck said. "Yesterday, Germany's Kriegsmarine got into a battle with the British Navy off the coast of Norway. One ship was sunk by the German heavy cruiser *Admiral Hipper.* Many signs that a Nazi invasion of Norway is imminent. Is it conceivable that Hitler already knows about Norwegian heavy water from a different source?"

"That's possible. Regardless, as of tomorrow, Diebner will have his answer from me, and who knows to what lengths this government will go to increase production from Vermok?"

"If Hitler learns that Norway's product could guarantee his winning this war . . . for the love of God, he *can't* be allowed to possess this substance."

CHAPTER 24

INSTITUT DU RADIUM

"One never notices what has been done;
one can only see what remains to be accomplished."

Madame Curie, letter to her brother (1894)

I T HAD BEEN AN UNEVEN morning for Alex Drake. An aching head and a foul stomach had hijacked his body. He didn't know what was causing it since he hadn't had any out-of-the-ordinary consumption of strong drink or food. Still, he knew that if he'd possessed any smarts, he would have stayed back at his apartment, downed a few aspirin powders, and attempted to sleep it off. But, instead, he'd discarded good sense in favor of quenching his thirst for a story and gone to the *World Week* bureau office.

His thoughts replayed the flow of dispatches from the frontlines over the past few weeks of fighting. A clash of powerful nations can result in a prolonged, blood-soaked stalemate such as the World War of 1914. Yet, if one of the combatants acquires a better grasp of the tactical situation and adds a dash of inspired creativity, the result can be a quick victory. And so, Drake had observed this very occurrence in the spring of 1940 as the German *Sichelschnitt*—sickel cut—fell upon France.

At the start, the German invaders closely matched the British and French allies in the count of troops, tanks, and guns. The Luftwaffe possessed an advantage in numbers and technology. Still, the French were fighting for their nation's life behind massive defensive installations, notably the heralded Maginot Line—a mighty fortification of buried pillboxes connected by underground railways and reinforced concrete walls.

Hitler's imaginative attack plan was based on the idea that a high-speed invasion of Belgium and the Netherlands, backed by massive air support, could quickly destroy the Allied armies. This scheme was intended to bring the Germans across the River Meuse only a few weeks after the initial thrust, thus side-stepping the debilitating trench warfare that exhausted and ultimately destroyed Germany in the last war.

And so it went. The Luftwaffe controlled the skies with sleek, effective Messerschmitt Bf 109E fighters powered by Daimler-Benz DB 601 V-12 engines. At the same time, bombs from Junkers Ju-87 Stuka dive bombers pummeled British and French armies. Maybe it was nothing more than dumb luck, but Hitler's strategic triumph was his decision to ignore the Maginot Line. He shot his troops northwest through the Ardennes forest's thickets, which the Allies had foolishly assumed were impassible. Field reports related that German Army Group A, comprised of thirty-seven regular divisions and seven Panzer divisions, had squeezed between the trees and into Belgium virtually unchallenged. At the same time, Allied soldiers wasted their blood and ammunition fighting smaller Groups B and C.

The foyer of the bureau office was dominated by a black and white checkerboard-tiled floor. Across from the receptionist's desk, four Siemens teletype machines in a small, brightly lit room did their duty of providing battle information. In front of each gray hammertone-finished teletype console was a cardboard placard identifying it as specifically receiving transmittals from Associated Press, United Press International, Reuters, or "Division IV"—the Domestic and

Foreign Press unit of Goebbels' Ministry of Public Enlightenment and Propaganda. Drake hovered over the Reuters teletype machine like a hawk looking for a field mouse.

The reporter had learned from his informers that the French military had come down with a severe case of *crise de tristesse somber*—a kind of dismal melancholy resulting in a paralysis of will. By May 15, the Panzers were across the river Meuse and on their way to the English Channel. In a few more weeks, the Germans waded across the shallow Seine.

Drake conjured one of the teletype machines into clattering to life under his gaze. The yellow paper unrolled from the spool behind the platen as the device produced the latest Reuters News Service dispatch coming from the Picardy region north of Paris.

REUTERS NACHRICHTENDIENST ENGLISCH

14 JUNE 1940 GERMAN ARMIES AT EDGE OF PARIS <STOP> IN LESS THAN FOUR WEEKS HITLER HAS DEFEATED NATION THAT ELUDED GERMAN CONQUEST FOR FOUR YEARS IN LAST WAR <STOP> FRENCH MARSHAL HENRI PÉTAIN YESTERDAY DECLARED PARIS AN OPEN CITY MEANING UNDISPUTED OCCUPATION BY GERMAN ARMY <STOP>

Drake walked away from the apparatus and shoved the sheet of teletype paper into the outstretched hand of Jimmy Keene.

"The French have their huge army," Drake said, "lots of modern equipment, fighting for their families, and they're out of it after just a few weeks. There's a lot more going on here than the battlefield statistics can explain." He gazed out the window toward the Berlin Zoo.

"Right. And how long will this occupation last? If this war doesn't end with Germany defeated, it might be hundreds of years."

The telephone buzzed. Drake nodded at the editor's words as he grabbed the black instrument.

"This is Drake." He paused to listen to the voice at the other end of the line. "Yeah, we know—Paris is now an open city. German occupation starts today."

Drake turned toward Keene, who sat atop a low bookcase on the office's window side. "It's Ulbrich at Division IV," he said to the editor, then nodded a few more times.

"Okay, that might work. Let me talk to the boss and get back to you." He slammed the handset onto the stirrup switch. "You, me, and some other foreign correspondents are invited to fly to Paris on Friday. There and back in one day."

Drake's journalistic instincts flared. He must learn of and write about how the rape of France was being carried out. While the soldiers and politicians would do their labors, his job was to let the readers understand what living inside the conquered nation was like. What would they find to be their new reality if Hitler conquered more nations? And, maybe a brief trip would be of help in improving the rapport with his boss.

Keene laughed. *"Invited?'* More like *commanded.* What the hell. I haven't walked the Champs-Élysées in three years. This time, though, there won't be anyone singing *La Marseillaise* in the streets unless they're suicidal. Call 'em back and say we'll do it."

"I'll be back to feeling normal by then, God willing. If you don't mind, I'm going home right now."

"Take care of yourself. See ya tomorrow." As the editor closed the door and started down the hallway, Drake reached for the candlestick-style telephone and dialed.

"Hallo," said the voice on the other end of the line.

"Red Vixen. Taverne."

"Okay, 20 minutes."

The phone clicked dead, and the handset went back on the base. Drake grabbed his hat and grabbed the doorknob.

The Taverne was nearly empty as he took a table in the darkened corner of the restaurant. The heavy curtains along the walls ensured that the place never lost its smell of stale tobacco smoke. The ever-present band returned from a break and took up their instruments— horns, an accordion, and a guitar, getting themselves girded for more hours of German and Italian music. A waiter had detected his presence.

Drake's aching stomach turned him away from beer, so he ordered tea and waited. Despite the offer of a visit to Paris, which could prove beneficial, he had a bad hunch—but why? German planes were sturdy. His disquiet was nothing more than a product of irrational imagination. His eyes caught sight of an approaching figure with a large mustache and thick black hair.

"Good evening," said *Oberleutnant* Schoe. "Do you like the mustache? I bought a new one, and I'm not now so reluctant to wear it."

"Just make sure that thing doesn't fall off just as SS men walk past."

"Okay, why the meeting?"

Drake motioned for the waiter to take Schoe's drink order.

"Engelhardt Biere, bitte," the SS officer said.

They stayed quiet until the server moved out of earshot.

"Here's why. I'm going to Paris on Friday. Staying a day, a guest of Goebbels' gang of villains."

"Nazi-occupied Paris. Interesting. The French have been at the forefront of atomic energy research. If conquered, they would have to turn over all their scientific equipment to Germany. And scientists, and heavy water. They won't waste any time. I'm thinking of this as a way to learn what the Germans are up to there."

"My thoughts precisely."

"You won't be able to swim around Paris like a nosy shark. So what are your limitations?"

"No idea yet, but I might be able to suggest things. Nazis want to show off the undamaged city, that they're not the barbarians that the world thinks they are, and so comes a tour for journalists from neutral countries."

"They'll treat you nice. Go to the Curie radium laboratory if you can. See what the Germans are doing with Curie's equipment, especially the heavy water the French have been buying from Norway."

"Where's the lab?"

"It's at the Collège de France, within the Latin Quarter, I think. I'll find out exactly for you. An envelope with the directions will be delivered to your office within an hour after I get back to my desk."

"If I can find out that the Germans are taking the heavy water, that'll tell us more about how much time we've got to work with."

"Think clearly before climbing into this spider web. I don't want your life to go dark in the City of Light. Our work of recruiting you, what you've added to our alliance—all wasted. So ask yourself if it's worth the risk you'll take going to the Institut."

"If American contacts know that the Nazis have seized the French heavy water, that could help us ring louder alarm bells within the United States. Facts can build a real sense of urgency to make them understand that Germany is moving fast. They must get going on an atom bomb project."

"I'll get my people to find the name of a specific person—a French scientist—at the Institut. Go to his office and say you're one of Diebner's transport coordinators, and ask him a simple question: *Where is the heavy water?*"

"Could succeed."

"Might. Might not. So go to work, Alexander."

Drake folded a clean shirt and shoved it into the side pocket of his valise, which could be a good thing to have if they stayed overnight in Paris. The itinerary couriered over by the Ministry of Propaganda showed them leaving at 7 am and back to Berlin before dark. Still, this tour of the conquered city was going to be such a special occasion— every reporter will have "exclusive" dispatches. Certain reporters might be laggards, and the entourage could wind up staying overnight.

He lit a cigarette and stared at the blue paper invitation. Then, finally, he dropped heavily on the edge of the bed, his hair falling across his forehead as he thought about the hours ahead, the story to come.

A firm knock on the apartment door shook Drake out of his contemplations. "It's open," he said.

Keene stepped into the room. "Ready?"

"I'm right behind you."

They walked down the stairs and into the morning sunshine bathing the row of apartments on the Invalidenstrasse in gold light.

Cars and trucks rumbled past, only a meter from the two men on the sidewalk.

FLUGHAFEN BERLIN-TEMPELHOF

The Ministry of Propaganda staff car drove the pair of journalists out of the central city, south through the heavy traffic leading toward the Tempelhof airport. Nearly 100 foreign and domestic flights arrived and departed daily from the terminal, now the busiest in Europe. In the background, workers continued the construction of the monumental new terminal building. Looming over them as they approached the main entrance was a massive carved stone Nazi eagle. Drake had read that the new building would be the largest structure in Europe when completed. The airport's site was originally the property of the Knights Templar Catholic military order in medieval Berlin, hence the name Tempelhof.

The four-engine Focke-Wulf *Kondor* was vastly more comfortable than the old *Deutsche Lufthansa* "Iron Annie" tri-motor planes with their horrible wicker seats, which were usually employed to fly foreign journalists. The 1200-horsepower BMW-Bramo motors hummed effortlessly as the sleek transport cruised over Belgium in the bright sunshine. Multiple hues of green filled the rectangles of farmland far below.

The 350 mile-per-hour cruising speed meant they would be in the air only slightly more than two hours before landing at Le Bourget field, north of Paris. The *Kondors* had entered civilian airline service in late 1938, with twenty aircraft sold to Lufthansa and more to Danish and Brazilian airlines. Drake was especially enamored of the sleek lines of the Kondor, which made it look like a much bigger version of America's Douglas DC-3 Dakota. He glanced around the cabin. Some of the journalists who regularly gathered at the Taverne, maybe ten in all, were spread around the cabin, along with an equivalent number of men from the Party propaganda office.

"Looks like we're flying over the Belgian border with France,"

Drake said. "Right down there—see all that concrete? The esteemed Maginot Line. Hitler's troops just looped around all the barriers and gun turrets. Then, up that way, right through the Ardennes forest."

"Your eyes are a stretch better'n mine. All I see is a lot of trees and sky. We'll be landin' pretty soon."

Drake studied the checkerboard landscape below, all green, brown, and yellow rectangles. No aircraft, no equipment, no troops visible on the ground. The plane banked, allowing the passengers a sweeping view of the City of Light.

"Look at that," said Keene. "Eiffel Tower, the Arc de Triomphe—see there? Down the Seine, there's the Île St. Louis, beyond it Cathedral Notre-Dame de Paris. Ah, so many memories."

The pilot smoothly banked the *Kondor* onto the final approach, then touched down so gently that Drake could barely feel the wheels meet the runway. Awaiting the aircraft were a half-dozen black Peugeot sedans, two of them long limousines, swastika flags on the front fenders identifying them as appropriated Wehrmacht staff cars. German soldiers lined the walkway leading to the small terminal building. Canaries chirped from the eaves as the reporters walked to the waiting vehicles.

"They're going to show us how much the Parisians love their new overlords," said Drake. "The French are as fine actors as they are cooks. We might start believing them if we're not careful."

Drake took a step through the airplane's door and looked at the bright, French-blue sky. The irritating voice of Dr. Würms sounded. "Gentlemen! Welcome to the Paris District of the Greater German Reich!" The propaganda officer looked outward from the top of the deplaning stairway.

They made their way down Air France's portable stair and followed Würms to one of the idling limousines. Looking across the tarmac toward the stone terminal building, Drake saw no other human beings, no aircraft in motion. The swastika flag flew atop the control tower structure that bore the white vertically arrayed letters Le Bourget.

"Paris! A magnificent city," Würms said as the boxy Peugeot lurched into motion. A glass window separated the three passengers from the driver. "Note that there is no bombing damage to Paris. I can tell you that the Luftwaffe had no plans whatsoever to bomb the city and risk the fabulous treasures of art and architecture." Würms rubbed his small, blue-veined hands together as he looked over the top of his tiny *pince-nez* glasses.

"You're telling me that Paris would have been spared even if things hadn't gone Hitler's way?" Drake asked.

"The German people and our first citizen, Adolf Hitler, love the arts at least as much as these French," said Würms. The underpowered car lumbered onto the four-lane southbound motorway. "The French may enjoy more notoriety with their famed artisans, but artistic talent and the love of technique are as strong inside Germany as you might find here." Würms smiled. "Eventually, these noble *objects d'art* may have to be removed from France for safekeeping. I'm sure you agree that would be wise."

Keene frowned. "Maybe hang the Mona Lisa up at Göring's huntin' lodge with all the other artwork he's so kindly guardin', eh, Würms?"

Paris looked like a ghost of itself, nearly deserted, its citizens in hiding. Beige and dirty white stone buildings loomed ahead; their casement windows flung open, curtains fluttering in the light breeze, newspapers blowing along sidewalks devoid of people. The journalists' cars veered onto the Rue d'Amsterdam, past a row of German troops marching in the opposite direction.

"I'd like to grab a copy of *Le Temps*—if it's still publishing," said Drake. "I'm curious about what it's able to print in these times."

A convoy of camouflage-painted German Army trucks was parked to the right of the intersection, laden with a dozen German troops, rifles ready for action. The park Les Tuileries and its immense flower gardens were spread out on their left, Avenue des Champs-Élysées off to the right. Their car swung onto the broad boulevard. A boy of about fourteen stood on the grass between the road and the banks of the Seine. Seemingly unconcerned about German invaders, he pushed a green cart with large wheels, holding three red miniature sailboats. The Arc de Triomphe stood at the head of the broad, tree-lined street, the sun illuminating its fifty-meter height. Drake and Keene stopped talking for a few moments and concentrated on the beauty of the city.

"Napoleon started building the Arc in 1806," the older correspondent said in English. "Ever seen it before?"

"Yeah, in '37, when I was here for a day, I caught a look."

The German host twisted toward them and broke into their exchange. "We wanted to show you the city's unharmed state, talk to its happy people, and give you time for a relaxed lunch along the river. Doesn't that sound splendid?"

"It's your party, Würms. So lead on," Drake said as he turned his head back toward the car window.

"Where is France's Little Corporal when his countrymen need him to defend them?" Drake asked Keene quietly. "These latter-day Napoleons aren't up to his style."

"Think maybe they've slipped a little, eh?" Jimmy half-smiled as he spoke. The driver selected the Avenue Victor Hugo, one of the twelve avenues radiating from the Étoile, the Star, on a roundabout route to the Tour Eiffel.

Paris, beautiful Paris on a bright June morning—maybe someday, when this war ends, he would walk with Sondra along these streets. She would absorb every image, make her clever and vivid comments on each creation.

As they crossed the Seine on the bridge Pont d'Arcole, they passed a few Parisians trying to maintain normalcy in their lives. A fishmonger laid out his meager goods on a thin bed of ice under a canvas canopy. On the Parc Royale, *Bouquinistes* tended their displays of prints and books as a column of uniformed German Army troops marched past.

"France has collected a lot of brilliant thinkers. Is there a monument or location where we could see some of that grand history being preserved by Germany?" Drake asked. Just traveling along a prearranged route of yours doesn't show us much. How do we know that you only display what's left intact?"

"Unquestionably, we would not do such a thing!"

"Then prove it. Show us you are telling the truth by taking us a little off course." Drake thought of historical landmarks that would be too far away to be acceptable. "Take us to the Palace of Versailles."

"Oh no, that is at least an hour away. Impossible."

Jimmy Keene shuffled in his seat and averted his eyes from the others.

"Then what about *Madame Curie's* place where she discovered radium? Nobel prizes there, maybe a display we could photograph. Mr. Keene has his nice little camera there."

"I do think that is within acceptable limits, gentlemen. We want our guests from the neutral nation of America to see Germany is protecting Parisian institutions. The Collége de France is to our left, not far."

Würms spoke on the intercom. The driver nodded, taking the Peugeot onto a new street. "He says we can be there in minutes. You will see it is perfect. Take a photo, of course. Then we must rejoin the others in the city center. We would not want to miss lunch, especially in this city of cuisine and wines rivaling only those of Berlin."

Drake glanced toward his editor, who opened his mouth and eyes simultaneously like a cartoon character expressing his horror. Then he gave a tiny smile as his expression returned to normal, and he swung back to the window to contemplate the passing storefronts

The car headed south onto a narrow campus street. Ahead on the left was a three-story building bearing the inscription Institut du Radium Pavillion Curie carved into the stone above the double glass doors. White swastikas marked the cab of a large dark green German army truck parked in front. Two men in gray business suits stood alongside several soldiers in front of the building. Others were pushing heavy equipment up a metal ramp and onto the truck.

"This is it," Drake said to his host. Würms again spoke into the phone, and the car stopped quickly. Four soldiers emerged from inside the building, pushing a large dolly carrying more machinery.

"What in hell's goin' on?" Keene asked Würms. "Soldiers here on campus takin' things out? You said your conquering army was preservin' things, not lootin'."

It was a risky, dangerous move, but Drake recognized an opening by taking advantage of the escalating conversation to slip out of the vehicle.

The German swung around as he caught sight of the quickly-moving Drake. "Stop!" he shouted. "You have no permission!"

The journalist hustled across the Travertine tiles and cut through a row of evergreens. He turned toward the street to see Würms clambering out of the limousine.

One of the soldiers approached the car. "Who are you? What is your business?" asked the man, his eyes wide.

Würms smiled and extended his hand. *"Heil Hitler!* We are from Berlin," he declared. "Here on Ministry matters. I am *Herr Würms* of the Ministry of Public Enlightenment and Propaganda, Berlin Headquarters. And you are—?"

"Hauptscharführer Splittgerber of the SS Paris Division. Show me your papers! Who is this?" he said, pointing toward Keene.

"Guest from the neutral United States. We were displaying the preservation of Paris under German power. However, we must be on our way back to the rest of our group. So nice to have met you, sir."

"I saw someone else. Where is he?"

"Had to take a piss," Keene said in German. "He went to find the toilet."

"You and your foreigners do not have access."

While Würms fumbled in his oversized wallet for identification, the SS man shouted at the soldiers. "Someone went into the building. Unauthorized! Find him and get him back here!"

Drake entered the building through an unlocked door and walked down a corridor of the Radium Institute. Dr. Jules Bougain was the name of the scientist Oster had identified as the one overseeing heavy water experimentation at the Institute. As he passed the windows of the laboratory rooms, he saw that they contained no scientists or students. *Probably still in hiding—that's where I'd be,* he thought. Then, walking as fast as he could without breaking into a run, he approached a large open area. A directory board! Dr. Bougain—105. Drake looked back at the last doors he'd passed. Back a few—105 should be just there. *Yes.* He glanced at the number plate and tried the door handle. It opened, revealing a short man with a white lab coat standing in front of a worktable crowded with glass beakers and rubber tubing.

"Excusez-moi, monsieur," Drake attempted a language he barely knew. "Are you Dr. Bougain? I'm from Berlin—the Kaiser Wilhelm Institute."

"Another one from there? What do you want from me?"

"I'm sent here to coordinate the removal of your deuterium oxide—heavy water—from the building."

"Coordinate? That makes no sense at all. Don't you know that it all went out yesterday? What's your name?"

"Yesterday? That must have been a different agency, not the KWI. Nobody is communicating these things properly! Nobody told me that it was already gone. How much did they take?"

"I don't have any idea. Ask the Germans who took it. Again, your name?"

"Je vous remercie," Drake said, grasping the brass door handle and exiting the room.

On the way back to the car, Drake realized he hadn't paid enough attention to the surroundings and didn't know which corridor to follow. To the left—those doors looked familiar. Then three uniformed men rounded the corner of the hallway ahead and ran toward him. Their pistols were drawn.

"You!" came a loud voice. "You have no permission to be in this building."

Drake forced his forehead muscles to relax. Finally, he mustered a disarming smile. "This historic institute is off-limits? I didn't know that."

One of the advancing soldiers dropped his sidearm back into its holster and grabbed Drake's arm. "This way!"

They exited through the front door. Würms had the car door open, waving vigorously to get him inside. The other gray suit headed toward them, accompanied by four soldiers.

"I've come a long way, and I wanted to meet *Madame Curie,"* Drake said as he approached the car. "Or at least to see her research laboratory—where she worked to earn her two Nobel Prizes."

"Ah—no, bad mistake. We shall be on our way. *Heil Hitler!* And have a fine day, gentlemen," Würms shouted to the uniformed men. In moments, the car was speeding away from the Radium Institute. Würms wiped his scowling face with a handkerchief. "That person could have made a lot of trouble for us. What if they would have shot you? That would bring disaster to our relations with America! *Lieber*

Gott! I could have been held responsible. I had no idea the Army was—you shouldn't have gone in there alone."

Drake looked at the Nazi. "My apologies, but I meant no harm."

"Even so—we'll get back to the others now—have some lunch." He picked up the intercom handset and shouted angry German words to the driver. The car picked up more speed as the spire of the Eiffel Tower again rose over them. From its apex, the hooked-cross flag of Hitler fluttered over the Seine.

"Lovely city, isn't it?" Drake said. His eyes played on the stores and bicycle stands, black and gold street signs, and a few people, but his mind was replaying the images of a scientist saying that the heavy water had gone into Germany's hands and soldiers pushing big machines into swastika-emblazoned trucks. The prospects for the end of civilization had gotten more powerful in just the past hours.

The *Kondor* leveled off someplace over the Champagne region northeast of Paris, heading away from the setting sun. Spring was dying early this year, soon to be replaced by the start of summer rains and heat coming to Europe. Swelling gray clouds appeared on the south side of the plane, and the passengers and crew felt the first sensations of turbulence. Drake and Keane finished off their inflight supper, concluding with a bit of German Underberg aperitif, a welcome antidote to the quantities of food and drink they had consumed during the afternoon. Both men embraced relaxation for the first time in days. The Parisian trip was behind them now, and they had material with which to fashion more than one substantial piece of writing for the magazine.

Another solid bounce of air turbulence. Keene leaned toward his associate. "You like plane rides?"

Drake turned his head. The editor's eyes tossed a challenging look toward him. "This one's getting a little uncomfortable. Why do you ask?"

"You're gonna be takin' a real long one soon."

The younger journalist shifted in the seat, clenching his hands in a gesture revealing he was momentarily taken aback. "Oh? Where to?"

"You remember my piece a few months back that I wrote about the new Pan American Clipper route flyin' from Lisbon to New York?"

"Yeah, sure, I remember."

"Since '37, after the aerial cremation of the *Hindenburg* airship in New Jersey, there's only been one way to cross the Atlantic, and that's by steamship—until a couple of months ago. Henry Crown's willin' to pay a lot of money for you to take that flyin' boat. He wants you to write a story about the seaplane travel experience when you're back. And more. Think *Berlin at War*."

Drake shoved the hair off his forehead and sighed. "New York—a meeting with the owner—why me? Why not bring in the bureau chief, the top dog?"

Keene pulled his pipe out and fished for his tobacco pouch and lighter. "If I leave Germany, they might not let me back in. Goebbels and his people hate my guts. Or I might get a heart attack on that plane bouncin' across the Atlantic, and they'd throw my corpse to the sharks." He stuffed two pinches of leaf strips into the pipe's bowl and lit a match to start the ritual. The smell of pipe tobacco was soothing. "I'm stayin' right here."

Loud voices emanated from the front of the cabin. The correspondents on the plane had not left their penchant for arguments at the Taverne, and a good quantity of German liquor lubricated this exchange.

"C'mon. What's the real purpose of sending me to Manhattan? And why would the Nazis permit me to leave the country?"

"I told you why. Think I'm not bein' straight with you? I talked to the Ministry folks myself, and they're all for it. Goebbels wants to read 'bout the New York World's Fair and American sentiments on sending troops to Europe. They see you as the perfect insider to do this. So, they'll let you go and come back. Maybe you'll go to see little doctor Goebbels himself. Since there've been no more censor's rejections on your articles, they are trusting you more nowadays."

"That's going to make me a reporter for both Germany and the United States."

"A little crazy, ain't it? *World Week* wants to hear first-hand what's going on here in Europe. Crown said he's not gettin' a sense of what Europe feels like in this war—the stinkin' censorship—and wants to talk directly. Maybe they want a book written. I think Crown also wants to interview you for bigger things down the line. Can't hurt you if you don't screw up."

"When?"

"Get a bigger suitcase, 'cause you're leavin' day after tomorrow," said Keene between puffs on the pipe stem.

CHAPTER 25

CHAIN REACTION

"The airplane reveals to us the true face of the earth."

Antoine de Saint-Exupéry, *Wind, Sand, and Stars*, 1939

A LEX DRAKE REACHED OUT TO grasp the firm handshake of General Ludwig Beck. The hand was trembling more than he'd previously noticed. The general had an insatiable hunger for details, and this meeting of Black Orchestra in the basement of the Speier warehouse would quickly devolve into an interrogation.

"What did you find in Paris—Nazified Paris, that is?" Beck inquired.

Drake leaned forward and looked first at Sondra and then at the general. "People stayed out of sight. Nazi flags flew everywhere." He rested his foot on the rung of a wooden chair. "I heard their propaganda pitches a dozen times in a few hours of sightseeing. But I found something that means big trouble for us."

"Go on, said the general."

Drake twisted in his chair before continuing. "I convinced my host to take me over to the Curie Radium Institute on the Rue d'Ulm."

Schoe interrupted. "Atomic scientist Frèdèric Joliot, the husband of the late *Madame Curie*, is here right now in Berlin, being interrogated by the SS on orders of Dr. Diebner who is leading the questioning. I suspect I'll get pulled into it tomorrow."

Drake gathered himself up, then continued. "I slipped away on my own. I didn't play it very smart and thought for a few moments that I would get a bullet. Instead, I found your scientist there and twisted him into telling me that the Curies' heavy water was already gone from the Radium Institute," Drake declared, "taken by the Germans the day before my visit. And, an army truck and soldiers were moving large equipment out of the laboratory building."

"*Scheiße!*" exclaimed Schoe. "Got French heavy water, their best brain, and their equipment, including the world's most powerful cyclotron, all at the Virus House."

Hans Oster nodded. "My well-paid spies confirm they'll force Joliot and other French scientists to continue their atom research here. And another thing. This morning, I learned that Germany has shipped thousands of tons of uranium mined in the Belgian Congo from Nazi-occupied Belgium to Berlin."

Schoe closed his eyes and sat back. "That's bad, but not unexpected. And since the German conquest of Norway in April, Diebner is starting to get a little heavy water directly from the Vermok hydro plant. Soon, they can start experiments on conversion of uranium to the fast chain reaction explosive element."

Drake looked at the others. "What are we going to do about it? It comes down to Diebner and Heisenberg. We have to kill them."

"There are many outstanding physicists in Germany," declared Schoe. "You're dreaming that we're going to kill those two, plus Hahn, plus von Weizäcker, plus Bothe? Do you seriously think we will dispose of them all before the Nazified police catch and kill us?"

Goerdeler slumped in his chair. "Impossible. Nothing can be done anymore."

"General Beck," the cleric Born declared, "We swore we were not going to allow the Nazis to have the most powerful weapon imaginable! Our Munich bomb attempt failed, but now we must regroup with even greater, stronger resolve. Do you want the corpses of five million citizens of London on your conscience? Doesn't that scare the stink out of you?"

"If you're discouraged and want out, then get out," Beck banged his fist down hard on the tabletop. "Any of you!"

"No, nobody is quitting, General," Goerdeler countered. "I'm sorry for that nonsense. On the contrary, we move forward bolder than ever! We invent new ways to let the world live."

"All right then, I'll tolerate no more defeatism." Beck turned to Drake. "You sent that communication to the American scientists months ago. Where's your damned answer? What are the Americans doing to get their own carolinum for an atom bomb?"

Drake brushed his hand across his forehead as Sondra and the others looked at him.

"Nothing. No reply. My contact succeeded in finding Dr. Szilard and gave him a means to get information back to us, yet it didn't happen. But, in two days, I fly to New York at the orders of the owner of *World Week*. I will search out Szilard and get answers."

Beck leaned back and looked at Drake with wide eyes, his mouth agape, showing his straight teeth and deep creases next to the temples. "You are *flying* to New York? It has been now, what, ten years since your Lindbergh flew the Atlantic and was hailed as a big hero, and now newspaper men fly it as a matter of routine. The mind of man— amazing capability for good, but when perverted—well, no wonder that limitless destruction is coming."

"It's a flying boat operated by Pan American Airways. My U. S. passport will get me to Marseilles on the south coast of France. The Pan American seaplane will fly from there to Lisbon, on to the islands of the Azores, then across the wide Atlantic to Long Island Sound. Almost two days total."

"That's very dangerous, Alex." said Sondra, "All that time above the open ocean."

"If it weren't safe, they wouldn't be flying it. I've gotta get answers for Black Orchestra. One, how far have the Americans gone in developing an atom bomb? Two, if America is doing nothing, how can they get motivated to move forward? Three, how can we get their help in preventing Germany from making even more progress in their quest for the moderator substance to create carolinum?"

"A valued gift from your magazine owner," Beck said. "It comes to us at a time when we badly need your investigative skills in New York. You did well for us in Paris. Now we will see if you are equally productive in New York."

PART TWO

THE WORLD
OF TOMORROW

CHAPTER 26

TRYLON AND PERISPHERE

"I have seen the future"

—Inscription on pins given to visitors exiting the General Motors
"Futurama" exhibit, New York World's Fair of 1939

THE MORNING SUN BATHED THE seagulls in an ocher glow as they circled against the backdrop of New York's surreal, multifaceted skyline. An old man slowly padded across the lawn, looking for scraps, anything of even the tiniest value that the late-season picnickers and fairgoers might have left.

A few minutes of peace in a peaceful land.

Alexander Drake heard the deep moan of a foghorn coming from somewhere off to the northeast, sending the few remaining earthbound gulls winging skyward. The air was thick with an ammonia tang of dead vegetation, intermingled with the aroma of dew-moist earth. He sat on a black wrought-iron bench and let the sun's rays warm his face against the crisp air. A taxi had brought him to the Corona Avenue entry of the New York World's Fair a half-hour before the gates opened. He was still rocked physically and mentally from the long, exhausting flight across the Atlantic aboard the Pan American B-314 Clipper seaplane. Dragging on his earlobe, he thought for the hundredth time, *how do those pilots endure it?* The journey ended with a water-splashing landing in Manhasset Bay, off Port Washington, Long Island, that jacked Drake's pulse rate into the stratosphere. His magazine had given him explicit orders to develop an article, maybe a book, contrasting the Fair's unbounded optimism with the harsh realities of life in war-torn Europe, told from his vantage point as a witness to the terror tormenting the citizens of Germany. And the crossing gave him the better part of four days, including the journey by rail from Berlin to Marseilles, to think through the many moving pieces simultaneously churning in his life. Finally, at his hotel, he'd slept deeply, the effects of the arduous excursion pushing him into slumber minutes after hitting the pillow.

The bold, blazing white icons of the Fair, the towering phallus dubbed the *Trylon* and the adjacent spheroid *Perisphere* auditorium, had become symbols of hope in a time when new war made it look as if there was no hope. The lofty promises of the fair, this magnificent utopia called the *World of Tomorrow,* had vanished with the cruel conflagrations of war like a lifting Long Island fog. Drake had boned up on the background and perspectives of the exposition, and he'd learned that thirty-three nations had constructed magnificent buildings on the site before the Fair's opening in April 1939, the only remarkable exception being Germany. What if the Hitler regime had agreed to take part in the exposition? After all, they'd hosted the 1936 Olympiad in Berlin. Why turn down the World's Fair and a chance to show off the supposed grand accomplishments of National Socialism? The logic escaped his mind. Like everything about Nazi Germany, it disobeyed rationality and clear thinking.

Drake killed the remaining minutes before the gates opened by scribbling notes in his leatherbound pad. After a while, he shifted his eyes to focus on the white spike and the single globe. There were quiet speculations in Germany that Hitler had one undescended testicle, possibly responsible for his aggressive urges meant to prove his manhood. Were these symbols of the Fair actually icons of Germany's dictator? *The World of Tomorrow* dominated by Hitler's genitals? He wagged his head in disgust and spat on the manicured lawn next to his bench.

The ticket booths now were accepting money for the fifty-cent tickets, reduced from seventy-five cents the prior season, and Drake headed for a window occupied by a pretty redheaded counter clerk. He gazed at the surrealist vision towering above what once were weedy marshes, home only to snakes and loons.

The Corona Avenue Gate's turnstiles yielded to his push, and immediately ahead of him loomed the General Motors pavilion. Turning to his left, he spotted a coffee stand and paid a dime for a cardboard cup of black java. He leaned against a pillar of the Chrysler exhibit and took a deep breath as the grandeur of the World's Fair buildings sank into his brain. There were just a few people around him as he walked along the *Avenue of Transportation* and approached the General Motors exhibit entrance ramp. He went inside its dark, shadowy interior, a striking contrast to the sunshine he'd left behind. He slid into a seat on one of the chair cars carrying rows of three-across seats. Only half-filled, the cars moved smoothly forward as the overhead lights dimmed, spotlights illuminating the *World of 1960*—an acre of animated models of a new America spread out below him, a utopia seemingly defined by an assortment of remote-controlled motor vehicles rolling along multi lane-highways, futuristic power plants and apartment buildings, farms for artificially produced crops, and rooftop platforms for individual flying machines. An idyllic, thoroughly sanitary, worry-free society.

He studied the dazzling lights, formidable sounds, and dramatic color effects as the tram transited along a continuously curved pane of glass. So optimistic, this land of grand technology, perfection, and happiness. A world without the destruction of war, with education and work for all. And all this to come in just twenty years? What might such a city look like if the carolinum bombs fell on it? He thought of the striking contrast in front of him—this vision of a safe, harmonious world versus the specter of a Nazi-ruled planet with constant fear, the extermination of the weak, adherence to strict party doctrines, and freedom only a distant memory. Then the ride was over, and he was standing again on solid ground, looking at the brightly floodlit lineup of 1940 General Motors cars surrounded by gorgeous, bored female models and brightly painted cutaways of engines, transmissions, and axles.

Drake sat down on a bench near a display of a spiffy bright red Buick Roadmaster convertible with beige leather seats. Four years had passed since he had last set foot on American soil. Atoms, electrons, and neutrons were only vague college-course concepts to him back then. In Germany, every action provoked a risk for reaction—by the Gestapo. Drake had become so accustomed to that milieu that he had to force himself to readjust to the freedom that was America. New York City was nirvana compared with Berlin. Here, he was free to be himself, to breathe, to visit the great restaurants, enjoy the nightlife, and listen to the music of Bennie Goodman, Glenn Miller, or Duke Ellington. Compared to Berlin's inane oom-pah bands—well, there *was* no comparison. He imagined the places he could take Sondra if she were here, without fear of the wrong people seeing them together. So many opportunities to smile, to laugh, to be in love. *Someday.*

New York was a magnet that drew many expat European scientists. Along with Einstein, Drake was familiar with the names Szilard, Segrè, Fermi, and Wigner. They would undoubtedly know the state of American atom development. If he found his way to link up with them, he'd tell them that the Germans were working on a bomb. They would have no choice but to take the threat seriously and get moving, although he would have to use General Ludwig Beck's name to gain credibility with them. It was well-known that Beck had been thrown out of the German military after a struggle with Hitler, so his name should carry authority. On the other hand, an immense danger lay in revealing too much information, which would leave Black Orchestra vulnerable if some American scientist proved to have German leanings and betrayed them.

It had been months since Drake's friend Herb List in New York had met with Szilard and given him the code-speak information about Hahn's atomic energy release. List had never heard anything back from the Hungarian scientist. *Why? Wasn't he concerned?* Drake had been given the address of Szilard's New York residence from the Abwehr: the King's Crown Hotel on West 116th Street in Manhattan.

He looked at the outside of the World's Fair brochure he had picked up at the airport and focused on the cover notes:

The eyes of the World's Fair are set on the future — but not peering toward the unknown nor attempting to foretell the shape of things to come.

He laid the booklet down on the bench next to him and looked toward the Trylon tower. *I've seen those words—or damned similar,* thought Drake. The phrase was probably pinched from another H. G. Wells work, *The Shape of Things to Come*—one more novel about the struggle for the mightiest bomb ever conceived. It was a story that was playing itself out in reality—and only a tiny handful of individuals knew.

The yellow Dodge taxicab pulled up at the King's Crown, across the street from the Columbia University laboratories. Drake paid the driver and went to the curb where the doorman stood.

"I'm here to see Dr. Szilard."

"Go ask the man at the desk."

Moving through the ten-story structure's heavy black doors, Drake crossed the small lobby and banged the silvery bell on the swirled gray marble countertop.

A short man with heavy glasses emerged from behind a dark red curtain. "Help you please?"

"Dr. Leo Szilard."

"Are you expected, sir?"

"I'm a friend from Europe. He will want to see me."

"I take it that means no. I will call his room if you wait a moment. Shall I give him an indication of your business?"

"Tell him," Drake paused, "that I come with news of the nucleus."

"The—what? I don't know that word."

"*Nu-cle-us.* Just say it as I told you."

The desk clerk turned and went back behind the curtain. Drake heard the scratching of a rotary phone being dialed, then the murmur of conversation.

The clerk reappeared and said, "Seventh floor, room 713. Elevator right behind you."

A uniformed, dark-skinned elevator operator smiled with brilliant white teeth and dragged the folding metal screen closed as Drake went to the back of the car. She moved the rotary control to start the rise, pushing the wheel clockwise, then counterclockwise like she was driving a bus. As they approached Szilard's floor, a flood of wariness swept over him, not knowing what kind of reaction awaited. The lack of a response to the message from List probably signaled a refusal to cooperate.

"Have a good day, sir," she said as he turned right and headed down the corridor.

713. Drake knocked above the number plate.

The door opened against a safety chain. A shadowed face appeared in the opening.

"Who are you?"

"Doctor Szilard, my name is Alexander Drake, and I come from Berlin to give you urgent information. Can I come in?"

"Berlin?" Szilard's eyes went wide. "Do I know you?"

Drake made his voice quiet as he said, "No, but you will be very interested in what I have to say. I have spent much time in Germany, and I understand your concern. You have nothing to fear from me. Do you know of H. G. Wells' book, *The World Set Free?*"

"Know of it?" The safety chain was slid off its rail. "This book I have carried around with me for ten years." The door opened, and the scientist made a sweeping wave of his hand. "Come in."

Drake entered the small apartment, strewn with books and folders. Another man, thin, high forehead, sat on an overstuffed sofa. A pitcher of water sat in the middle of a coffee table laden with notebooks and newspapers. A big, brown mahogany Grundig radio console under the lace-curtained window spilled out a J.S. Bach fugue.

"Please sit, Mr. Drake. This is Eugene Wigner, my friend and one of the world's most noted scientists. Now, who are you? Why have you come?"

Drake found a small open space on the sofa and sat as Szilard removed the cigar from his mouth. His face was composed of dark

Semitic features set off by a large nose, but his eyes were his most outstanding feature—they sparkled with deep, penetrating intelligence. "I am an American but live and work in Berlin. I have come here, a long journey, to see you. Have you heard the name of General Ludwig Beck?"

"Yes. German military leader. I recall reading something about him leaving his post over a disagreement with Hitler. But I am finished with Germany and care nothing about that despicable regime in power."

"I am associated with Beck and others in Berlin."

"'Associated?' What does that mean? What do you—and Beck—want of me?"

Drake hesitated before answering, realizing he was about to cross a dangerous bridge. "It means this: I work with him to bring down the Nazis."

"I will not discuss Germany or German political issues with you, a stranger to me."

"I don't come to speak politics. A message was given to you at the Empire State Building by Mr. List. He confirmed with me that he'd met you and conveyed the information, but he never heard from you again. Two more times, I had him try to contact you, and you didn't respond."

"I'm not a fool—I won't communicate with unidentified foreign agents. There must be hundreds of Nazi spies roaming around New York, fully prepared to cut out my heart if I'm identified as working with anti-Nazis. I won't be duped. Besides, I lost his card, and there is the same problem with you that I have with him. How can I be sure that you—and List—are not Nazi agents?"

"What List told you was from General Ludwig Beck and me. We believed you would *use* the information to energize the Americans to get their own project moving—"

Sounds of footsteps from the terrazzo-floored hallway outside the apartment door stopped Drake's words. The echoes rapidly and rhythmically passed beyond the door.

"I couldn't put Beck's name in the communication delivered to you by List. It came by open telegram to him, which is why it was in strange words."

"I did more than you might think, Drake. I went to Einstein and told him of Hahn's discovery at the Kaiser Wilhelm Institute. I drafted the letter to President Roosevelt, which professor Einstein signed, to alert the president of the danger, but still, they have done nothing! Even with Einstein's worldwide recognition and status, the letter sits somewhere in the government bureaucracy."

Drake leaned back on the sofa. "The Germans are working hard on atomic energy. Heisenberg and Hahn are very involved—and being pushed hard. The German army has stolen the French supply of heavy water from the Curie Institute. We think heavy water is necessary to make the explosive element from uranium. Without heavy water to create Wells' carolinum, no explosion. With it, explosive millions of times more powerful than dynamite."

"*Oy gevalt!* But my calculations led me to believe it could be that powerful, yes." said Szilard.

"The central question," Drake said, "will the Nazis be first with it? Will they melt this city into a black pile of radioactive lava?"

The scientist swallowed several times, his eyes darting back and forth. "But, first, we must decide whether to trust you."

"Gentlemen, annihilation is the ditch we fall into if we *don't* trust each other."

And that was the point.

Szilard looked toward the floor, his hand resting loosely against his temple. "Then let us talk, Alexander Drake. The sorcery of physics will allow scientists in Germany and America to seem to defy the laws of thermodynamics. Impossible quantities of energy created from nothing if they can make the artificial element, then find a way to *instantly* bring it together in the right amount. Only a few kilograms of it, a slug the size of a can of beans. New York—gone in a heartbeat."

So he knows, Drake thought. He focused on the scientist's face, which had become pinched like that of a man just told he has a terminal disease.

"Now tell us about your situation—and Beck's—before we go any further."

The American journalist laid out their knowledge of Otto Hahn's historic splitting of the atom for the first time, the Virus House project, of Heisenberg and Diebner, of the heavy water obtained from Paris, the uranium coming in from the Belgian Congo. Szilard nodded at crucial points, occasionally raising his heavy eyebrows or contributing a few words to indicate his comprehension.

Wigner looked up. "This is far, far worse than I imagined, Leo. Diebner—you said that's the name of the project leader? This Virus House is much further along than I had ever dreamt possible."

"Here's what's going to happen," Drake continued. "Based on the information the Underground has, Hitler could get the atom weapon in his hands by the middle of 1943. Hitler's people are also working on big rockets capable of sending the atom bomb to New York from Europe, a missile for which there is no defense."

Drake paused. Wigner and Szilard looked at each other and simultaneously produced guttural noises expressing trepidation.

"Maybe we should go to the FBI and tell them." Wigner declared. Szilard frowned at the words. "What suggestions do you have, Mr. Drake?"

"I don't think you take information this sensitive to bureaucrats. And I don't trust that publicity hound, FBI Director J. Edgar Hoover—rumors are that he's possibly pro-Nazi. This is too important. Use your access to Einstein to get an appointment *right now* with the President. It's the only way to ensure American actions will begin."

Szilard had been nodding slowly. "Two years I've been gone from Germany—seems like an eternity. I lived under Hitler, as you do now. If that monster comes to devastate this world and I have let that happen . . ."

Szilard stood and paced, then walked to a window and looked out. His back arched so that his face was almost parallel to the floor. He turned, chewing hard on the cigar stub, and sat down again across from his visitor. "The Dahlem laboratory must be stopped totally, immediately. All risk of atom bombs in Hitler's hands must be ended."

Wigner smoothed his hair, then spoke. "I completely agree with you, Leo."

"How can we communicate if you are back in Berlin?" Szilard said. "We have this slight little problem of wiretaps and letters opened. Every correspondence or telegram into or out of Germany is scrutinized."

"We will use photographic microdots," Drake replied. "The dot is minuscule, less than the size of a period produced by a typewriter. The equipment to make such photos is available in America, manufactured by a company in Latvia but distributed here. Embed a microdot in the paper of a letter and cover it with a spot of glue. Mail it across the Atlantic to me, and I will use my machine to read it. Another way is to slip microdots into slits cut in the edges of postcards. Buy a microdot machine using one of your university laboratory budgets."

"Microdot. Yes, we can make do with your microdot communications, Drake."

Drake knew that the Abwehr had several of the machines which Black Orchestra could access. "I must be back in Germany in a few days. We have problems there that seem insurmountable. When I need your help, I'll send a letter from fictitious 'D. Alexander' to Dr. Szilard, and the very last period on the page will contain the message."

They sat in silence for a full minute. The World's Fair and conferences in the *World Week* offices would get his time and energy, of course, but Drake had joined forces with the essential American scientists. He stood and shook hands with them, then walked to the door and opened it.

"Good luck, gentlemen." Drake turned toward the elevator. The most crucial purpose of his Pan Am Clipper ordeal was accomplished, but would it help in the long run?

Szilard waited nearly a minute after the door closed before speaking. He turned toward the room, face downturned, index finger touching his lower lip.

"The Germans are still pissing around with heavy water, meaning only one thing. Do you realize what Drake *doesn't* know, Jenó?"

"Of course I do. If he is as informed as he says, the Germans don't comprehend the one tremendous advantage which the Americans will possess."

Szilard sat down on the sofa, then reached over to the table and picked up a stubby yellow pencil. "Carbon graphite, my friend, plentiful graphite, right here in my hand. Clay and carbon graphite mixed, not lead at all. Cheap as dirt—and our testing with Enrico Fermi has shown it to be as good as heavy water for use with uranium. It's the perfect moderator to create the new explosive element. *Graphite* is the key to making an atomic bomb. And it's available instantly."

"*Gross Gott,* Leo. If Heisenberg and Diebner learn this secret, it changes the world forever."

"Yes. If Drake becomes aware of this and is a spy, or he's real but gets captured and tortured by the Gestapo, the knowledge comes out. Germany quickly moves from unobtainable heavy water to refocusing their work on abundant graphite to make their bomb. Therefore, Drake must not be allowed to possess this secret!"

"What about our group of scientists? Not a word of this can be spoken!"

"This is the Armageddon secret, Jenó. We will protect it with our lives, and we become the pressure point for mounting an American atomic bomb project."

CHAPTER 27

CONFRONTATION

"... This planet will, as it did thousands of years ago,
move through the ether devoid of men."

Adolf Hitler, *Mein Kampf,* 1923, Volume I, Chapter 2

NOVEMBER 13, 1940

THE LEADER OF THE VIRUS House atom research project glanced at
his watch. *Seven-forty.* He'd been ordered to arrive at the Reich
Chancellery at eight. The call from Himmler's adjutant had been terse
and very specific: "Be prepared to report on the Virus House project
and its potential for success. No papers or presentations, no parcels."

The word *nervous* didn't begin to explain what Kurt Diebner was
feeling. His steps were slow and measured, his lips moving in a silent
recitation of the explanations he'd been rehearsing for the past two days.

He walked along the center of the Pariser Platz at the intersection
with the broad Avenue Unter den Linden. The boulevard was bordered
by the bare, straight trunks of linden trees, trimmed to lift the foliage

high in the air, as was the German custom. Across from his vantage point at the city's symbolic heart towered the Brandenburg Gate, hung with red and black Nazi flags. His eyes fixed on the bronze sculpture that topped the colossal monument, the *Quadriga*, a golden chariot drawn by four horses. Diebner stopped in front of one of the windows of the Hotel Adlon and spent two minutes adjusting his tie in the reflection. Then, he walked briskly to the entranceway of the Chancellery, embellished with four monumental pillars. A huge Reich eagle carved into the stone façade occupied a commanding position above the portal.

"*Grüße—was ist Ihr Zweck, Herr—* greetings, what's your purpose, sir?" asked the guard seated at a marble-topped desk. A large portico window arched behind him, allowing the last light of the day to make passage into the antechamber.

"My name is Doctor Kurt Diebner. I'm ordered to come for a meeting with *der Führer.*" The vestibule was ornate, grand crystal chandeliers suspended over gleaming marble walls and floors. Diebner had followed press reports of the work of Hitler's Architectural Minister Albert Speer as he'd gutted the old Chancellery building to fashion this cold, modernized design. It was intended to be powerfully evocative of the icy determination of the Nazi government.

"The official schedule has been disturbed somewhat, sir. You will wait until we receive notification from the third floor that you will be permitted the audience."

Diebner was thoroughly patted down by one of the SS guards, his coat opened, each pocket emptied, contents placed on the desk for examination.

"And," said the younger officer, "these are your identification papers?"

Diebner's inquisitors nodded to one another, signaling their satisfaction with the other's scrutiny.

The man from the Virus House was escorted to a substantial silk-covered blue and gold striped sofa. There were no books or magazines, no music to help loosen the nervous tension of people waiting to see the *Führer* or one of his underlings. Diebner used the time to review his explanations once again. He felt uneasiness from what seemed to be a prominent omission: why wouldn't Himmler or one of the top generals be summoned to explain the atomic program? Why wouldn't one of them at least accompany him to this meeting?

Some have said that Hitler was a *chimera*, a human being made up of two or more individuals inhabiting the same body. He was sometimes "Little Adolf," fretting about the most humane way to boil a lobster or fawning over babies, and moments later metamorphosing into "The Great Dictator," screaming orders at frightened army generals and ordering the cold-blooded executions of thousands. So which person would Diebner encounter on this November night?

Thirty minutes passed. His nerves made it feel like the wait had been three hours—then the sound of a buzzer. The official picked up a telephone handset and glanced in his direction. Replacing the instrument in its cradle, he looked directly at Diebner.

"Mein Herr."

Diebner stood and approached the desk. "You are to go up now. Wait here for your escort."

He felt the dampness of his armpits. The wool of the uniform was going slightly rank from perspiration.

Behind him, the doors of an elevator parted, and a slim, bun-haired woman in a dark-blue suit walked toward the desk. Diebner turned.

"Doctor Diebner? I am the *Führer's* appointments secretary. This way."

They walked back toward the elevator. She was all business, attractive with long-lashed, frosty blue eyes.

"No smoking at any time, and do not make any unusual movements during your visit with the leader. No shaking of hands. You will have about half an hour for this appointment, depending, of course, on the wishes of the *Führer*."

The elevator's doors slid silently shut as a female operator dressed in a gray tunic activated the controls.

On the third floor, Diebner and his escort walked through a dimly lit, paneled hallway carpeted in thick material. Reaching the end of the corridor, she swung open double doors and gestured for him to precede her into a small, windowless room. "Please wait here."

Five more minutes of angst. Then, the doors reopened.

"This way, please."

A man sat behind an immense desk, staring at papers illuminated by a brass lamp at the edge of the work surface. He wore glasses in thin silver frames, the kind that a priest might wear. Diebner had never seen a photo of Hitler wearing glasses. The Nazi leader didn't look up as the secretary escorted Diebner to a chair facing the desk. The assistant nodded and wordlessly slipped out of the room.

Several minutes of silence followed. Diebner noticed the large table topped by a huge bouquet of multicolored flowers next to the window. Hitler scrawled something that could have been a signature and continued reading, oblivious to the presence of his visitor. Then, suddenly, he looked up and uttered a single word. "You are—?"

"*Mein Führer*, I am Doctor Kurt Diebner."

Hitler remained seated and slipped off his glasses. "Are you a National Socialist?"

"I have been a party member since 1933 and proud of it."

"You should be. We will dispense with formality, and I will call you Kurt. Be candid and clear in talking to me." The man behind the desk was not large. His hair was mostly brown, some gray showing above his forehead and in his trademark mustache. The staring eyes—misty gray and unblinking.

Diebner knew it could be suicidal to 'dispense with formality' in discussions with the utterly ruthless dictator of the Third Reich.

"We will sit over there by the fireplace," Hitler said, pushing back from his desk and standing.

The *Führer* seated himself on the sofa nearest the hearth, his back to a pair of tall, ornate lamps that rested on a carved table set against the light-colored wood wall. He motioned to Diebner to take the other sofa. "The Party appreciates your academic achievements—not many with your scholarly triumphs gravitate toward the hard discipline of the National Socialist movement. Why did you decide to join the Party?"

Diebner allowed himself a slight smile. "The ideals of National Socialism closely parallel my personal beliefs. Germany must make certain that the useless lower races are eliminated or enslaved. Therefore, I had no hesitation in joining once I understood the Party's goals."

"Good answer, regardless of your true feelings. Now, this business of atoms. The little building blocks of the universe, are they not?"

Diebner nodded, his right index finger pushing his heavy glasses up the bridge of his nose. "They are, sir."

"And I understand you are working on ways to use atoms somehow in warfare. Big bombs. So the tiniest of things making the greatest of explosions. Ironic, is it not?"

Diebner nodded slowly.

"Last year, I turned fifty. Half a century. Where do you think Germany will be when I'm sixty, a short nine years from now? Have you ever thought that far into the future?"

Diebner recalled Hitler's proclamations of a *Thousand-Year Reich.* "I'm certain we will soon be victorious over the British," said the Virus House scientist-leader. "Peace shall be not far off. Then will come global prosperity due to National Socialism. That will be the world of 1949. A world of German glory."

"Yes, there will be a great German empire and *Welthauptstadt Gemania*, the German World Capital, celebrating the Reich and our ideas. But achieving such an empire requires winning this war, and the Wehrmacht can't mount my invasion of England until the aerial situation is totally, unquestionably in our favor. I've had to postpone the invasion several times until this is fully under my control."

Diebner had seen many German press reports on the progress of the Luftwaffe air offensive over Britain. Everything written in the newspapers was positive. However, the truth seemed to be a bit different.

Hitler continued, "It is proving to be more of a task to defeat the British than we originally expected. Once . . . they were weak and indecisive. But, suddenly, they have a backbone. Instantly, something completely changed them. They do not want to make peace. Why do you imagine they have this new outlook?"

"It has been nearly nine hundred years since the last successful conquest of England. They've come to see themselves as invincible, despite the reality of the situation."

"Perhaps. Or maybe it has something to do with your business of atoms."

"Sir?"

"The British must have a card to play that I cannot see. A powerful and newly dealt card that they could play in a crucial situation. What card could that be, Diebner?"

Diebner felt droplets of sweat running down his temples. This had to be ignored, lest it signal his growing terror. "*Führer,* they may be progressing in research and development of atomic energy."

Hitler scowled. "Himmler has told me of your atom project. Unfortunately, he possesses not much of a scientific mind—no sense for technical issues. So, I asked him to send me the top authority in the entire Reich regarding this energy source. It appears that's you. No ignorant sycophants to interfere and confuse the issues."

"The project is under my leadership. Therefore, I am indeed your subject matter expert. However, a pure scientist such as Heisenberg might be a better judge of the potential of the British or Americans."

The dictator sipped from his cup. "I shall talk with him at some point. Speak candidly with me now. Is this just an interesting science project or the arrival of the most powerful weapon ever imagined by man? How realistic is it that someone can make a super-bomb from invisible little atoms? Is that possible?"

"I believe so. Eventually, maybe by your sixtieth birthday, sir. All of our information gathered from scientific literature and intelligence networks indicate that nobody knows how to get that power out all at once."

"What if the British know already? What if they have this super bomb hiding in the basement of Westminster Abbey?"

"Then, sir, our defeat is possible—ah, no—our defeat is *certain.* The power of a single such bomb could be greater than all the bombs in Germany's arsenal put together."

Hitler's face grew red. Diebner shifted in his seat.

"And if they had this weapon," said Hitler, his voice rising to a shout, "they would suddenly be unconcerned by our strength and unwilling to negotiate!"

The scientist remained silent.

"Do the British have this weapon at their disposal or not?" Hitler spat out the syllables, thrusting his arm out and away from his chest.

Diebner paused before replying, thinking carefully about his words before delivering them. "I sincerely doubt the British or the Americans have an atomic bomb. The element needed for a bomb must be manufactured by a process that is presently believed to be extremely costly and difficult. Knowledge of how to do that is years away."

He paused to gauge the leader's response. The natural color was returning to Hitler's face.

"An all-new element must be created," Diebner continued, "through the combination of purified uranium and a moderating material. Unless German intelligence sources have uncovered a huge industrial plant in England or America, taking in natural uranium in at one end, they don't—*can't*—have an atom bomb."

Hitler looked up and down several times, and then his head motions became an emphatic nod. For a moment, Diebner anxiously contemplated that Hitler might possess factual knowledge of this kind of factory somewhere.

Then *der Führer* spoke again. "A plant like that could be underground in Scotland or Canada, in the American desert, or anywhere. But—your point is not lost. I will have Canaris put on a high-intensity search for such a facility. You will provide details as to what to look for."

"I pledge full cooperation with anyone who would help verify the status of atomic bomb development outside of the Greater German Reich." Diebner nodded, relaxing a little. His bladder was signaling distress.

"Which leads me to my final question—presuming you have all the resources you need, when will Germany get this bomb? And let me caution you, nine years is an intolerable response." The mesmerizing gaze was in full force. Diebner could feel the press of Hitler's eyes on his brain.

"I cannot be precise, sir. In two years, we will know if it is even possible to have in our hands this new element. It could be several years after that before an actual weapon can be fabricated. Five years—1945."

Hitler spit his tea onto the carpet. "*1945!*" His face again reddened as he set the cup on the table in front of him. Then he jumped to his feet. "Ridiculous! That will not be accepted!"

Diebner stared at the pattern in the thick carpet.

"One year! No more! What do you need? Name it, and it will be provided."

"Time is the only thing I must have. Things must be built. Tests run. Results analyzed."

Hitler's face grew more solemn. He paced faster. "Do you need more scientists? More machines? What is it? *Take profit* from Germany's technical greatness. *Make that bomb!* Your success will mean that when I build my Great Domed Hall, Germania's showpiece, your sculpted figure in Norwegian marble will stand next to mine. You will be revered as the inventor of the weapon that conquered the entire world for the Aryan race. The spotlight of German history will shine on you for a thousand years. A billion schoolchildren will admire your brilliance, your heroic preservation of Germany."

Hitler's pale gray eyes drove hypnotically into Diebner's, his voice dropping to something just above a whisper. "And if you fail? If Germany does not get this weapon first? Then you will simply be incinerated along with the rest of us by atom bombs created by the enemy. I assure you—if I find that everything is not being done as vigorously as is humanly possible . . . I am wasting my breath with you! Report to me in one month. Go back to work."

Erhard Langen, the outspoken physicist at the Max Planck Institute, was startled by the unexpected buzz of his telephone. He grabbed the handset.

"This is Diebner. Get over here to my office right now. No excuses." The line went dead. Langen sat back in his office chair and looked toward the light fixtures above. *Why does this filth summon me?* he thought. Whatever the reason, this wasn't going to be a good experience. At this point in his life, he was willing to take any risk to bring down the Nazi monsters who had ruined his beloved country. Now he was being forced to cooperate in atomic research, which could give the Hitler regime world dominance. He needed to fight this in any way possible until he had no life left in him. He'd been brave up to this point. Nothing else mattered. Reaching for his car key, he bit his lower lip and stood.

The trip through Berlin was twenty minutes of calm. He walked through the Virus House building's center door and turned left into the main corridor. The sounds of machinery and the energetic activity all around gave visible evidence of frenetic effort concentrated within the converted municipal building. He turned a quarter circle and entered an office where uniformed men waited, hands clasped in front of their bodies. One of them stepped forward and grabbed Langen by the upper arm.

The man with heavy spectacles spoke first.

"Langen, sit down."

"What is this, Diebner? What do you want with me? Tell this idiot to release my arm."

The guard pushed the elderly scientist hard onto the chair. Diebner walked in front of him and said in a loud voice, "What about your publishing of information in the university journal about military use of atomic energy? You know it is a state secret. Yet you chose that method and many others to imperil our work. Should we be impressed with an intellect that does those kinds of things? Should we, Langen?"

"Diebner," he said quietly, deliberately, knowing these might be the final words he would speak in this life, "you, once a legitimate scientist, are a lackey of the Nazis. You have become a disgrace who will do anything to please them. You have sold your intellect, and you aspire to destroy the world in their service."

"How dare you speak to me like that! Hold him down!"

The Gestapo officers dragged the gray-haired scientist off the chair and onto the floor, pinning him down. Diebner walked over and stood above his adversary, whose black eyes burned into his own.

"You have done nothing to move the atom project forward. You are a smart man and could have been of great help, but you've become an obstacle—a roadblock that I won't tolerate. So now you will become an example to others who might think about doing things that could jeopardize our project. It will be a shame to lose your intellect, but it's already lost."

The leader of the Virus House stepped back and nodded to the Gestapo officer on his left. "Kill him now." Diebner's eyes bulged as the braided wire garrote went around Langen's neck. The old man's screams were cut short as the cable shut off his breathing tube.

The calendar had become the cruelest enemy of Black Orchestra. The members knew that each day that passed without halting the German atom bomb project brought Diebner's organization one day closer to possessing the superweapon. The lost hours flowed by and became lost mornings and evenings. Days snapped by, turning into weeks. Nights brought to Drake a problem that few young men experienced—sleeplessness.

Two empty wine bottles rested on his nightstand. Alex Drake said as he sat on the edge of his bed and looked across the room at Sondra. "Don't you see that we have a problem?" he said. She held a half-filled glass in one hand, the other holding the flowery, quilted blanket pulled up to her chin; it stretched to the floor and gathered at her feet. Her face looked like that of a distressed little girl looking for a kindhearted friend.

"No, Alex, I don't. What are you talking about?" Her eyes shimmered in the lamplight.

"Our feelings for one another are wrong for lots of reasons. I will get caught, and by being together, we're going to make our ending more likely and more painful."

He didn't sound sincere even to himself. *What am I doing,* he thought, *pushing away this amazing woman?* Yet he knew without a doubt that their relationship would speed the cataclysm which awaited Black Orchestra. The secret police would catch them together, at his apartment or her home, a high-society widow of an associate of Beck, with an American journalist, and start digging deep. Questions would lead to an investigation. The Gestapo had already killed her husband and kept watch on Beck, and their quest for information would intensify. Then, more of its members would disappear into the night and fog until they were all gone.

"You want to stop seeing each other? That's quite what you're saying, isn't it?"

The clock on the nightstand ticked loudly. Sounds of the Polish couple making love in the apartment above didn't help the conversation. "For now, yes. I don't want that, but I also don't want you to be exposed to the secret police if they know about us. The possibility that they'll make the connection between you and me, then come after you, is huge. We can't see one another again until Black Orchestra has done its job successfully."

"No. You're using that excuse to cover up something. You can't accept the image of my damaged body. That's it—I know it."

"You're totally wrong. You're beautiful, and not just physically. That's not it at all."

"Then you're scared, aren't you? You know what? You're carrying around more scar tissue than I am. Your brain—it's not working well."

A hundred thoughts were flashing through his mind. He realized that he was still emotionally hobbled by his lingering love for Viola. Did Sondra agree that this break was what they needed, what Black Orchestra needed, what humankind required right now? *Maybe it's all of these.*

She was standing, fussing with her clothes, pushing her hair around, looking everywhere except at Drake.

"Then, *Mein Herr,* as you wish. My coat's over there. I'll see you around Berlin or in a basement meeting sometime. I'm a tough girl from the *Kabarett* life, and I land on my feet."

There were no tears.

Drake smoothed his hair back from his forehead. "Look at me. This is just for a while—until we get through this. It'd better not take long to do what we've set out to do. If it goes on much more, the world goes under because we foot-dragged. We might be too late already."

"Then I'll say good night and good luck." She pulled the coat over her shoulders, straightened her back, and slammed the door behind her.

Good luck, Drake thought, the same words he'd used a week earlier at the conclusion of his meeting at the King's Crown. *Good luck, dumb luck*—he'd take any kind now except more bad luck.

CHAPTER 28

VIRUS HOUSE

"Force and fraud are in war the two cardinal virtues."

Thomas Hobbes, *Leviathan* (1651) pt. 2, ch. 13

THURSDAY, NOVEMBER 14, 1940

GENERAL LUDWIG BECK ADJUSTED THE snap-brim on his black fedora hat. The sun slanted into the side windows of his car, the bright light falling on Alex Drake, who sat next to him in the vehicle's rear compartment. They leaned slightly as the car curved onto the entrance ramp of the westbound Reichsautobahn.

"I called you out on short notice," Beck said. "There is something I want you to take a look at."

"Okay. Go ahead. What have you got up your sleeve?"

"Remember that you and Born are the youngest and most athletic of us."

Athletic? Drake thought. *What the hell is this going to be? A soccer match against the SS?* He tried to anticipate where this line of conversation might be heading, and his journalist's sharp eye for a story's trajectory brought a sense that something dangerous was about to be tossed toward him.

"How old is the Reverend?"

"About forty, but he's in first-rate shape—he has a little gym where he trains every day, in the basement of his church."

The car slowed as they approached a construction site. A laborer waved a red flag and gestured to the driver to change lanes, a quick maneuver that paused the discussion for a few seconds, which Drake needed to get his concentration set for a new test.

"At Diebner's request, Hitler has appointed atom physicist Heisenberg as the scientific head of the bomb project. Won the 1932 Nobel Prize for his work on quantum physics, whatever the hell that is. Helga informed Schoe of this move earlier today."

Drake's eyes widened. "Well, General, that means now Heisenberg is directly under Diebner's command. That nails down the top star for them and hands to Diebner all the scientific know-how he'll need to complete the project. They might be close to making the first batch of carolinum if they now have enough heavy water."

"And our lady Helga has been moved from the Kaiser Wilhelm building along with her boss, Hahn, to Virus House. She is now secretary to Diebner also. So that's good for us."

"Puts her right in the project's center," Drake added.

"And it means that we have a better view of what's happening at Virus House, find a way to paralyze this monster while we work to behead it. We must get rid of their priceless heavy water. That will set them back years."

The general's pronouncement triggered a chill in Drake's shoulders. "Of course, sir, you realize that destroying their heavy water will push them harder into looking for alternatives."

"Which I'm sure they're doing already. We have no choice but to get rid of the immediate threat." The general looked toward the trees rushing past as they hurtled along the superhighway.

"What's your proposal?"

Beck reached into the breast pocket of his jacket and yanked out several pieces of folded paper. "This is a map of the building now occupied by Virus House—as it was in the year 1895. Oster's people searched the city archives for engineering projects involving the Virus House when it served as an electrical generating plant for the KWI. Long ago, the power station was made part of a test—the city fathers awarded the university a contract to build a prototype of a subway system featuring cars powered by *air pressure*. Think of the pneumatic tubes used to carry money in banks and department stores—big, people-carrying versions of those. The objective was to demonstrate the possibilities of the new transport mode. It flopped—unreliable. The cylindrical cars got stuck in the tube too often!"

"Fascinating, even a bit comical. Oster's people turn up the damndest things."

"They do indeed. Case in point is this engraving he gave to me. You can see the open door of the air-propelled approaching car with the operator standing there. The tube ran southeast from Virus House, less than one kilometer to the basement of the Post Office branch, which was already using much smaller air tubes to move mail around. The air-powered subway project was a failure, but the abandoned tube is still below the ground there, according to Oster's snoops." Drake added up the information coming to him and saw the outlines of the general's plan. Beck wanted him to put his life on the line once more to stop the German atomic bomb. It was becoming something of a routine; he was the late-inning relief pitcher whom the manager called on time and again to pitch the team out of dire straits. But when he committed to Black Orchestra, he'd bound himself to travel a road scattered with deathtraps.

"If that's true, you're going to tell me the idea is to use it to break in and pour out their heavy water."

"Yes," he said in a low, solemn tone.

Drake turned his head to look across a sunlit field toward a German farmhouse standing alongside a gray barn. Its silo was in the shape of the pneumatic cars, turned vertically, and dozens of times larger. The old tunnel would have been airtight to develop the pressure to push the car one way or the other, and so, fifty years later, what would be the condition of the air inside? A poisonous miasma made up of the gasses of decomposing bacteria, the oxygen gone out long ago?

"Men might not be able to breathe inside that tube. The doors are likely sealed up by now—bricked over or blocked by equipment. Maybe one of the transport cars is stuck inside there. Maybe the whole tube has been filled in."

"Maybe many things. I haven't said anything to you yet concerning your involvement with this attack idea, Alexander." The general's vision swung back to his companion in the resistance movement. "You are a person who seems to embrace no fear. At this time in your life, your unusual boldness imbues you with a willingness to take on grand risks. You don't have much in this world to anchor you to it, and a person with no family, no partner, might be cavalier with his life. Before you plunge yourself into this, ask yourself a simple question. *Why?* Because you have a sense of calling, or something else? Think about my words before you say anything more."

"General, this is reminiscent of my work in Munich. Count me in. I just hope it ends a lot better and we accomplish our goal this time."

Beck sat back in the Mercedes. His face was utterly noncommunicative. Finally, tapping the end of his nose with his index finger, he said, "then so it will be. I have already spoken to the Reverend Born about this stratagem, and like you, he knows well the astronomical stakes and showed no hesitation. He's another man alone, but regardless of how it ends, I believe God will protect you and give us success to protect His world."

"How do we start, General?"

Beck let loose a little laugh which seemed to declare, *where can I begin?* "We'll need Schoe for his Helga connection. We can't have any chance to do this unless she gets precise information about the condition of the tunnel door on the Virus House side—if it even exists."

"We will have to get someone to check the Post Office side, too. One of us needs to dress like a postal worker and go down there," said Drake.

"Or like a plumber or maintenance worker. One thing more. I know you're still concerned about Würter. There is no proof that he has done anything against us, but I'm ready to err on the side of utmost caution. I want him to know *nothing* about this operation. Anyone not absolutely needed to pull it off will not know about it. Total secrecy."

Drake felt a lucid serenity, knowing that he would take action against the Nazis once more. Another chance to make good on the promise from the Black Orchestra card pressed in his hand many months ago—*preserve civilization, avenge the murder.*

"No question about it, sir. You, me, Schoe, Oster, and Reverend Born. Born and I go in and get rid of the heavy water as soon as Oster and Schoe confirm the passage is possible."

Helga felt the pressure deep in her chest. The note she found in her velvet bag yesterday asked her to become not just a document finder but now a detective of sorts. She was uncomfortable with the dangerous but lucrative request. Her hands shook as she reread it for the tenth time:

ON THE LOWEST FLOOR OF VIRUS HOUSE, ALONG THE WESTERN WALL, THERE IS A LARGE DOOR, PROBABLY UNUSED. DETERMINE IF IT IS LOCKED OR BLOCKED OFF. DRAW A MAP OF BUILDING AND INDICATE THE LOCATION OF LARGE GLASS JARS HOLDING CLEAR LIQUID. THEY MIGHT BE MARKED D_2O OR HEAVY WATER. YOUR PAYMENT FOR THIS INFORMATION WILL BE TWO THOUSAND REICHSMARKS. URGENT.

Two thousand Reichsmarks! She only made six thousand for a full year. She looked at her watch. Most of the daytime workers would be gone by now, and the afternoon people were in their work locations. If she carried a small box in her arms, it would look like she was delivering a parcel to someone. If anyone inquired about whom it was for, she would use the name of someone she knew who had already gone home. She had a good memory, so she would keep a mental count of her paces as she walked, then use these dimensions to sketch the requested map.

Canceled stamps were on the box. She pulled off the address label and pasted a new one in its place, then wrote on it the name of 'Viktor Schornn," a clerk who worked downstairs and would be gone by now. The box was stuffed with several reports she had pulled from her files, just in case anyone got nosey. She adjusted her dark-rimmed spectacles and started walking. The stairs to the lowest level were fifty paces from her desk near Diebner and Hahn's offices.

She took the steps down to the basement and turned toward the western side of the building. Steam hissed from valves on the piping, and yellow conduits snaked along the gray-black walls. Electric motors hummed, but the sound of someone hammering metal overcame all other noise.

A voice from behind her. "Halt! What is your business down here?" She swung around and saw a uniformed man with a menacing look on his face.

"*Guten Abend,*" she said in a calm voice. "I'm delivering a package. A problem?"

"Do you know where you're going? Not many people down here."

"I'll find him. It has been a long day sitting at my desk. A little walking is good for me. Thank you for asking."

The man in the uniform shrugged his shoulders, turned away, and started up the stairway.

She felt a sense of relief and congratulated herself on thinking of carrying the parcel with her. She continued along the hallway toward the west foundation wall of the building. Turning right, she stepped past dust-covered desks and file cabinets stacked in rows along the wall. No door portal could be seen. She continued, but the light was becoming weaker, and it was hard to see the wall at all.

Then something. Behind several tables pushed against the concrete, she saw what looked like a sizeable rusty door. She looked all around for people, saw none, then placed the box down on one of the tables and went closer. She twisted the handle, which showed no signs of a lock.

It moved a quarter turn on the second try, and the door sprung open five or six centimeters. The steel tables prevented her from opening it further. Then a quick motion at her feet. She jumped back and suppressed a scream as a large rat ran from the portal and into the darkness of the room. Reclosing the door and picking up her files, she moved on, keeping count of her paces.

Between machines and boxes, another corridor lay ahead—no signs of any workers or guards. No glass jars or containers were marked as indicated in her instructions. She turned left—a worker stood directly in front of her. She stopped short, almost dropping the box.

The man nodded.

I need to get back upstairs, she thought.

Helga offered a calm greeting and kept walking. As she continued along the corridor, she saw the stairs to the left. At the top, she turned toward her office and then remembered that she'd seen something . . . in the direction of Dr. Heisenberg's office, a new installation had gone in a few months ago. She decided to head that way. After about 3 minutes of walking, she caught sight of a large steel mesh rack—big glass jars inside, maybe fifty of them, a padlock on the metal door. A chill rushed through her body—was this what the note referred to? There was nothing else remotely similar that she'd seen in the building. *Yes.* An inscribed square of cardboard was wired to a metal mesh enclosing the jars:

$$D_2O$$
ZUGANG VERBOTEN!

Access Forbidden!

She now desperately needed mental composure to finish this excursion.

"Still looking?" The same man. He'd followed her up the stairs. "You must be lost."

"I—well, sort of. I thought *Herr Schornn* was in the basement, but no worry, I'll take care of this tomorrow."

"Give me that. I know where his desk is. You just go home."

"Oh, no, it isn't any problem, sir."

"And whom did you say you work for?"

"I'm sure you have heard of him," she said, a dose of mockery in her voice. "Dr. Otto Hahn."

"Oh yes! I didn't recognize you in this poor light. I—why, of course, *Madame*. I am sorry to have detained you. Have a pleasant evening." The man smiled at her, bowed slightly, and clicked his heels together.

Hans Oster's apartment was elegantly furnished but small. The Deputy Chief of the Abwehr lived alone and entertained his many friends here, preferring to engage in exhilarating intellectual exchanges about just about any topics except Nazis and war—things forbidden to discuss, thus avoiding risking awkward, unpleasant trails of conversation. The *Generalmajor* was an unlikely bet to ascend so high in the super-secret branch of government. Son of a Protestant minister from Dresden, he'd won an iron cross for bravery in the World War but was kicked out of the military after his love affair with an army general's wife was exposed. By the early 1930s, he'd found a way to reenter the Army and quickly rose to prominence due to his brilliant mind and excellent connections. This night, he'd summoned Beck, Drake, Schoe, and Born to his residence on short notice, knowing well that any such meeting carried tremendous risk, but there came times when no other choice existed. The men began arriving in the hour before midnight and sat with lights dimmed. No one spoke as one-by-one the members appeared.

"Oster, this must mean you have important news," Beck declared as Schoe, the last man, took a seat on the sofa.

Even in the most threatening of circumstances, Oster maintained a facial expression that was at the same time serious and deceptively elfin. "That's right, sir. My man, dressed as a maintenance worker, went into the post office building unchallenged. He got to the basement where the tunnel entrance should be, according to the 1895 map. It was there but obstructed by filing cabinets. He got close enough to try the handle—not locked, but he couldn't get it to twist fully open. Then more news. Helga found the tunnel's other door. It cost Black Orchestra plenty, but she made her way to the western wall of the Virus

House basement and completed her reconnaissance. She went all the way to the section where the old map indicated the tunnel entrance should be. *Voilà!* Big steel door, rusting, but no sign of a lock. Our way in."

The Reverend Dietrich Born stood up, hands in his pockets. A cigarette drooped from his lower lip. "What do you mean 'our' way in? You'll be sound asleep in your sweet bed, with your even-sweeter wife, while Drake and I are crawling through the piles of rat crap inside that wet tunnel. Sounds like the wretched, stinking trenches of Verdun in the last war."

Oster turned his head. "The irreverent reverend. You, a minister of God, you volunteered! Helga has provided a map of the bottles and the layout of the place, and we follow it!"

Born scowled.

"It's not that simple," said Drake. "We have to be very precise and plan carefully. This place will be guarded like Fort Knox."

"Fort what?" asked Schoe.

"Never mind—just remember this is no run-in-and-smash job. We've got to use this map, sneak past—or kill—any guards, *then* smash. On the wild assumption that we even get that far, then there's the little challenge of getting out alive."

"Helga's map," Oster continued. "Very likely, she's hit upon the shelves holding the heavy water. Her 'X' marks the zone where the bottles of water are stored inside a wire cage on the main floor of the building. This means you must penetrate the cage, and we don't have any way to practice that. We don't even know what the bottles look like or how they are kept secure. You'll only get one crack at it."

"Not very encouraging," Beck replied.

"Born," Drake said, looking at the clergyman. "You and I will take a slow walk around the outside of the Virus House building just before dark tomorrow. We'll compare her map with what we can see of windows, exterior doors, possible ways out, look for guards and where they might be stationed. Going back through the tunnel will work only if we are undiscovered. Unless things go perfectly, we'll have to get to a doorway and smash through, then run for it."

Oster cleared his throat, then spoke again. "I have something else.

At a huge risk to myself, I have obtained firepower. The Polizeipistole Kriminalmodell Walther semiautomatic pistol—the PPK—one for each of you," Oster pulled the guns from a small box and held them toward the light, one in each hand. His face glowed in admiration of the craftsmanship of the weapons.

"I hope to God those are not loaded," said Beck.

"They're not, General," Oster replied, banging a steel ammunition clip onto the oilcloth table cover. "I'm not stupid, although I sit here with a news hack and a preacher—ordinarily not experts in the use of guns." Oster's face displayed a thin, closed-lip smile.

"I might remind you, *Generalmajor*," said Born, "I didn't always wear this collar."

"Truly, I know that, and I apologize for my mockery," said Oster. "I'll remind us that our good parson was a sergeant in the Great War. Highly decorated soldier."

The clergyman took a gun from Oster. "I could have used one of these as a nice little backup in the trenches of Verdun."

"You did all right for yourself and Germany with a plain Gewehr 98 rifle," General Beck declared, staring at the weapon. "Can you do as well with a pistol?

"Count on it."

"I know how hard it is to get guns, Hans," Beck continued. "You've risked your life to obtain these."

Beck looked around the apartment. He grabbed the edge of the table with both hands as he shrugged his shoulders and glared intently at Drake. "Ever shot a gun?"

"When I was a boy. So, I'll drive out into the countryside and practice with a few tin cans. Don't worry about me. I'll be ready."

"I know you will. Don't get caught with that gun. Now—something else." Beck spoke in a steady, low-pitched voice that compelled confidentiality. "This is a mission that cannot be compromised. If you don't see someone here, it's because I intentionally excluded them. Say nothing to anyone about this attack. We are reforming into a smaller group. I have struggled mightily with this decision, but the others will not be included in future actions."

Born's face lit up in surprise. "Why not?"

"Himmler must have received a tip about our Munich bomb, including the exact time it was to go off. It could have been someone inside our group. I have sifted through the evidence for quite some time and concluded that you men here could not be responsible."

"General," Drake interjected, "we have the people we need here, tonight, for this operation. You've made the right decision."

"I am a man of loyalty," said the general as he folded his hands slowly and carefully, then rested them on the table. "I am troubled by casting them aside since I recruited them all. But this is the way it must be."

"We move ahead!" said Dietrich Born. The others nodded.

"But know this," Born declared, adjusting the small gold-rimmed glasses that gave him the look of a burly college professor. "God will judge our actions, and He will be pleased when we have achieved this, even though blood may flow like water . . . *heavy water.*"

Dressed in dark blue janitors' coveralls and carrying toolboxes, Born and Drake entered the Ministry of Posts basement in the blackness of five a.m. along with the morning shift of postal workers trudging toward their workplaces to handle Dahlem's mails of the day.

They separated themselves from the flow of workers and turned toward the dimly lit corridor which they believed led to the stairs to the abandoned tunnel. A staircase was located to the right, blocked by a rusty padlocked chain which they quickly ducked under. In moments, they were standing in near-total darkness at the bottom of the stairs. Drake pulled the battery-powered handheld light from his toolbox and switched it on. Brick walls enclosed them. Little rivulets of water dribbled from cracks in the mortar. The smells were of mustiness and mold.

Born nodded. "Hold your light there—a door. I don't see a lock."

They tried to be as silent as possible as they pulled three file cabinets away from the portal and pushed themselves between the steel panels. The handle twisted slightly but not enough to release the bolt. They each tried, but nothing happened until they put four hands on the lever and pulled hard. It rotated enough to allow the door to spring open just a crack. They struggled to open the iron entry. It didn't give up easily.

"*Scheiße!*" Born kicked at the rats as they scurried past their feet.

"Now," declared Drake, "we find out if we can breathe the air in there." As they closed the door behind them and began moving through the long-abandoned tunnel, their shoes became soaked in several centimeters of cold, muddy water. Its presence, along with the appearance of vermin, indicated that holes or gaps existed in the tube, explaining why the atmosphere was breathable. They stood inside a brick-lined circular passageway, about three meters in diameter, covered with orange-red rust picked out by the beams from their flashlights. In the near darkness, the invaders traversed the length of the tunnel. Sounds of sloshing water and the squeals of rodents moving along the tube were their accompaniment. Finally, their lights illuminated the portal to the Virus House. The handle was caked with rust and refused to turn. Born's light caught the L-shaped handle as Drake put all his strength into another twist. It moved.

"Good. Keep going," said Born.

The door finally relented, creaking open and making unwelcoming noises as it pivoted. They forced it against a stack of tables. A groaning, scraping sound emanated from the hinges—the noise brewed up possible trouble.

They entered a cavernous space, the walls and ceiling reflecting a dim, blue glow from a distant source. Drake scanned the room for clues about where they were, some sign he could relate to the crude map sketched by their informant. He shifted the pouch containing tools to his left hand.

In the darkness lay what would be the storage area for the beakers of heavy water. The nucleus of the German atomic program lay not far ahead.

They passed through an archway and entered a second room.

"There!" whispered Born. "Look at that!" An eerie deep-blue illumination filled the room, bathing the walls and ceiling with shimmering color, an unearthly radiance emanating from the bottom of what looked like a compact swimming pool.

As they drew nearer, they saw that the light was coming from objects deep below the surface of the water.

"Is that it?" Born asked.

"This couldn't be the heavy water—Helga had marked another area on the map as *bottles* of water." They moved forward.

"She said there would be guards," whispered Born as he patted the PPK in his pocket. It was loaded with 7.65 mm lead-core Parabellum rounds, which spread open upon impact to cause devastating wounds. Its magazine held eight rounds, and each man carried two extra clips.

"Keep that light aimed low."

There were sounds of pumps, running water, and the steady hum of alternating electrical current. A *whoosh* of steam sounded several times as radiators vented.

"Hear anything human?" Born asked.

"Nothing."

The cleric looked at his watch, the radium-decorated dial and hands glowing faintly in the darkness. "Just after five-thirty. There's nobody down here but the two of us, plenty of rats, and a few cats," Born declared. "May the God of Abraham be with us."

They found the stairs and ascended to the main floor of the structure. The smell was a mixture of humidity and oil, sounds coming from air compressors and heaters sending off their effluents into the building's atmosphere. A few dim lightbulbs glowed from overhead sockets, providing some illumination for the benefit of guards as they made their rounds.

Drake glanced at a row of office doors. It was too dark to see nameplates, but according to the map he'd memorized, Diebner, Heisenberg, and the other Virus House leaders spent their working hours behind those doors.

He took two steps, then stopped cold at the sound of a door slamming shut with a metallic *thwack*. Laughing voices echoed from a distant part of the building. Heavy boots stomped in the far reaches of the Virus House. Two voices were barely audible, and more doors opened and closed again. Drake listened to the sounds a toilet flushing.

"Must be guards," Born whispered. Helga's map said the bottles would be ninety paces down this corridor to the south."

They started walking. Born counted under his breath and stopped. "That's ninety."

Drake moved to his right.

"Dietrich. I've got something." Drake felt the wire matrix of an enclosure. "I think we've got Helga's metal cage here."

Drake walked along the enclosure and took another chance with the light, playing the beam across the mesh. The cage was about eight meters long, roughly equally deep, with a woven-wire top. The shaft of light fell on rows of racks, greenish metal structures that resembled huge double-decked troughs. A cardboard sign: D_2O. Barely visible at the top of the channels were silvery shapes, the necks of glass containers—Drake estimated about fifty. Inside would be the heavy water supply for the atom project. Each beaker was probably two feet tall and held maybe five gallons. Drake did quick mental arithmetic: if the big jars were all full, there was nearly a *ton* of heavy water inside the enclosure, roughly the quantity of a moderator Schoe had said was needed to get a uranium converter started.

Drake spoke in a whisper. "So near and yet so far. Look how thick this wire is. And the padlock there—a stout bastard."

The sound of another metal door slam. Drake and Born waited in silence, listening for more sounds.

"At least one of them has gone back outside, could be both. If we shoot them, it will wake up the neighborhood and bring police faster than we can work. We get it done now," said Drake.

He slid the hacksaw from his toolbox and began sawing on the padlock. The shackle was hardened steel, and his blade was making almost no progress. "Got anything better than that?" asked Born. "Need a stinkin' acetylene torch."

"Three spare blades, but they are all the same kind. This is going to be tough. Real tough," Drake got the words out between breaths, keeping to slightly above a whisper.

"I'm ready when your arms get too tired." Born held the light, allowing Drake to stay in line with the cut. He worked the hacksaw as quickly as he could, trying to keep the blade in the tiny groove he had started. Seven or eight minutes went by. His forearm muscles stung with fatigue.

"You're not making headway. Give me that blade—there's no room for both of us to work on it. Hold the light and be careful!"

Anxiety and darkness conspired to produce a cruel result. The cleric's elbow hit Drake across the forearm, sending the flashlight toward the concrete. Drake's desperate grab for it sent it spinning, throwing an arc of light across the windows above the Virus House corridor.

"*Damn!*" he said as he leaped on top of the light to cut off its beam.

CHAPTER 29

DISCOVERY

"No pain is felt from a wound sustained in the moment of victory."

Publilius Syrius, *Sententae,* ca. 43 BCE

"**WHAT THE HELL WAS THAT?**" The tall Gestapo sergeant's cigarette fell from his lower lip. He squinted into the darkness. "Did you see something?"

"See? See what?" The two uniformed men stood together about thirty meters from the north wall of Virus House, atop a slight rise, usually clear of snow and ice. The air was almost entirely still. The condensation from their breath was visible in the light of a single small bulb illuminating the door to the wagon house behind them. A passing breeze wafted their breath toward the laboratory.

"Right *there*." He pointed over the shoulder of the other guard toward the outlines of windows. "A light flashed."

"There's no light. You just seein' things. That place is locked up as tight as a can of fish."

"I'm telling you—it was there."

"You're just cold. It's affecting your mind."

The other guard shook his head. "No. It's something."

"Maybe boss Diebner came in. He gets here early. He's about due."

"The main lights would have turned on."

"All right. We go inside, warm up, and have a look around. I might try making another pot of that stinking tar while we're in there."

The sergeant stopped walking and pushed his cap back by the brim. "I don't like this. If somebody got in there, it's your ass and mine. We'd better have a good look."

"I hope nobody saw that," Born said in a hoarse whisper. "I'm through this damned thing, but help me pivot the shackle."

The two men grunted as they tried to force the padlock to move. "Give me the saw handle," said the parson. "I'll use it as a lever, you hold the lock."

"Ahh—ahrg!" Born gave a mighty twist and felt something give. "There! Let's get it open."

They wrenched the padlock off and swung the heavy wire gate. Born pointed the flashlight low, toward the beakers.

"Dump them," Drake said. "If we have trouble, we shoot the jars and run like hell. I stepped on the cover of a drain over there, so pour that way and hope the floor slopes more than it feels like it to me."

The darkness was making their work nearly impossible. Drake placed his gun on a barely visible box next to the cage entrance and walked to the racks of beakers. Born was already swinging one of the big jars. The heavy water splashed into the blackness. He rolled the glass bottle aside and grabbed another as Drake joined him. In moments, the two were moving in coordinated labor, pulling the beakers out and hurling the contents onto the floor. Drake heard the liquid dribbling down the drain. They had cleared the first half in two minutes as the minister worked the top row, the reporter concentrated on the lower one.

"*Hell*. My arms are getting heavy, Alex."

"Taking too long. Keep moving. Let's get done and out of here."

"Must get done," said the huffing cleric, "while my arms are still—"

A door slammed, and they jumped.

"Bad timing. Faster!" Only a dozen bottles remained to be shattered—then came the sounds of running footsteps.

"Blast the rest," said Drake, "and we hide."

Born dropped to one knee and leveled his PPK at the glass beakers. The roar of the gun meshed with the sounds of shattering glass, the precious heavy water splashing on the concrete floor. He snapped the second clip of bullets into the gun.

Glass everywhere—Kristallnacht *again,* Drake thought.

Suddenly, the overhead lights flashed on.

The two Black Orchestra members ducked around the back of the wire mesh.

"Try to get around them." Born said. "Find a door."

Each man went in a different path through the rows of boxes and machines. The guards were cursing and shouting for them to come out and give up.

A guard came into Drake's view and aimed.

Born swung around and fired twice, one bullet knocking the gun from the guard's grip. More explosions of gunfire from both sides. Spent slugs clanged against steel cabinets and girders. The guards split up and circled.

Born fired once more, the bullet smashing into the forehead of the taller guard, the Parabellum round blowing off the back of his skull, and then—only clicks. His clip was empty. At that moment, the remaining soldier blasted more shots from his pistol.

"Run!" shouted the cleric. Drake sprinted toward his single chance for life.

"*Nein!*" Born flew forward as a bullet ripped through the right side of his head. Another shot hit his right calf and exploded his leg. He sailed headlong into a pile of shiny pea-grained coal, gasping as his body convulsed. Drake twisted to see Born writhe and tumble across the black lumps, then glimpsed a new figure running toward him. The American saw a door and ran toward it full stride, then leaped shoulder-first through the glass, tumbling in the snow. He wobbled, regained his balance, and sprinted into the night.

A row of tin garbage pails clattered as he smashed into them. He hurdled the cans and felt the power of adrenaline rushing through his body.

Two shots echoed. Drake felt a sudden impact and a searing pain on the back of his head as he fell across a small hedge and tumbled forward. As he rolled in the snow, he saw only blackness. Hot blood flowed down the side of his head. An alarm screamed from the roof of Virus House. An automobile engine—*close by!* More shots. Bullets zipped directly over him as he lay in the snow. Then strong hands grabbed him under both arms and pulled him up.

"I have you, Alex."

Drake recognized the voice—it was Oster. "Born is still in there!" said Drake as he was shoved into a car's back seat.

"We go now or die," said Oster as he jumped behind the wheel and jammed the accelerator pedal to the floorboard, headlights off. The car lurched forward and fishtailed on the slippery stone roadway, gaining speed, disappearing into the predawn Berlin traffic.

Kurt Diebner barked orders, his voice sounding like a loudspeaker, "Shoot out the tires! Shoot!"

The guard fired at the car with no apparent effect.

"Where are the police? Why aren't they here yet?" Diebner ran back into the Virus House. The guard ran alongside the laboratory leader as they went back to the basement coal pile.

"Don't kill him!" screamed Diebner as the Gestapo guard put a gun to the cleric's head.

The sounds of sirens—vehicles were coming to a stop outside.

"A car went north. Go after it!" Diebner shouted to the approaching policemen.

The figure on the coal pile was hemorrhaging, spurting crimson blood from his neck. He moaned in a semi-delirious stupor.

Diebner stepped closer to the bleeding figure. "Who are you? Who sent you here? Who was the one who escaped?"

He spun and looked toward the racks that once held his heavy water. He spat on the floor into the trickle of fluid running down the drain, knowing his career and probably his life were flowing with his heavy water into the same sewer.

"God sanctify me as I come home." Dietrich Born whispered the words repeatedly as the Berlin police officers bent over him, screaming questions at him. Blood poured from his wounds.

Born knew his heart would lose its prime with the loss of another liter of blood. He concentrated on trying to get the pump to push more out. His prayers took away his pain completely, and he kept his mind focused on the story of the beggar Lazarus going off to heaven. He felt a shudder in his chest.

Shouts of "Who are your accomplices?" entered his consciousness. Yes! The flesh was yielding! Another wild quiver came from deep within him. Something, a glutinous plug of blood, possibly a clot that had made its way from his neck, shut down his heart. He vomited again as the Nazi attacker jumped back.

Diebner kicked at the pile of coal, scattering black fragments across Born. "You! I've learned nothing from you!" The body went fully rigid, then limp.

His sole source of information lay dead, sprawled across ten thousand lumps of coal.

Oster drove north out of the city and watched for police vehicles. Black Orchestra had set up a safe house in the wooded suburb of Rosenthal to hide the attackers for as long as needed. Drake, silent in the back seat, was bleeding heavily from his head wound.

He drove until he felt that he had thoroughly intermingled with the traffic. The slight hint of purple sky signaling sunrise didn't affect the darkness. Scant light from the headlamp blackout hoods made driving extremely treacherous. He stopped the car behind a telephone booth. Oster walked quickly to it, dialed, spoke in staccato fashion, then slammed the phone down.

They traveled along a forested trail. As the car made its way to the front door of the tiny building, Schoe came out. Oster stopped, and both men pulled their unconscious colleague from the back seat.

"This is bad. Have you any idea where Reverend Born is?" asked Schoe.

"No. There was a lot of shooting." They carried Drake into the main room of the cottage. Oster lowered the injured American onto the small bed. "Get out of here and call Doctor Koenig."

CHAPTER 30

BRINK

"Death cancels everything but truth
and strips a man of everything but genius and virtue."

William Hazlitt, *Lord Byron* (1825)

THE PHYSICIAN PULLED THE STETHOSCOPE off his ears, stood upright, and exhaled with a sigh. His patient lay on the bed, head swathed in bandages, his breathing shallow, irregular. Two other men stood at the foot of the bed, faces gray with anxiety.

"I don't know what I can do. If we could take him to a hospital—I feel like a useless appendage here in this house. No x-ray, no experts to help me."

Oster and Schoe both looked toward the floor. A strong wind whistled and howled outside in the early morning light.

"I've stopped the bleeding, but his skull is broken. The bullet passed through the upper layers of the dura matter and exited. His heart sounds are weakening, and he's lost a tremendous amount of blood from both the head wound and the deep cuts on his arms and shoulder. His breath is shallow, and I have no oxygen here to give him. And there is another challenge to deal with."

The members of Black Orchestra remained entirely still. They watched Drake's chest expand and contract ever so slightly under the sheet.

"The size of his pupils indicates his brain may be swelling. If this continues, he will die very soon. If he lives, his mental functions may be damaged permanently. Or, if the swelling is less than I think, he could be all right. His test will take place within the hour. We'll have our answer—one way or the other."

The door opened. General Beck stepped in, accompanied by a blast of cold air and snowflakes. He dragged the door shut.

"What's happened?"

Schoe rubbed the stubble on his chin. "It's not good. We can thank God that Oster was able to get to the Virus House with his car, then stayed on the lookout as things unfolded. He saved Alex and brought him here."

"What about Dietrich Born?" Beck asked.

"We don't know a damned thing," Schoe said.

Oster lifted his eyes and spoke. "I was there as we'd planned and grabbed Drake when he went down."

"And so, of course, we have no idea if Alex and Dietrich were able to accomplish anything while they were inside the building," said Beck.

"Correct, sir," replied Schoe. "I will go to my office, and perhaps there will be word of our attack and the outcome."

"Excuse me, gentlemen," interrupted the doctor. He was kneeling at Drake's bedside. "His breathing is becoming much more labored. His heart rate is slowing perceptibly."

The other members of Black Orchestra came to the doctor's side and looked down at the stricken American.

A deep rattle emanated from Drake's throat. Schoe covered his eyes with his thin hand and whispered, *"Nicht sterben*—don't die."

Doctor Koenig bent down and pressed his stethoscope on the chest of the unmoving figure. Then he stood. "I am sorry."

Oster slumped in a chair. Beck remained motionless, holding the stilled hand. No one spoke. A strong wind whipped snow against the tiny house, branches of the tall pines swayed as the rushing air buffeted them. The shingles on the roof slapped in the wind. The air in the house smelled of iodine and alcohol.

"I did what I could. All I could." Shaking his head, the doctor opened his case and began loading his instruments.

Beck jumped. *"Was ist das!"* he thundered. "His hand moved!"

"Moved? Well, that would be nerve release, General. Please, I think you should—"

"No! Look at him! Something is . . ."

The physician stepped quickly to the bed and grasped the wrist. "Yes, a pulse!"

Drake's eyelids fluttered.

"He lives!" Beck said, a tiny smile crossing his face.

The doctor wafted a vial of smelling salts under the American's nose. Drake took two short breaths and then began breathing deeply and regularly.

"The pulse is stronger than before. The eyes." Koenig lifted Drake's eyelid and shot a flashlight beam against the cornea. "Pupil dilation is slightly less."

The doctor laid Drake's hand back on the white knit bedspread and waved the others away from the patient. "We must find a way to move him to a hospital."

"Impossible," Beck replied. "The SS will be looking for any gunshot wound coming into a hospital. He must either live or die *right here.*"

"Then, I must insist that you all leave now," said the doctor.

Schoe volunteered to return. "What shall I bring in the way of supplies?" he asked.

"Let me check a few other things with him, and then I'll write up a list. And before you leave, get me more ice for this compress. I don't give a damn if it's icicles from the roof."

CHAPTER 31

DESTINATION

"I will remove your heart of stone and give you a heart of flesh."

Ezekiel 36:26 (NIV)

DECEMBER 15, 1940

STRENGTH WAS BUILDING BACK IN the body of Alex Drake with each passing day. He found a certain comfort in the fact that neither he nor the doctor could thus far detect any symptoms of permanent brain damage. The hours of recovery were appallingly dull, but General Beck had been effective in rotating a very few Black Orchestra members to visit him at the cottage, feeding him or bringing him encouragement.

By the second week, Drake was strong enough to feed himself with food provided by his visitors. The good doctor had provided an ample amount of barbiturates for the pain. The house was warm, quiet, and he was healing. Then again, the physician had made the situation clear. "You must rest and be as still as you can." Twice, he repeated his warning: A re-injury of the fractured area could trigger renewed intracranial bleeding and death.

His nemesis was the headache. It would start around the wound, then crawl like a family of worms across the bones of his skull toward his eyes, enveloping the sockets and burrowing back into the center of his head. Sometimes, he'd see flashing lights in front of him, only to realize the room was dark and the lights were inside his brain. Then he would manage to swallow one of the big yellow pills, and in a half-hour, he would fade into sleep.

The pain was coming again. He took medicine, then touched the ring on his finger. *Father knew so much about everything.* Above all, he had a deft touch in communicating with his son, so the eleven-year-old could comprehend the ideas while never feeling like his dad was talking down to him. They went on about baseball, cars, astronomy, religion, writers, steam engines, even pretty girls. For an intellectual, the senior Drake laughed a lot, especially when he was with his son. *Damn,* he missed him, even fifteen years on.

A wolf or wild dog howled in the night as Drake drifted toward unconsciousness. His mind began to play something like movie scenes, a slow-motion film of events past. There was a comfortable home on the street named Allendale in Detroit; then, he saw his friends playing in a small park in Munich. Soon, the *Sturmabteilung* Brownshirts were marching and carrying big, flapping red and black Nazi flags; his father, lying dead. The scene changes. He's holding Viola's hand in the Warwickshire General Hospital as she took a final breath.

The troubling reel of film inside his head began to play again, but he jumped as an intense beam of light reached through the cottage's ice-frosted kitchen window. The pill was having its usual effect, strong as always. It couldn't be morning already. Automobile lights? It wasn't time for his familiar visitors. A stab of apprehension hit him. *Gestapo?*

He sat upright. A knock sounded on the door. The light continued to shine through the small window. He swung his legs onto the floor and stood, looking toward the back door of the cottage. If he made a run for it, in the snow—

Sondra Speier strained to look out into semidarkness through the windshield from her position in the back seat of the Mercedes. The road was impossible to see, and she could only make out tall, looming evergreens off to the sides, heavy with snow. She thought back to her telephone call that afternoon with General Ludwig Beck. Employing their code-speak, she'd asked him to meet her at the Pfaueninsel. The questions poured out of her. *Where is Alex Drake? Why has he not been heard from? Is he in trouble?* And his answers were straightforward but not reassuring. *He's had an accident; he's alive, don't be concerned.* When she asked for directions to go to him, he refused. *It's nothing of your concern.* She demanded information, and finally, Beck relented. *It might be good for him to see you.* But the general added a stern warning: *He's been hurt, weakened. Be exceedingly careful—have your driver take extreme evasive measures to shake off any followers. Ask him nothing about how he received his injury. And erase from your mind any romantic muddle until we succeed in depriving Hitler of his wonder weapon.*

"This looks to be the place," the chauffeur said as he braked the car to a halt. "Shall I go in to check?"

"No, just help me out of here, and I'll go myself."

Joachim pulled the car's rear door open and held her around the shoulders as they stepped through the snow and crossed in front of the headlamps. He helped her up the steps to the small porch, then let go of her and returned to stand next to the car.

"Alex, open up! I must see you. Are you all right?"

She saw the outline of a man's head appear in the side window, followed by the sound of the bolt being thrown open.

"Oh, God," she said as she threw her arms around him. "I didn't know where you were! I went to General Beck. He directed me here, but I wasn't made aware of what happened."

As she released him, he wobbled slightly. "Thanks, I'm . . ." He spoke in English, then corrected himself and switched to German. "It's so beautiful to see you."

She closed the door.

"Please, sit down. Here, let me sit beside you. My driver will wait. What have they done to you? Are you getting medical attention?"

Drake sat on the edge of the bed. "Driver? Does your driver know I'm here? Who the hell is he? You shouldn't have brought anybody here, Sondra."

His slurred speech and disheveled appearance took her aback. "Alex, don't worry about Joachim. He looks out for me and is my shield. He's kept my secrets and saved my life. I trust him completely."

"You trust, so I trust. Simple as that."

"What has the doctor said?"

"I know I look bad and sound bad, too. But I'm getting better. Don't worry. I'm just sloppin' my words a little. I took a strong pill before you came. It helps with the headaches, but I can't see too well. Was just going to go to sleep . . ." His voice trailed off.

"I've been so worried about you." She put her head against his shoulder and grasped his hand.

Drake snapped back to attention. "I felt death coming to me. I was bad off for a few days—but if the pill for pain hadn't hit me right now, you'd see I'm pretty normal. Well, normal for *me*, at least." He smiled.

This tiny trace of humor was slightly reassuring. "What about food? How can you build your strength in a place like this?"

"One of the men comes here each day—brings me meals. Nobody else knows I'm here. You've got to keep this quiet."

"I will tell no person, not even within Black Orchestra. This has been hell, not knowing what happened—not knowing how badly you were hurt."

"What . . . what's been going on with Würter? Have you been seeing him?"

Sondra slid closer and put her arm around his shoulders, holding him up.

"Yes, I've seen him, as we'd planned before this. And I still don't trust him. General Beck may trust him, but I don't."

Light from the single lamp on a small, white-painted table fell across his face. Even with his bandaged head and hollow eyes, he looked handsome. Yet, there was something more than just his face that compelled her to risk her life to come to this place. Sondra laid him back on the bed, resting his head on the pillow. She gently covered him with the randomly patterned quilt folded at the end of the bed. She sat for a moment and held his hand in hers, feeling his pulse through the skin and veins.

Drake stirred, then sat upright.

"Alex, please rest. You look so tired. I must leave you now." She watched his pale face, realizing her own had grown sour with worry. There was nothing else she could do in this place. The *tincture of time* would be the most crucial medication in his recovery. Yes, he had forced them to end their emerging relationship, and she'd been strong, entombing her feelings. But seeing him drugged, at the brink of death a short time ago, made her realize how deeply she cared for this man.

She brushed a kiss on his cheek, then pulled her coat closed. Turning to smile and look toward him one more time, Sondra braced herself against the snow-flecked wind and closed the door behind her.

CHAPTER 32

NEW YORK ROCKET

"Life, forever young and eager,
will presently stand upon this Earth as upon a footstool,
and stretch out its realm amidst the stars."

H. G. Wells, *The Outline of History* (1920), Ch. 41

DECEMBER 20, 1940

THE VIRUS HOUSE WAS A swarming hive of action, hundreds of men and women moving about carrying notebooks, boxes, or tools, in a supercharged atmosphere of urgency, driven by Kurt Diebner's desperate need to show results that would please Hitler.

And results? He had none. It was all busy motions, a theatrical stage preserving men's jobs, temporarily protecting them from being sent to the battlefront. The raid on the laboratory had deprived them of the most vital fragment of this puzzle. Diebner dreaded the aftermath of this security failure and the loss of irreplaceable heavy water. Both guards involved were dead, one killed by Born's bullet, the other executed, but that didn't bring the heavy water back up from the sewer. When Hitler hears of this disaster, Diebner would be as lifeless as the rats that took too much radiation in his biological testing laboratory.

Sitting in his office at the center of the Virus House, the plump German scientist pulled off his black-framed glasses and scratched his eyes, his face tight with worry over the break-in—the blow to his project that it had delivered, his need for answers *now*. He saw the great peril he was facing, one of those branches of life where one is right at the verge of great success and the next moment devastated and without possibilities. He looked down at a letter laying across his desk from Dr. Wernher von Braun, the handsome, intelligent, precocious leader of the Peenemunde Rocket Development Center in North Germany, which occupied a three-mile-long swath of shoreline along the Baltic Sea. According to the communication, the Amerika Rakete, a missile that could not be intercepted and designed to be capable of lifting a four-ton bomb and delivering it to New York City, would be ready no later than July 1943. In addition to himself, copied on the letter were Himmler and the man heading the war production effort, *Reichsminister für Rüstung und Kriegsproduktion* Fritz Todt.

Now Hitler had a date, and he would use it to pressure Diebner even harder. The atomic bomb would have to be done in time to hitch a ride to Manhattan atop the giant rocket.

Virus House had burned more than a year chasing heavy water. Diebner had planned to get enough of it under his control by now to sustain a chain reaction and make a small amount of carolinum—element 94. Since Germany's conquest of Norway, the heavy water plant had been owned by Hitler. But Vermok was proving to be incapable of delivering increased amounts of heavy water, and despite enormous pressure from Berlin, they were not improving their output. Almost all of Diebner's precious liquid was gone. Other materials to feed the uranium-to-carolinum furnace would be far less effective, according to Heisenberg's calculations.

But a vital assumption had suddenly changed. Diebner's newest scientist at Virus House, Frunz Obeerst, had just days earlier returned from Russia. He had academic stripes galore, having joined the University of Moscow's physics faculty immediately after the German-Soviet Nonaggression Pact was signed in August of 1939. Initially thrilled at the opportunity to run the fledgling Russian atomic research work, Obeerst eventually jumped on a train to get out of Moscow, barely escaping to Berlin when the Soviet NKVD secret police organization began investigating his political points of view. It seemed he'd made a few ill-chosen comments to fellow workers about rumors of the Red Army conducting mass executions of Polish civilians in the "pacification" of Poland. But during his year-plus with the young Russian scientists, he'd kept abreast of nuclear power developments. He and his Soviet minions had developed a clear picture of the destructive potential of atomic bombs.

Diebner summoned him to a meeting. From it, Obeerst received a simple directive: "The great Heisenberg says over and over that heavy water is the only conversion material possible to make element 94. PROVE HIM WRONG."

Obeerst had his orders.

In these five weeks since Alexander Drake had been shot and nearly died, he'd languished in the safe house, the snowy, cold, gray days passing with excruciating slowness. Time had stopped—for him, for Black Orchestra, and possibly for atom weapons development. Black Orchestra was relying on the notion that the destruction of heavy water at Virus House had knocked back Diebner's development of carolinum for several years. Maybe America was now working on a bomb to stalemate the Germans. Maybe lots of nice things. And the war between Germany and its adversaries remained a battle of inactivity. This inertia was a blessed hiatus from constant fear and angst for German citizens. After all, Christmas had almost arrived. Although his body continued to heal, Drake was still in no shape to do anything for their cause.

"Alex!" A familiar voice and heavy steps on the porch of the safe house. General Ludwig Beck unbolted the door and let himself in. The former Wehrmacht leader put a paper bag on the table. "I have brought you food. My driver will bring the rest in."

Drake stood up. "I'm feeling better. It's time for me to get out of here."

"You will wait until the doctor says so. Not one minute earlier."

Another sound of the door being pulled open and a gust of winter's wind. Beck's chauffeur came in carrying metal trays and containers.

"Regardless, I think you are going to like what my cook has prepared for your dinner. Roast beef, excellent sliced potatoes. I hope you have an appetite."

Drake drew himself up to a sitting position. "I do. Thank you, General, as always."

The driver placed the food on the table, then turned to grab the door handle. "I shall wait for you in the car, sir," he said, giving a quick salute.

"Very well, I will not be long."

Drake moved to light the oven. He produced a long match and turned on the gas valve, creating a loud hiss that subsided in seconds. The ignition of the gas made a pop, followed by the rumble of combustion. The general dragged over a chair and sat across from the journalist. "It's an intricate game getting here. Takes two hours for any of us to come to this house undetected. You're looking better. The baggage is gone from under your eyes. The headaches?"

"Fewer. They still come, but only three today. And when the good doctor looked at the hole in my skull this morning, he thought it was healing satisfactorily. Eyes getting better, too. Has anyone heard what the Gestapo is doing about the Virus House break-in? It's been weeks."

Beck nodded slowly. "Oster has seen a preliminary copy of their investigation report. No mention of me or any of us, except Born, of course. It only says that he died before he could reveal anything useful to them. They know he had an accomplice who was taken away by a waiting car. The overall conclusion is that Virus House security was terribly mishandled, and the break-in was probably engineered and carried out by the British Secret Service."

"What exactly did they say about Dietrich?"

"The report stated the British recruited him, and he was working with them. Said Born had a reputation of being anti-Nazi."

"We'll see if that explanation holds. They'll be looking for a way to link the Resistance to it."

"Maybe not, Alex. The Nazis refuse to admit that a resistance movement could even exist. That's good for us but shows how arrogant and stupid they are."

"I'm strong enough to go back to my apartment tonight, but there's nothing to eat at my place." Rubbing his arms and looking around, he said, "That reminds me, my rent is overdue."

"I'm continuing to protect you. Don't worry about food. I'll be sure you have plenty. And your rent has been paid. Your job status is fine—I went to see your boss. I told him you had made an impromptu visit to Italy and were in an accident. He's covering for you. *Herr Keene* was glad to hear you are recuperating, and no more was said, except that your job is safe, not to worry."

"Thank you, General. Have you figured out if there is a turncoat in our midst? That's a fundamental question at this moment."

"That's my problem, and I'll take care of it."

"I'd say it's a problem for all of us. We've been told a couple of times that somebody in our group is a traitor. So how does this bunch continue without answering that?"

"I told you it's my business. Leave that to me, and don't question my authority. I'm a general of the armed forces, and I command." Beck's ears were reddening, his voice increasing in pitch and power.

"Our greatest threat is having a double-crosser inside this group waiting to destroy you, me, and everything we're doing to prevent a global catastrophe."

The general's hands were moving in jerks, and he shifted his weight from one leg to the other.

"If there *is* a traitor, it has to be one of the people in our group whom we have chosen to keep in the dark."

It was patently obvious that Beck didn't know and wasn't doing much to find out. The general pulled his overcoat tight and pulled the door open.

"All right. Enough for tonight. *Guten Nacht.*"

Helga sat upright as the door to Dr. Diebner's outer office was pulled open. A large man in a rumpled blue serge suit walked in.

"And may I help you, sir? I don't believe we've met," she said.

The blue suit moved toward her and raised his arm to show a sheaf of papers in his hand.

"I'm new here. This document is for Dr. Diebner."

"What shall I tell him about this?"

"He asked me for a report two weeks ago; here it is. Self-explanatory. You will see to it that he gets it right away."

"Indeed. Your name?"

"It's right there. Dr. Obeerst."

"Oh yes, I see. He will get it, although he's gone for the day. Meetings in town."

"Good evening then." Obeerst shut the door quietly.

Helga looked at the top sheet.

Konversion von Uran zu Explosiven

F. Obeerst

The title—*Conversion of Uranium to Explosive*— portended that this might be important for her grocery market contact man. She read the first few pages. The author discussed in understandable terminology an unstable artificial element, possessing more neutrons in its nucleus than the heaviest natural element, uranium. There were swirls of mathematical symbols, none of which she even remotely understood. She saw Heisenberg's name. The words said Heisenberg's analysis rejected substances such as ordinary water, paraffin, carbon graphite, and carbon dioxide for making an exploding element. Then Obeerst's comments veered off into a different direction. He contradicted the great Nobel Prize winner. His concluding paragraph:

> Therefore, based upon the above calculations, in addition to heavy water, purified carbon graphite must be tested empirically for usefulness in transmuting ordinary uranium to element 94.

Helga's eyes went wide. She knew enough to realize this was something important. Stuffing the report into her generously sized purse next to the little camera, she started for the restroom.

CHAPTER 33

TREACHERY

"Ask, and it will be given to you; seek, and you will find;
knock, and it will be opened to you."

Matthew 7:7 (ESV)

T HE BIG SEDAN TRAVELED THROUGH the tree-lined road toward the
safe house of Black Orchestra. The sky was almost black now, the
deep purple twilight transitioning into night.

"I'll get him," *Oberleutnant* Schoe said. *Generaloberst* Ludwig Beck's
driver slowed the vehicle to a halt. "Open the trunk and prepare the
hidden compartment for a rider." He climbed out of the car and walked
up to the house.

"Drake!" the SS officer shouted as he knocked on the door. *Is he in
there?* Schoe thought. *Has the Gestapo paid a visit?*

The door opened. Alex Drake stepped aside and motioned Schoe
to enter.

"Gather your things. We'll hide you at Beck's house to check you
over before you go to your apartment. You'll stay there a day or so."

"Time to get out of this damned box—I'm going nuts here."

"It's dark already, but you'll get in the compartment built under the trunk. I will meticulously check this place to make sure nothing's left behind."

The trip to Beck's home took an hour. It was nearing nine o'clock as the sedan entered the frigid garage. The two Black Orchestra members and the driver traversed the concrete floor, just a single bare lightbulb to illuminate their way into the house.

The distant deep-toned chime of a clock traveled through the house, informing those who could hear that the ninth hour of the evening had arrived. Snaps and hisses sprang from the logs blazing in the hearth. The fire's glow flickered across their faces, the orange light softening the shadows made by the lamps. "Sir, we are here," said Schoe as Beck came into view.

"There is much danger in your coming to my home, Drake," the general said, "but I need to assess your health before sending you off to your apartment."

"Thank you, General. I'm thrilled to be out of that place and damned happy to be alive."

Schoe sat down on the edge of a desk as the other two men went to the sofa.

"*Thrilled?* See if you're even more thrilled by this," Schoe said, pulling a sheaf of photographic prints from his waistband. "Something extremely crucial comes now. Helga's camera has again brought forth a big result—this time, it's a report to Diebner. We don't know who this author is, but it's dangerous—there are fresh calculations about neutron moderator substances. He concludes that *carbon graphite* might be as effective as the scarce heavy water in producing carolinum. Carbon graphite is cheap and abundant—it's just purified pencil lead. Think of what this means if proven to be correct."

The dark figure of the butler stepped into the room from the unlit hallway. He gripped a fireplace poker to rattle the fire logs into new vitality as the telephone issued a staccato buzz. The servant moved quickly from his duty at the hearth to answer it.

"Excuse me, sir, a call for you."

The general grabbed the handset. "Beck speaking." He listened and nodded, a look of unease creeping across his face. *"Verstanden."* He dropped the handset onto its cradle.

"Gross Gott! Here we sit, talking about your new revelation concerning the carbon graphite material, then at this instant comes a call from Oster. He took a chance and cut out the code speak this time. Virus House is already moving with precisely Schoe's information. They've ordered a pure carbon graphite sample to be shipped via rail from Siemens Chemicals in Berlin to the University of Heidelberg for testing, taking place there only about three weeks from today. They will test it as a substitute for heavy water."

Beck stared out the window at the clear night sky. "It's December 22, 1940, and Hitler has never been stronger—France, Holland, Poland, Denmark, Norway, Belgium—all of them conquered. America is neutral, out of the war, and stays that way for now. England teeters on the brink, and Stalin is covering Hitler's *arse.* He's doing just fine at present and has time to work out the atomic bomb without worrying about much more fighting right now."

Drake started to talk, but the rising blare of air raid sirens cut him off.

"RAF on the way!" Beck declared. "We go to the basement."

They clambered down the stairs, followed by the servant. The scream of the sirens quickly overpowered the thunder of aircraft engines.

"Get in here!" shouted Beck.

They followed him into the cinder block coal bin as the *ack-ack-ack* of antiaircraft guns and explosions sounded. As they waited with growing angst, Drake thought about this carbon graphite test. From every scrap of knowledge he'd gleaned about Germans, going back to his boyhood sojourns to Munich, he knew one thing: *Germans are planners. You can win if you trap them into having to improvise.*

The blast of a massive explosion rocked the home. Dishes hit the floor above.

"Some of my neighbors might be having a bad night, gentlemen," said Beck.

The men stood for ten minutes in the coal bin in the farthest corner of the darkened basement, illuminated only by a single distant bulb. The sounds of the air raid died down.

"Let's get back upstairs," Beck said. "Entertainment's over for tonight."

The general led the way to the main floor but stopped almost at the top of the stairs. "Smoke! Something's burning!" he said.

Darting around a corner and into the kitchen, Drake looked for signs of fire, his nostrils picking up an acrid smell. He could see no signs of damage to the house, but he headed toward the fireplace of the main room. He ducked under the intensifying smoke. Beck followed right behind him.

The woodwork around the fireplace smoldered, and black smoke roiled upward from the fire. Materials of some sort were burning on the floor and along the right side of the hearth. The butler came at them, sloshing water on the mantle and surrounding woodwork from a large canister, dousing the flames in a plume of steam.

"This had nothing to do with bombs," Drake said. "We'd know it if one had hit this house."

They switched on more lights, illuminating the fire scene.

"*Ja!*" Beck said, raising his arm to point to the hearth. "My red ribbons are gone. The bomb concussions made them fall from the mantle and into the fireplace. There were newspapers here, where that black mess is. Papers set fire to the painted wood."

"The impact from the explosion must have dislodged the decorations," Drake declared. "They fell into the fire igniting everything while we stood downstairs."

Beck turned to his butler. "Dirk, open the doors and set up a fan to blow this smoke out. Alex, get back downstairs and out of this stink. We will come and join you after we have aired out this place."

Drake tried to ignore the onrushing headache as he descended the wooden stairway. He made his way to the bed and dropped himself on top of the yellow blanket. He wanted to see Sondra again, let her know he was safe and his health was returning.

His thoughts bounced back to finding a way of stopping the Germans from testing graphite. And then he had it. The holiday decorations had yielded a Christmas gift to him—the beginnings of a plan which just might work.

CHAPTER 34

A PLAN OF ACTION

"In war, whichever side may call itself the victor,
there are no winners, but all are losers."

Neville Chamberlain, British Prime Minister, 3 July 1938

DECEMBER 23, 1940

"I'LL BE A SON OF a gun, Alex Drake! You're a darned sight!" Jimmy Keene yanked off his gold wire-rimmed glasses and jumped to his feet.

Drake walked into the *World Week* bureau office, flanked by two laughing female office workers and followed by three writers.

"Rough trip! Ya look a little bit worse for wear." Keene said. "But here you are, walkin' and breathin'! Welcome!"

"Uh-huh," he replied.

"You didn't eat much spaghetti there—you've lost lotsa weight, and that's a terrible haircut. You'll have to tell us about Rome—*Il Duce*—Mr. Mussolini. But first, take it easy. Come, sit down."

Moving toward a chair, Drake remained standing. The receptionist hugged him for the fourth time, then walked back to her desk. She returned with a brown paper bag and held it out to him. "Alex, please take this. It is from all of us. We went in together, a remembrance of our admiration for you and your long journey."

Drake grasped the package, turned it over in his hands, and removed a small box. Inside was an engraved silver money clip. He looked at the inscription:

ACD

World Week BERLIN **1940**

He smiled and looked around at his colleagues. "I'm so happy to see you all. Thank you. Now, if I had some money to slide into this!"

As the last well-wisher went back to work, Jimmy Keene crossed the shiny tile floor and put an arm around the reporter. "Let's go into my office, eh?"

Keene shut the door as Drake took a seat in front of the older man's desk. Sunlight slanted in through dusty Venetian blinds, throwing stripes of light and shadow across the typewriter, pencils, and books.

"I got a call from General Ludwig Beck," said Keene. "We met at the Münster Café. He told me about your predicament. She said you'd rented a car in Rome and somebody hit you, you were injured, you had to go into a hospital. Then he got you back to Germany, and you were healin' up at his country home. He asked me not to go any deeper than that. Somethin' damned important was takin' place. The stories I filed for you were 'bout the Italian offensive into southern France and their occupation of French territory along the Franco-Italian border. I had plenty from my sources to write with about it, and that was that. When we talked again, he told me you were comin' back. You're lookin' better than I'd expected for bein' hurt as damned bad as he'd said you were."

"I didn't know how long you could keep me on. I know it was hard;

the stories made up, filed under my byline. Did you have to tell your bosses?"

"Look, I'm in charge of this office. I make the decisions. All I know is you were hurt, and it's nobody else's business 'bout your life and times. New York doesn't know a thing. And *I* don't want to know any more about what the hell you are screwin' around with. Beck is Hitler's noblest enemy who still manages to survive in this country, but if he gets arrested, he might suck you right in along with him."

Pipe tobacco smoke drifted around Keene's head as he leaned back in his chair and put his feet up on the desk. He swiveled slightly to look out the window.

"New York's been happy with your articles—the World's Fair and the war, and they're tellin' me good things 'bout you. They even like the stories I ghosted for you—so I must be learnin' from you, not the other way around like it's been for a couple of years. Just don't have me runnin' your obituary in the magazine." His voice trailed off.

"Boss, someday you'll understand. Not now, but someday. For a while, I worried about—what's a good word—your trustworthiness? I thought you had told someone about Munich, about my father. You didn't."

"Of course I didn't. But stay healthy from now on. I don't want to try to cover for you again if you get in trouble. Next time, you're gonna drag me into your conspiracies along with this magazine and maybe America. You're *American*, not German. Remember that."

Drake opened his hand and held it in front of Jimmy Keene. A little packet labeled Kaugummi lay in his palm. "I keep this nearby twenty-four hours a day."

"Chewing gum? Worried 'bout bad breath botherin' a lady friend?"

"If I get in a bind that I can't get out of, I'll have a chew. Special gum—with cyanide."

"If you put it in your mouth, I'll see you in hell next."

CHAPTER 35

CARBON

"There are two great jars that stand on the floor of Zeus's halls
and hold our miseries in one, the other our blessings.
When Zeus mixes gifts for a man,
he meets with misfortune, then good times in turn."

The *Iliad* of Homer 24.525

DRAKE PUSHED UP HIS SLEEVE and glanced at his watch. He'd waited now nearly half an hour for Beck beyond the agreed meeting time, and he was growing edgier with each minute. He cursed himself for not thinking of a better place, one even more secluded.

It had been two weeks since the waters of the Havel surrounding the park named Peacock Island had frozen over. The youngsters of Berlin had wasted no time in clearing patches of its shiny, icy surface for skating. Across the smooth gray-black surface, women and children spun and glided, their breath revealed in puffs that vanished alongside their rose-colored cheeks.

Ludwig Beck approached, the usual "get right to the point" look on his face. No greetings of *Frohe Weihnachten*—Merry Christmas— even though the day of celebration was coming tomorrow.

"I wish there'd been time to think of a better place for this, but I need your immediate agreement and total support, General."

The two men walked down a path into a cluster of pine trees.

"Sir, I've been thinking of a way to foul up the Virus House graphite test."

"I can't wait to hear what you have to say," Beck said, turning his head to look at Drake.

"When they test carbon graphite, Diebner and friends will very likely find it works. So. we've damned ourselves either way. Had we not destroyed their heavy water stocks, their uranium conversion furnace might be up and making carolinum already."

Beck cut him off. "We knew that destroying the heavy water would push their interest toward a different solution."

Drake leaned away from the cold wind. "So, let's get them to reject carbon graphite. Make them think heavy water stands as the only option."

Beck nodded, his brow deeply furrowed. "Nice idea, but we're not scientists. How could we have any chance of knocking them off course?"

"*Deception*, General. Dupe the German scientists into deciding once and for all that carbon can't make carolinum. And they can never have the slightest suspicion that they've been tricked. They must have complete confidence in their test so that it's never challenged or repeated."

"Easily said. Practically impossible to carry off."

"You know ancient history. Do you remember the tale of Menelek I, the Emperor of ancient Ethiopia? Ethiopians believe he stole the Ark of the Covenant from Jerusalem by sneaking in and grabbing it, then replacing it with a perfect replica."

Beck scratched his chin and eyed Drake with a look of uncertainty. "A Menelek deception," he said.

"We've had terrible failures, General, but we push on. We have to keep trying. To fight this evil is not just our pledge to each other; it's in our core."

A sudden movement in the bushes startled both men. A big male peacock jumped out and ran across their path.

"Walk with me through the woods," Drake said. "I'll tell you what I'm thinking."

PART THREE

TESTS

CHAPTER 36

TEMPTATION

"Again, the devil took Him to a very high mountain and
showed Him all the kingdoms of the world and their glory.
'All this I will give you,' he said, 'if you
will fall down and worship me.'"

Matthew 4:8-9 (ESV)

JANUARY 1, 1941

THE CHIRPING NOTES OF HER antique Black Forest cuckoo clock
reminded Sondra that she was the only person who would hear it.
She looked again at the card in her hand, delivered to her home in a
sealed envelope by courier minutes ago.

I need to see you in a safe place.
Victory Column at four.
Call me with code speak if not possible. AD

She expected that something like this would eventually come from Alex and had decided that if such a message were to come, *yes, she would see him.*

The late afternoon sun in Tiergarten Park threw long shadows across white patches left from Sunday's snow accumulation. Berliners had given the gilded statue atop the 70-meter high Column of Winged Victory the nickname Goldelse, which meant something like "Golden Lizzy." At the eastern side of the Großer Stern—Great Star, a prominent roundabout intersection on the axis leading from the Brandenburg Gate to the east, Joachim pulled the car to the curbside to let out his passenger. He left his door open as he moved to open hers and help her out and onto the sidewalk, then jumped back in and sped off as instructed. She looked up at the monument in the roundabout's center, then scanned the pedestrians along the sidewalks. A tall figure walked south toward her from the street named Spreeweg. It was New Year's Day, and traffic was nil. He crossed the circular roadway and approached her, his bright grin shining. A floppy hat covered Drake's head, and he wore his favorite Harris Tweed overcoat.

"Sondra, you're the picture of loveliness!" He hugged her tightly.

"Alex Drake lives." She smiled and, for a moment, wanted his kiss but knew this wouldn't be a great idea with cars passing nearby, even if there were few. "Come, let's walk."

They took the southeast sidewalk lined with fir trees into the woods. A single bicyclist passed them. The mournful song of an early nightingale came from the west.

"I almost decided not to meet you," she said.

"I'm persistent. I'd have found you anyway."

"How are you? I'm so glad you are here strolling along with me, not in a hospital or a cemetery."

"Surprising that I'm not. Thank you for coming out there—to the house. You did that despite my words about not seeing one another."

Sondra clasped his hand around his. "How could I stay away when I heard you were hurt? I was so worried."

"The view of you coming into that house, the wind blowing snow all around you, then to hold you even for just moments. The impact that had on me, how it helped my healing—I can't describe it, Sondra. It was like a blood transfusion, but no blood crossed. Maybe some part of you came into me."

She grasped his hand tightly and pushed her arm against his as they walked.

"It's been only a few days that I've been feeling strong enough to be out and moving around. I've walked almost a kilometer from my place to here, no ill effects." Their pace slowed, and he released her hand, then put his arm around her tiny waist.

"Well, neither of us is an excellent walker right now, are we? she said with a sweet laugh.

"Let's sit here." Drake pointed to a wooden bench between two towering pines.

"Only for a few minutes. Joachim will be circling back around the Großer Stern to watch for me." She brushed her hair away from the side of her face.

"Then I'll get on with it. I need your help with our final shot at stopping the German atom project. If we can't do this, Diebner will have a clear pathway to the bomb, and we'll never again have a chance to block them. They will have gone too far for us to do anything. So Black Orchestra's going to be finished, and along with it, the planet."

"How can I possibly help?"

"Here it is, Sondra. I need you to be a diversion. We're still working on the details, it's tremendously risky. I'll tell you all about it when it's completely figured out."

"I'll do whatever you need. You know that."

"It's almost dark. So, for one thing, what I need is for you to kiss me."

It was long and passionate. She felt the same desire for him as before and didn't want this moment to pass. His hands found her waist, and she didn't push him away.

Then he drew back, clasped her hand again, and stood, pulling her to her feet. "You must go, but I'll be in touch soon. Very soon, Sondra."

They walked back to the column. He kept his arm around her as they waited wordlessly for the Mercedes to return. Within two minutes, it came around the traffic circle, barely visible in the deep twilight. Sondra waved to the driver, and the car slowed. Drake stepped away from her, turned toward the forest, and began walking. She knew they couldn't be together. It was, of course, so that they wouldn't jeopardize Black Orchestra's work. She also knew this state of being existed because he couldn't break through his self-imposed nautilus shell.

"Klaus, I've dismissed the housekeeper, cook, and chauffeur," Sondra said as she put her cup of tea down on the bone china saucer. "It's time we talked about something I've wanted to say to you for awhile."

"Then let's get out of this kitchen and go someplace comfortable."

"Take your cup and come this way," she said, waving a hand toward the large living room.

"Your home—charming, but nothing like I will have for you soon, my dear. Nonetheless, thanks for inviting me here. Don't be afraid. I'm not going to attack you," he said with a smirk.

She walked to the velvet-upholstered sofa and moved the pillows before sitting.

"I know that. I think we've come far enough in our relationship that I can trust you. Sit down here next to me."

He sat on the sofa. "For now, Sondra, we have become what I once said to you. 'More than friends but less than lovers.'"

"'More than friends' is the sentiment that led me to invite you to come to see me." She looked at his scarred face and oddly shaped ears. A queasy feeling lurched in her stomach as she considered the possibility of "lovers." But he was better-mannered than usual, and she might find this conversation to be tolerable.

"We have come to know one another, and I confess that I have developed feelings for you that did not exist before," she said, trying to sound sincere.

Würter picked up his cup of tea, his eyes widening. "Your dead husband was not right for you. He provided you with a comfortable existence, but your life with me will be exciting and passionate."

"Don't move too fast, Klaus."

He leaned back, exhaling through pursed lips. "You must make a choice, my darling. You know that I am moving to great success one way or the other. Either as the military leader of a post-Hitler Goerdeler government or, maybe more likely, I'll be the number-two man in Himmler's SS. I shall take you to the heights of wealth and power." He paused, folding his arms, and made direct eye contact with her as a grin crawled across his face.

"Unfortunately, as we both already know, you have just about drained all your husband's wealth. My Wehrmacht people do such excellent research for me. I've learned that the Speier department store is losing money. It's worthless in this wartime economy and cannot be sold. Your inheritance from him is worth nearly nothing at this point. You're broke. That would have happened regardless of whether your feeble old husband would have gotten himself killed or not. It's good he's dead—leaves you for me. Don't trifle with me, my love. If you choose to brush me off, not only will you have no way to support your lifestyle, which means so much to you, but you'll be arrested just like the rest of Black Orchestra, if and when the time comes."

She put the cup and saucer aside. "Did you betray Holger to the Gestapo? You had something to do with his murder by those bastards?"

Würter's eyes went black, looking like flat circles cut out from crepe paper. "Why, how could you think something like that of me? I am what I am, above all else, a nice person." His reply was almost mocking in tone.

"So, now I wonder—what *is* the truth, Klaus?"

"The truth is, I offer you pieces of gold, lovely Sondra, but if you choose wrong, you get lumps of coal. Opportunities with me—are they starting to sound better?"

"Maybe my feelings for you are growing, Klaus. I need time to think."

"Kiss me," he demanded.

They stood and embraced. Sondra kissed him, then backed away. "We will talk again soon, Klaus. Very soon."

Black Orchestra's "code-talk" afforded some degree of safe communication. Even at that, making a connection between the telephone sets of, say, Hans Oster and Ludwig Beck was a potential tip-off to the Gestapo of a conspiracy. The cell members had memorized about 20 code words and used phones only in times of critical need. Hours earlier, Alex Drake had used code words in a call to summon Sondra Speier to another rendezvous.

"You're going to risk your life again." Sondra's eyes glared, her head tipped slightly.

The Bismarck was a small place, empty in the late afternoon, not familiar to either of them. It was a recently-opened eating spot, just a block off the Charlottenburger Chausee, about a kilometer east of the Olympic Village. It was out of the center city, so unlikely that anyone knew them, yet reachable by taxi or car without much difficulty.

Behind the counter, on a glass shelf above the embossed brass cash register, the little Volksempfänger—people's radio—was tuned to the Reich Broadcasting Corporation news. An announcer was reporting on the New Year's Day bombing of the port city of Bremen by the RAF. Then the recorded voice of Hitler boomed from the radio's speaker. "For every English bomb that falls on Germany, a thousand bombs will rain down upon England." His voice sounded like the snarling of a mad dog.

"Bombs," she said quietly, almost whispering. "If he gets his hands on that big bomb, he will only have to drop *one* on London to get his revenge."

Drake twisted his ring as he thought through his reply. "Exactly why we push on with this."

"Our record has proven that this little handful of people can't stop the German Nazi government. I think you've got a death wish. From whom are you trying to escape? Yourself? Your childhood demons? Maybe from me?"

"You know damned well why I'm going this route again. You know the stakes. You've pledged your help."

"I say it because of the traitor to our cause. He'll destroy us."

"We tried to tell Beck it's Würter, but you've found nothing, no proof."

Sondra sat on the edge of the wooden chair and played with the cut glass salt cellar. Her mouth was a straight line. Then, finally, she looked up at him. "I've learned more."

"Oh? What do you know now? Tell me."

"I've said this much to you before—he began to press me for a relationship almost right from the beginning of Black Orchestra—months before they recruited you. I resisted, but not entirely, because he seemed untrustworthy, and I wanted to know if he would demolish the effort and kill my husband."

"And—?"

"He's said something which makes it clear to me that he set up Holger's murder with the Gestapo to make me an unattached woman, even if it destroyed Black Orchestra. He will stop at nothing to achieve his obsessions."

"Then he's both a traitor and a murderer." Drake turned away from her and looked around the café. The door jangled open, ushering in a storm of January air. A young couple walked arm and arm to a booth on the other side of the room. The waitress who had served Alex and Sondra reappeared and headed for the newcomers.

"Alex," Sondra said in a low tone, "we are in a terrible situation if this continues on longer. He knows so much about Beck and Black Orchestra, and he'll spill everything to the Nazis whenever he thinks it will help him. But General Beck won't move."

He turned closer toward her. "Beck should have had Würter killed long ago."

"I've said enough. We both know the danger. So now, what are we going to do?"

The Bayerisches Gasthaus—Bavarian Inn—resort hotel lay across the Havel River from Spandau. In its quiet barroom, Klaus Würter had a table by the window overlooking the frozen water. He could think more clearly when he could see the ice and the trees, stripped of their leaves but delicate and beautiful. The unencumbered view provided him a serenity, which, when combined with alcohol, calmed his demons for a while. If he believed in the existence of souls, he'd think the landscape he observed was strengthening the one inside of him. Long ago, he'd become convinced that absorption in religious piety and superstition was the stuff of old women and puny men. But something like a miracle might be happening within Sondra. She might be starting to believe in his dreams and see that he could achieve his grand victory. He'd dealt with so many obstacles in his time of existence that he knew he would overcome this final adversity and rise to the heights which should already be in his possession. Pain and rebuke would have crushed others who were weaker than he. But for Würter, incidents like these had forged him into the ultimate German superman, the quintessence of Arayan masculinity. Experience and anguish had taught him to ignore the problems of others and concentrate solely on himself. People were mere commodities to be used and exchanged for his gain, and he felt nothing negative about that. Long before Adolf Hitler had shown up with his ideas about German men "as hard as Krupp steel," he had known this to be his destiny. He was a distilled version of the all-inclusive German way of thinking under Nazism, and damned proud of it.

The snake Himmler had lied and not followed through with his part of the bargain for the Bürgerbräukeller information, which had saved Hitler's life. The dictator lived on, and Himmler continued to enjoy his privileged position only because of Würter's tip-off, but his reward was nowhere. So now, he would have to force Himmler to provide the status Klaus knew must be his. And when he moved ahead in his ascendancy to real power and wealth, Sondra wouldn't be the only woman who would submit herself to him. Many of the top men in government, politics, and industry openly kept several mistresses. A life of women, wealth, and satisfaction lay ahead of him when he leveraged his knowledge.

His glass of Kornbrand schnapps was almost empty, and he waved for a second shot. He could sense Sondra was losing her faith and commitment to Black Orchestra and Beck. The Underground group would be wiped out soon, and he needed to distance himself from them. Würter stared out at the icy river and drummed his fingers on the tabletop. A plan was coming together in his mind. A lot of people were going to get killed, and maybe long ago, he might have even given a damn about that. The bartender brought him his next glass of liquor, which he drained in a single, quick motion. He set the glass on the bar and checked his watch. It was time for war.

"Don't think I have forgotten," said Heinrich Himmler. "Your information enabled our great leader to achieve near-martyr status and to unify Germany further. I meant to thank you personally, but you know how hectic things have been since the outbreak of war, and I haven't had a moment." Himmler's eyes were looking out the window beyond Klaus, to the daylight of Prinz Albrecht-Strasse. Würter fidgeted, filled with impatience. He knew immediately where these words were leading.

"You can stop with the excuses. It's long overdue for you to make the public announcement that I'm second in command around here. Do it *now*, or there will be the repercussions which we both know about."

Himmler's eyes returned to look blankly into Würter's face; then, he let go a chuckle. "Oh? Just two days ago, I had a visit from my man Kaltenbrunner. Remember him? He told me about something he claimed he'd just found out, something that I would have thought you would call me about, perhaps stop by and have a friendly chat. He told me of the loss of an urgently needed material for the big bomb project. It happened *weeks ago*. People have kept that trifle of information from me. Many, including you, must have known about it."

Würter's head jerked back—Himmler's words had grabbed him entirely off guard. "What are you talking about?"

"A break-in at the secret project headquarters building. Two *Schurke* criminals entered through an abandoned tunnel and destroyed the stocks of an extremely hard-to-obtain substance. It puts the project back by months—maybe years. I've blamed it on the British, but do you know something?"

Würter stared blankly at the pinprick eyes of the SS leader, unsure of what he would hear next but realizing he was in serious trouble.

"I think it was Ludwig Beck, your old boss and mate. He must have found some traitors to do the work for him. One miscreant bastard was killed, and we eventually identified him—a person we've known to be hostile to the Party and a friend of Beck. Name was Dietrich Born, a churchman. Know him?"

"Hell no. What are you insinuating? Do you think I was somehow involved? I know nothing about it."

"Nothing about it? You should have known about this attempt to destroy something of such importance to the Reich—through your Beck connection. You should have told me. Do you have any idea what's going to happen to the people who knew of this but didn't tell me?"

"I said I didn't know anything about it."

"You are a high-ranking officer in the Wehrmacht and have sworn an oath of loyalty to the *Führer*. Perhaps you remember that little item?"

"Everyone in the military has sworn that oath."

"Does it occur to you that your failure to report Beck's activities makes you nothing more than a traitor? You won't be surprised to learn that I've denied your promotion. By the way, my best people have worked hard to find your accomplice and capture his photos and recordings. Have you tried to call him lately? No answer, perhaps? That's because neither he nor his materials exist anymore. Can you guess what happened to the wire recordings? The steel recording wire was wrapped around his neck to strangle him. You can try going to Bormann with your copies, but the same fate which met your friend awaits you. Checkmate, General Würter."

Würter felt more hot blood rushing to his face. *Dietrich Born*, he thought. *Those swine held this from me!*

"You'd better find out everything you can about this clique of Beck's traitors and report their crimes directly to me. Don't come back until you are prepared to spill everything about them, and when you come here, bring your pictures and recordings with you. Make that tomorrow. It's simple for you, Klaus, become a hero to Reich—or become a corpse," Himmler stood and walked toward his intercom box. "Get out of here, right now!"

Würter stood and snatched his hat from the table.

"Information about Beck, Klaus. All of it this time."

Würter went through the door, his heart throbbing under his uniform jacket. He strode quickly through the office containing Himmler's underlings and pulled open the door to the corridor.

He walked to the elevator and, in minutes, was out of the building and onto the sidewalk. He realized he'd been caught—maybe fatally—between his twin intrigues with Black Orchestra and Himmler. But, by handing over Black Orchestra, he could still reach the top of the government. He would spill Black Orchestra members' names and simultaneously implicate his superior officer General Halder as Beck's accomplice. That would reinstate his power with Himmler and revitalize his plan for eminence. His mind was starting to clear; a slow smile began to spread across his face. All these conspiratorial clowns, especially the damned American Drake, were about to depart this planet. A planet Klaus Würter would rule.

CHAPTER 37

ENERGY

"A coward turns away, but a brave man's choice is danger."

Euripides, *Iphigenia in Tauris, ca.* 412 BC

SONDRA FELT SLIGHTLY MORE SPIRITED after walking a few blocks around her neighborhood in the sharp, cold air of early January. The artificial lower leg made walking mildly painful and uncertain, but the exertion coupled with the sight of people helped to diminish some of her unease which had been building for days. She looked back, trying to ascertain if anyone was following her. The side door to her house was slightly ajar—very odd. For a moment, she thought about her husband's killers. *Just walk away—find a pay telephone. Call Alex or Joachim for help.* She dismissed her fears and pushed the door open.

Würter! He stood in the same place where months earlier, the Gestapo thug had confronted her.

"Why, good afternoon, my love," he said in a harsh voice, the ceiling light washing across his facial scars, accentuating them. He walked across the tile floor and took her arm in his fist. "Shocked to see me so soon?"

"I—yes, I'm surprised. What made you come back?"

"The Black Orchestra vermin. I just now learned that there has been an attack on the atom bomb project building. They kept me ignorant of this. Why did you and the rest hide it from me?" He stepped closer to her, his ears red. For the first time, she was genuinely afraid of him.

"No, Klaus. I know nothing of an attack. Believe me."

He watched her face intently. "I thought you'd say that, and I've made a decision. It's time that you and I cut all ties with Black Orchestra. Get away from them. You know as well as I do—they are all rabble and will be caught up in a mass arrest. Soon."

"Why do you say that? What's going on?"

He grinned, the whites of his eyes invisible as the lids narrowed. "I, of course, know nothing specific. But the day can't be far off when Himmler pounces like a jaguar on a jackrabbit."

"What do you want from me?"

"Pack a few things. I'll come back for you in an hour. We're going away for a long-overdue week together, someplace far from here. I don't want you anywhere near them. We'll stay in a chalet in the Bavarian Alps for a while. I need to keep you in my sight to be sure you are safe."

She shifted her hips uncomfortably as her index finger found her lower lip. The walls were closing in around her. "Klaus, I don't want trouble for either you or me. We'll just back away from them. Let them figure out that we're no longer involved. My feelings for you have changed, and I've come to loathe Beck and the others."

Würter, startled to hear these words he'd longed to hear, leaned over, pulled her close, and kissed her deeply. She surrendered a kiss back, struggling not to flinch. He kissed her again, and his body pressed her against the wall as his hands dropped down along her hips.

Sondra pushed back. "No, it's not a good moment for that. Let's wait until we are out of this town and can enjoy each other. Let me pack my things, bathe, and get ready for you."

"I didn't sense much passion in your kiss. That's fine. It will change, and soon you will show me all the emotions you have pent up inside."

"Maybe you're right, Klaus. Now, let me get ready to go with you."

"I'll come back in an hour with my things and pick you up. Tell no one of this trip—it's just you and me."

She turned and walked along the hallway. Pulling the bedroom door behind her, she clutched her arms around herself and looked in the mirror. She barely recognized her own face—worn, tired. She bent across the washbasin and splashed cold water across her mouth, her thoughts tangled and strange. Dark hair fell across her face as she stepped back and twisted the door handle again. The sound of a car's starter motor outside. "He's gone," she said in a soft voice.

Doubts about Black Orchestra's chances to stop the Nazi atom bomb washed over her again. Würter could be her deliverance—her way to get free of all the worry and risk—to quell the fears of being arrested and tortured in the same way as Holger, no financial ruin, a top-level position in the hierarchy of the Nazi Party, a life of protection and riches. All she needed to do was go with Würter, enter his sanctuary, and let the gods sort out the world's future. Shrewd, beguiling temptations were hanging out in front of her.

Sondra couldn't control her hand tremors. She cried out at the ceiling. "Holger, what now? Where do I go?"

She returned to the table, clenching her hands. Images of the last night in the *Kabarett* played back in her brain—the Nazi's knife, the shock of those moments after she awakened from the surgery to see only one foot pushing up under the sheet, the pain of fitting the prosthesis to her stump. She thought of her vow to never again be in a position where she would be poor, as she was before becoming a Beauty Girl. She had survived all those troubled times. But now—the stakes at this instant were far more significant than just her situation. Now the world must endure. She turned her head. Sondra had her decision.

She stepped into the kitchen and looked to the table where the telephone sat on a white silk cloth. Touching the back of her neck and glancing around, she walked toward the black instrument, lifted the handset, and dialed.

The phone buzzed in her ear for what seemed like a long time. *"Hallo."*

"Mars—apothecary, right now!" She slapped the handset back down onto the telephone box.

Sondra saw Alex Drake's wavy black hair as she entered the lunchroom of *die Apotheke*. In a dimly lit corner booth, he was looking down, scowling, moving his finger around the rim of his cup.

"Thanks for coming so quickly. I hate to add to your anxiety," she said.

"'Anxious' is our life these days." Drake stood and grasped her hand. "What's this about?"

"Sit with me—we must talk, and don't have much time."

They took a booth with high backs and a blue oilcloth table cover. Drake motioned to the waitress, and soon, black coffee was delivered. They didn't talk until they were sure there were no unwelcomed ears nearby.

Sondra was out of breath before she started. "Würter has been at my house, and he is going to tell the SS everything he knows about Beck and our group. He told me his plans. I was right the entire time—he's the traitor, and everyone's going to be arrested."

Drake studied her face for a moment. "*Damn.* Here it is, finally. Where is he now?"

"I think he's on his way to his house—to get his clothes."

"His house? Then what?"

"Then probably to SS headquarters—to Himmler. He said he's coming back for me in an hour, so he's moving fast."

"Pray that he doesn't go to the SS first. I'm going to try to catch him at his house. You go to the general's home to tell him what's happening."

"No, Alex! Don't go there alone!"

He grabbed his coat, stood, and turned away.

He'd been to Würter's home with Beck. It was on the south side of the city, a half-hour by U-Bahn. The Berlin telephone directory provided the general's address and telephone number. A hang-up call from a telephone booth to Würter confirmed he was in there. Drake felt pressure on his skull wound as he looked at his fellow riders in the subway car. He had no gun, no knife, a hole in his head—which meant he had only his diminished athleticism to rely on. He sensed death pressing in on him like a vise. But Würter must be stopped.

It was nearly seven o'clock, and north German winter darkness had descended on Berlin as Drake pushed his way through the exit turnstile of the Bahnhof and out onto the street, opening then clenching his hands as he walked.

Würter had a small home, built in the pre-1914 compact style. Leafless trees lined the boulevard, and each block had a streetlight hanging in the roadway center, suspended from iron posts with ornate latticework. He counted seven of them before his eyes caught the shape of the house he sought. The address number was barely visible in the dim light of the streetlamp's illumination. He walked up the pathway. His heart pounded faster as he knocked.

"Who's there?" The voice came loudly.

"Drake. Open up."

The door swung. A scarred, scowling face came into view.

"You! What do you want?"

"Let me in."

"Get the hell out of here, *Müll.*" In English, the word meant garbage.

Drake jammed the door against Würter's body, driving him backward and into the main room. In an instant, he was inside and standing less than a meter from his adversary.

"Who have you told about Black Orchestra and our work?"

"A stinking foreigner, coming here and talking like this to me. I'll tell anybody I want to about anything, and you're not going to stop me." His breath came heavy with liquor.

"I know you tipped off the Gestapo about the Bürgerbräukeller bomb."

"You're a fool." Würter threw his cigar toward the wall and took a step toward Drake. "Gonna whip you good. Wouldn't that be funny? All that crap about 1923, your father being there at the Munich *Putsch* and getting in the way of the revolution. I was there! Ha! They took good care of him. And now you're gonna get your own damned head opened up!" Würter's glassy red eyes fluttered as his rage built. Then, suddenly, his hand darted upward to toss the remaining contents of his glass into Drake's face.

Drake lurched backward, blinded by the alcohol in his eyes. Würter sprang toward his foe and whipped a knee into Drake's groin, doubling him over in agony. He dropped and rolled under the dining table.

Würter circled, laughing, kicking the chairs toward him, then grabbed something from the cabinet behind him.

Drake squinted and saw his opponent's legs lined up with a chair. From under the table, he kicked out at the chair with all his remaining energy.

The chair legs flew sideways, and Würter grunted as Drake rolled and jumped to his feet. Then he glimpsed Würter's hand, the fingers squeezing the handle of a foot-long knife.

The German recovered his balance and wiped his forehead, his eyes bulging from their sockets.

"See this blade? Your father—a half-Jew bastard. Shake hands with him again."

Drake's smirking opponent was coming faster, waving the shiny blade.

Suddenly, Würter leaped at him with surprising speed, whipping the knife, missing Drake's throat by less than an inch. Drake's quickness, although diminished, bought him another chance.

The German neatly swung back with his other hand and caught Drake solidly with a stone-hard fist to the side of his skull, just below the area of the fracture. Drake's field of vision became a blinding bright yellow wall. He rolled onto the floor again, to the center of the room, spinning across the braided carpet.

Würter slashed at him with the knife, another narrow miss. Drake kicked at the ghostly image of his attacker, his shoe finding a leg, forcing Würter to stumble back, clutching at his thigh, his mouth twisting in agony.

Drake got to his feet and backpedaled toward the fireplace, trying to blink away the fog which clouded his vision. He had to take advantage of the one hard blow he'd landed. Würter came toward him, jabbing the knife toward his midsection. Drake caught his outstretched arm, and they fell to the floor and rolled. The German got the upper position, holding the blade between them, their arms locked in a vibrating struggle. Drake groaned, his back pinned against the floor with the knife above his face. Then, something moved—his vision was still no good, his eyes not aligning right. *Something—*

"*Ja*" Würter made a sound that was part moan and part scream as a wooden object came out of nowhere and hit him solidly on the side of the head. His grip on the carving knife went limp, and its handle shot upward, slamming the underside of his jaw, snapping his teeth together with a loud *clack*. The knife clattered to the floor.

Drake glanced toward the figure holding the wooden piece and gasped.

Sondra Speier was balancing herself against a chair back, holding her prosthetic leg in one hand. It had smashed Würter's right ear—he was dazed, blood starting to run down his neck. She dropped the prosthesis and fell toward the knife. She seized it and sprung toward Würter.

"*Traitor!* You bastard! Months of faked feelings for you! Nazi filth like the one who cut me—made me wear this leg, you rotten *pig!*"

Würter's eyes bulged as he glimpsed Sondra coming toward him, the knife gripped in her small fist. The handle rhythmically whacked the wooden floor as she used her hands to crawl toward him.

"*Aaag! Nein!* The dazed German tried to sit up. The knife thrust toward his neck, but he unwisely jerked in the wrong direction, the blade finding his left eye socket instead, plunging through until her hand was hard against his face. His head slammed back onto the wooden floor as he expelled a final gasp of air.

Sondra fell backward, her fingers clawing at her cheeks as her body shook uncontrollably.

"Oh God! I've killed him. I've killed Klaus!" She sobbed, rolling over to glance at Drake. "Blood—it's everywhere, coming out of his face!"

Drake raised himself to one knee, utterly exhausted but ignoring his pain.

"How did you get here?"

The beige leather jacket she wore was splattered with blood. She sat up and leaned against the wall, burying her face in her hands.

"You saved my life!" Drake said, gasping for air. "If you hadn't done that, the knife—"

She cut him off. "We've got to go!" she said in a quaking voice.

His arms were trembling, his breath still coming out in gasps. "Würter was *there*—the day of my father's murder in Munich—said he saw it all. Body's gonna stay right there until I figure a way to dispose of him," said Drake. "Why didn't your driver come in with you? Can you trust him with knowing what happened here?"

"I told him to stay in the car, to let me talk to the two of you. But, yes, I've told you before that he's to be trusted."

"Then have him come in. We'll wrap the damned body in that rug and take it on a one-way ride into the woods north of the city."

Sondra touched his hand. Her face was pale white. "Alex, my leg—please hand it to me."

Drake obliged and looked away as she took the prosthesis and raised her skirt to reattach it to her lower leg. He stood slowly, his head throbbing where the blow had landed, then helped her to her feet. They kissed for a brief moment. She headed toward the door and went out into the blackness of the December night.

He walked over to one of the overturned chairs, swung it upright, and then dropped himself heavily on the seat as he experienced a startling new sensation—like a too-tight jacket had been stripped from his body, releasing him to breathe, to feel human again. Death lay next to Alex Drake, but life was flowing into him, derived from the destruction of one of his father's killers. Four times he'd tricked the grim reaper, but he sensed deep in his chest that this had been his final free pass—there would be no more deliverances.

CHAPTER 38

DIVERSION

"If Adam had seen in a vision the horrible instruments
his children were to invent, he would have died of grief."

Martin Luther, *Table Talk*, sec. 820 (1569)

KURT DIEBNER HADN'T HAD A decent night's sleep in the month
since the Virus House break-in, not more than a couple of hours of
rest each night. Today was the accursed day that would most probably
result in the end of his life. He was under orders to revisit the Reich
Chancellery to report on the progress of the Virus House project to
Adolf Hitler. This time, however, he would not be going alone—
Heinrich Himmler would accompany him. The limousine picked him
up at precisely 2 p.m. in front of the Pickelhaube, then drove to SS
headquarters. In the basement garage, the SS leader stepped out of the
elevator and walked to the vehicle. The driver moved quickly to open
the right rear door as the thin man got inside.

"Well, *Doktor Diebner*," Himmler said with a mocking, derisive
tone in his voice, "prepare yourself for an extremely ugly discussion

with *der Führer*. Both he and I have just learned that you've had a major setback in your atom project. A break-in. How could you be such a damned buffoon as to let this happen? I hope you've put your personal matters in order because I can't tell you what the outcome will be of this discussion."

Diebner felt fear overtaking him and fought to summon calm. "It may not be as bad a setback as you are thinking, sir. Yes, the material we were planning to use in the uranium conversion process—called heavy water—was far too difficult to obtain. It would have required this nation to invest in a lengthy hydroelectric dam-building project in Norway to obtain enough to be of use in manufacturing the new explosive element. It took the Norwegians *decades* to make their first drop of it. We would have had to expand the plant a hundredfold, taking years."

"Save your explanations for the leader and hope that he accepts it because if he doesn't, it will cost you dearly. Neither he nor I will accept incompetence with this project."

"Yes, sir, and I remain optimistic." Diebner's positivity was belied by the shaking in his hands and the sweat rolling down his forehead, neither of which he could control.

The limousine ride was only five minutes, terminating in front of the main entrance to the Reich Chancellery. The two men were quickly admitted through the vestibule security apparatus and taken to Hitler's third-floor office.

Himmler closed the door and walked toward the sofa where the dictator of Germany sat with his hands folded in his lap. *"Mein Führer*, we are here to discuss the atomic bomb project with you as you have requested."

"Now, it's a month since you were here, and I ordered you to report progress within that time. Sit over there. *Herr Atomic Bomb*, I'm told you've gone backward! What the hell did you and your idiots do to cause this?"

Diebner saw black dots in front of his eyes—was he passing out? He wondered if these next minutes would mark the end of his life. That probably depended on how well he could explain the break-in, the loss of the heavy water, and his plan going forward. *Oh, no!* Two guards entered the room from a side door. They'd clearly been watching for some kind of signal from the dictator.

"Sir," Diebner said haltingly, "Indeed, there has been a setback in our progress. Criminals broke into our laboratory; we don't know where they came from or who they are affiliated with. Our guards killed one of them, the other escaped, and the Gestapo is still hunting for him. They destroyed material we were planning to use in experiments to make the explosive for a bomb, but that material was already problematic due to its extreme scarcity. Moreover, to make enough of the heavy water substance to begin manufacturing the explosive material would take years of expansion of the plant in Norway, or in the alternative, creating a new plant within this nation. Either one requires a long period of construction. And thus far, there is not the slightest actual proof that this substance would even work in the conversion of uranium."

Hitler seemed to be trying to control himself, perhaps realizing that an outburst would gain nothing. "When *Herr Himmler* informed me of this situation, my immediate reaction was to order your execution and for your replacement to be a military general. However, I recognized that would probably lead to even more delays because such a person would know nothing of your science. So, I am going to spare your life and your position for now. I will listen to whatever alternative plan you have come up with." He looked beyond Diebner. "You men—go back into your places there."

As the guards turned away, Diebner felt an enormous surge of relief—he would be able to live on, accomplish his work using a different path. "My leader, yes, I have a better plan than the original, and we are taking steps now to identify a superior and more readily available ingredient to be used in an all-new process. Testing is imminent on this material, and if successful, it should enable us to move even faster than originally anticipated. When I came here before, sir, I tried to clarify that there was a lot of work required to find materials and processes of which we know nothing yet. But as we discussed, the potential payoff for success is so colossal that we do not take failures as being dead ends. We continue on until successful."

"You've lost valuable time! You'd better get this right!" Hitler said, the volume of his voice swelling. "I'm not sure at this point if any of your scientific double-talk is going to lead anywhere, but you must find out. So keep going, and no more security lapses or stupidity! Your new boss is sitting right next to you, and henceforth you will report to him on your progress every week."

"Yes, thank you, *Führer,*" said Himmler, straightening the front of his uniform.

"One other thing," Hitler said. "Diebner, I told you before to determine if our enemies were getting this weapon. What have you found?"

"My people and *Herr Himmler's* scientific staff have searched every international publication and found nothing indicating progress on the other side. Nothing's been published, no scientific papers presented. So that means, sir, that everything has been classified secret by these foreign governments, or there's just nothing going on because someone's already found out that the atomic bomb is not possible."

"Heinrich, tell Canaris to make his spies figure this out without delay. I want another report from you and him by Monday. Now get out of here and back to work."

"I will see *Generalmajor* Oster at once!"

The office secretary's gray hair was pulled back into a small bun on the top of her head. She gave out a sneering snort, seemingly unimpressed by the black SS uniform of the man in front of her. Schoe was puzzled since it usually evoked fear and provided access to just about anywhere for anyone wearing it. She was probably well-accustomed to the sight of SS coming and going from Oster's office and was no longer intimidated.

"I cannot interrupt him. He is busy. Write your name here, and when it looks like I can break in on him—"

"*Madame,* you will break in *now.* He will want you to interrupt. My name is not important. Just tell him one word: Wells."

She stood, shot a frown at the SS officer, and showed no haste as she went through the door to the office area. Schoe pulled a slip of paper from his lapel pocket, looked at it, and then glanced up and down the lobby.

Minutes later, she returned, accompanied by a jovial-looking man in a gray army uniform.

"*Oberleutenant!* SS business cannot wait. Please, into my office, and tell me what *Herr Himmler* has for the Abwehr to work on." Schoe recoiled slightly—Oster's ebullience was, as usual, somewhat overwhelming to the mild Ph.D. chemist-turned-SS officer. He stood and shook hands with the Intelligence leader, who turned to walk ahead of him down the marble-walled corridor.

Oster motioned toward a leather visitor's chair across from his broad oaken desk as they entered the spacious, thickly carpeted office. "Please, sit. To cause you to come here, this must be something about the carbon graphite test."

"Precisely. Let's go for a walk."

"Yes. I will meet you at the northeast corner of the library building in a few minutes."

Schoe looked down as he walked past the receptionist. Dragging the door open, he felt the snow falling, the cold wind causing him to pull the collar of his outer coat up around his neck. He walked three blocks and waited in the January cold, facing toward the granite wall of the building.

He heard footsteps coming fast.

"Very well," Oster said. "What do you have? The seventeenth is only days away."

"Drake has come up with something, a possible pathway to derail the experiment. Beck and I think it could be made to work, but it will take a tremendous effort by you and your Abwehr laboratory."

Schoe's words were interrupted by the approach of three men in army uniform.

"This way, Schoe. Keep walking."

"We need answers. If you must bribe, blackmail, or threaten, do it. Besides us, only Beck and Drake know anything about it—the fewer exposed, the less chance that something will get out."

"Go on."

"Your spies and operatives must get a photograph or very accurate sketch of the packaging for the shipping crate, labels, and anything else, down to the most intricate detail."

Oster nodded. They stopped walking. "How in God's name would I do that?"

"That's not all. First, you have to find a way to create a duplicate of the carbon graphite sample being made for Diebner's test."

Oster was swaying back and forth, eyes downcast. "You must be kidding."

Schoe continued. "No contaminants—the graphite must be perfectly pure, except for one huge thing. It must be poisoned so that it plausibly fails the test, and therein rests another overpowering problem for us. Yesterday morning, Drake and I composed and sent a microdot message to Leo Szilard in the United States, seeking an answer for how to spoil the carbon graphite, a way to make it fail, but in a manner in which our tampering cannot ever be detected."

The SS officer looked around and then pulled a sheaf of paper from his jacket pocket. "Look—here is what was sent. An earlier transmission has verified that Szilard had purchased the microdot decryption machine."

Oster scanned the words.

To LS from AD—New Virus House report states CARBON GRAPHITE may function for making explosive element 94. If so, need exact instructions on how to spoil carbon to make it fail test. Use telegram, no time to mail microdot. Nazis will see telegram, so use extreme caution, send code-speak message addressed to Drake at <u>World Week Berlin bureau</u>. All is at stake. MUST HAVE ANSWER BY TENTH OF JANUARY.

"If Szilard can give us direction—what to do to nullify the graphite, then whatever is the material to be added, it must be located and compounded into the sample, and the sample must be switched with the original coming from Siemens."

Oster's face clouded over with a leaden frown. "Good Christ! You don't want much, do you? You can't even tell me what kind of fairy dust

I'm supposed to sprinkle on that *Scheißedreck* to fix everything. How in hell can I do all of this in a few days?"

Schoe cocked his head while raising his eyebrows. "Can you?"

"It's impossible! But, unless we screw up this test for them, Hitler has the carolinum for his nice little fifty-million-times-TNT bomb!"

"We destroy their test, or our world is destroyed."

"I don't know where to begin. This, I must discuss openly, directly with Canaris. I will need every gram of his help."

Schoe scratched his forehead, mulling over the overwhelming job ahead. In addition to the microdot, a code-speak telegram from "AD" to Dr. Szilard had gone out to alert him to the incoming microdot message, but the letter containing the microdot would require at least four days to get to Szilard in New York via the Pan Am Clipper airmail service. If the plane falls out of the sky, the world perishes with it. After that, Szilard would have to read the microdot, figure out the answer—if there was one—and get an ordinary-appearing telegram containing coded instructions back within a day to give the Abwehr a chance to contaminate the faked sample of carbon. Of course, Oster had to accomplish all the things that had been asked of him. Then, somehow, pull off the switch. He suddenly felt like a poker player looking at the hand being dealt to him, realizing that the cards had to reveal themselves as nothing less than a royal flush in exact sequence.

He grasped the truth: *it couldn't be done.*

CHAPTER 39

SUNBURST

"Mighty events turn on a straw."

Thomas Carlyle *ca.* 1840

WITH ALL ITS UGLY CONNOTATIONS, *extermination* was the lens through which Drake viewed Würter's demise, but Beck would see it differently—maybe. The general's butler stepped aside when Drake barged through the front door and made his way to the study.

"Würter is dead."

"Dead!" Beck shouted.

"It happened yesterday. We fought. He tried to kill me, General. A knife. Him or me—it was that simple." Drake walked around the end of the wooden table and put one foot up on a cane-back chair.

"And you wait to tell me now? What the hell's happened? How will this not come back to destroy Black Orchestra?"

"He told Sondra that he was going to spill everything about Black Orchestra to the SS—he was done with us and was going to turn us in. She managed to get in touch with me, and I went after him, to stop him before he went to Himmler. He almost had me, but she'd come to the house and saw the fight. She hit him while we were battling, and his knife went into him. Sondra saved me. She typed a suicide note telling of his agony in dealing with his failures, and it said he'd jumped in the Havel River. Her chauffeur and I cleaned everything up and took his corpse to the forest. Wolves will finish him off in a few days; no trace will be left."

"Würter was our single conduit to the Army," Beck declared. "Now, there's no connection between General Halder and us. This happens on the eve of our most important mission!"

"It also means that the betrayal of the Bürgerbräukeller will not be repeated."

"How could you have beaten him? You've been recovering from your injuries for only weeks—you were dead yourself a short time ago. Where could you get this strength?"

Drake played with the diamond ring on his finger. "I'll tell you about it someday."

The stairs squeaked loudly in protest as Drake began his descent to Black Orchestra's meeting place. A single bulb dimly lit the first few treads; light from the room below fell across the remaining steps. *Voices*—he was probably the last to arrive again. He hadn't been to this room under the Speier warehouse in months, but his key still worked in the lock, and nothing seemed to have changed. Tonight, their courage and unity would be ruthlessly tested.

General Beck was sitting at the head of the table, his head lowered. Next to a glass-shaded lamp, Schoe and Oster stood talking. "Sit down. We start immediately," Beck said. "We have agreed that Drake's plan has only a slim chance of success, but it's all we have. Time and realities have converged, so we take action now, regardless. Your update please, *Generalmajor*."

"Time is absurdly against us, my colleagues," said the Abwehr spymaster. "Today is Sunday, the fifth of January. Bothe's laboratory will test the carbon sample at the University of Heidelberg on Friday, the seventeenth. That's only *twelve days,* and we have nothing yet. The date of its shipment from Siemens in Berlin to Heidelberg is set for fifteen January. Therefore, the substitute, which I am having made at the Abwehr *Gruppe I-K* technical research unit, must be ready no later than January fourteen. That's our final deadline for completion."

"Ten days," Beck said, "that's all we have to accomplish what's needed to put a tainted carbon graphite sample on a train when we have started nothing yet? Do you even know what you're supposed to do, for God's sake?"

"One big thing's done, General. Yesterday, the Abwehr embedded a mole at the Siemens plant," Oster said. "He took an amazing risk to photograph Diebner's sample shipping container, labels, even a photograph of the shipping box to be used, enabling my exact duplicate to be constructed by *Gruppe I-K.*"

General Beck's face registered skepticism.

Oster continued as his mouth drooped into a vinegary expression. "We've learned a great deal. The Virus House sample is a six-and-a-half kilogram—fourteen-pound—sphere of the purest available carbon graphite. Siemens will put it through cleaning with deionized water, then conduct spectroscopic analyses to detect any foreign substances. That brings me to the most irresolvable problem. My *Gruppe I-K,* cloaked in complete secrecy, must know the answer to the most fundamental question: How do we make our duplicate material fail the Heidelberg testing?"

Beck turned to his right. "Schoe, what, if anything, have you learned about means to scupper the carbon graphite?"

"The Telex radiotelegram system is our only reliable communication with Szilard in New York. Since the Reichspost operates it, it's certain that the Nazis carefully monitor any messages sent. Even code-speak telegram communications between Szilard and us risk the chance of being traced to us. We sent the microdot message to Szilard in New York yesterday. Our question is too complex to be understood by telegram. It requires information to be sent back to Drake by Friday the tenth, via telegram," Schoe said. "Takes five or six days for our letter to get to New York by airmail—at best. It's going to be extremely tight. If it takes a week or more, we're dead."

Oster rubbed his chin and spoke. "Let's hope it works because, in our Abwehr laboratory, nobody knows a *damned thing* about atomic physics. If I try to recruit a Virus House scientist to help, I might get an answer, but at huge risk that I'd hit upon a Hitler loyalist who would tip off Diebner. Tenth of January—unless we get Szilard's directions by then, we are *erledigt für*—done for."

"Now six days," Schoe said quietly.

No one moved or conversed. Drake saw the image of a carbon sphere in his mind—like a miniature black Perisphere from *The World of Tomorrow*. Rumbles of thunder reached the cellar, sounding like RAF bombs for a moment, but the rolling reverberations signaled that it was nature's audible calling card.

The door above the room was being unlocked and pulled open. All four men swung their heads toward the stairway. The sound of footsteps could be heard on the treads, but it wasn't of heavy police jackboots. Slowly, in the dim light, small black shoes came into view. A few more steps, then the oval face of Sondra Speier was before them, her dark eyes shining.

Drake pushed back, stood, and approached her. "Gentlemen, I asked her to come here tonight. There is an important part missing in the plan. It requires something that only she can do."

Sondra pulled the woolen scarf from around her neck. "Whatever I must do to stop Nazis, to bring them down, to keep them away from that awful weapon, I'll do."

General Beck turned to look directly into her eyes. *"Frau Speier,* please sit. There is a vital role for you in this." He folded his hands on the tabletop and leaned toward her. "It's to effectively catch the attention of—call it *lure away*—anyone who tries to interfere with the most crucial seconds of this plan."

She sat straight. "Sounds like you're asking me to become a whore."

"Don't worry, you'll keep your clothes on. But your appearance qualifies you to do a little play-acting. Drake will instruct you on exactly what you've got to do. Are you all right with this?"

"Yes. I am, General. He's already taken me through the basic idea, and I've long ago learned 'play-acting.' I can do it pretty well. So, what about this professor who will oversee the Heidelberg test and report the results?" Sondra asked. "Can't we flip him to our side? Forget the switching of samples. Get him to fake the test result!"

Twisting in his chair to look at her, Schoe spoke. "We know things about Professor Bothe, this man designated by Diebner to test the effects of graphite. In 1934, Nazis in Heidelberg tried to have him removed from his academic position, and Bothe lost his job as the university's Director of the Department of Physics. *Why?* Because his wife was Jewish."

Sondra shook her head. "Disgusting, but not surprising. But what I said works, doesn't it?"

"How the devil do we know what his attitude toward the Nazi regime is seven years later?" Beck said. "Would he cooperate with us against them? If Bothe fears that a later test could reveal his lie, would he work with us or turn us in to the SS to save himself?"

"Here's the thing," Drake said. "We've decided that we would leave Bothe a virgin and make him an unwitting pawn in the game. In that way, we spare him the knowledge of our substituting contaminated carbon graphite, and he could never reveal anything. Moreover, Bothe's Nazi troubles in the past give us plenty of reason to believe that he won't be too aggressive in searching for a retest which might threaten the secret of our contaminated sample."

Schoe followed up on those words. "If our swap falls apart, we'll be left with trying to appeal to Bothe's anti-Nazi leanings—an ultimate last-ditch effort to keep the secret of carbon graphite safe. I'll bet he'd turn us in simply because he can't assume that we weren't putting him to the test for the Nazis. He can't take that chance."

Sondra's face showed skepticism, but it wasn't her decision to make. And now they were five—Drake, Beck, Oster, Schoe, and herself, a tiny group of souls bound together in a final, frantic, impossible effort to halt the Nazi atom bomb project.

"From here on," Ludwig Beck said, "we communicate individually. We may never see one another again, so I wish you God's protection and inspiration."

Sondra Speier was last to leave, locking up her warehouse for the final time for Black Orchestra.

After the others had said their *Guten Nachts* to one another, Drake waited for her outside the building.

She opened the door. He was standing in the glow of the bare bulb which hung outside the entranceway. "Alex! You frightened me."

"Sorry. I couldn't leave you in there alone."

"I'm glad you stayed. Come back inside."

He pulled the door closed as she touched the sleeve of his woolen overcoat, then put her hand on the gentle fold of its lapel.

"There is one other thing I couldn't say in front of the others, Alex. I don't entirely know what it is yet that you need me to do, but you can trust me with it because I've fallen in love with you."

He moved closer. "I feel the same," he said.

This time, their kiss was going to take much longer. When it stopped for a few seconds, she grasped his hand and led him back down the basement stairway.

CHAPTER 40

TELEGRAM

"We are never deceived; we deceive ourselves."

Johann Wolfgang Von Goethe (1830)

NEW YORK CITY, SATURDAY, JANUARY 11, 1941

"JENÓ! OPEN! IT IS ME! Szilard knocked hard, six or eight raps, and pressed his body against the door.

Wigner swung the door open. "Leo—what?"

"Information from Berlin, from Drake and the others. It is about the carbon—we must give them help."

Wigner clasped his hands to his chest, waiting for the sentence to follow.

"Jenó, a microdot message, sent to me—I read it with the machine. Drake requests information on modifying a carbon graphite sample to cause a German test of it to fail. We must tell them today! Coded telegram must be sent back—no time for transatlantic mail delivery of a microdot."

"This certainly means the Underground is trying to deceive the Nazi atom program, throw them off the carbon secret. There's no other explanation, and they *must* succeed!"

Szilard paced in circles around Wigner's living room. "Enrico Fermi and I had very bad problems with graphite tests last summer. We could not get the graphite blocks to give consistent results. Something was wrong—some sample blocks did not measure correctly—very different from others when they should have all been the same. *Impurity.* Some contained an impurity, made them no good."

"Yes, that's right, I remember," said Wigner. "Off by two hundred percent."

"Finally, we identified this impurity as the element boron and eliminated it. Boron—a dark powder—that is what we tell Beck to use! But how much? Too little or too much will make results questionable, might be retested with new samples. I must find my notes from last year—make calculations of how much boron."

"You say *today* it needs to be communicated back to Drake?" asked Wigner. "Impossible!"

"We have to get him a message by a simple code-speak telegram sent through an open channel which Nazis will monitor. Jenó Pál, you must help to compose a telegram. We must word it so it cannot be detected for what it is."

"We will call Fermi long-distance in Chicago *right now,*" Wigner added. "God, I hope he can be found. When we get our calculations done, he will need to run tests with his cyclotron, even if it takes all night. We only have a few hours. Our answer might come a day late, but the continued existence of humanity depends on us getting this right."

Drake had been seething in his apartment all day. Szilard's reply was a day overdue. It was already the eleventh—late in the afternoon. He sipped a glass of water and put the copy of the Nazi Party newspaper *Der Angriff–The Attack*—on the table in front of him.

Then, at 4:50 p.m., a knock at the door. *"Herr Drake, bitte?"*

*"Nur einen Augenblick—*Just one moment."

He swung the door open. The yellow envelope was placed in his hand by a uniformed delivery boy, not older than sixteen. *"Danke,"* he said, and the courier was gone.

Drake slid the envelope open and pulled out the page with five narrow yellow tape strips glued to it. He read the words pasted to the page, then kept staring at the sheet, thoroughly puzzled.

Telefunken Telegramm

Datum: ZEIT 23:08 11 JANUAR 1940

Nach: HERR DRAKE BERLIN 150 INVALIDENSTRASSE HALTEN

Von: HERR LEO S HOLSTEN WESTERN UNION OFFICE NEW YORK HALTEN

Nachricht: SIE MUESSEN TEST ZERSTOREN HALTEN MENDELEEV B HALTEN SEHR KLEIN HALTEN POINT 0004 GRAM SQ CM ZUR OBERFLACHE HALTEN

"Gibberish," he muttered. But the first four words translated as YOU MUST DESTROY THE TEST. "Halten"—STOP, like a period, was just about the only other thing he understood. *Mendeleev B*—what was that? A chemical? Drake pushed his hair into place and, shifting his weight from one leg to the other, unbuttoned his jacket.

"Now *think!* 'Leo S Holsten,'" he said aloud. "'Leo S' means it's from Szilard. Holsten—the main character in *The World Set Free,* the fictional discoverer of carolinum, so it's how to block the test."

Drake picked up his telephone handset and dialed. Schoe's voice answered.

"Red! Starlight zebra!" he said.

Drake walked back and forth for half an hour, struggling to understand how this peculiar telegram message provided any useful information about adultering the graphite test sample.

A knock on the door. As Drake pulled the handle, Schoe dashed in.

"Look at this!" the American declared. "How's *this* tell us the way to poison the graphite sample?"

The SS *Oberleutnant*, dressed in street clothes, wearing dark glasses and a large hat, took the telegram and scanned it several times. "So, 'Leo S' is Szilard, and 'Holsten' is Wells' discoverer of carolinum."

"I've got that. What's the rest?"

Schoe continued staring at the sheet, then said, "Mendeleev B?" As a chemist, I can tell you Mendeleev was the Russian who created the periodic chart of the elements. So, 'B' . . . that's the chemical symbol for the element boron."

Drake nodded. "Okay, we're getting someplace. "If the material is boron, then 'Sehr Klein'—Is Szilard saying, 'very small' amount of boron?"

Schoe put his black hat on the table and scratched his forehead. "Yes. This means—apply a very small amount of the element boron to the sample. ZUR OBERFLACHE—means TO THE SURFACE. 'POINT 0004 GRAM SQ CM'—that would be four ten-thousandths of a gram of boron per square centimeter, applied to the surface. I think we have something for Oster's Abwehr laboratory to work with."

"Amazing." Drake's mouth was dry. "Damned clever communication, but can Oster's chemists do this fast? Do they even have any boron?"

"We'll find out very soon. First, we've got to find him," Schoe said, buttoning his coat.

"Let's move."

CHAPTER 41

SUBSTITUTE

"Courage is resistance to fear, mastery
of fear - not absence of fear."

———

Mark Twain

SCHÖNEBERG DISTRICT BERLIN, WEDNESDAY, JANUARY 15, 1941, 16:20 HOURS

ALEX DRAKE SAT BEHIND THE wheel of the idling Daimler 660 rental sedan, looking beyond its vacuum-powered windshield wipers, which juddered as they swept wet slush off the glass in a slow cadence. Schoe's information had been exact in the description of their target. The SS corporal designated to act as a sentry aboard the train was tall, with a solid build, narrow eyes, and a slightly receding chin. *Mole on left upper lip. Required to be on duty at 6 p.m.* Drake pulled up in front of the apartment 20 minutes early.

His guts were churning as he went over the many complex facets of their Emperor Menelek-style carbon substitution blueprint. Now that Szilard had provided the vital information identifying the sample-poisoning material and how to apply it, five critical steps in this battle were in progress or completed. To start with, Oster's technicians, trusted workers at the Abwehr equipment test building, had heroically acquired a small amount of laboratory-grade boron. Next, the substance was carefully applied to the duplicate sample. Then, following Szilard's directions, a tiny quantity of the neutron-guzzling element was metered out and dusted into the pores of the sphere. It would be just enough to sop up atomic particles and render the judgment of *no good* for boron, but not so much as to render the result unbelievable—so they hoped. There was no way to test the effect until the Nazis did it for them, so everything depended on Szilard's wisdom and know-how from the United States.

Thirdly, working from the photos and verbal descriptions provided by the Siemens infiltrator, trusted Abwehr technicians had carefully replicated Diebner's shipping container. And then came arrangements to get the false shipping box aboard the train. One of Oster's trusted contacts had found a railroad clerk named Hubinger, assigned to the mail car on the day and hour the shipment was scheduled to go to Heidelberg. Heavily bribing this agent resulted in an agreement to make sure that a man identifying himself as recently transferred conductor *"Herr Wolf"* would get access to the fake sample secreted among the rest of the parcels. Schoe agreed to a face-to-face meeting with this clerk as arranged by Oster's man, and money crossed hands, sealing the deal. Schoe thought that the likelihood of this going as planned was reasonably decent since they were paying Hubinger a lot of money for his cooperation and silence. Moreover, this somewhat dopey-acting man had no reason to doubt that this involved a "secret SS operation," as he'd been told, or to question that Schoe was, in fact, a railway conductor. And lastly, Abwehr agents had identified the SS sentry assigned to accompany Diebner and his colleagues on the journey to Heidelberg. He had to be eliminated so Drake could take his place—Drake's and Schoe's mission in the minutes ahead. So far, Oster's team had accomplished nothing short of miracles on a routine basis. Still, a crushing number of extraordinary acts remained.

The January sky was hung thick with clouds, a deep violet twilight descending upon the city. Drake sat behind the boxy Daimler's steering wheel and kept his eyes focused on the small lamp in SS corporal Jürgen Bals' apartment window. A big blackbird cawed noisily as it flew just over the windshield, and when Drake's eyes blinked and refocused on the source of the light, it had been shut off. He rolled down his window and waved to Schoe, who loitered in the cold behind a thick tree trunk a dozen meters across the street. The door to the apartment opened, and a black-clad figure stepped out and began walking toward the road. Drake glimpsed the silver "death's head" SS *Totenkopf* insignia above the brim of his hat.

"Jürgen?" he asked, a cigarette bobbing at the corner of his mouth.

"I—who are you?" The SS officer wore a heavy overcoat. He stepped toward the Daimler. Over Bals' shoulder, Drake glimpsed Schoe, who pivoted away from his station and started moving toward the car.

"We met a few weeks ago. My name is Bauer. You said I should stop and see you about the information on my application for an SS position."

"Bauer? I don't know you." He leaned against the car's running board to try to see Drake in the dim light. As he studied the American's face, the unseen form of a slightly-built pedestrian crossed the street behind him. "No, I—*aaargh!*"

The SS officer's words caught in his throat as the syringe with a seven-gauge stainless steel needle plunged into the base of his neck just above the hairline. A quick motion by Schoe pushed five cc's of concentrated liquid hydrogen cyanide, the super-toxic main ingredient of Zyklon B, into his cranial cavity. He squealed and twisted. The needle bent and came out of his neck as he wrenched backward in a sharp convulsion. The corporal stopped breathing and slipped into the frozen slush beneath the sedan.

Drake threw the car door open and jumped out as the SS man's body went rigid. His muscles all contracted simultaneously in a single dying seizure. The liquid forced under his skull was instantly absorbed by his tissues, leaving no residue. The homicide would be impossible to detect if the body were to turn up. Curiously, the leftover Zyklon B from Schoe's assignment of genocide investigations for the SS was being used to destroy Nazism.

"Help me get him in the back seat," Drake said to his accomplice. "Grab that needle, and let's get out of here. Get in the back seat and strip his uniform off."

Drake drove west, toward the deep woods that stood five kilometers outside of the city limits, his second trip to the area to dispose of a corpse within twenty-four hours. Bals' naked body went to its permanent resting spot—a shallow grave dug hours earlier in the hard-frozen earth by one of Oster's trusted aides.

Drake drew the window shade and switched on the electric light in the tiny bathroom of his apartment. His byline article had been in Keene's office at 3:00 p.m., a story reporting on Berlin bomb shelter social manners. Having entrusted the typewritten pages to the copy clerk, he'd walked out of the *World Week* office and made his way to the U-Bahn station. As his mind fired its cylinders, he meticulously retraced the things that had gone wrong during the break-in of the Virus House. His nearly fatal injury and the horrific death of Born were the results of stupid things they should have avoided. *People haven't died pointlessly,* he thought. *Their deaths teach what's needed for victory this time.* Black Orchestra's primary error was that they didn't have a well-planned exit strategy, failing to reasonably anticipate that they would be discovered once they started making noise. Nothing had been adequately rehearsed, and a workable plan to get out of the building never ripened. Their attack plan had been faulty—incomplete and overly optimistic. Experience is the best mentor, and although they had such little time, *attention to detail* was now their maxim.

Each facet of this plan had been talked through, memorized, and walked through with his fellow performers, Schoe and Sondra, like the dress rehearsal for a Broadway musical. They repeated the crucial maneuvers, rechecked the words and costumes, the planning and preparations, the step-by-step logic. Then yesterday, the three players had made a dry run, taking the train from the Zoo Station to Zossen to get a feel for the layout of the Reichsbahn passenger coaches. That meant getting familiar with the lavatories, the coach doors, the interconnecting platforms between cars, even measuring the time required to traverse a railcar. Each washroom had a small window and a wall-mounted light switch, as did the wood veneer-lined passenger spaces. Schoe slipped into an empty compartment, and while Drake stood watch, he dismantled one of the ceiling lights to examine the wiring and insulation. Everything seemed right, but an unexpected event, an unanticipated factor, could trigger their downfall.

Drake took his shirt and necktie off, dropped them on the end of his bed, and stood in the light of the bare bulb illuminating the sink. The uniform was still wet, but it fit. Now, as he put it on, he became the very thing he hated—an SS officer. Drake had appropriated the corporal's identification papers and uniform decorations, but he couldn't assimilate the man's training and memory.

Now would begin his test. For a moment, the thought crossed his consciousness of abandoning this impossible, suicidal excursion. *Go home,* he thought, *go to Detroit, picnic on Belle Isle, write for the* Free Press *newspaper, sail on Lake St. Clair as he'd done with his father, live another fifty years.* The German atomic bomb meant such an idyllic world would never exist unless the project was stopped. *No!* He had this singular opportunity, and he despised himself for even considering for a moment that cheap alternative.

Sondra's Genève watch sparkled as she stood in front of the mirror in the Bahnhof restroom. She knew that at this moment, the others playing roles in this intricate drama—Alex, Schoe, Diebner with his sample of carbon material, and Diebner's entourage—were preparing to board the train bound for Heidelberg.

She checked her appearance in the mirror one last time and liked what she saw. Her deep red dress looked right. The years of comfortable and undemanding life with Holger had possibly dulled her keen survival instincts, but they hadn't disappeared.

As she exited the lavatory, she caught sight of Schoe sitting on a bench in the large waiting hall. He wore a worker's baggy lightweight coveralls. She almost missed him. Yet, that is precisely why Drake and

Beck had included him in the blueprint. Schoe could blend into the crowd and disappear entirely. He was translucent gray, without a single feature that would cause an eye to be diverted in his direction. When he wore his military uniform, it provided a glimmer of attention, but wearing coveralls, he might as well be colorless glass.

Sondra sat opposite the waiting room and watched the train begin to load with people. Beyond the passageway to the platforms, clouds of white steam boiled upward from the locomotives' hissing underbellies. The monstrous engines lined up at their marks next to the platforms, groaning with the steam pressure within their boilers. Passengers scurried along the ramps bordered by shining brass guardrails.

A group of soldiers passed, several turning to look at her. *Good*, she thought, *seduction is going to be a part of my role in this performance.*

Fifteen minutes passed. The Berlin train should be arriving. A fashionable young woman strolled by, accompanied by an older man, reminding her how she and Holger must have looked together. She wished he could see her tonight, sitting here in this place, about to put her life on the line carrying out the work he had started. He would be proud.

Angry-sounding loudspeakers blared a new announcement: the train to Heidelberg was loading. Passengers sleepily stood and gathered their possessions for the walk to the platform. Schoe glanced toward Sondra, then moved toward the turnstile. Striding toward the queue, she fished the rail pass out of her brown alligator-skin purse. Helga had provided a photo of the tickets bought for Diebner and his cohorts. It indicated car 2403, compartment 1. After the coal tender, the first car would be the Postamt Reichsbahn postal car containing Black Orchestra's Emperor Melenek sample. Diebner and his test box would be in the second car back from the coal tender. She held a ticket to the third car. The porter grasped her white-gloved hand and assisted her as she stepped into the car's interior. She took off her cashmere coat, stowed it in the overhead rack, and sat on a velvet upholstered seat. As she adjusted her skirt and smoothed her hair, she saw Schoe making his way past her, heading for his predetermined place in the rear of the car.

She glanced at her watch again, noticing that her hand was shaking.

What if Alex had already been detected as an imposter? What if Diebner had sent additional guards? What if other passengers were also riding in that car despite Helga's indication that she'd been ordered to buy tickets for all the compartments and seats in 2403 to ensure Diebner's privacy and security? *God help us all,* she thought. *We're free-falling.*

A sharp jolt—the train was moving. So was their plan of attack.

"All is well, sir?" asked Alex Drake, his head projecting into the compartment occupied by Dr. Kurt Diebner and his companions. A long whistle sounded from the locomotive. The train's acceleration continued. Drake smiled as he awaited a reply from the people he was assigned to safeguard. Then came a slight nod from the man with heavy glasses.

"The conductor asked me to mention to you that the dining car will soon open," Drake said, "and tonight's special is Black Forest ham, spaetzle, and good Bavarian mustard." The evening's menu was the first thing Drake had checked when he boarded the train.

Would Diebner and his associates eventually be tempted to abandon their sample box for dinner? If they all moved to the dining car together and left the sample unattended, the swap would be relatively simple. But the chance of that happening was tiny. It was much more likely that they would take turns going to eat or not go at all, having a meal brought to them by one of their group. If they stayed in the compartment for the entire five-hour trip, Black Orchestra's scheme was destroyed.

Diebner looked up from a magazine and grunted something that sounded to Drake like *Sehr Gut*—very good.

Drake took two steps back, looked up and down the corridor, and then took his place by the door. The carbon graphite sample box was on the floor of Diebner's compartment. Except for their presence, the entire coach was unoccupied by the command of the Virus House leader.

Darkness had enveloped the speeding train. Schoe sat between a snoring man and a foul-smelling, obese woman wearing a heavy coat. The man's body leaned toward the windows, allowing at least some space to get away from the beast on his left. The woman had a pocketful of stale-smelling peanuts someplace, and she fed herself constantly during the first half-hour of transit. Schoe was exhausted mentally and physically. Not three hours earlier, he had killed an SS officer.

The fake conductor waited for the start of this complicated maneuver, watching for the real conductor. As soon as he'd passed through and moved to the next car, things would start happening. He felt his heart rate accelerate. The battered black leather portmanteau briefcase with two straps, like a doctor's bag, rested on his lap. His heart started missing beats—missing a lot of them. He realized he was squeezing its handle so tightly that his knuckles had turned alabaster. His breath was short—not getting enough air again. He consciously worked to relax his muscles, hoping to relieve what would probably become a very nasty chest pain in a few moments. It was time to down a nitroglycerine pill. *Where was that conductor? He should have been through by now.* There was no space for error or the unexpected. Schoe's armpits were soaked.

The railcar door slid open, the sharp *clack* of the latch, the sound of rushing air announcing the entry of the conductor. He shuffled along the aisle, motioning for the travelers' tickets, snapping through each one with a metal punch. Schoe grasped the coupon in his pocket and positioned it for his turn. The conductor reached out for Schoe's card, snapped the punch, and shoved it back with a sniffle, which he seemed to give out with every ticket punched. The wind roared into the car as the conductor opened the door and went out onto the platform. Schoe had only minutes for their plan to be carried out while the conductor finished his duties in the remaining cars.

He gripped his case and squeezed past the woman next to him. The train rocked, nearly buckling his legs as Sondra gave him a split-second glance, then brought her head down. He adjusted the blue identification badge on the left lapel of his coverall suit and pulled his neck scarf tighter, steeling himself for the performance of his life.

Clutching the valise and keeping his face lowered, Schoe made his way to the front of the railcar. He pushed against the flat metal door panel, shoving with all his strength. It gave way, revealing a red light illuminating the platform. Another bulb lighted a connecting structure on the next car. The coach's interior appeared identical to the previous one, with a single huge exception: no passengers visible. Shafts of yellowish light beaming from tiny ceiling fixtures fell across rows of empty seats.

The car's lavatory door was to his right. He slipped inside and opened the valise, pulling out the conductor's uniform and hat. Then, moving as fast as possible, he changed clothes, put the coveralls into the valise, and slid it under the sink. He straightened himself, put the hat on his head, and went back through the doorway. He saw that a single compartment at the forward end of the car had a light on, its door pushed partially open. He glanced in as he moved past silently. Three men sat inside. Ahead of him, near the door, stood an SS guard. He recognized the sturdy build and dark, unblinking eyes.

Drake was looking toward the back of the car. Schoe followed his glance and understood. He had only minutes to retrieve the parcel and get it positioned. All was moving as planned—so far.

The postal car was forward of the coach where Schoe and Drake stood. Within its neat stacks of parcels would be a wooden crate, the kernel of their deception. Schoe pulled the door open and stepped out into the bone-chilling cold.

Unlike the other platforms between railcars, the Reichsbahn postal unit's connection to the adjoining passenger car had no canvas diaphragm cover. Instead, he saw menacing openings at the sides of the inter-car bridge plate, guarded only by minimal metal handrails on either side of the connection. The platform plate was no more than one meter wide and swayed violently.

He blinked twice as he grasped the handle of the door marked with a polished brass sign:

Verboten!
Postamt Reichsbahn

CHAPTER 42

STRIKE

"A show of daring often conceals great fear."

Lucan (Roman epic poet, 39–65 AD)

"**H**ERR *HUBINGER!*" **SCHOE DECLARED AS** he pulled the coach's door closed behind him. Turning at the sound of the opening door, the balding man was met by a blast of frigid air rushing into the windowless postal railcar. He wore a cheap gray sweater and sat at a small desk, a backless stool supporting him. Schoe squinted at the surprised look on the man's face, illuminated by a small, green-shaded desk lamp. If the clerk assignments had been changed, if this were not the same man Oster had bribed, there would be trouble now.

The postal employee pushed his eyeshade up higher on his forehead and looked cautiously at the uniform of his visitor. "*Guten Abend, Eisenbahnoffizier!* Can I help you?"

Schoe breathed in the air of relief and straightened his necktie. "I'm *Zugleiter Wolf.*"

"Ah, yes, Conductor—yes indeed! We meet again. I have been

looking forward to your visit to my small domain—that is, mine until we reach Heidelburg. Our arrangement continues to be in effect, of course."

"You have brought the special SS package on board, put it in a safe place, and you will now give me access to it. The other half of your money will be given to you when you return to Berlin. That is our bargained-for exchange. So, return to your duties. You have already forgotten you saw me here."

"Ja! Heil Hitler!" said the rail clerk, tossing his head in the direction of the stacks of packages placed along the length of the railcar.

Schoe unfolded the bows of his gold-rimmed spectacles, slipped them over his ears, then began looking along the piles of parcels. He knew the size and color of the box, but there were many containers along the aisles with similar dimensions, stacked high and in sloppy disarray. As orderly as Germans usually were, especially in government settings, this mail car was unexpectedly chaotic, and the poor placement of lightbulbs made for deep, concealing shadows. *There wasn't any time.* While he was burning minutes looking for the box, Diebner and his men might already have left the genuine container behind to go for their dinner, and Drake would have nothing with which to make his substitution.

"You require help, perhaps?" Hubinger stood at the end of the row of packages, his form silhouetted by a bare bulb swaying from a ceiling-hung cord. "The package you left with me yesterday per the agreement we have—I have placed it where it will be safe from prying eyes and picky fingers."

"Give it to me."

"Of course. But one thing. The box is of substantial value to you, isn't it?"

"I said *now!*" Schoe's nostrils flared.

"I have kept it very safe for you and will gladly continue my help. Perhaps an additional fee of a hundred Reichsmarks? A paltry sum to ensure you will be so much more comfortable about the future security of our relationship."

"Security? Hubinger, if you try to be cute with me, an SS guard is standing in the next car who will be glad to make your acquaintance.

You're outnumbered two to one. During our conversation, you might make an unscheduled departure from this train."

Hubinger took a step back. Schoe watched a look of alarm crawl across the man's eyes. "SS? I—why certainly, no harm meant. I just wish to help."

"Sure, you do. Get the box."

The clerk disappeared behind a brown wooden panel. Schoe listened to the sounds of things scraping the floor of the car as he waited. Finally, Hubinger reappeared, carrying a container. "Here. Here it is. As I said, sir, no harm meant."

Schoe grasped the wooden box. It was heavy—ten kilograms or more and bulky. Simultaneously, he clutched his leather case.

"Open the door for me." Schoe surprised himself with the firmness of his declaration. "And I will say it one more time: if you utter a word about this, you know well what will follow."

"Of course, sir." Hubinger pulled the door open as he wiped beads of sweat from his forehead.

"I'll be bringing this back shortly, so keep that door unlocked."

The clerk sat back down in his chair and adjusted his eyeshade. "Of course, sir. Thank you very much. *Heil Hitler!*"

Schoe exited into the immobilizing gale of freezing wind produced by the speeding train and struggled to keep his balance as the narrow platform swayed. After crossing in the blood-red illumination, he propped the parcel against the coach's bulkhead, freeing his hand to grip the door handle. The door to the railway car that carried Diebner, his entourage, and Alex Drake didn't give way until the third try. As he clasped his load and stepped into the corridor, he passed by Drake standing in his black SS garb, making momentary eye contact in the dim light.

Schoe started down the nearly dark corridor toward the rear of the railcar. He needed to get past the door of the occupied compartment as speedily as possible without attracting any attention. He shuddered at the incredibly vulnerable position he'd crossed into now. The nitroglycerine pills had worn off, and he didn't have the time or the hands available to fetch another dose. A thin shaft of light shone into the corridor from the door of Diebner's space. He risked a glance. Two of the three occupants inside were asleep.

He neared the end of the empty coach. On his left was the door to the lavatory. His arms ached from the weight of the box as he entered the small compartment and flicked on the light switch with his elbow.

Schoe dropped to his knees as he put the precious parcel on the floor, then stood to lock the door behind him. The heavy wooden box had two labels pasted on it. One said *Zerbrechlich*—fragile—the other inscription read *Doktor K. Diebner, Privat und Persoenalich*. Had he been seen by Diebner or his men with this in his hands, the end to this escapade would have been swift. Was a label added or anything changed on the corresponding box that sat in Diebner's compartment? He knew this was one glaring weakness in their plan. Leveraging the entire operation on the assumption that the two cases would be indistinguishable meant the original would have to be unchanged since it left the Siemens manufacturing plant. That was a colossal supposition that they had no way of confirming.

Schoe patted the substitute box as he slid it under the sink, next to his valise as rehearsed. He stood and switched off the light. In the darkness, he waited and recited a prayer for success, a plea to the Almighty that in the next minutes, they would save the world from Nazi atomic destruction. He opened the door just a crack, allowing him to see out to the corridor.

Drake glanced into Diebner's compartment. One of the men seemed to be asleep; the other two were speaking in low tones. The train was picking up speed, swaying more than before. A voice—words about food. *Exactly what he needed to hear.* A visit to the dining car wouldn't be far off if things continue to go as hoped.

The counterfeit conductor opened his leather case. Pushing aside the wadded-up coveralls, he removed two razor blades, a wire cutter, and a small sack of tissue paper containing something that looked like black soap flakes. He placed the package of chemical chips wrapped in tissue on the floor next to the door to the corridor. Then, taking two *Easy-lite* matches and putting them next to the tissue, he took five steps to the light fixture hung by two wires from the ceiling's center. He carefully stripped the brown fabric insulation that encased both wires, making it look like natural wear abrasion of the sheathing. He avoided touching the bare copper, which would create a premature short. If anyone walked in on him now . . . he forced the thought out of his mind and put away the tools. It was time to go to the unoccupied compartment ahead of the washroom and await Drake's "go" sign.

At the front of the car, Alex Drake straightened as he saw the door opening at the far end of the coach. A figure came into view—the train conductor was walking toward him, going by the lavatory containing the bogus sample box and past the door with Schoe on the other side. So far, nothing had gone wrong, no mistakes. The drama was being acted out seamlessly, even by actors who didn't even know they were performing in Black Orchestra's theater.

"Is everything in order? No problems?" asked the railway officer.

"Yes, all is excellent," Drake replied. "We must be making good time."

"Indeed, we are. I am going to the locomotive cab to speak with the engineer, and then I will go back to the other coaches. Maybe to the food car. I will return later."

"Very well, Conductor." Drake touched the brim of his hat with this right hand and saw the railroad man's eyes flick upward for a second to the *Totekopf* skull-and-crossbones badge above the brim of the hat. "Say hello to the engineer from the SS." He instantly regretted the hint of sarcasm leaking out.

"*Heil Hitler!*" The conductor was gone, at least for now.

Drake slid the door to the first compartment open further and leaned in, smiling. "Perhaps you are considering the dining car, gentlemen? The conductor told me it might be closing before long," he lied.

A plump, bespectacled figure looked up and scowled. The size of his midsection indicated that he was a big eater and would probably be hungry. He rose and walked toward Drake before glancing down the passageway. "Rinsch—stay here and keep your eyes on that box. Bockman, come with me to eat. He will go later."

Drake gestured toward the rearward end of the coach. "Fifth car is dining, sir."

Sondra Speier sat in the third rail car, waiting for her cue to act. Her index finger picked at her lower lip.

The door opened. She heard the *whoosh* of rushing air, the clatter of steel wheels against rails. The conductor was back again, heading toward the rear of the train. Then, after a few minutes, two other men came through the portal. She studied them and compared the smaller man's appearance with the photograph she'd been shown of Kurt Diebner. *Oh, my God*, she thought. *Yes—definitely*. Her heart fluttered: the time had come. She began the slow count—one hundred seconds until she and Drake would come together as rehearsed.

Diebner and his accomplice walked the length of the coach. She glanced back at them as they approached the railcar's rear door. *No box—it must still be somewhere in the forward coach*. She had to follow through with the ballet, missing leg be damned, using her razor-sharp awareness. It was time to make her move, to become the distraction for anyone who might interfere with the plan.

Coatless, Sondra pushed open the door and made her way onto the platform. The canvas diaphragm between cars only partly held back the freezing wind. As quickly as she could, she thrust open the door to the next carriage and entered.

The lights inside the coach ran along the corridor's ceiling, met by a small shaft of illumination coming from a forward passenger compartment. The light was dim, yet she could make out Alex Drake's form at the far opposite end of the corridor. His head nodded toward her, and then he turned away. She disappeared into the tiny washroom, where the smell was of disinfectant, the chlorine-based kind used by janitors throughout Europe. As she snapped on the light, she noticed a puddle of water on the floor below the basin, alongside the fake box. She considered for a moment doing something about it, but there was no time. She thought, *did I just say thirty-five or forty-five?* She'd lost count of the seconds! The Tarot card—*The Queen of Swords*—shouted at her—intuition would stir her powers of improvisation. She must now invent all her movements.

Schoe heard a *thump-thump-thump* against the wall of his compartment—Drake was moving past. The time to strike had arrived. As he waited in place for the predetermined two minutes, he dropped another pill in his mouth, swallowing it quickly and praying it would relieve the pressure in his chest. He focused his eyes on the second hand of his wristwatch. He lit the match, then ignited the tissue paper wrapped around the Abwehr-prepared granulated chemical as the time expired. It gave off a massive plume of smoke, even more than in the test he'd tried yesterday. He cracked the door and slid the smoldering material twenty centimeters into the corridor, then returned to work on stripping the wires. The next step—he used another big kitchen match and more tissue paper to ignite the wire insulation itself. Burned, melted insulation and black soot would deposit on the wall for the fire investigators' benefit, who would eventually examine the area for evidence. His eyes watered with the arrival of smoke from the smoldering resin flakes. He paused, holding the two wires by the remaining braid, then turned his face away and braced himself.

The revolting smell of the combination of burning rubberized fabric and sulfur spread rapidly down the corridor. The lights flickered once, twice, then went out. A dim battery-powered emergency bulb came on at each end of the car, sending shafts of yellow light through the smoky haze hanging in the corridor.

"Achtung! Feuer!" he heard Drake shout.

"Verdammt! What the hell is burning?" roared Diebner's remaining associate as he stumbled out of the compartment.

"Move to the next car immediately!" said Drake.

"Damned smell—I'm getting sick!" yelled the Virus House emissary as he reached back into the compartment to grab Diebner's briefcase along with his own.

Drake approached him. "It's an electrical short and a fire—lights gone. We must get out of here—let me help you." Drake bent to grab the sample box from the floor.

"No!" The bodyguard coughed hard and pushed the black-cloaked Drake back. "Leave that alone!" he shouted.

"Your container can't be left here. It could be destroyed. I'm SS—let me handle this!" Drake grabbed the sample. "I've got it—*go!*"

Diebner's assistant started down the corridor.

Drake braced himself as the smoke bit at his throat and lungs. The slight glow from the overhead emergency light revealed the lavatory door—half-open as planned. He veered toward the side of the corridor and thumped the wooden wall with his hip. Diebner's lackey slowed ahead of him, coughed deeply, and let out another curse.

Sondra stood in the slightly open lavatory door, eyes huge, her hand over her mouth as she held back a cough. The man from the Virus House glanced toward her, went by, and approached the car's rear exit. As Drake neared her, Sondra slid their deception box out into the passageway. Drake bent toward it, still holding Diebner's parcel, keeping his vision focused on his adversary. The bodyguard started to twist around for a look—Drake instantly kicked the counterfeit box back into the darkness of the washroom before it could be seen.

"This smoke—" the German exclaimed.

The swap had failed.

Sondra saw the miss. "My eyes!" she cried, stumbling out of the lavatory, past Drake, choking, moving toward Diebner's man. "Help me! I can't breathe!" The Nazi stepped toward her, grasping her as she fell into his arms. She tilted her head back, brushing her long, lightly perfumed hair across his face, then threw her arms around his waist and maneuvered him so that his eyes stayed away from Drake. They moved together toward the steel door in a sort of dance, out onto the connecting platform between coaches.

Her distraction gave Drake the seconds he needed. He dashed into the dark washroom, twisting to close the door behind him. His foot hit the puddle of water and he shot sideways. His right knee buckled as it slammed onto the tile surface. Diebner's box squirted from his arms, then crashed hard to the floor. Drake turned onto his back, hands clutching his leg. If it were broken, their plan was shattered.

The knee straightened, although painfully. *Where were the boxes?* He rolled into a sitting position and shook his head side-to-side, trying to get rid of the multicolored dots of light he saw before his eyes. He hadn't struck his head on the way down, and the leg felt like it might bear weight. Drake groped in the darkness along the floor. His hand brushed around the top and sides of one of the cases. In a second, he felt the surfaces of the other. *Which was their substitute, which was Diebner's?* There was only an instant to decide. He rubbed his palms across the first box again—something—an irregularity—on the corner of the case.

Fighting off the pain, he stood, lifted the container to his chest, and moved back into the corridor.

Ahead on the platform, Diebner's bodyguard was still trying to help the coughing Sondra. Drake moved past them, trying to hide his newly-acquired limp, and carried the box through two more coaches back to the dining car where Diebner stood, arms crossed, swaying to and fro. He wore a sullen, threatening scowl on his face. Drake placed the box in front of the Nazi scientist and stared at it, pondering the question: had he made the right choice in the darkness?

CHAPTER 43

DIAMOND

"All warfare is based on deception."

Sun Tsu, *The Art of War*, 500 BC

S CHOE SCRAPED UP THE RESIDUE of burnt resin and shoved it into his valise. Squeezing the leather case to his chest, he made his way to the rear of the smoke-filled coach with only seconds left to complete his work. The train crew would already be rushing to deal with the smoke and damage. He was dizzy—so much of the poisonous fumes had gone into his lungs. He had stayed too long, too close to the source. If Drake had successfully made the switch, the original sample box was someplace still inside the lavatory. He had to get to it before the toxic fumes sapped every speck of his strength.

He felt his way along the corridor back to the open washroom door, and in the smoke, groped for the wooden box. There—he felt it! Clutching the valise containing his discarded clothes and the tools used to short out the wiring, he picked up the carbon sample box, then turned back toward the Postamt car.

Schoe's legs were leaden. He staggered forward in the shadowy coach. The emergency lamps were faltering, their bulbs becoming glowing red torches high on the bulkheads at the end of the car. Although they helped him keep his direction, he could see nothing else. The center of his chest burned. His mouth gasped for air.

He slid open the steel door. The speeding train shot into a curve and swayed sharply, tossing him off balance. He regained his footing, then gripped the box tighter and made a few steps across the platform. Dizziness intensified, and the inferno in his chest was overwhelming. He had to get to the car door ahead, put the label on the box addressing it to Drake's Berlin apartment, and get it back into the stacks of the mail car. He staggered to his right. His grip on the wooden container and the valise stayed firm, but his vision was quickly failing. He fell to the left, slammed his knee against the tubular rod guarding the bridge plate, and glimpsed the red lights reflecting off the rails hurtling by below. Still, he didn't release his grip on the items he carried as he lurched headlong into the gap between the cars. In the freezing January night, a hundred wheels of the train sliced Schoe, the valise, and Diebner's carbon sample to strips and shreds.

Diebner stood at the dining car table. Wordlessly, he looked intently at the box held by Drake, then swung toward the aisle and abruptly stepped back to avoid the train crewmen dashing through the car. They looked a bit cartoonish as they rushed down the corridor, all in a row, wearing red fire hats, carrying axes, fire extinguisher tanks, and lanterns.

Diebner's bodyguards had commandeered the entire fifth coach on the train. All passengers had been driven into cars further back, and Diebner had the sample box secured next to him. Finishing their food, Diebner and his cohorts ordered more beer as Drake took his position at the front of the coach. The conductor announced that the train was passing the outskirts of Wurzburg. Heidelberg was two hours ahead.

Moonlight glinted off the clear eyes of the lead wolf as the last car of the train passed the pack. Over the years, these animals had learned to drift toward the sound of an approaching train because occasionally, one would drop garbage scraps through a chute inside the dining car, down onto the tracks. It was cold, and the pack hadn't eaten in two days. They slept through most of the hours of daylight in a state of semi-hibernation and scavenged during darkness.

Moving along the tracks, the wolves found nothing that was edible. The leader raised his snout toward the moon, sniffing the air. He turned back, away from the sound of the train, and began plodding toward the scent—of blood. Then there was another smell in the light breeze, which caused the fur on his neck to stand on end.

Another wolf pack.

The first troupe heard sounds of ripping flesh, the yapping of animals fighting, and railway ballast stones being kicked about. The rival pack was feeding on something. The leader pressed closer, edging his way toward the tumult. The others stopped their gorging and turned toward the newcomers. Suddenly, the two groups of wolves were in full confrontation, howling and snapping their teeth, circling the food, and lunging at one another. The pieces of meat were not large. Both packs soon ignored each other and were satiating themselves on the human remains, carrying away uncontested body parts deep into the thick woods. Within a few minutes, the combined wolf packs had eaten or dragged away the entire corpse. Jackals and weasels would be by after daylight to take care of any tiny leftovers, leaving nothing on the tracks.

Alex Drake put his key into the lock cylinder of the latch on his apartment door. He walked to the bathroom, snapped on the light, and opened the tap. As warm water flowed, he splashed it onto his face with cupped hands. He grabbed a towel from the hook and headed to the bedroom, then sat on his bed and turned on the lamp. The picture of his father on the nightstand looked more lifelike than ever. The smile in the picture didn't look noncommittal to him anymore. Drake extended his finger toward the glass bordered by the black wooden frame. He drew an imaginary curve on the glass, a line lifted at the corners of the mouth. *You've done well*, the image said to him.

Drake fell back against the pillow, exhausted but with an emotion new and strange to him. *Triumph*. He was asleep in seconds.

Ludwig Beck had called Drake, Oster, and Sondra Speier to his house. They sat around the familiar table, the smoke from cigarettes drifting toward the ceiling as they talked.

"All right, Hans Oster," said Beck, "tell us what you've learned."

"Our old friend Helga at the Virus House," said Oster. "Always Helga, time and again. When Hitler is defeated, she should get a medal for bravery for the help she's been to us. I located her at the camera drop store and told her that her contact is dead. She thought I was Gestapo trying to trap her, but I managed to convince her that I was Schoe's fellow operative. Then she confided in me."

"Oh my God, she's seen something?" asked Sondra, her eyes flaring with anticipation.

"Yesterday, Professor Bothe got his apparatus to run for a second time in Heidelberg. The test results were identical to the day before. Carbon graphite is *useless* in slowing neutrons. It has the wrong—Alex, what is it? Absorption cross-section? Bothe's report to Diebner and Hahn stated the only known material with the correct cross-section is deuterium oxide—*heavy water!*"

They sat in silence as they processed the words.

"Diebner oversaw every step of Bothe's procedure in Heidelberg. Still, carbon graphite failed the test!" Drake declared, jumping up from his chair.

Oster, Drake, and Sondra were now on their feet, hugging.

"You, Sondra, and our absent Schoe, you've saved this planet from Hitler's destruction!" shouted Oster.

Drake stopped smiling. "And still we don't know where he is. Our waiting at the station and searching the train produced nothing. I so wish he was here with us to hear this."

"He must have performed his tasks perfectly," declared Beck. "In the end, he truly had a core hard as diamond."

"Now we must pray," said Oster, "that the Germans don't do more tests and discover the boron element in the sample. I believe that Professor Bothe's circumstances with Nazis may make him less than enthusiastic in pushing very hard for answers. The same goes for any decent German scientist!"

They stood in silence. Finally, Oster asked, "And what hymn does this orchestra play next, General?"

"It'll be a funeral march unless we stay out of sight," Beck replied. "I'm heading to my son's home in Samswegan to settle my thoughts, but it's not the time to clear off the desk and start a new mission. There's a world war upon this planet. Hitler's not going to let Diebner and the others give up on his key to salvation. We have much more to do before civilization eliminates this criminal regime."

"Those two boxes," Sondra said. "They both wound up on the floor in the washroom, in the darkness, all that smoke in there. Alex, how did you decide which one to give to Diebner, which one to leave for Schoe?"

"When I touched the corners of the boxes," said Drake, "I felt that one box had a corner slightly dented in, which I figured must have been from my dropping it in my fall. The other one had all of its eight corners come to perfect points—so it had to be the faked box. I took it."

"You have sensitive hands, *Herr Drake,*" she said, smiling. Drake's chin dipped down, and he looked toward the floor to mask the unease shown in his thinly drawn smile and flushing face. There were a few quiet chuckles to be heard.

And there was one final item. *Generalmajor* Oster and his anti-Hitler contingent inside the Abwehr acted to ensure the secret of the carbon exchange *stayed* secret. A day after the Black Orchestra members returned from Heidelberg, the Berlin police were called to a subway station washroom where a body had been found, an apparent suicide. The corpse, sprawled across the toilet in a stall with both wrists deeply slashed, was identified as a railway postal clerk named Hubinger.

Berlin had one of the largest populations of any city in Europe, but it was much like a small town in many ways. There was little crime, and an incident such as the disappearance of two SS officers on the same day drew attention. *Reichsführer* Himmler ordered an official investigation. The family of SS officer Bals wanted to know how he had vanished without a trace. The Reichsbahn authorities had sent an inspection car along the railway line to look for signs of foul play. They turned up nothing except a few smashed pieces of wood and something that looked like pulverized charcoal along the tracks.

Schoe had no family. Nobody inquired on his behalf. SS investigators searched his room. Nothing was found except some old love letters, his university diploma, and a dozen faded sepia-toned photographs of a beautiful woman. The official report concluded that he had vanished without a trace, no explanation.

And, for Black Orchestra, so it remained.

CHAPTER 44

DEMONS

"A misty morning doesn't mean a cloudy day."

Ancient proverb

BERLIN CENTER CITY, JUNE 29, 1941

EVERY FACE IN THE CITY seemed to wear the same mask. Walking along the Budapesterstrasse on his way to the Café Kranzler, Drake marveled at the similitude of expressions: bitterness and fear showing above wide eyes and forced smiles. All except the most fanatical Nazis had been thunderstruck a week earlier by the astonishing news of Germany's invasion of the Soviet Union. These two powerful nations that had joined in a non-aggression pact only twenty-two months earlier were now at war. Hitler now faced the hideous prospect of a two-front war against England and Russia by his reckless action. Yet, German citizens were powerless to voice dissent or challenge the decisions of the government.

Their smiles were simply a means to retain a scrap of sanity.

The warmth of the June evening coaxed the patrons of Berlin's outdoor cafés into sipping coffee or beer and talking of art, politics, and friends—anything but war. While they sat in comfort, German soldiers, three million of them at that very moment, were encamped for the night in the mosquito-infested marshes of western Russia. They had shot across hundreds of kilometers of Soviet territory since the invasion started not even a week earlier, encountering hardly any resistance. Drake thought Hitler might seize another quick victory like he'd enjoyed against France a year ago, yet there was something vastly different this time. Russia was an enormous, forbidding place a long way away, with three times as many inhabitants as Germany.

Drake looked along the sidewalk of the Kurfürstendamm at the tables set up outside, marble pedestals topped by flower boxes guarding the boundary of the sitting area for the well-dressed clientele. Barely visible against the deep violet sky was the towering steeple of the Kaiser Wilhelm Cathedral looming over the leafy boulevard. Small candles, perched in the centers of the tables, gave off little points of light. Yet together, they provided enough illumination to enable him to distinguish the facial features of some of the patrons. Blackout hoods covering car headlamps made their beams look like tiny shafts of light zigzagging through the misty air.

Drake watched Sondra approaching. She looked to him like something out of a dream, her hair catching and reflecting the pinpricks of scant light.

"*Guten Abend, Mein Liebling,*" Drake said, taking her hand. "It rained a while ago. I wasn't too sure if we could be outside tonight, but it seems to have cleared."

"Yes, Alex." She gave him a quick kiss on the forehead and sat down. Germans didn't show affection in public.

"This darkness makes it hard to see your face," she declared.

"Well, from what I can see of yours, you look exquisite. But then I'm kind of working from memory."

"Oh? It's been two days. Perhaps your memory needs refreshing." She touched his arm and rested her hand on his elbow.

Her flirty remark made him feel warm inside, like he'd just knocked back a generous shot of Kentucky bourbon and maybe as intoxicating. But Drake straightened his back, his urge to return the flirt cropped off by the barriers imposed by a lifetime of bad memories. Sondra watched his reaction in the dim illumination, her smile transforming into lips pressed tight.

"My news of the day is that *World Week* is closing the gap with *Time* in worldwide circulation." His remark deflected the conversation from tenderness to business. "Only five thousand copies apart now."

Sondra folded her arms and stared someplace far beyond him. "Well, that's good, especially since you're a significant part of the reason."

"Believe that if you want, but it does make me happy. I'm going to kick the butts of those guys at *Time*. Keene said he'd join us tonight."

"It's your intelligent insights combined with Jimmy's clever editorial columns. More and more, the byline *Alexander Drake* is on the magazine's feature articles. You're becoming a journalist known to the world, despite the conditions here in Naziland." Sondra's eyes were downcast.

"Thanks for saying those things, but something's bothering you. Tell me."

"When the Americans join the war against Germany, you'll go to New York to write. You'll be pulled back to America soon. You've become too valuable to risk here."

He poured them each a glass of wine

"My favorite," she said after the first sip. "Médoc Château Beychevelle. How'd you manage that?"

"Nothing but dumb luck. Not much good wine left in this town."

"My luck, bad luck, would be that you'd leave me here when this war expands."

"America neutrality still holds," said Drake. "Unless there's a direct attack on US territory, they'll stay out." He shook a cigarette from the pack and offered it to Sondra. She waved it off and raised her gaze to meet his.

"But this invasion of Russia inserts lots of twists," he continued, looking around to ensure their conversation remained private. "Instead of Hitler just coveting Europe, he's moving against the whole world. If he comes to own Russia, he's on to India and China. Then where? Japan? The United States? We've created an eggshell shield over our secret. If the Germans were to break the egg, they'd find the pathway straight to Hitler's bomb. So there are a thousand risks and scrapes still ahead."

As was his habit, Drake scanned the street for signs of Gestapo or SS activity. He kept his voice low. "I'm not leaving here soon. Count on that."

Sondra's face showed relief at those words. She grasped his hand. "Alex, if you go, I can't stay here—not anymore."

"I was certain we'd both be killed in the carbon graphite deception," Drake said.

"Remember the Queen of Swords?"

"The woman's ability to improvise solutions," Drake replied. "For us, it worked."

"Together, we did the impossible."

"And do you remember what was inside the wooden box on the train?"

"Well, of course, Alex. *Carbon.*"

Drake twisted the ring on his pinkie finger. "Heat and pressure transform plain old carbon into the hardest material in the world— diamond. Our fight against Nazis always seems to come back to carbon. As I lay there in that safe house, I looked at my mother's diamond every hour I was awake. It reminded me of the heroes we lost. Dietrich Born's life bled out on a pile of coal. Gunnar Schoe disappeared with the box of graphite. It surrounds us—I read that carbon makes up something like twenty percent of the human body."

Sondra was silent as he slipped the ring off his finger.

"The ways your eyes shine with the reflection of that candle, they make me think of diamonds."

She leaned toward him and rested her cheek against the back of his hand.

Jimmy Keene strolled up to their table. "How are you both? No bombs fallin' yet, just that rain an hour ago. The clouds should keep the bombers away tonight, givin' us a good evening for jawin' a bit."

Alex shifted his eyes away. "Hello, boss." He pushed the ring back on his finger.

"Just a while ago, Bill Shirer and I were talkin' about this invasion of

Russia. How far do you think the Wehrmacht has gone by now? He hears they're slicin' through her like a hot knife through lard. Germans had better be careful, or the army will get ahead of their supply chain. Then, if the Red Army prepares a welcome for the Wehrmacht somewhere on the way to Moscow—pillboxes reinforced, a million troops brought by train from Siberia, a cache of tanks and trucks, Adolf Hitler may find himself pushed over a cliff . . . okay, I'm shuttin' up before somebody hears me."

Drake was having trouble centering on Keene's words.

"Look at you," declared the editor. "This is a helluva place to be moonin' over each other. The worst damned place I can think of. Clouds or not, Churchill might drop a big old bomb right on top of this table. The whole town's in a bull's eye. So why don't you two get the hell outta here? You've got your whole lives ahead of you—why stay in this God-awful hole? Get your butts to New York."

Drake smiled and looked toward Sondra. "I've got a lot of work to do in Berlin." He sipped more wine. "Have some, boss," he said before continuing. "German long-range rockets and other wild inventions in warfare will begin appearing before long. These things can still hand victory to Hitler."

From far beyond the leafy hedges surrounding the patio of the café, a deep rumbling sound rolled over them. Simultaneously, they looked toward the railroad cars moving slowly through the intersection of the tracks and the boulevard. The diffuse light from shrouded automobile headlamps fell across the painted red crosses on the sides of the coaches.

Jimmy Keene turned his head back toward the table. "One of the first hospital trains returnin' from the Russian front. Inside those railcars—hundreds of armless, legless, eyeless German boys—bodies ruined after their run-ins with death. This crappy war has a whole world of misery yet to deliver."

Another sound rose over the clatter of the train, causing Drake to sit straight up. *Air raid sirens!*

Keene jumped to his feet. "Here comes Churchill's messengers—let's get outta here." The café's patrons were standing, knocking over chairs and beginning to charge toward the steel archway marking the stairs to the U-Bahn subway station.

Drake grasped Sondra around her waist, supporting her as they moved together with the others in the direction of the shelter. Keene stayed right behind them. Someone ahead tripped and fell to the Belgian block pavement, and nobody offered help. *Survival instinct in wartime Berlin,* thought Drake. He twisted his face toward the heavens to glimpse the crisscrossing searchlight beams.

The sirens quieted for just a moment, letting the distinctive choppy drone of the big four-engined British Halifax bombers further frighten the fleeing residents of the city. For a moment, the sounds were only of screaming people and distant aircraft engines. Then came the first big explosion, followed by a dozen more with immense orange and yellow bursts of flame. *The archway was only ten meters ahead.* He had to be careful not to start dragging Sondra, which could cause her to trip—the tempo had to go fast enough that she could keep her steps matched with his and yet not get bumped by other scared citizens.

The bomb detonated three hundred yards above the square, its shock wave driving down into the crowd, blasting a heavy oaken cornice from a building's façade. Wood, stone, and concrete spun downward, smashing Drake across the shoulders and pinning him against the pavement. A shower of heavy fragments rained onto the sidewalk.

Drake opened his eyes and realized that he'd been knocked senseless—for how long, he didn't know. As the last shards of stone and wood fell to the pavement, he heard screams and shouts merging with the blaring sirens of ambulances and fire trucks. Drake struggled to push a heavy timber off his back, then rolled onto his side. The massive beam had missed his head and spared his life, but his shoulder wouldn't move. He tasted blood in his mouth. His vision was out of focus. *Sondra! Where is she?* he thought. The Day of Death! *It's here again!* His thinking cleared slightly. *No, it's summertime—can't be.*

Wails came into his ears, the moaning voices of dozens of injured people simultaneously crying out for help. Bombs exploded to the east as the British continued their raid over the Nazified capital.

Drake slowly sat up, moving his right hand across to touch his injured shoulder. There was no sensation—the arm was numb. He swung his gaze along the Kurfürstendamm. The rising clouds of smoke veiled some of the destruction revealed by the fires.

"Sondra!" He shouted her name ten times—twenty times. Nothing. No reply.

"Sondra! Jimmy!"

A wall of the Berlin Zoo had partially collapsed, opening a path to freedom for a terrified gazelle that flashed past the place where Drake stood. He went quickly from one pile of rubble to the next, stepping past the injured and the dead.

"Alex." The voice was unmistakable but shaky.

"Jimmy! I've got you!"

Drake used his good arm to lift and shove three or four timbers aside, then moved a table off the figure that lay in the darkness.

"Get me up, for God's sake."

Drake extended his hand toward the old editor, and in a moment, both men were standing.

"Sondra—I've got to find her." Alex reached in his pocket for the Zippo and flipped its lid open to spark a flame from it. It didn't help much. He kept moving, repeating her name. The roar of the British bombers had at last evaporated. A few lights inside undamaged buildings were coming back on.

"We'll get her. Help me find my glasses," said Keene.

Drake felt the ground next to the editor. "Here." He grabbed the spectacles and passed them to the other man.

"One lens cracked. It's okay—go."

He kept moving, pushing debris aside. A dazed young man staggered past, blood streaming down his face.

"Alex! Over here!" Jimmy Keene was ten meters away.

Drake held the lighter flame above the shape of a twisted, broken prosthetic leg on the pavement. A fractured stone cornice lay across it. He sensed movement out of the corner of his eye and turned to glimpse a slender figure partially covered by bricks and fragments of wood. *Sondra!* He knelt beside her, removed debris from her face and body, and then spoke her name quietly. His fingers found her wrist, and he felt for a pulse. *Nothing.* He touched her soft throat. Again, only stillness.

He handed the lighter to Keene and lifted her head off the concrete, putting his face next to hers. He tasted the saltiness of her blood, then cradled her stilled head in his arms and again felt her hand. Finally, he slipped his father's ring off and gently placed it on her left ring finger. The encircling blazes heightening the faint glint of the diamond reminded him for a split second of Kristallnacht.

The air raid sirens blasted the clipped all-clear signal as Sondra coughed and gasped for air. He brought his hand up to force her mouth open.

"Take another breath!"

Jimmy Keene knelt beside them. "Lift her head a bit more."

More coughs and another jagged breath. "Alex—are you here?" she whispered.

"Yes—I'm right next to you!" He pulled a handkerchief from his lapel pocket and held it to the gash in her forehead after blotting up the blood on her cheeks.

Keene stood and shouted at two passing air raid wardens carrying a stretcher. "*Du! Kommen Sie hier mit dieser Bahre!*" They quickly dropped the stretcher to the ground next to Sondra and slid her across the pole and onto the canvas.

"Get her to the bomb shelter's infirmary—U-Bahn stairs, that way," said one of the wardens, pointing toward unseen arches.

As they began moving toward the portal, Drake walked alongside and continued to hold the handkerchief to her forehead. The right side of her dress was torn and soaked in blood, but her breathing seemed steady. He had forgotten about his own pain and pulled his shirt off to make a bandage

The reporters followed the stretcher-bearers down two long flights of concrete stairs, wedging their way past a crowd of frightened Berliners.

Emergency lamps flashed intermittently in the smoky stairwells as people stumbled over one another. Drake fought to stay alongside the stretcher, holding the shirt against the fissure in her side with his functioning arm, clumsily attempting to halt the outflow of blood. At the end of the final corridor, under steadier light filtering from a few overhead bulbs, he was stunned by the image of Sondra. So much of her white dress was stained crimson.

They shifted her onto the hospital cart.

"Drop that soaked shirt," shouted one of the wardens. "Hold this sterile compress on. Careful of her ribs—probably broken!"

Drake touched her warm skin, running his fingers along her face. Sondra's eyes opened. "Alex—my side hurts. How'd I get here?"

"Bombs exploded near us."

"You're all right?" she asked.

"I might have a broken arm here. They're trying to find a doctor for you."

"This place—where am I?"

"About twenty meters beneath the streets of the city—first aid station in a subway."

His arm hurt like hell, but it was starting to move a little. This fierce new physical pain was like a surging wave displacing the ghosts who had been his constant companions for nearly two decades. Drake realized he was in the environment where he'd started this journey with Black Orchestra—deep under the streets of Berlin. Then came a sound, something like the snap of a dry twig, but it didn't resonate through his ears. Instead, it originated from someplace *inside*, maybe from his heart, a big hole in it being closed. He caught a deep breath and tapped a loose fist against his chest, feeling the warm sensation of again loving another person. He was, in some sense, free.

Sondra seemed to be slumping into unconsciousness again. *Damn,* he thought, w*here is that doctor?* His good hand fumbled with the other one, then he took her fingers in his grip. She began blinking, moving her lips, trying to be heard. He tilted to listen to her faint voice.

"Alex—"

"Just be still until the doctor gets here."

"Alex—you saved this world. You're a hero."

"No, it's *we*. You and I crossed into the world of Black Orchestra at almost the same time. You rescued me from Würter's knife, then sidetracked the guard aboard the train to preserve our deception. And no one will ever know about it."

And so it was. Throughout the uncountable generations of humankind, only a tiny number of individuals found themselves in a place where they changed the direction of what was to come for the planet, be it for good or evil. The names of some of these people are well known—Moses, Julius Caesar, Einstein. Others have been lost to the ages or were never known at all. Alexander Drake comprehended that Black Orchestra had been the source of one of those world-shaping events. And someday, when Hitler and his unique strain of ruthless, destructive evil were well past, when again sanity ruled, maybe he, a journalist, could communicate this story to the world. But in time, all kinds of tales will be told about the atomic bomb, so people might not believe it or even care anymore. And he needed to live long enough to tell their story.

He shook off those thoughts and turned toward Sondra, then gently lifted her left hand toward her face.

Puzzlement showed in her eyes. "Your old diamond ring," she whispered. "What's it doing on my finger?"

"I put it there, and I want it to stay forever."

He took her hand, knowing he'd found the person who could enable him to conquer his demons and free him from his past. Alex Drake pushed the lock of his hair away and let his head fall back. Germany's atomic scientists were running fast—but, at least for now, sprinting down the track to failure. As long as the carbon graphite secret stayed safe, the lights of hope, decency, and democracy could continue to burn.

And a Nazi Armageddon would not consume the planet Earth.

AUTHOR'S NOTES

PROFESSOR BOTHE'S ERROR IN CALCULATING the suitability of graphite in creating plutonium—H. G. Wells' carolinum—has never been demystified. In his Pulitzer Prize-winning book *The Making of The Atomic Bomb*, Richard Rhodes relates that the January 1941 carbon graphite test sample was likely contaminated with boron. Bothe's erroneous measurement ended German work with abundant carbon, and nothing in the historical record explains how this mistake happened.

Dr. Otto Hahn in Berlin was the first scientist in the world to split the atom. He was awarded the 1944 Nobel Prize in Chemistry for his 1938 discovery of nuclear fission.

In late 1942, Enrico Fermi's team at the University of Chicago used ultra-pure *carbon graphite* blocks to build the world's first functioning atomic reactor. It led directly to the production of the human-made element plutonium—Wells' carolinum. America's "Fat Man" plutonium bomb exploded thirty-two months later.

Adolf Hitler narrowly escaped death in November 1939, when a bomb was detonated thirteen minutes after he left the Bürgerbräukeller meeting hall in Munich. The man who planted the bomb, Georg Elser, characterized by some as an excellent technician but "almost like an innocent child," was never tried for his assassination attempt and was eventually executed at the Dachau death camp. After the war, Allen Dulles, the future Director of the CIA, summed up various Bürgerbräukeller conspiracy theories when he wrote, "This event still remains unresolved. Some evidence suggests that [the bomb] was exploded with the knowledge of Hitler and Himmler in order to consolidate the German sense of community, or, as in the case of the Reichstag fire, to give rise to a new wave of terror." Today, a plaque marks the position of the white post where Elser had concealed his bomb.

Black Orchestra existed and fought heroically against the Hitler regime. Founded by General Ludwig Beck in 1938, several of its members played roles as described in this novel.

Black Orchestra succeeded in placing a time bomb aboard Hitler's plane on March 13, 1943. It failed to explode.

Johannes von Dohnanyi was arrested in April 1943 and murdered by unknown methods in the Sachsenhausen concentration camp a year later.

General Beck was arrested and shot to death in the aftermath of the July 20, 1944, *Operation Valkyrie* assassination attempt on Hitler.

On April 8, 1945, Hans Oster and Wilhelm Canaris were hanged in the Flossenbürg concentration camp. The camp was liberated two weeks later by the American 90th Infantry Division.

Dr. Leo Szilard wrote the letter to Roosevelt signed by Einstein, alerting America to the danger of German atomic bombs. He later worked with Eugene Wigner on America's Manhattan Project and founded The Council for Abolishing War. He died of a heart attack in 1964.

American forces arrested Kurt Diebner near Munich on April 30, 1945, the same day Adolf Hitler committed suicide.

No nuclear weapon has ever been detonated in war after America's atomic bomb, made with plutonium-carolinum, fell on Nagasaki, Japan, on August 9, 1945, killing approximately 65,000 people and ending the war.

I realize the tragic significance of the atomic bomb . . . thank God that it has come to us, instead of to our enemies . . .
—*President Harry S. Truman, August 9, 1945*

ABOUT THE AUTHOR

Robert Burnham is a licensed professional forensic engineer with two University of Michigan engineering degrees and is a member of the National Academy of Forensic Engineers and the National Society of Professional Engineers.

A professor of engineering and statistical quality control, and lifelong student of science, history, and atomic energy, he lives in Ft. Myers, Florida, and Traverse City, Michigan. He is currently completing his next novel featuring journalist Alex Drake, to be released in 2022.